# BETTER DEAD

# BOOKS BY MAX ALLAN COLLINS

## The Memoirs of Nathan Heller

*Better Dead**
*Ask Not**
*Target Lancer**
*Triple Play* (novellas)
*Chicago Lightning* (short stories)
*Bye Bye, Baby**
*Chicago Confidential*
*Angel in Black*
*Majic Man*
*Flying Blind*
*Damned in Paradise*
*Blood and Thunder*
*Carnal Hours*
*Stolen Away*
*Neon Mirage*
*The Million-Dollar Wound*
*True Crime*
*True Detective*

## The Road to Perdition Saga

*Return to Perdition* (graphic novel)
*Road to Paradise*
*Road to Purgatory*
*Road to Perdition 2:*
*On the Road* (graphic novel)
*Road to Perdition* (graphic novel)

## With Mickey Spillane

*Murder Never Knocks*
*Kill Me, Darling*
*King of the Weeds*
*Complex 90*
*Lady, Go Die!*
*Kiss Her Goodbye*
*The Big Bang*
*The Goliath Bone*
*The Consummata*

## With Barbara Collins (as Barbara Allan)

*Antiques Fate*
*Antiques Swap*
*Antiques Con*
*Antiques Chop*
*Antiques Disposal*
*Antiques Knock-Off*
*Antiques Bizarre*
*Antiques Flee Market*
*Antiques Maul*
*Antiques Roadkill*

## Quarry Novels

*Quarry's Choice*
*The Wrong Quarry*
*Quarry's Ex*
*Quarry in the Middle*
*The First Quarry*
*The Last Quarry*
*Quarry's Vote* (aka *Primary Target*)
*Quarry's Cut* (aka *The Slasher*)
*Quarry's Deal* (aka *The Dealer*)
*Quarry's List* (aka *The Broker's Wife*)
*Quarry* (aka *The Broker*)

## Writing as Patrick Culhane

*Red Sky in Morning*
*Black Hats*

## With Matthew Clemens

*No One Will Hear You*
*You Can't Stop Me*
*Fate of the Union*
*Supreme Justice*

*A Forge Book

# BETTER DEAD

## MAX ALLAN COLLINS

A Tom Doherty Associates Book
*New York*

BETTER DEAD

Copyright © 2016 by Max Allan Collins

A Forge Book
Published by Tom Doherty Associates, LLC
175 Fifth Avenue
New York, NY 10010

www.tor-forge.com

Forge® is a registered trademark of Tom Doherty Associates, LLC.

The Library of Congress Cataloging-in-Publication Data
is available upon request.

ISBN 978-0-7653-7828-6 (hardcover)
ISBN 978-1-4668-6078-0 (e-book)

Our books may be purchased in bulk for promotional,
educational, or business use. Please contact your local bookseller
or the Macmillan Corporate and Premium Sales Department
at 1-800-221-7945, extension 5442, or by e-mail at
MacmillanSpecialMarkets@macmillan.com.

First Edition: May 2016

Printed in the United States of America

0  9  8  7  6  5  4  3  2  1

*For Ken Levin,*
*Nate Heller's Chicago mouthpiece*

Although the historical incidents in this novel are portrayed
as accurately as the passage of time and contradictory source material
will allow, fact, speculation, and fiction are freely mixed here;
historical personages exist side by side with composite characters
and wholly fictional ones—all of whom act
and speak at the author's whim.

Communism to me is not a dirty word. When you're working for the advancement of mankind, it never occurs to you if the guy is a Communist or not.

—Dashiell Hammett

Oh God, don't let me weaken.

—Motto on Senator Joseph McCarthy's office wall

Now listen, Mike. Listen carefully. They're harmless words, just a bunch of letters scrambled together. Try to understand what they mean. Manhattan Project. Los Alamos. Trinity.

—Pat's speech in the film *Kiss Me Deadly* (1955)

America fundamentally wants to think of itself as being good, and that we're fundamentally right in what we're doing . . . because if America does have a darker side, it threatens your hold on your view of America.

—Nils Olson

The most efficient accident, in simple assassination, is a fall of seventy-five feet or more onto a hard surface.

—CIA assassination manual, 1952

# – BOOK ONE –

## RED SCARE

# CHAPTER 1

I was there when the Commies took over.

You won't find it in the history books. But for one day in 1950, in a certain Wisconsin hamlet, the Red Menace came alive in America. I was only an observer, protected by an armband that identified me as such, provided by an armed guard at a checkpoint at a bridge leading into the downtown of Mosinee, population 1,400.

On this first day of May, there would be no dancing around streamer-flowing poles or handing out of baskets of flowers—in this little town (so perfect for a *Saturday Evening Post* cover) citizens would celebrate not May Day but International Workers' Day, the worldwide Communist movement's favorite holiday.

The timing of the takeover was in perfect sync with these early days of the Cold War. Just last August, the USSR had conducted its first successful atomic bomb test, while Mao Tse-tung's People's Liberation Army had kicked ass in the Chinese Civil War. Two months ago, at the Old Bailey in London, atomic spy Klaus Fuchs had been sentenced to fourteen years, a slap on the wrist to American eyes. Meanwhile, Wisconsin's homegrown hero, Senator Joseph McCarthy, was making a national name for himself blowing the whistle on Commies in the U.S. State Department—all 205 of them. Or was that 81? Or maybe 57? Like Heinz.

At a precise predawn 6 a.m., a froglike form in metal-framed glasses, black fedora, and matching baggy suit strode to the front door of a modest brick home. Wearing a white armband that provided him with a sole splash of color (a red star), the squat scowling figure knocked four times with a fist, cannon shots that echoed in the early morning air.

Then the fat little man loudly announced himself: *"This is Chief Commissar Joseph Zack Kornfeder! Open up at once!"*

And he knocked four more times.

When he got no response, he shouted a chilling command: *"Come out now—with your hands on your head! Or we're coming in after you!"*

Backing up the commissar's demand were six heavily armed soldiers with red-star armbands. When Mayor Ralph Cronenwetter, still in his robe, pajamas, and slippers, finally answered his door, two of them dragged the middle-aged man out across his porch and down into the snowy street. Spring in Mosinee was in no hurry, the air chill, the trees skeletal.

Eyes wide in a doughy round face, his thinning hair askew, the startled mayor listened as Kornfeder informed the "enemy of the state" that his town had been taken over by "the Council of People's Commissars."

*"Mosinee, Wisconsin,"* Kornfeder decried ominously, a cigarette dangling, gangster style, *"is now part of the United Soviet States of America!"*

As two armed men dragged His Honor along, the commissar led his squad of invaders on foot to the police station, where they stormed in and yanked Chief Carl Gewiss away from his desk to deposit him in one of his own cells. A shouted third-degree interrogation began, conducted by a club- and knife-wielding pair in dark fedoras and matching overcoats.

Following this, the Mosinee *Weekly Times* was similarly stormed, its editor arrested and informed his paper would henceforth be known as the *Red Star*. By noon, an edition would be on the streets with Stalin's picture sharing the front page with a Communist manifesto and a list of regulations, courtesy of the new regime.

Quickly the commissar and his bully boys took over the public utilities and then did the same with the town's chief industry, the paper mill, where a sign was hung above the double doors saying, "Nationalized—Operated by Authority of the Council of People's Commissars."

Gradually wide-eyed citizens in winter apparel—topcoats, plaid hunting jackets, hats, gloves—filled the sidewalks, taking all this in, eventually spilling into Main Street. When enough gawkers had gathered to form a crowd, the quasi-military strangers with rifles and red-star armbands herded the good people of Mosinee into the village park, which they were stridently informed had been renamed Red Square.

Here a platform had been erected overnight, above which hung a banner that said, "One Party—One Leader—One Nation." The citizens watched dumbfounded as the compact commissar, looking like a cruel caricature of James Cagney, stepped up onto the platform to a waiting microphone.

"The United Soviet States of America," the amplified gravel voice intoned, the eyes behind the round-lens glasses as cold as the morning, "is nationalizing all industry. In addition, all political parties are now abolished, with the exception of the Communist Party. All civic organizations are disbanded as well. All religion is forbidden, all churches to be confiscated as representing an institution against the working class. Hereafter, you will live in an atheistic world, your minds unclouded by superstition."

Here and there, citizens protested, only to be arrested and marched into a large vacant lot that had been transformed by barbed wire into a concentration camp. Adjacent was the American Legion Hall, where a banner read, "Commissariat of USSA Information." As the day progressed, this concentration camp would grow to include the rounded-up likes of nuns from the Catholic school, local clergymen, and paper-mill executives.

But right now it was only 10:15 a.m. and the fun was just beginning. Up on the platform, the squat commissar announced that rationing was now in effect, and that restaurants would be serving black bread and potato soup only. For those who could not afford that, an outdoor soup kitchen would be available.

"Those of you who do not cooperate will be assigned to slave labor camps," Kornfeder said, almost casual now in his recitation of atrocities.

Finally, gray-faced Mayor Cronenwetter was dragged up onto the stage at gunpoint. Still in his robe and pajamas, His Honor at the microphone rather pitifully read to the captive audience a prepared statement: "Police Chief Gewiss has been liquidated for failure to cooperate. I now urge all citizens to comply with the new socialist order."

Throughout the day, most Mosineeans did comply, having been issued ration permits for food and gasoline as well as red-star lapel pins to signify their cooperation with the new regime. Anyone not willing to wear the lapel pin would be marched to the concentration camp.

Midday, an enforced parade was held with signs provided saying, "The Communist Party is the Only Party," "Stalin is the Leader!" and the like. A big wooden circle with a red star that resembled a Texaco service-station sign (albeit superimposed with a hammer and sickle) was posted over the door to city hall, while all around town red-star-emblazoned flags were draped over doorposts.

Students were corralled in the high school gym and made by armed guards to stand in rows to hear lectures on Communist doctrine by visiting faculty. At the grade school, children were encouraged by teachers to join the Young Communist League, if for no other reason than the local sweet shop only sold candy to card-carrying members.

Elderly Reverend Will La Brew Bennett put up the biggest fuss, saying to those padlocking his church, "When America is taken over by Communists, I will hide my Bible in the church organ!" Then he was marched to the barbed-wire camp.

Elsewhere in Mosinee, Commie storm troopers entered the library with lists of books to remove, which they did, making a pile on the front lawn (apparently for eventual burning). Prices in the local A&P—renamed the Red Star Grocery—were raised to exorbitant rates, and the front window was painted with a borscht advertisement. Down the block, the movie theater replaced its current feature, *Guilty of Treason* (with Charles Bickford and Bonita Granville), with the 1945 Russian musical *Hello, Moscow!* (with Oleg Bobrov and Anya Stravinskaya).

Under third-degree interrogation, I would have to admit the musical was better than the Bickford picture, a turkey I'd suffered through a week ago back in Chicago. I mean, *Hello, Moscow!* was in color at least and had some catchy tunes.

I had slipped into the theater mid-afternoon when I'd become cold from the Wisconsin weather and bored with the Mosinee theatrics. I was pleased to find the popcorn machine hadn't been confiscated, and that a good old American quarter could still get me a bag, a Coke, and change. Plus, the little blonde behind the counter gave me a smile for free. Shouldn't she be attending a lecture on the new order at the high school gym?

Maybe they gave her a pass. Possibly even Commies needed somebody to hand out popcorn at the movies.

The mock coup, staged by the Wisconsin American Legion, was an elaborate daylong piece of street theater put on for members of the press, an international contingent that included television networks, newsreel outfits, wire services, *Reader's Digest*, *Life*, and *Time*, and even the Russian news agency, TASS. A few dignitaries had been invited as observers, and I'd rated one of their rarefied armbands because the unofficial guest of honor for the Red takeover was Senator Joe McCarthy himself.

I was along as McCarthy's guest because we'd done some business over the last couple of years and were friendly. When I learned he'd be back home in Wisconsin for a short stay, I arranged for an audience with America's newly self-appointed Commie-Hunter-in-Chief. A client of mine needed help and McCarthy was the only path.

The business I represented was my own—the A-1 Detective Agency, of which I, Nathan Heller, was president. The firm had started back in 1932 as a one-man, one-room affair in a fairly dingy building at Van Buren and Plymouth, and had grown to include a Los Angeles branch office and an expanded main one in the celebrated Monadnock Building in the South Loop. Today I had half a dozen operatives, not counting my partner Lou Sapperstein (my old boss on the Pickpocket Detail) or our secretary Gladys Fortunato (with us since before the war).

You might wonder why the forty-four-year-old president of the A-1 would go chasing into the wilds of Wisconsin on behalf of a client when he had plenty of young operatives who could do that for him. But when it's a United States senator like Joe McCarthy you make exceptions. Not that there really were any other United States senators like Joe McCarthy.

My forty-four years, by the way, were well-preserved ones, assembled into six feet and two hundred pounds, including features considered by some female types to cause no eyestrain. I was in a dark blue Dobbs hat and a gray Albert-Richard greatcoat with a black fur collar and lapels, its lining in (I'd been to Wisconsin in the "spring" before), over a lighter blue Botany 500 suit. Buying clothes on Maxwell Street was out these days, unless I needed a suit cut to conceal my nine-millimeter, which I had not brought to the party.

Good thing—it might have been confiscated by the Reds.

I admit to reporting some of the early morning activities second-hand, having flown in that a.m. from Midway to Downtown Wausau Airport, where a young aide of McCarthy's waited in a black Buick to drive me the half hour to Mosinee. But I got there in time to fall in beside McCarthy where he lurked with the press on the periphery, as the mayor gave his surrender speech at pistol point to the assembled community in the park. That is, Red Square.

McCarthy wore neither Dobbs nor Botany 500—he was in a rumpled raincoat over one of those dark blue ready-made suits he seemed to buy in bulk. His red tie was showing—an irony that had escaped him, like most ironies did—and sported random polka dots that were really food stains.

He was grinning at the dark proceedings, and occasionally laughing under his breath—"Heh heh heh!"—in an almost girlish fashion that hardly suited such a bullnecked, barrel-chested, blue-jowled brute. His black hair was thinning, his eyebrows heavy and grown together over hooded sleepy eyes, his Bob Hope–ish nose flat from bridge to tip, a condition possibly dating to collegiate boxing days. For all that, the oval face on the big head could almost be called handsome.

No legislator had as many enemies in government as Joe McCarthy—then again, no legislator had as many followers outside of government. The junior senator from Wisconsin's notoriety and popularity on the national scene had, in a matter of months, grown exponentially.

Nothing in McCarthy's history hinted at the fame and power awaiting him. He'd been a chicken farmer and a grocery store manager, and had not gone to high school till he was twenty-one, although admittedly he'd then raced through. In college he majored in frat-house beer and poker, but did manage to graduate with a law degree. As a New Deal Democrat, he lost a run for district attorney of Shawano County; but as a Republican he became a Circuit Court judge. Running on a self-inflated war record ("Tail-Gunner Joe"), McCarthy became a U.S. senator in 1946.

Today, standing behind the newsreel and television cameras in the park, McCarthy was keeping an uncharacteristically low profile, begging off interviews, saying, "This is the Legion's day. I'm just a spectator here. A guest."

He explained to me from the sidelines, as we'd watched the mayor surrender his town, that the national American Legion was the real author of this Commie-takeover melodrama.

"Well, heh heh heh," he said quietly, lessening the nasal drone of his baritone, "the Legion and *J. Edgar.* Everybody's favorite G-man's got the Legion wrapped around his little pinky, and good for him."

As we passed the concentration camp on our way to a soup-kitchen lunch (vegetable—not bad), the senator pointed out among many unlikely prisoners in hats and business suits the owner/editor of the Mosinee *Weekly Times,* a tall distinguished-looking fellow in his forties who turned out to be retired Brigadier General Francis Schweinler.

"He was the local mover and shaker," McCarthy said. "High mucky-muck on the state Legion's Americanism committee. Really put it together."

"Oh?"

The big bucket head nodded. "Sent a letter out all but ordering that citizens here join in. Told 'em they were being asked to play along for the greater good, and to voluntarily subject themselves to a few harmless inconveniences." His small smile was almost a sneer as we took in the dazed faces of the concentration camp crowd, their breaths pluming. "Afraid the good people of Mosinee didn't really know what they were getting themselves into."

Later, as we watched the May Day parade, citizens trudging along with grim faces, a grinning Joe said, "This is wonderful— *wonderful!* A real object lesson in what it's like to live under Communism. It's no bed of roses."

"Who are these troops, anyway?" I asked. Red-star-emblazoned jeeps were parked on either side along Main Street with helmeted rifle-bearing soldiers spotted all around.

"Ex-servicemen," he said gleefully, "from all over the state. Seem to be having a darn good time."

Maybe a little too darn good.

About that point I excused myself to take in *Hello, Moscow!* And two hours later, when I rejoined McCarthy in back of the camera crews, a dusk the color of the senator's five o'clock shadow had fallen. A quietness settled in only to be shattered by bullhorns demanding everyone's presence in Red Square.

There, under bright lights, the froglike commissar with his gangster overcoat and hat, wire-rim glasses and droopy cigarette began to speak again, extolling the virtues of Communism. *"You have had today a small taste of the superior way of life represented by Soviet Russia!"*

McCarthy, his mouth a slash in the blue-cheeked face, said quietly, "Good, isn't he?"

"He's a believable Commie, all right."

"That's because he used to be one. Name really *is* Kornfeder. He's Czech, a real leader in the American Communist movement back

18

in the thirties. Ten years ago he turned friendly HUAC witness. Now he's what you'd call a professional anti-Communist."

Took one to know one.

The commissar was still yakking when from nowhere the mayor—finally out of his pajamas and into a dignified suit and tie, hair neatly combed but face still gray—emerged to walk up onto the platform and push the commissar out of the way. Suddenly blue-uniformed police came up onto the stage and dragged off the pro-testing commissar, Kornfeder feeding corn to the wildly applauding audience to the very end.

With an austere dignified smile, the mayor said into the microphone, "I am here, good people of Mosinee, to announce that democracy has been restored to our fair city."

More, even wilder applause now. Whistles and hoots and hollers.

As if in reaction, the mayor's eyes widened.

But then he clutched his chest and seemed to be working at keeping his balance, as blurts of concern blossomed around the crowd. Finally he slumped to the wooden flooring, first on his knees, then onto his side, feet drawn up into a fetal position.

A collective gasp came up.

"Now what?" I asked McCarthy.

"That's not scheduled," the senator said, eyes disappearing into slits. Not smiling at all now. He took me by the arm. "Come on, Nate, let's find my man and get out of here. This looks like something not to be a part of."

Screams and wails were going up from the assemblage and we passed a screaming, wailing ambulance as in our black Buick we headed out of the liberated little community, making a getaway worthy of bank robbers.

Robbers back in Dillinger days were said to have escaped coppers via tunnels below the Hotel Wausau. But Joe McCarthy and I, in the downtown hotel's restaurant off its Gothic cathedral of a lobby, weren't hiding from anybody.

A scattering of diners exchanged glances and stole looks as the senator and I sat in a booth, the dark, rich wood around us typical of the hotel. McCarthy was working on a well-done porterhouse steak about the size of a hubcap and a buttered baked potato not much larger than a hand grenade. His short arms were pumping and his big hands were balled as he carved with knife and fork.

Delicate eater that I was, I had settled for a club steak, rare, and some hash browns with onions. McCarthy was drinking beer, and so was I. Schlitz. Made Milwaukee famous, you know.

We were inside an eight-story 1880s brick structure courtesy of Chicago architects Roche and Holabird—who turned out such little numbers as Soldier Field and the Art Institute—which might have made a Chicago boy feel at home. It didn't. I had come to Wisconsin and Joe McCarthy's table on a mission of mercy, or seeking mercy anyway, and right now my dinner companion didn't seem merciful at all. Certainly the porterhouse was being shown none.

"There's no *question* this friend of yours was in any number of Communist *front* groups," he said between bites. When he said things like that, McCarthy fell into public speaking mode, forcing his baritone up into second tenor and emphasizing random words by dropping them back down.

"Youthful college days," I said. "He didn't know better. It was the Depression. You remember the Depression, don't you, Joe? Lots of folks out of work. Weren't you an FDR man back then?"

He grinned and had some more steak, chewed, swallowed, said, "But he's a scientist. They're the worst kind. Damnit, Nate, he worked on the Manhattan Project! Think what he had access to."

"Early days at the University of Chicago. A minor figure, Joe. And back then the government gave him a full security clearance."

"Quit assin' around, Heller! In those days Uncle Sam let more Commies in than a half-ass henhouse fence does foxes. My boys tell me your pal is just another State Department Red."

"He doesn't work for the State Department, Joe. He's a full-time professor now."

"Filling empty young minds with dangerous propaganda."

"No. Just physics. He does a little consulting with State, that's all. Did your people find any Soviet ties?"

". . . No."

"Can you give him a pass, Joe? As a favor?"

He moved on to the baked potato, using the steak knife to cut down to and through the skin. "How are you and our buddy Drew gettin' along?"

This was not the non sequitur it seemed. Reporter Drew Pearson, easily the nation's most powerful syndicated left-of-center columnist, had once been very friendly with McCarthy, who had provided him and his man Jack Anderson with all kinds of inside dope from the Hill. But lately Pearson had been running negative items on McCarthy. The bloom could well be off the rose.

"We fell out," I said, spearing some hash browns and onions, "after what he did to Jim Forrestal."

Former Secretary of Defense Forrestal, a client of mine, had committed suicide in the midst of a heavy Pearson smear campaign. I'd stopped doing investigative work for Drew because of that.

"Glad to hear it," he said, as he chewed potato. "As for your professor pal . . . let me sleep on it. I'll let you know in the morning. When do you fly out?"

"Ten o'clock."

"Come by my room at eight and we'll have breakfast."

As for the name of my friend at the University of Chicago, that isn't pertinent to this narrative. Just in case you thought I was somebody who named names.

We were having apple pie when McCarthy's slender young staffer came around and leaned in. His name I can't give you because I don't remember it, but I can tell you he had a nicer suit and tie than his boss.

"Senator . . . turns out Mayor Cronenwetter had a heart attack back there. He's in the hospital in critical condition here in Wausau. Did you want me to arrange to go out there and . . . ?"

The hooded eyes flared. "No. We, uh, don't want to intrude on the family."

The staffer nodded and disappeared so fast I expected a puff of smoke.

McCarthy said, "Damn shame."

"Yeah. Too bad."

"Really casts a pall on a great day."

That evening I kept McCarthy company on a walking tour of downtown Wausau bars. He put away more beer than a bachelor party and yet circulated among the citizens, pumping hands like they were so many more porterhouses he was carving. I'll give him this: He seemed to know them all by name, and he sat and laughed and talked with maybe a dozen of them.

Shanty Irish Joe had the common touch, all right. This was his base—Wisconsin's German, Polish, and Czech voters. My Irish looks, courtesy of my mother, made me fit right in. Would I have been as welcome, I wondered, if my apostate Jewish pop showed more clearly in my features?

I also wondered if I'd be this welcome at Joe's table if he knew my pop had been an old union man, a Wobbly who ran a left-wing bookstore on the West Side.

We wound up back in the hotel bar. I hadn't had near as many beers as him, but enough to ask some questions that might have been ill-advised.

For example. "Joe, you used to be a Democrat. Civil rights, race relations . . . a damn moderate. How you'd get to where you are now?"

Drunk, he was in full-blown nasal speechifying. "I was a Democrat *because* I was ignorant. I know *now* they're all a bunch of Commie-crats. Whether they know it or not, they're part of a *conspiracy* on a scale so *immense* it dwarfs anything in human history."

"You really believe that."

"Damn right I do. And we have our friend Jim Forrestal to thank."

"Oh?"

"He's the boyo who clued me in about the Commie threat in government."

He was also the boyo who jumped to his death from a high window in an insane asylum.

I said, "Well, it's sure working for you. That speech you made in Wheeling, it really started the ball rolling."

He didn't deny it. He grinned a little and the droopy-lidded eyes glittered. "I got hold of something here, Nate, something really good. Something that'll help me *and* our country."

"But some of these people you're accusing, Joe—you're painting them with an awful wide brush."

He shrugged and sipped from his pilsner. "If I'm right in the larger sense . . . and I *am* . . . *it* doesn't matter a damn that the details are wrong."

I was pretty drunk myself, but not enough to buy that bullshit. Still, I was sober enough not to say so.


The next morning I stopped by McCarthy's suite at eight o'clock. The door was answered by the young staffer, who was in a silk mauve dressing robe. He looked tired but I didn't sense I'd woken him.

"I'm afraid the senator's indisposed." He was blocking the way.

"Joe said to stop by and get him for breakfast."

"Oh, I don't think he's in shape for that."

I pushed through. "I need to talk to him before I head back."

There was a living room area and two bedrooms. In one of the latter I found a nude Joe McCarthy sitting up in bed, pillows propped behind him, pouring himself a glass of something from a pitcher. I thought at first it was water.

But raising his glass, he asked, "Care for a martini, Nate?"

I will spare you any description of a naked Joe McCarthy, other than to say it would have involved hair, muscle, flab, and an appendage that was limp, which was fine by me.

"No, Joe, I better grab a quick breakfast downstairs. You want to throw something on and join me?"

"No. No, I'm fine." He set the pitcher on the nightstand next to a little pile of pulp westerns. "Listen, I gave it some thought."

"Uh, yeah?" I wasn't sure what he was referring to, but I hoped he meant my University of Chicago friend.

"How did you *know* I was looking into that professor guy? That pinko scientist . . . *how?*"

"The private detective agency you hired to investigate him in Chicago is one I farm things out to sometimes. A colleague there clued me in. Professional courtesy."

"Breach of trust, I say. Bastard shoulda kept that name to himself." He grunted. "But you, Nate, you're a good guy, looking out for a pal. What the hell. I'm gonna give him a pass."

Right then he could've wrapped one of those sheets around himself and passed for Nero, even without a laurel wreath—*thumbs-up, thumbs-down.*

"I appreciate that, Joe."

He grinned goofily and held out his hand for me to shake. Handshaking was a staple of his approach, though I found it as clammy as it was vigorous. And I wasn't comfortable being that close to the naked senator.

Not that the image put me off breakfast—you develop a strong stomach in my line—and I made the ten a.m. flight just fine.

That was the end of my Mosinee adventure, but there is a postscript: Mayor Ralph Kronwetter, forty-nine, died on May 6. And Reverend Will La Brew, seventy-two, who had so indignantly promised the fake Commies he would hide his Bible, was found dead in his bed the next morning. A spokesman from the Mosinee American Legion called it "a terrible, tragic coincidence."

But the doctor who'd treated them both said "the excitement and exertion of the day" had likely "contributed" to their untimely passings.

On the other hand, it was still relatively bloodless for a coup.

CHAPTER

## Washington, D.C., March 26, 1953

I'm not sure I would trust anybody in my business who read private eye novels. Reading the "true detective" magazines was a different story, because there was always a chance you could place a case of yours there and get some publicity, or possibly a little dough if you split with a reporter or even wrote it up yourself.

The pulps and the paperbacks were such a travesty on what a real private investigator did that I had no time for them, and I was perfectly capable of giving rise to my own sex scenes, thank you, and as for violence, that was mercifully rare in coming.

But scratch somebody in my profession and you'll find a one-time reader of the romantic version of what we do. For me it was Sherlock Holmes and Nick Carter and eventually *Black Mask*, a pulp magazine I read in the twenties as a very young man. All that stuff had gone into the hopper and helped point kids like me toward police work. It hadn't strictly been the graft.

One of the *Black Mask* boys, as the editor liked to refer to his stable of writers, was an actual ex–Pinkerton operative, and his stories had an understated yet gritty reality the rest of the pulp-paper yarns lacked. When the writer graduated to publishing actual books, I had stayed with him, through my early years on the Chicago P.D. and even later as a private detective. I might have kept reading him, but I hadn't seen anything new by him in the book-stalls for a while.

"Samuel Dashiell Hammett," the frail thin man said, seated at a table with a glass of water, two microphones trained on either side of him like rifles, and a glass ashtray where he had stood a pack of Camels upright.

A flat nasal voice from the dais, where a brace of senators sat with various staffers behind them, asked: "And what is your occupation?"

"Writer." He had a full head of brushed-back white hair, darker eyebrows, salt-and-pepper mustache, and a handsome if ravaged, sunken-cheeked face the color of typing paper. In a medium-gray suit with a dark gray tie and a breast-pocket handkerchief, this was the kind of man who seemed dapper without trying.

The kid playing prosecutor—and he *was* a kid, still in his twenties—was Roy Cohn, who'd made a name for himself in the Rosenberg "atomic spy" case, as assistant to District Attorney Irving Saypol. With his slicked-back black hair, high forehead, reptilian hooded eyes, and cleft chin, he might have been the son of the man he sat next to—Senator Joseph McCarthy.

Referring pointlessly to his notes, Cohn said, "You're the author of some rather well-known detective stories. Is that correct?"

Hammett leaned forward, elbows on the table. He looked comfortable, or at least not uncomfortable. "That is right."

"In addition to that, you have written on some social issues. Is that correct?"

The emaciated-looking writer's shrug involved his whole upper body. "Well, it's impossible to write anything without taking some sort of stand on social issues."

I was seated off to one side, just behind the press tables, in the gallery of the Caucus Room in the S.O.B., as the Senate Office Building was nicknamed. The vast rectangular room with its trio of grand sun-streaming windows had an oddly French-derived style, from the black-veined marble floors to the ceiling with its gilded rosettes. The smell of cigarette smoke—allowed between witness appearances—did cut the elegance somewhat, as did the rumpled suits of reporters and politicos.

This was a hearing of the Permanent Subcommittee on Investigations into the use of federal funds to purchase books by known Communists for State Department libraries abroad. I recognized one of the senators—loquacious Everett Dirksen from my home state of Illinois—but it was Cohn, the young committee counsel, doing the talking right now.

The young prosecutor turned to McCarthy and they exchanged sleepy-eyed looks. "Mr. Chairman, some three hundred books by Mr. Hammett are in the Information Service today in some seventy-three information centers."

"That's a lot of books," Hammett cut in, with a smile that managed to be both wide and barely perceptible.

"I'm sorry—three hundred *copies*, eighteen books." The young prosecutor offered up a slight smile to his witness. "I realize you haven't written three hundred books. About how many *have* you written?"

"Five, I think."

"Just five books?"

"Yes, and many short stories that have been collected in reprint books."

Cohn nodded, thumbing through his papers. "There are eighteen books in use, including some collections. Now, Mr. Hammett, when did you write your first published book?"

The author's head tipped to one side. "The first book was *Red Harvest* in 1929."

"At the time you wrote that book, were you a member of the Communist Party?"

Hammett's chin came up, as if inviting a swing; but his voice was quietly nonconfrontational. "I decline to answer on the grounds that an answer might tend to incriminate me, relying on my rights under the Fifth Amendment of the United States."

Cohn had expected that. "When did you write your last published book?"

Hammett's frown was as barely perceptible as his smile. "Well, I can't really answer that . . . because of the short story collections. I imagine it was sometime in the thirties or forties."

Cohn nodded. "And at that time were you a member of the Communist Party?"

"Same answer."

McCarthy hunkered toward the microphone, gesturing with his black-rimmed glasses, the beast awakening.

"Mr. Hammett," he said, his voice dripping cold contempt, "let me ask you this. Forgetting about *yourself* for the time being, is it a safe *assumption* that any member of the Communist *Party* . . . under Communist *discipline* . . . would propagandize the Communist cause *regardless* of whether he was writing *fiction* books or books on politics?"

McCarthy's oratorical style was in full sway, that familiar nasal second tenor randomly dropping and raising register for emphasis.

Unimpressed, Hammett shrugged. "I honestly don't know."

McCarthy leaned in farther, teeth showing in nothing like a smile. "Refusing to *answer* on the *grounds* that it might *incriminate* you is normally taken by this committee . . . and by this *country* . . . as meaning that you are a *member* of the Communist *Party*. Therefore, you should know *considerable* about the Communist movement."

Hammett's eyebrows were up; there was something lazy about it. "Was that a question, sir?"

Now McCarthy accompanied his emphasized words with bobs of the head. "That is just a *comment* on your *statement*." He swung toward Cohn. "Mr. Counsel, do you have anything *further*?"

Cohn flashed a nervous smile and sat forward, the smartest kid in class. "Oh yes . . . Mr. Hammett, from these various books you've written, have you received royalty payments?"

"I have."

"And I would assume that if the State Department purchased three hundred copies of your books, you would receive some royalties."

A tiny nod from the author. "I should imagine so."

Several nods from the prosecutor. "Could you tell us what your royalties are, by percentage?"

Hammett flipped a hand. "On the books published by Alfred Knopf, I think it starts at fifteen percent."

McCarthy—sitting back now, as if trying to get as far away from this odious witness as possible—asked brusquely, "Did any of the *money* which you received from the *State* Department find its *way* into the *coffers* of the Communist Party?"

Hammett again matter-of-factly declined to answer.

Cohn, showing no opinion of the witness at all, asked, "Is it a fair statement that you have received substantial sums of money from the royalties on all of the books you have written?"

"Yes, that is a fair statement."

"And you decline to tell us whether any of these moneys went to the Communist Party?"

"That is right."

McCarthy shook his head and smirked at several other senators on the dais.

Cohn pressed on. "Is it a fact that you have allowed the use of your name as sponsor and member of governing bodies of Communist front organizations?"

Hammett declined to answer.

Now Cohn raised his voice somewhat, but his youth made that seem like he was trying too hard. "Mr. Hammett, is it a fact that you recently served a term in prison?"

A tiny nod from Hammett. "Yes. I did six months on the bail-bond matter—actually, *five* months." The writer smiled again, just barely. "I got time off for good behavior."

Some mild laughter rippled across the spectator section. I admired the wry good humor of this long-in-the-tooth *Black Mask* boy; but the thought of this frail-looking individual being incarcerated was anything but funny.

McCarthy, irritated, snapped, "That was a *contempt* citation, was it not?"

The chin came up again, daring his inquisitor. "Yes, over the bail-bond fund."

Cohn craned to address McCarthy. "After certain Communist leaders jumped bail, three trustees, including Mr. Hammett, were called in and refused to answer questions about the whereabouts of the fugitives, and they refused to produce books and records of the bail-bond fund, and were sentenced to jail."

This little speech was disingenuous, because of course McCarthy already knew all that; but both the senator and his committee's counsel wanted it said in public, and got into the record.

Now Cohn turned back to Hammett, a cobra eyeing its prey. "Is that a fairly accurate statement?"

"Fairly."

"Do you know the whereabouts of any of these fugitive Communist leaders today?"

"No."

"You say you don't know?"

"I don't know."

Sitting forward again, McCarthy asked, rapid-fire, "Did you *know* where they *were* at any *time* while the government was *searching* for them?"

"No."

"Do I *understand* that you *arranged* the bail bond for these *fugitives?*"

Hammett declined to answer, and then also refused to say whether he'd contributed any funds to the bail-raising effort.

McCarthy was hunched over, ready to pounce. "Have you ever engaged in *espionage* against the United *States?*"

Firm but quiet: "No."

"Have you ever engaged in *sabotage?*"

"No, sir."

The bobbing big head punctuating, McCarthy pounded, "Do you *believe* that the Communist *system* is better than the *system* in use in this *country?*"

Hammett thought for a moment. Then: "I don't think Russian Communism is better for the United States, no."

Grinning, McCarthy leaned back, tapping his black-rimmed glasses on the table. "You seem to *distinguish* between *Russian* Communism and *American* Communism. I cannot see any *distinction,* but would you think that *American* Communism would be a good *system* to adopt in this *country?"*

Hammett thought about that, as if he were taking part in a reasonable conversation, then said, "That can't be answered 'yes' or 'no,' Senator. Theoretical Communism is no form of government—there *is* no government. I doubt I could give a definite answer."

McCarthy pressed: "Would you *favor* the adoption of *Communism* in this *country?"*

"You mean right now?"

"Yes."

"No."

"You would *not?"*

"It's impractical when people don't want it."

That stopped McCarthy momentarily. "Did you favor the Communist *system* when you were writing these *books?"*

Hammett declined to answer.

The writer was then questioned about testimony against him by a friendly witness who had identified him as a Communist, and declined to answer those questions as well.

Openly sneering now, McCarthy asked, "May I ask one *further* question, Mr. Hammett? If you were spending over a *hundred* million dollars a *year* on an information *program* allegedly for the purpose of *fighting* Communism, and if you were in charge of that *program* to fight Communism, would you purchase the works of Communist *authors* and distribute their works throughout the *world?"*

Hammett shrugged again. "Well, if I were fighting Communism, Senator, I don't believe I would give people any books at all."

That sucker-punched McCarthy, who muttered, "Unusual, coming from an author . . ."

Hammett was excused. He collected his Camels and made his way down the aisle through a lightning storm of camera flashes. He smiled a little and shook his head, refusing to answer any press questions without having to resort to the Fifth Amendment.

But that had slowed him down enough for me to catch up with him in the marble two-story rotunda, where he stood lighting up a cigarette.

"Mr. Hammett," I said. "Nathan Heller."

He gave me a nice grin and we shook hands. His grip was bony but firm. "I was expecting to meet you later at the Ambassador. That's where the gentleman with Bradford said we'd connect."

Bradford Investigations and my A-1 Agency backed each other up in our respective cities.

"Right, but I had to be over here today for another appointment, and figured I'd drop by the Caucus Room and, uh . . ."

"Catch the show?"

I grinned, a kid caught climbing over a stadium fence. "Something like that. Shall we find a bar with a quiet corner?"

"This is so sudden, Mr. Heller." He exhaled smoke; his face had length and a bony angularity. "But maybe a coffee shop instead. I gave up drinking, so why tempt fate?"

"How about lunch? I mean, it's only fair—you were already somebody else's main course."

He liked that remark.

We put on our respective hats and stepped out into a day breezy and cool but not enough so to inspire topcoats or even a London Fog.

I waved down a cab and told the driver, "Seventeenth and L Streets NW."

As we rode, Hammett was concentrating on his smoking and maybe the wind-tossed skirts of the government girls on the sidewalks.

I said, "I thought writers were hard drinkers."

"Oh, I've done far more drinking than writing. It's just that I promised someone important in my life that I'd stop."

"Who was that? If you don't mind my asking."

"My doctor."

Duke Zeibert's was a brick-fronted cavern impressively overseen by a massive white-on-black neon sign—

*Duke Zeibert's*
## RESTAURANT

—and a red-and-white canopy.

I'd been here a number of times, but I couldn't say whether Duke himself really recognized me when he came over in his trademark white jacket and black bow tie to slap my back and shake hands. Bald and mustached, he was (as someone once said) like a cross between Ben Franklin and a bookie.

Giving Hammett a respectful bow, Duke said, "This gentleman looks very familiar to me, Mr. Heller."

So he did recognize me. And this was his way of finding out if yet another celeb had wandered into his realm.

"Dashiell Hammett," I said, making the intros, "Duke Zeibert— our host. Mr. Hammett's the Sam Spade author, as you probably already know."

Obviously Hammett didn't love this kind of public fuss, but it might get us comped, so I took a shot.

"Mr. Hammett, sir," Duke said, grinning and pumping the author's hand. "An honor. Tell me, if I may be so bold. What is Humphrey Bogart really like?"

"Short," Hammett said.

Duke laughed and led us past a glassed-in case of Redskins trophies on through the bar into the long narrow brick-walled dining room. He half-bowed and left us at our table. Mid-afternoon found Zeibert's underpopulated for a place so often littered with politicians, sports figures, executives, and entertainers (if not Bogart yet). Today the three other tables taken had nobody recognizable.

A white-jacketed waiter in his fifties—all of the waiters here were at least fifty—brought us a basket of onion rolls and a bowl of pickles. We both ordered Duke's Delight ("boiled beef in pot") and coffee.

"I understand," I said, after a bite of perfect pickle, "that you called my new Manhattan branch and inquired about my availability."

Hammett nodded. He discreetly chewed and swallowed a small bite of onion roll and said, "I have an apartment in New York. Greenwich Village."

Our coffee came.

I said, "Why inquire about a Chicago detective's availability? Or do you have a job needs doing back on my turf? Even so, why me? Why not Pinkerton?" I gave him a small smile. "Or maybe Continental?"

I got a small smile back for my trouble: Continental was the fictional detective agency he used in some of his stories.

"So you've read me," he said.

"I plead the Fifth." I shrugged. "But you might say you inspired me to go into this trade."

He shivered, and I doubted it was the tart taste of pickle. "Then I owe you an apology. It can be a dirty business."

"It can."

His eyes drifted to one side. "But you know, I really did enjoy it." Then a gaze that was at once hard and soft somehow returned to me. "As for why *you*, Mr. Heller . . . I read about you in *Life* magazine, although it painted you as more Hollywood than Chicago."

He was referring to an article calling me the "Private Eye to the Stars."

"Overstated," I said, embarrassed again. "Just a bunch of puffery for the branch office I opened out there."

He sipped coffee, black. "But it included some interesting background material. You were in the thick of some big jobs."

I liked that he'd used the word "jobs," not "cases." He still had some real private op in him.

"Everything from the Lindbergh snatch," he was saying, "to the Black Dahlia killing."

"I was also bodyguard for Mayor Cermak, Huey Long, and Amelia Earhart. And you may have heard how they fared. But I'm flattered. What do you have in mind?"

"Your father was involved in the union movement," he said, not exactly a direct answer.

"Yes. He ran a socialist bookshop on the West Side. But we didn't see eye to eye."

"On politics, you mean?"

"We didn't even define the word the same way. To me politics was just getting ahead. I used a family connection that my father had severed, a long time ago, to get onto the Chicago P.D. You may recall it was the Depression, and that was a good job to have."

"He didn't appreciate you becoming a Cossack."

That got a laugh out of me. "Aptly put. He killed himself, actually—over what a disappointment I'd become. I lied on a witness stand, you see. You should try it sometime."

"I didn't mean to pry."

"But you kind of already have. You checked up on me. Which is hard for a detective to resent, but I do anyway. I vote straight Democrat, Mr. Hammett, but then I'm from Chicago so don't take that too literally."

"I do apologize."

I waved it off. "No need. It's just that if you're looking for a . . ."

"Fellow traveler?" he asked, something like a twinkle in those dark serious eyes.

I had to grin. "Let's just say I'm a capitalist. I don't do pro bono work, no matter how good the cause."

He lifted the eyebrows and sat them back down. "Well, it's a good cause, all right. But we're not looking for a free ride."

" 'We'?"

Our waiter came over, accompanied by Duke, and put down two big servings of prime rib in front of us. And I hadn't seen baked potatoes that size since I'd dined with McCarthy in Mosinee.

Leaning in, Duke said, "Now, I can still get you the boiled beef if you like—it's perfectly delicious—but I thought you might enjoy this more. All right, gentlemen? And either way, it's on the house."

My Chicago instincts were serving me well in the District of Columbia. I thanked our host profusely (Hammett just said, "Well, thank you") and Duke went off grinning.

Stunned by the size of the serving, Hammett began to cut himself a bite and said, "As I say, the cause is a good one, and a number of us have put together a fund . . . not a bail fund this time . . . but a fund."

"A number of you."

He nodded. "The names, which in this case I'm happy to give up, are ones you'll recognize . . . but keep in mind many of us do not make the kind of money we once did."

"It's a rough climate," I said.

He shrugged. "In my case, all the radio shows based on my stuff have been canceled. State and federal people have heavy income tax liens on me. And Hollywood is out till this Red Scare is over."

"Okay. Money is tight. I'm listening."

He named names, all right: Dorothy Parker, Howard da Silva, Paul Robeson, W.E.B. DuBois, Alfred Kreymborg, Howard Fast, Ring Lardner Jr., John Howard Lawson, Leonard Bernstein, Arthur Miller, Thomas Mann, Lillian Hellman, and Albert Einstein.

"These are names," he said, "that you must keep to yourself."

"If we wind up doing business," I said, "you'll be covered. I work through an attorney so that I have client confidentiality."

"Wise," he said. Another shrug. "We can give you a flat three thousand dollars. It's not a retainer but payment in full, to conduct an eleventh-hour investigation into the alleged crimes of two people who are sitting on Death Row at Sing Sing right now."

"Not the . . . no . . ."

"Rosenbergs. Yes."

Shit.

And I'll be goddamned if Hammett, this old man of less than sixty sitting across from me, didn't look like my father for a second there.

"You know that little prick Cohn," he said, spearing a bite he made, "helped that D.A., that crook Saypol, put me away on the bail bond. And together they railroaded the Rosenbergs."

"So you have a personal stake in it."

"I'm human," he admitted. "Julius and Ethel Rosenberg are no atomic spies, Mr. Heller. They're innocent. We want you to prove it."

I had a bite of prime rib dipped in horseradish sauce. Excellent.

"Call me Nate," I said.

"Make it Dash," he said.

CHAPTER 3

Around four-thirty, a cab dropped me back at First and C Streets—
the Senate Office Building, one of three imposing white marble
structures facing the Capitol grounds. Even this late in the day things
were bustling, sidewalks full of well-dressed professional types,
male and female, mostly under forty, lugging briefcases, hugging
file folders, in a huge white-collar hurry. And yet government itself
was a snail.

I went up the broad flight of steps on the S.O.B.'s southwest
corner to a terraced landing, then through the main doorway,
which opened onto the second floor. I was back in the marble
two-story rotunda with its balcony and conical ceiling, a vast
space where worker bees flitted around over-forties who were
laughing and talking and ambling along—senators and senior
staff.

A uniformed elevator operator delivered me to an endless tunnel of a hallway lined with office doors tall enough to accommodate Abe Lincoln, stovepipe hat and all. Conversation echoed as
I slipped unnoticed into a steady two-way stream of people who
belonged here, the sound of footsteps on the marble-and-tile
floor combining into an awkward tap dance.

When I got to McCarthy's office, a tall shapely brunette in a tailored blue-trimmed white dress was just about to go in. Not quite
thirty, Jean Kerr looked like the beauty queen she'd been, but she

was much more. Among other things, she'd ghosted McCarthy's anti-Communism book last year.

"Well, Nathan," she said, beaming, her bright red lipstick completing a patriotic pinup, "hello."

I held the door for her. Her hair up, her eyes a sparkling blue, this fairly ravishing Irish rose had gone to work for McCarthy straight out of college. Now she was his chief of staff.

"He's in with Roy," she said, with a fresh-faced openness that wasn't quite flirtatious, "but I'll let him know you're here. . . . Can I take your hat?"

"Sure."

She did so, then walked me into a conference area where staffers were at work before we took an immediate right through a short filing-cabinet-lined hall into the central area. Staffers were evenly split between females and males, some at their desks typing or bent over research, others filing or on their way back from or to somewhere. Most were no older than their mid-thirties.

Jean deposited me in one of a row of chairs along the wall near McCarthy's office door and said she'd let the senator know I was here. While I waited, one of the young staffers in shirtsleeves and loosened tie looked over from his desk and squinted at me, removed his reading glasses, and squinted again.

He got up and came quickly over, a slight figure with tousled dark brown hair and boyish features. Until he gave me a buck-toothed grin, I didn't recognize him.

"Bob Kennedy, Mr. Heller," he said. "You probably don't remember me."

He held out his hand and I shook it, then started to get to my feet. He motioned me to sit back down and settled in next to me.

"I remember you, Bob." His father, Joe, had been an occasional client of mine since the mid-'40s, back when the onetime big-league bootlegger had bought the Merchandise Mart much as I might buy a new car.

"My dad and my brother," he said, still smiling, "always speak warmly of you. You really helped us out of a jam that time."

He was referring to a job I'd done half a dozen years ago, getting Jack out of a quickie marriage the young senator had screwed and boozed himself into one ill-advised night. It had taken bribing a courthouse clerk, playing with matches, and paying off the socialite bride, just another day's work for a Chicago-bred PI.

Typical that Bob would credit that as me helping the family and not just a brother whose brain went soft when his dick got hard.

I said, "You must be a lawyer by now."

He nodded. I put him at around twenty-seven, maybe twenty-eight. "Graduated last year. I was, uh, at Justice for a while, now I'm working for Joe. Family friend. Assistant counsel."

"Does that mean you assist that Cohn character?"

His smile disappeared, and his voice lowered to a near whisper. "I keep my distance as much as possible. We don't, uh, exactly get along. He thinks I'm a spoiled rich kid, which *is*, uh, rich since he's a judge's son with his own silver spoon."

"So—you're married, I understand."

The grin returned with some shyness mixed in. "Coming up on our third anniversary. Two little ones, boy and a girl, Joe and Kathleen."

Missing his cue by maybe half a minute, sleepy-eyed Roy Cohn—similar to Bob in height, weight, build, and age but cheerless and darker—emerged from McCarthy's office in shirtsleeves and crisp navy silk tie.

"Mr. Heller, the senator will see you now. . . . Would you like coffee?"

"That'd be fine," I said.

Cohn nodded. Without looking at him, he said to Bob, "Coffee."

I could almost hear Kennedy bristle. Maybe he missed "waiter day" at law school.

Cohn held the door for me while the assistant counsel went off to do his master's bidding.

I went into the rather barren-looking office—beyond a few framed certificates of election, the brown-paneled chamber lacked the usual framed photos and honorary degrees, the only memento a baseball bat on a pedestal between file cabinets on a counter. Burned into the bat were the words "DREW PEARSON."

In rolled-up shirtsleeves and food-stained tie, McCarthy was in his big-backed swivel chair behind his massive standard-issue senatorial desk, its top littered with files and papers. A pair of button-tufted leather armchairs sat opposite him. He wore black-framed glasses, which took nothing away from the bullnecked-brute effect.

Giving me a tight smile, he flipped aside a stapled report, tossed his glasses on the desk, and waved me over.

"Saw you in the gallery this morning, Nate," he said, the nasal baritone muted now, the oratorical eccentricities absent. "Hope you enjoyed seeing democracy in action."

I took one of the leather chairs; Cohn took the other. His face looked like putty awaiting a sculptor to make an expression out of it.

I shrugged. "I thought the mystery writer held his own. I saw *The Maltese Falcon* during the war and didn't have any particular urge to overthrow the government. Except maybe my sergeant."

McCarthy, who like me had been a Marine, smiled but I knew he didn't like what I'd said. His big shoulders lifted and left his barrel chest behind.

"I agree," he said, "that it's probably unlikely there's much *overt* Communist content in those books of his. But why should the government put money in the hands of some fool who's going to funnel it into the Communist cause?"

I nodded. "He seemed to agree with you on that point."

"He's a strange character. One of these oddball left-wing artistic types." McCarthy shook his head, then his dark eyes bore in on me. "But you're probably wondering why I sent you a plane ticket to come and talk to me."

"I am. But since you're paying my day rate, too, how could I say no? Like you, Joe, I'm in favor of the capitalist system."

A big off-white smile blossomed in the blue-jowled face. "I was always impressed by your investigative abilities, Nate . . . and I got to feeling bad about how I've underutilized you of late. Ever since that bastard Pearson betrayed me."

In 1953 retrospect, rabid Red hunter McCarthy and arch-liberal columnist Pearson seemed unlikely bedfellows. But in the early years of McCarthy's first term, Joe and Drew had worked together ferreting out governmental corruption.

After all, from 1947 up to '50—possibly due to his New Deal roots—McCarthy had been a liberal Republican, his seat partly won by courting the Communist vote. As Joe said on the stump, they had "the same right to vote as anybody else." And for several years, the junior senator from Wisconsin had swapped Senate secrets with Pearson's man Jack Anderson for flattering squibs in the nationally syndicated "Washington Merry-Go-Round" column.

I had worked for McCarthy and Pearson, helping them expose D.C. influence peddlers getting 5 percent kickbacks on government business. Then I'd fallen out with Drew over his merciless haranguing of my friend and client Jim Forrestal.

McCarthy dropped Pearson, too, after the columnist attacked him in print as a reckless witch hunter. McCarthy retaliated with an all-out assault on Pearson on the Senate floor ("a Moscow-directed character assassin!"), where Joe had immunity from slander charges.

"I'm gearing up for a major *investigation*," McCarthy said, the weirdly hypnotic oratorical rhythm kicking in, "into the darkest *shadows* of this *government*—from the *military* to the Central Intelligence *Agency*."

"That sounds ambitious," I said. And foolhardy.

"Our country is *riddled* with military bases with security so *lax* it's *criminal*. Roy here is *convinced* that a spy ring rivaling the one that gave the Soviets the atomic *bomb* is operating out of an army base in New Jersey."

I shifted, uncomfortable in my comfortable chair. "Joe, you do know your Republican president—I believe his name is Eisenhower?—has a certain affection for the military."

He waved that pesky fly away. "And the *CIA*—its own *director* admits he's well *aware* Communists have infiltrated his organization! But he *justifies* it because other countries have the same *problem*! *Something* must be done."

"Okay," I said.

He almost crawled across the desk at me. "But I need trained *investigators*. Most of my staff is not *qualified* or *experienced* enough for what I intend to do. Roy here is the *best* I have—and don't be *fooled* by his youth!"

Now McCarthy sat back and interlaced his hands on his belly, getting chummy and conversational. "I guess you know Roy helped put the Rosenbergs away . . . but he also put a dozen *other* Commies away, as assistant U.S. attorney in New York, *and* nabbed counterfeiters and narcotics traffickers."

I gave Cohn a grudging smile and said, "Nice going."

He looked at me with an unsettling blankness. "Doing my job."

The door opened behind us and a glum Bob Kennedy came in carrying a wooden tray with coffee cups, sugar and cream dispensers, and a pot of coffee issuing steam like the Little Engine That Could. The nearest corner of the big desk had room for the tray and Kennedy leaned past Cohn to set it there. He gave McCarthy a small nod and smaller smile, and was turning to go when Cohn spoke to him.

"I'll have sugar and cream. Cream for the senator. Mr. Heller?"

"Black is fine," I said.

Kennedy winced and then returned to the tray and started serving us up.

McCarthy went on: "This young man here, Senator John Kennedy's brother Robert, is probably our second-best investigator on staff, after Roy."

Kennedy spilled just a little as he poured a cup.

McCarthy continued singing the gopher's praises: "Bob spent half a year at Justice, in the Internal Security Section, Criminal Division, investigating Soviet spies. Here in this office he's been helping expose trade between U.S. allies and Communist China, doing a crackerjack job. . . . Thank you, Bob."

Kennedy had just handed the senator his coffee.

Cohn took his filled cup from the tray, as if to minimize contact with Kennedy, who I gave a knowing look and a nod as he came around and handed me mine with half a smirk. Then the assistant counsel gathered whatever dignity he could salvage and went quickly out.

"I am well aware, Nate," McCarthy said, the speechifying style lingering but muted, "that you're a very successful businessman—three branch offices now. Really something. But your country needs you, Nate."

I risked half a grin. "The last time I answered a call like that, I wound up with malaria and a Section Eight."

A veteran of the Pacific himself, McCarthy let out a chuckle; then his expression turned serious. "I assure you I have the budget to pay you a respectable sum. I don't expect you to be a dollar-a-day man, like our late friend Forrestal."

"How long would you want me on staff?"

He rocked in the chair a little, tossed a hand. "Six months should do it. And it would be excellent publicity for you. A real boon to your business. I don't expect an answer right now. Take some time and mull it. Personally? I think we would be doing each other a *great* service."

I sipped the coffee. Cohn was watching me. I felt like a fly an iguana was contemplating sending a tongue out after.

I placed the still mostly filled cup on the tray. "I don't need any time to think it over, Senator. I really have to take a pass on this one. I'm flattered, but—"

"Now," McCarthy said, holding up a big hand, as if swearing me in on the witness stand, "don't be hasty. This could take your career to a whole new level."

Or depths.

I said, "I just opened a Manhattan office, and I still run Chicago myself. I'm the only one coordinating the three branches. Really, I don't have anybody on staff who could take my place."

Cohn was still looking at me with those cold hooded eyes. He had skin the color of the scum on butterscotch pudding. "Maybe there's another reason why you're turning down this opportunity."

A question, even an accusation, was buried in that statement.

I gave him my own cold look. Slapping him would have been rude. "And what would that be?"

Tiny toss of the head. "Maybe we're not on the same team."

"Care to clarify that?"

Cohn shrugged one shoulder, placed his as-yet-unsipped coffee cup on the desk, though he could just as easily have set it on the tray. "You were seen talking to Hammett. After he testified."

"So what?"

"You were then seen getting into a cab with him. You were also seen going to a well-known local restaurant, where you talked for over an hour."

I swiveled in the chair toward him. "I had lunch with the man. He hadn't eaten before he testified. Again—so what?"

"Is he a friend of yours?"

"He's a writer I admire who I took the opportunity to meet. Don't you like *The Thin Man*, Roy? Nick and Nora? Asta?"

Cohn ignored that. "Did *he* offer you a job? Did *you* turn *that* down?"

Was this humorless little prick psychic? I noted that McCarthy, sitting there like a blue-jawed Buddha, fingers laced on his belly again, was just letting his hatchet man do the dirty work.

Unsettled in spite of myself, I said, "How is this your business again?"

Cohn, folding his arms, gave me the tiniest smile in human history and said, "We know all about this 'concerned citizens' group of pinks he's assembled. He should spend more time writing and less time raising funds for traitors."

Now McCarthy spoke, no oratory this time: "Were you approached to reopen the Rosenberg case, Nate? To look for new evidence to clear those two Soviet spies?"

"Suppose I was," I said. "What then?"

"If you didn't say yes," McCarthy said, "I'd encourage you to reconsider."

That made me blink. I admit it.

I said, "What?"

The off-white smile blossomed again in the plump sea of blue beard.

He said, "I'd like you to say yes to the slippery Mr. Hammett, and look into whatever his little Who's Who of Commies think they have."

"Why in hell?"

Cohn summoned a bigger smile. The second smallest on record, but a smile. "We want you to work for us, Mr. Heller. Undercover."


The headquarters of the journalist called by *Time* magazine "the most intensely feared and hated man in Washington" was hidden away on a quaint Georgetown corner within a rambling faded yellow-brick Federal-style town house. I didn't recall ever coming here in the evening before, and in the street-lamp glow, the old house, with its many shutters, brick sidewalk, and brass trimmings, had an almost soothing effect.

Not at all soothing was the bustling newsroom-like office area a few steps down from the entry, typewriters chattering, news tickers ticking, telephones shrilling. As in McCarthy's Senate suite, half a dozen or more young professionals were lost in work at desks or at the long gray row of filing cabinets, sometimes moving in or out of smaller offices. This was mid-evening, so some late-edition-style deadline had to be driving them.

I'd been greeted by a lovely, shapely redhead in a simple, simply astonishing green dress. She was the married boss's latest secretary, the current "fair-haired girl" (actual hair color not an issue). The other young women in the office were attractive enough, but in a pencil-behind-the-ear, hair-up, horn-rimmed-glasses way. As opposed to the *Esquire* magazine cartoon way.

Her boss was in a small office that looked more like a den—dark plaster walls with framed original political cartoons and signed celebrity photos; a working fireplace with an amateur rural landscape over it and family snapshots lining the mantel; windowsills stacked with books, magazines, and a slumbering cat; and the big central scarred wooden desk with an in- and out-box, a telephone, a glass jar of Oreo cookies, and a battered portable Corona, where the boss in his maroon smoking jacket was in action.

No ashtray, though. I wasn't a smoker, though many people who stopped by here would be. But the man behind the Corona was a Quaker and smoking was out, office-wide. His only vices were some light drinking and of course his fair-haired girls. His wife, who lived on their farm, didn't seem to mind.

The redhead announced me at the open door, got a "Send him in," and stepped aside and gestured for me to enter, as she and I exchanged warm glances. I'd had an affair with the previous "fair-haired girl," and had nothing else going on tonight. Who could say where a warm glance might lead?

I just stood there while he finished his current page. Even sitting down he was tall, a trim and sturdy middle-aged man with a little graying dark hair left on the sides of a chrome dome. With his egg-shaped head and waxed mustache, he resembled an American version of Agatha Christie's Poirot. (I'd read her in my youth, too. I somehow doubted she was a Commie.)

He finished the page and with a flourish sent it from typewriter to out-box, then sprang to his full six three and held out a hand. He had a winning, rather toothy smile, but he was trying too hard. We hadn't been back on decent terms that long.

As we shook, Drew Pearson said, "So what kind of mood did you find our esteemed public servant Joseph McCarthy in? Does he know about your late father's politics yet?"

"Somehow that's eluded his crack investigators."

He grunted a laugh from deep in his chest. "You mean that little weasel Cohn? His idea of investigating is looking under beds for Reds."

He gestured for me to sit opposite him in a wooden visitor's chair that was apparently designed to discourage a long stay.

"I wouldn't underestimate McCarthy's snoops," I said, "especially Cohn. I changed cabs three times coming here, making sure they didn't find me consorting with the enemy."

He sniffed. It was a habit of his, a kind of patrician expression of contempt. "That seems a little excessive."

I told him how Cohn had apparently had me followed after I left the Senate hearing.

He shook his head and said, "No. Probably it was Hammett they were surveilling. Did you change cabs because you saw someone tailing you?"

People always talked to me like that. Like in a private eye picture.

"No," I said. "It was a precaution. Or maybe just paranoia."

He fixed his light blue eyes on me and got a twinkle going. "So you met with Hammett, as I requested. How did that go? Did you accept the case?"

"First you should know that McCarthy and Cohn are already onto what Hammett and his friends are up to."

"Hell you say . . ."

I gave it all to him, including the offer of a staff investigator position on the committee and how they wanted me to accept Hammett's job and work undercover for them.

"Damn," he said. "What did you tell them?"

"Well, yes, of course."

"*What?*"

"The money was good. So is Hammett's."

"Well, who will you *really* be working for, man?"

"Same as always. Nathan Heller." I sat forward and lifted the lid off his glass cookie jar and got myself an Oreo. "Think it through. McCarthy may be able to open doors for me that you and Hammett and company can't. This is a closed case, with almost everybody I need to talk to in jail."

Thinking, Pearson said, "Not *everybody's* in jail. . . ."

"No, and that's where you and Hammett's All-Star Leftists can help out. I'll need to talk to several un-incarcerated folks, who'll be understandably gun-shy about opening up to any investigator."

The columnist had a cookie, too. He chewed, thought, swallowed. "I may be able to pave the way for that with the Rosenbergs' lawyer. He's refused to grant meetings to the justice committee members."

He was referring to the National Committee to Secure Justice in the Rosenberg Case, a grassroots group.

I nodded. "Hammett tells me this lawyer . . . what's his name, Manny Something?"

"Emanuel Bloch, yes."

"This Bloch is against the committee's push for clemency. He considers his clients innocent and apparently his clients agree. Which is why Hammett wants to look for new evidence, new witnesses. For a new trial."

"And that's what they *rate*!" Pearson said, and slammed a fist on the desk, rattling everything from typewriter to cookie jar. Even the cat opened its eyes. Momentarily.

"Nathan," he said, "that nice couple were convicted of a crime of which they were not only innocent, but which was never committed in the first place. The testimony against them comes from self-styled accomplices who sold them out, all of whom perjured themselves. They weren't charged with treason, as everyone seems to think, but with conspiracy to commit espionage in time of war. But the Russians were our *allies* at the time. And that this so-called conspiracy even *exists* comes from the lips of liars."

"Glad to see you're keeping an open mind."

He sniffed. "How much do you know about the case?"

"I followed it in the papers some. Looked like the defense botched it half a dozen ways, but also like the defendants were probably guilty. That's usually enough in this country."

He didn't argue the point. Instead he got a thick file folder out of a desk drawer and flopped it in front of me. "Here's everything I have on it. Get yourself up to date."

I folded my arms. "What—are *you* my client?"

He gave up a dry laugh. "Sounds like you already have *two*—McCarthy and the Hammett committee. Don't be greedy."

That was rich coming from the notoriously cheap Pearson. Part of why I fell out with him was because he could be slow to pay and always nickel-and-dimed me on expenses.

I said, "McCarthy called me, and then I called you. You put me with Hammett. I suppose the best I can expect is that you don't ask for a finder's fee."

He thought about that. "You're getting a decent retainer from Hammett. You've haven't said what McCarthy's ponying up."

"And I won't. Anyway, it's not a retainer from Hammett, it's a flat fee of three grand, as I expect you already know—maybe you contributed to it, but I doubt it—and Christ knows how long this will take."

His expression was grave. "They're set to die in less than two months. Isn't three thousand enough to hold you that long, man?"

I managed not to laugh at this tightwad's money management advice.

"You cover expenses," I said.

". . . What do I get for it?"

Now we were down to it.

"Everything I find goes to you first, Drew. I'll let Hammett know I'm giving you an exclusive because you put this all in motion."

He sniffed again. "Well, I suppose that's fair. I'll want the usual receipts and detailed accounting."

"Fine. Let's have it in writing."

He gave it to me, using the Corona.

Then he got a funny expression going, the waxed mustache twitching. "Listen . . . there's something else you need to keep a sharp eye out for."

"Oh?"

"I've been digging up plenty of dirt on McCarthy, and I've got hold of something that, if it's true, would sink him . . . but if it isn't, and I print it, I'll be the one circling the drain."

I put on mock shock. "You mean *he's* a Commie?"

"No." He breathed in. He breathed out. "I think he's homosexual."

"Oh, come on, Drew. Have you seen that doll who's his chief of staff?"

"The Kerr woman? Possibly a beard. Or perhaps his gate swings both ways. But I have three statements from witnesses who performed sodomy with him, or on him, or whatever they do to each other. And there was a boy on his staff who was let go a while ago after he was arrested for lewd acts."

I recalled the young staffer who'd chauffeured at Mosinee and later answered the door when I was ushered in to see the great Red hunter naked. Not an image I cherished.

But I hadn't seen that young man in the office today. . . .

"And then there's this Roy Cohn," he said.

"Now you're just indulging in wishful thinking."

"I don't think so, Nathan. Didn't you see the coverage about him and that matinee-idol Schine kid, that hotel heir? Prancing around Europe, snapping towels at each other in hotel hallways? When they were supposedly checking up on Commies in the Voice of America, and looking for books by Hammett to burn in State Department libraries?"

I held up a stop palm. "You're on real shaky ground, Drew. You know the Fifth Estate stays away from sex and drinking where these politicians are concerned. Anyway, who cares who sticks what into who, as long as the stickee is up for it?"

" 'Whom,' " he said.

I smirked. "Columnists who live in glass houses with stacked secretaries shouldn't throw stones."

He reddened. Actually reddened. Finally he managed, "Well, if they *are* queer, Joe and Roy . . . and they are so close you'd have to pry them apart . . . they're the worst kind."

"What kind is that?"

He raised a fist. "The kind that accuse others of it, to deflect such accusations from themselves. That bastard McCarthy implied *I* was a 'pervert' on the floor of the damn Senate!"

Innocently I asked, "What are you are supposed to have done on the Senate floor, Drew? And to whom?"

The sniff was almost a snort this time. "Tail-Gunner Joe makes a *big* to-do about his aversion to homosexuality, and rooting out the homos in government because they're bad security risks. But what if it's all to keep the heat off himself?"

I shifted in the wooden chair, lucky not to get a splinter. "The A-1 still takes divorce cases, Drew, but I don't snap photos through motel windows anymore. Even I draw the line."

"I'm just saying keep your eyes open."

"I promise. At least one." I stood. "Now . . . let me get to work trying to keep that 'nice couple' from sitting down where you don't stand up again."

I gathered the file folder and the one-page contract, took one last cookie, and was nibbling it and leaving when he said, *"Nathan!"*

I paused in the doorway.

"You'll need to exert extra caution. There are dangerous people involved in this, and Cohn and McCarthy may be the least of it. The prosecutor, Saypol, is in the mob's pocket, for one thing, and he surely wouldn't like his headline-making case overturned. And the Soviets would like nothing better than to make martyrs out of the Rosenbergs and close this matter. Then there's the FBI, who probably manufactured or concealed evidence, and God knows *what* the CIA is up to."

"Where is it you stay in New York, Drew? Waldorf, isn't it?"

I smiled and waved and went out.

Her name was Maureen, by the way, and she got off at nine. And again at midnight.

CHAPTER 4

In Manhattan, on July 17, 1950, Julius Rosenberg, thirty-two—
electrical engineer and civilian employee of the U.S. Army Signal
Corps during the war—was arrested by the FBI on suspected espionage charges. A month later, after the prisoner refused to cooperate
with his questioners, his wife Ethel, thirty-five, was also arrested.

The couple was indicted and tried for conspiracy to transmit
classified military information to the Soviet Union, chiefly on statements made by Ethel's brother, David Greenglass, and his wife,
Ruth. The Rosenbergs were said to have persuaded David in 1944
and '45 to provide them with top-secret data on the atomic bomb
project at Los Alamos, New Mexico, where David had been an army
sergeant working as a machinist. They also were said to have involved Ethel's sister-in-law, Ruth.

The arrest of Ethel, mother of two young sons, seemed obviously
designed as a cudgel to make her husband talk. No one seemed to
believe her role in the espionage reported by her brother was anything but minor. Still, after a relentless prosecution, both husband
and wife were found guilty on March 29, 1951, and sentenced to
death days later.

Julius and Ethel Rosenberg had said little since, stoic in their
Death Row cells. A codefendant, Morton Sobell, received a thirty-
year sentence, as did Harry Gold, another alleged conspirator

who testified against the couple, not terribly convincingly. David Greenglass got fifteen years. Ruth was never charged despite a role significantly larger than what the government claimed had been Ethel's.

The public seemed evenly divided between those who felt the world would be better off with this pair of Commie spies dead and those who felt the political climate had poisoned the jury pool. After all, the Rosenbergs had been arrested shortly after the start of the Korean War, their trial conducted in the shadow of McCarthy's Red-hunting crusade.

Others felt the trial itself had been a travesty—the only really incriminating evidence had come from a confessed spy willing to sell out his own sister, and few considered the death penalty called for, particularly in Ethel's instance.

For two years the case had been appealed over the constitutionality and applicability of the conspiracy charge, as well as the impartiality of a trial judge who, in pronouncing sentence, accused the Rosenbergs of a crime "worse than murder." Seven appeals were denied by the Supreme Court, and pleas for executive clemency were denied, first by President Truman and then by Dwight Eisenhower.

Now it was down to me.

Call it a Hail Mary pass or a last-ditch effort. Either way, if I succeeded, the A-1 would have a hell of a new slogan.

*When Harry and Ike fail you, call Nate Heller.*

In my suite at the Waldorf in Manhattan, I spent several days going over Pearson's fat file of clippings, trial transcript, and other background material. As promised, the columnist had arranged through Manny Bloch, their attorney, for me to meet with the Rosenbergs— individually, as prison protocol required.

Though not prisoners of New York State, the couple awaited execution at Sing Sing—the Federal Bureau of Prisons apparently fresh out of electric chairs.

So on a cool overcast Wednesday afternoon, I took the train from Grand Central Terminal for a quick trip north to Ossining. The scenic hamlet nestled on the east bank of the Hudson, which had given rise to the phrase "up the river," or anyway the famous prison there had.

A cab at the modest train station delivered me to where formidable brick-and-stone walls encased a fifty-some-acre sprawl of brick and stone buildings overseen by lighthouse-like towers where guards cradled rifles, spotlights craved sundown, and built-in machine guns bided their time.

I spoke into a mounted box and a uniformed guard with a badged cap but no gun emerged from a door near the gate. He looked over my letter of introduction, driver's license, and Illinois private investigator's license. This rated a shrug from him, but he let me in. There he patted me down thoroughly before leading me up a gentle slope to a low-slung tan-brick building with stone trim and a row of arched windows recessed into blackness, labeled "ADMINISTRATION BUILDING."

"Wait here," he said. His first words to me.

I wasn't going anywhere.

He went inside while I stood near a row of parked cars and took in the dreary landscape of walled-in brick buildings so quiet they might have been abandoned. Within three minutes the guard returned with another guard. Trained observer that I am, I couldn't have identified which was the one who'd let me in if that were my only way out.

But he identified himself by heading back to his post near the main entry, leaving me to the other guard, who indicated the rider's side of a black Ford sedan. I got in. We rode along in no hurry, the whole complex consisting of rough roads and weathered buildings on a hillside, massive walls stair-stepping down, assorted trees trying to make the surroundings less bleak without success. This might have been a factory complex, but really was a succession of warehouses.

This guard was chatty. He played tour guide, pointing out older buildings whose ancient marble was local stone used by long-ago prisoners forced to build their own hellish housing.

"Them old-time cells," he said, "didn't have no plumbing. Just a bucket. Older fellas here say it stunk to high heaven."

"Bet it did."

He chuckled. "Every morning, the prisoners got marched down, buckets in hand, to the river, and set their turds free."

I had a feeling this was his "A" material. Or maybe Cell Block "A" material.

We were rolling along by an endless several-story, windowless brick wall. This was the lower area of the prison. Must have driven half a mile before the black sedan pulled up to a two-story brick building facing a cement apron in a stunted, squared-off C, the side wings windowless, the central slab with half a dozen barred windows. My driver pulled in next to a half a dozen other cars and got out.

So did I.

My driver walked me inside, checked me in at the first office, where my credentials were again inspected and I got another efficient frisk. Then he escorted me through several locked metal doors, keeping up a running commentary, nodding to various guards as we went.

"East wing's six cells, west wing's six cells," he said, echoing slightly, "all boys. The girls got half a dozen cells upstairs. There's a lawyer room on the second floor, too. That's where you're going."

I said nothing. Sounded like I didn't have any more choice than the other inmates.

"Now your buddy Rosenberg," he said, "we keep him in the dance hall."

Apparently I was supposed to ask, so I did: "What's the dance hall?"

He chuckled again and threw me a sadist's smile. "Half a dozen cells, three on either side of the death chamber door. That's where your pal is, dance hall, 'cause his death date's been set."

"He's not my pal or my buddy," I said. "I'm an investigator. A guy doing a job, just like you."

"For that Commie's lawyer?"

That was an oversimplification, but I nodded.

"Well if you ask me," he said cheerfully, "and you didn't . . . that's one dirty damn job you got there, fella."

At a wall of metal bars with a door made of more metal bars—oddly labeled "NO LOITERING" (what else could a prisoner do; or was that for the guards?)—we went up a wide flight of stairs to a corridor where a wooden door said "COUNSEL ROOM," outside of which two armed guards were posted. One unlocked the door and nodded for me to go in.

Julius Rosenberg was waiting for me.

He was seated at a square, heavy, scarred wooden table in the small, stuffy, windowless space, the unadorned walls a faded institutional green, the single overhead light casting a jaundiced glow. No guard to eavesdrop. Rosenberg wore a typically ill-fitted gray prison uniform, his left hand cuffed to a metal ring screwed into the table, his ankles shackled. They had shaved off his mustache, which made him look a little like Wally Cox on the *Mr. Peepers* TV show, and about as dangerous.

He got to his feet—or nearly so, as best as his circumstances would allow. I'd gotten the impression from newspaper photos that he was tall, but now I made him at around five seven or eight. He summoned a slight smile, his eyes languid behind steel-rimmed glasses. His dark hair was combed back, face a narrow oval, forehead high, chin weak. His five o'clock shadow rivaled Joe McCarthy's, though he was otherwise prison-pale.

"Mr. Heller, I presume." This in a mellow second tenor.

"Don't get up for me," I said with a nod.

"Frankly, Mr. Heller," he said, taking his seat, "sitting down is nothing I much look forward to these days."

This I took as a wry reference to what lay ahead for him, in the room off the dance hall. But it made me like him immediately. He still had a sense of humor and I admired that coming from a guy in a tough spot.

I went to him and we shook hands. His was a firm if clammy

grip. Then I took my hat off and sat opposite him at what was little bigger than a card table, the result neither intimate nor removed.

From the Pearson papers, I knew both Rosenberg and his wife Ethel had been raised on New York's impoverished Lower East Side, his father in dry-cleaning, hers a sewing-machine repairman. They had graduated from the same high school (though were not acquainted there), she becoming a clerk, he going on to City College, where in his New Deal enthusiasm he'd gotten involved in unionism. He'd met Ethel Greenglass at a Seamen's Union fundraiser in a Delancey Street hall where the budding opera singer was a featured entertainer. That was 1936 and they would marry in '39. By 1950 they were raising two sons and living in a three-room apartment in Knickerbocker Village, a federal housing project.

"Mr. Heller," he said, "my attorney says I should cooperate with you. Answer any questions you may have. And I'm grateful for your willingness to help out, but—"

"I'm not helping out, Mr. Rosenberg. I'm a hired hand here, working for a group of anonymous supporters of yours. People mostly in the arts and entertainment fields whose names you'd recognize."

His dark eyes were understandably guarded. "What are your politics, sir?"

"I vote straight Democratic ticket. And my old man was a unionist going back to Wobbly days. But don't get too impressed. I'm also a former cop."

A smile twitched under the blue ghost of his late mustache. "Are you trying to talk *yourself* out of this, or discourage *me* from cooperating?"

I glanced around, including looking up at the light-fixture globe above us. Then right at him.

"You'd be well advised to provide me only limited cooperation, Mr. Rosenberg. The lack of a guard here is meant to give us a false sense of security, and privacy. This room is almost certainly wired for sound. But I'm guessing you already know that."

He flicked half a smile. "We'll do what we can, Mr. Heller. As I understand it, the idea is . . . you're looking for new evidence."

"I am."

A tiny head toss released a comma of dark hair onto his forehead. "I believe you are likely on a fool's errand—not meaning that personally. I believe clemency, thanks to continued public clamor, is our best, perhaps only, hope at this point."

"Not meaning it personally," I echoed, "you're a fool if you think there are any get-out-of-jail-free cards in your future."

"Even if there were," he said dryly, "I wouldn't have the two hundred dollars."

I liked that. I wasn't pulling any punches, and he wasn't ducking them. And despite what seemed a naturally morose countenance, he did have that wry sense of humor.

"You've been living this nightmare for a very long time," I said, leaning forward, elbows on the table, hands clasped. "I've only just taken a crash course over the last several days. So I'm afraid I'll be asking you some fairly rudimentary questions."

He lifted a shoulder and put it back down.

"I'm going to go over a lot of what was covered in the trial. If you feel comfortable going into more detail here, that would be fine . . . keeping in mind where we are."

He glanced quickly up, then nodded.

From inside my suit coat pocket, I got out the notebook and ballpoint pen that had been allowed in with me. I flipped to a blank page, turned the notebook toward him, and gestured with my pen—giving him a look that said private communications could be made this way.

He nodded again.

"Keeping in mind," I said, "that I'm playing catch-up—is it fair to say the government's case against you and your wife rests almost entirely on the testimony of her brother, David Greenglass, and his wife, your sister-in-law, Ruth?"

"More than fair," he said quickly, almost clipping my last word.

"One of the few things about this case that *can* be characterized as such."

I'd started taking notes but in my personal shorthand, maintaining eye contact as much as possible.

"At the time of the supposed espionage," I said, "David was twenty-nine and a soldier working as a machinist at Los Alamos on the fringes of big doings. In his testimony, he described two family meetings in New York with you and your wife while he was on furlough. This was 1945. He claims to have passed secret information about the atomic bomb project to you, which your wife Ethel then typed up."

Contempt curled his upper lip. "Nonsense. Lies." Then his forehead tightened under the dark comma. "But that is . . . *is* what he claims."

"There's no substantiation," I said, "because these supposed events took place in your apartment."

"That's correct."

"No outside witnesses present."

"Also correct."

I turned a page. "David admits, on one occasion, to passing secret information to another person, somewhere *other* than your home, and not in your presence."

He seemed to be taking my every word and turning it over for a better look.

"Yes," he said. "To this Harry Gold character."

"Your sister-in-law Ruth rented an apartment in Albuquerque, to be near David. There, both she and David claim this Gold picked up handwritten notes and rough sketches of a high-explosive device. Something David was familiar with from working at the Los Alamos machine shop."

Rosenberg nodded.

"He identified himself with your name—'Julius'—as his password."

"*They* say."

"And Gold further identified himself with a cutout part of a Jell-O box that fitted a piece that you supposedly gave David—after cutting the box up for that purpose, in your kitchen. At one of the furlough get-togethers."

Again his upper lip peeled back in disgust. "The Jell-O box farce. Cloak-and-dagger claptrap. Ridiculous."

"But Gold confirms it. The Jell-O box recognition device."

His eyebrows climbed. "*Coached.* The man was coached, likely by that weasel Cohn. I *told* you, Mr. Heller. It's a frame-up all the way. This is your government at work! Aren't you proud?"

I risked a grin. "I'm from Chicago, Mr. Rosenberg. I'm neither proud nor surprised. Well, I *am* surprised that you were convicted on such thin 'he said, she said' evidence . . . with nothing to back it up but this half-assed corroboration by Gold, likely the result of him cutting a deal."

Now Rosenberg smiled just a little. He was getting comfortable with me.

So much of what I'd been reading about the case, including the trial transcripts themselves, seemed lame even for a frame-up, much less one that would send the parents of two small children to the electric chair. Hell, Ethel was getting a ride on Old Sparky for typing up some notes! Julius was getting his ride in part because the name "Julius" had come from the lips of a couple of confessed spies who didn't claim ever even to have met him.

"Mr. Rosenberg, I'm not going to ask you if you were ever a member of the Communist Party, card-carrying or otherwise—I'm not Senator McCarthy. Unless you think that's something I need to *know* for my investigation . . ."

I turned the notebook toward him, proffered the pen. But he shook his head.

I went on: "Back in the early forties, a lot of us who lived through the Depression saw the Soviet Union as a successful political experiment. For the benefit of anyone besides yourself who might be listening . . . I wasn't one of them. And of course eventually the

Russians were our allies against a guy named Hitler who lately a lot of people seem to have forgotten about. What the hell, when was the last time he made the papers?"

He was expressionless. Tough audience. My Hitler jokes usually kill.

"So to me," I said, "whether you're a Commie or not matters not a bit."

No flinch at "Commie." Good.

"But," I went on, raising a cautionary forefinger, "if you're a spy who sold atom bomb secrets to Russia, I'm not all that inclined to try to help clear you."

"I'm not," he said flatly.

Then he held out his hand and wiggled his fingers, indicating the notepad. I slid it to him and rolled the pen his way.

He wrote something, held it up for me to see: *INNOCENT!* Then he flipped the notebook to me and tossed back the pen. This was, I guessed, his way of emphasizing that he wasn't just speaking for the hidden mikes.

"Now," I said, "your brother-in-law David also said you introduced him to a man named John, on the street somewhere—a Soviet spy. Did that or anything like it happen?"

"No."

He didn't bother prompting me for the notebook this time.

"Your loving brother-in-law says that when he was on furlough, you invited him and his wife Ruth over for dinner, and that a woman named Natalie Ash was there."

"No."

"That the purpose was to introduce the Ash woman to Greenglass so she could go southwest to play courier with atomic secrets."

His mouth tightened and so did his eyes. "I know her, she's a neighbor . . . but no such thing happened."

I leaned forward again, holding his gaze. "Do you remember what *really* happened, the night Greenglass claims your wife typed up atomic secrets and you cut up a Jell-O box to make a two-piece jigsaw puzzle out of it?"

A full shrug this time. "Just idle conversation. The war effort. That the Russians were carrying a heavy load, and we should have a second front. Nothing treasonous, or conspiratorial either for that matter."

I asked, "What about this Gold character? Do you know him?"

"I never met him in my life."

"What about this woman Elizabeth Bentley, who says she had calls from you?"

His nostrils flared. "The professional ex-Red? She said she had calls from someone named Julius. I'm not the only one with that name, starting with Caesar. But my understanding is that these spies use code names. So if she *did* talk to a 'Julius,' it was someone else."

"You didn't know her."

"I *don't* know her."

"And your codefendant, Morton Sobell?"

"He was at City College, an acquaintance. I bumped into him years later. Purely social and not much of that."

"There was a witness who claimed Sobell turned over some film to you."

"Never happened. But *what* film? This witness, Max Elitcher, was a friend of ours going back to City College days. First, Saypol and Cohn put the fear of God into him . . . then they put words in his mouth." He shook his head. "On *this*, Sobell gets thirty years? Incredible."

I finished my notes on that, then went back to the main point.

I asked, "Did your brother-in-law, on either of his two furloughs, come to your apartment and deliver to you—at your request or otherwise—information about an atom bomb?"

"Certainly not."

"What about a sketch of a cross section of the atom bomb?"

"No." A deep dismissive laugh came up and out from his chest. "Even if Dave had been capable of such."

"Why do you say that?"

Rosenberg smirked. "He's a machinist with a high school education. It's laughable to think that he would even *know* what he was looking at—much less memorize the 'secret' and carry it home in his head."

I held his eyes; they didn't waver. "What about the claim that your wife typed up notes David brought to you?"

"She did no such thing."

"*Can* she type?"

"Certainly. She was a clerk, a secretary, when we met. But she didn't type any such material." He shifted in his seat. "Mr. Heller, Ruth claims her husband's handwriting is illegible, and that's why Ethel was enlisted to type from it, since only his sister could decipher it. But Ethel says her brother has excellent handwriting."

I frowned. "I don't remember seeing where your attorney introduced samples of David's handwriting into evidence."

His eyes widened a little. "He didn't. Should he have?"

Underlining something in my notebook, I said, "Well. Let's just say *I'll* be looking for samples. My understanding is—after the war—that you and David went into business together, and that he left that business, a machine shop, under a cloud."

He tilted his head. "There *was* a strain. David felt I owed him money. I felt the failure of the shop was due to his lack of concentration, his general incompetence."

"But you finally paid him off."

"Certainly. A thousand dollars."

"Only to have him come back wanting more?"

Rosenberg nodded emphatically. "He said he needed badly to raise two thousand dollars. He was in some kind of jam but couldn't specify. I told him I didn't have that kind of money, then he sort of . . . shifted gears. Wondered if I'd check with my doctor for him, and see what kind of injections are needed to get into Mexico. Actually, he just wanted the doctor to give him a phony vaccination certificate."

"Did anything come of that?"

"Well, the answer was no."

"Yours or the doctor's?"

"The doctor. I conveyed the bad news to David. He started right in on the two thousand dollars again, that he needed it to get out of this, this *jam* . . . getting very agitated, saying I'd be *sorry* if I didn't help him out. I just walked away at that point. I don't respond well to empty threats."

Said the man on Death Row whose brother-in-law had put him there.

I asked, "*Was* he in some kind of jam, do you think?"

He thought momentarily, then said, "I think he was trying to squeeze me for money he felt was due him from the business. Of course, it could have had something to do with this . . . espionage activity of his."

"Which is why he considered skipping to Mexico."

He shrugged. "Possibly."

I sat back. Rubbed my chin. "What we need here, Mr. Rosenberg, is evidence. Physical evidence would be best. But testimony from witnesses would also help, people who saw the kinds of volatile interactions you had with your brother-in-law—possibly saw the two of you firsthand, him hitting you up for money, threatening you."

He stared into memory, then shook his head. "I can't think of anyone. He never approached me at the shop, so coworkers would be no help. Possibly somebody at Knickerbocker Village, where we live. Lived."

I let some air out. "What about this so-called console table in your living room? The special spy table given you by a Russian friend, according to the prosecution—outfitted for microfilming. Cohn made it sound like it did everything but play the banjo."

He turned his palms up. "It's in the transcript, Mr. Heller. We paid something like twenty-one dollars for that, at Macy's."

"Just a table from Macy's."

"Table from Macy's, yes."

"And where is it now?"

His eyes widened as he shook his head again. "That's the problem. We paid the rent on our apartment for a while after our arrest, but finally our funds ran out and we had our attorney, Manny

Bloch, get rid of our household things. All the furniture was sold to a Lower East Side secondhand shop."

Poised with the pen, I asked, "Could you give me the name of that shop?"

"No, but Manny might be able to." He was shaking his head again. "But Mr. Heller, our things are surely scattered all over the Lower East Side."

I shrugged. "I may get lucky. And we can check with Macy's about whether a console was available in the price range you mention. Maybe even track the purchase itself. That could blow a nice hole in the prosecution's case and even get you a new trial."

"A table could do all that?"

"This is the kind of table that could turn the tables."

"Why on earth?"

"Well, it indicates bad faith on the part of the prosecution—that they exaggerated that console table into some kind of exotic spy gear, to paint you as a master espionage agent. This is a damn good lead, Mr. Rosenberg."

This prompted the only full smile out of him in our session. "That's music to my ears, Mr. Heller." That sparked a thought and he sat forward. "Are you seeing my wife today?"

"Yes. As soon we wrap up here."

His expression turned instantly distant. "She's one hundred feet away from me when I'm in my cell, you know."

"Really."

"Sometimes I can hear her sing, above me, like an angel. Arias. She would have made a fine opera singer."

"Have they let you see her?"

"Yes. Once a week. They take me to her, up here on this floor. They drop a wire-mesh screen between us. We have an hour. A heavenly hour."

"And your boys?"

"They've been here a number of times. Manny brings them. They were living with my mother, but got to be too much of a handful. You know boys. They're with some friends of ours in New

Jersey." He looked from side to side, as if somebody might be sneaking up on us. "Is our time about up?"

"Afraid so."

He gestured with his free hand toward my notebook and pen. I slid them to him. He wrote something down, halfway through the book, then slid it and the pen back.

I flipped pages till I found it: "*N.A.K.V.*"

A rap on the door confirmed our time was indeed up. But I'd been keeping track on my wristwatch so it was no surprise. Not that it wasn't disconcerting in these surroundings.

Rosenberg didn't jump, either, just gave me another faint smile and a barely audible "Give my love to Ethel."

Two guards came in and undid his wrist from the metal ring and carted him off, his shackles making dissonant if rhythmic music.

I was told to keep my place—I'd be taken to see Ethel Rosenberg in a few minutes. As I waited, I sat staring at the notebook page, with initials that might have been a Russian secret police designation, like MVD or NKVD.

But it wasn't.

I smiled to myself.

*Natalie Ash, Knickerbocker Village.*

These secret agents had nothing on me.

# 5
## CHAPTER

I now knew why I'd assumed Julius Rosenberg was tall. Photos I'd seen had invariably shown him at his wife's side. And Ethel Rosenberg, it turned out, was less than five feet tall. No wonder her husband had seemed to tower.

I'd been escorted from the counsel room and down the hall through several steel doors to the women's east wing of the death house, three cells on a single corridor. Because Ethel Rosenberg was the only prisoner in the wing, talking to her from outside her cell had been deemed privacy enough.

A prison matron sat down the hall from us, out of earshot but in sight of my straight-backed steel chair facing the cell door. On the other side the prisoner sat in an identical chair looking back at me between bars.

As the lone prisoner on this wing, Ethel Rosenberg served a sentence of de facto solitary confinement, her cell maybe twelve feet by six with cot, metal table, washbasin, toilet, and the one chair. On the cot an orange-and-white paperback lay folded open—*Saint Joan* by George Bernard Shaw—the only thing in there not gray. This included the prisoner's complexion and some premature graying in her dark tangle of untamed curls, and her prison housecoat and slippers as well.

Pudgy but not fat, the prisoner had a rounded oval face with dark, wide-set, sleepy-lidded eyes, naturally arching brows, a straight nose, and a tiny red-lipsticked Betty Boop-ish mouth. It all added up to something at once haughty and childlike.

"Mr. Heller," she said, in a rather sweet soprano, "I am sure you mean well in your efforts. But Julie and I, our case will be determined in the court of public opinion."

"That may be true," I said, "but that isn't stopping your attorney from pursuing legal means. And I represent a group of anonymous benefactors who are funding my investigation."

She studied my face. "You say Julie spoke openly with you."

"He did—as much as possible here, anyway, where any conversation isn't likely *really* to be private."

The Betty Boop lips pursed into a tiny smile. "I can verify that my cell is 'bugged,' Mr. Heller. But only cockroaches and silverfish for certain."

Like her husband, she appeared to have maintained an admirable sense of humor. And when she smiled, a plain face took on near prettiness.

"You know," she said, something impish about it, "I have the distinction of inhabiting the same cell as the late Martha Beck."

The distaff half of the Honeymoon Killers.

"And," she continued coolly, "I read recently that the only *other* woman ever condemned to death in a federal court was Mary Surratt, for her *disputed* role in the assassination of President Lincoln. Rather stellar company, wouldn't you say?"

But this dark humor masked self-pity.

"As I explained to your husband," I said, "I was hired only recently and have had less than a week to read court transcripts and other materials. So forgive me if my questions cover what must be very old ground to you."

Her head cocked, her eyes narrowed. "What is the focus of your inquiry, Mr. Heller? The thrust, if I might ask?"

"Other than clemency, your best bet is new evidence turning up. That is, me turning up new evidence."

A small half smile now. "Best bet or only hope?"

"I'm not the only one working in your interests, Mrs. Rosenberg. But new evidence is the path to a new trial."

No smile now, and the eyes went distant. "How sad that facing such an ordeal again is the happy ending we seek."

"Yeah, well, it beats the unhappy one."

She only nodded at that sage observation. Like her husband, she could take a punch. And like her husband, she was winning me over right away.

I explained that I'd be taking notes. With that matron down the hall, I couldn't provide the prisoner with the option of private communication via ballpoint that her husband and I had enjoyed.

I shifted in the unforgiving chair. "We only have limited time here, Mrs. Rosenberg, so—"

"Excuse me, but would you mind calling me Ethel?" Damn, if there wasn't a twinkle in those dark eyes. "I believe we're about the same age, you and I, and if we're going to be friends in this, why stand on formality?"

"Well, that's fine. That's nice of you . . . Ethel. Though I'm sure you're much younger."

She liked that. "And do you prefer 'Nate' or 'Nathan'?"

"Six of one."

She gave me an emphatic nod and folded her hands in her lap. "We'll make it 'Nathan.' Preserve just a hint of formality at that."

I gave her a restrained grin. "All right. Now, because of the time constraint, I'm mostly going to skip things I already discussed with Mr. Rosenberg."

That twinkle again. "'Julie' didn't suggest first names, did he?"

"No he didn't."

"That's like him. He can be *too* serious, at times."

"I thought he had a nice sly wit. And we really hit it off."

"So are we, don't you think? Hitting it off?"

She leaned in through the bars to where she could see the matron down the hall; the woman was reading *True Romance* magazine.

Then the prisoner slipped her hand through the bars and

touched mine, squeezed momentarily, and withdrew it. She smiled at me and I smiled back. We'd gotten away with murder.

"Ethel, can we start with your sister-in-law, Ruth Greenglass?"

The arched eyebrows arched farther. "You mean the sister-in-law who hasn't been charged with anything because she sold Julie and me down the river? *That* sister-in-law?"

"Yes. That one." She had been so charmingly spunky about it I couldn't bring myself to point out that Ruth had really helped send her and "Julie" *up* the river. . . .

I said, "Ruth claims that in November of '45, before she left for New Mexico to join her husband . . ."

"My brother. Yes."

". . . that she visited you at your apartment."

"She did drop by."

I looked up from my note-taking. "But did you and Julius try to persuade her, against her will, to join you in espionage work? And to enlist her husband in the same, when she got to New Mexico?"

The eyebrows rose again but not so high this time; that haughtiness had kicked in. "It's difficult, isn't it?"

"What is?"

"Keeping a straight face, asking that. Poppycock. Twaddle. All of it."

I sat forward a bit. "Were you aware your brother was working on the atomic bomb project?"

Chin up. "Certainly not."

"But eventually you knew."

"Not till much later, when he came out of the Army, and wasn't working in Los Alamos anymore. And, Nathan, anyone who tells you Davey might have remembered things he *saw* there, and written them *down*, and made *sketches* that *meant* anything? They don't know Davey. Preposterous. Silly on the face of it."

"And why is that, Ethel?"

"He's just not that bright, Nathan."

That got a smile out of me. "You had *no* hint of it, his proximity to the atomic bomb."

Her forehead crinkled and she raised a finger to a plump cheek. "Well, he mentioned on one furlough or another that he was involved with a 'secret project.' Kind of bragged about it. Davey can be such a braggart."

"Braggarts often say too much."

"That's true. But all I recall is 'secret project' and a lot of puffed-up nonsense."

"And that's as far as it went?"

Chin up again. "He said nothing about atom bombs in front of *me*, I can tell you that. To me it still sounds like science fiction."

The survivors of Hiroshima and Nagasaki might have a different opinion; but I let that pass.

"Ethel, what about this Harry Gold?"

She shook her head. Firmly. "Never met the man. Never *saw* him till he tramped into court that day."

"Gold admits to passing secrets to the Russians. Did you ever know any Russian?"

"The language? No."

"I should say, 'Russian people.' Russians."

"I don't know *any* Russians. I don't think Julie does either. Well, second- and third-generation possibly, if I think about it."

I pressed a little. "Your husband never said he was engaged in spying or espionage work or giving information from various sources to the Russians?"

"He was doing no such thing!"

"You seem very sure of that, Ethel."

She leaned toward the bars, intimate. "We're very close, Julie and I. I think I'd know."

"He might have been protecting you."

"He never mentioned it to me. That kind of thing, it would be hard to hide from a loving spouse, don't you think, Nathan?"

Her hand darted out and touched mine again and withdrew just as fast.

*Was Ethel Rosenberg flirting with me?*

"There was this business of passport photos," I said, getting into something I hadn't gone over with her husband. "In May or June of '50?"

Chin back up. "They were *not* passport photos. They brought that photographer into the court, but I didn't remember him. I *don't* remember him."

"Was the man lying?"

"A *lot* of lying was going on in that court. But Julie and me, we were always kind of, you know, snapshot hounds—got our picture taken all the time. We have scrapbook after scrapbook."

I moved on. "Ethel, what's this about your brother stealing uranium from Los Alamos?"

The little mouth smiled as big as it could manage. "That's *almost* as big a farce as that silly Jell-O box thing! Only in this case there's some truth to it."

"How so?"

"A lot of the soldiers working at Los Alamos—this is what Davey told me, at least—took little uranium samples home, little hollow rocks, as tiny souvenirs. Used the bigger ones as ashtrays and paperweights. When the FBI first came around asking my brother questions, that's what Davey thought it was about. He told Julie, and we thought that, too."

"No idea the FBI inquiry might relate to the atomic bomb project?"

"Not at all. Of course, we were not in close, day-to-day contact with Davey and Ruth right then, because things had gotten, well . . . relations were deteriorating."

I nodded. "The business squabble between Davey and Julius, you mean."

"That's right. And after Davey got arrested, the FBI came around asking things, and hinted to Julie that Davey had implicated him. Tried to manipulate us into giving them information about Davey. Which we didn't have. Anyway, I would *never* have done anything to hurt Davey."

I let her bask in moral superiority for a few moments, then said, "Ethel, I have to bring up a sticky subject."

The little pursed smile again. "Nathan, this is no time for nice-ties. Ask."

"When you appeared before the grand jury, in August of '50, you refused to answer any number of questions on the grounds of possible self-incrimination."

Several nods. "Yes. That is true."

"You did this regarding questions concerning your brother's two furloughs, about whether you knew Harry Gold, various things that you later answered fully at the trial itself."

Chin and eyebrows up now. "When one employs the constitutional right of self-incrimination, one is not affirming or denying *anything.*"

I patted the air gently with a palm. "I know. But in this nasty climate, taking the Fifth has come to mean an admission of guilt to many."

"To many *fools.*"

"I don't disagree. But I'm curious as to why you *did* answer those same questions at the actual trial."

She shifted on the steel chair, gathering thoughts for a moment or two. "When I testified for the grand jury, Nathan, the ground under me was *not* firm. If the government had presented false evidence or false witness against me on those questions? Why, I could have faced *perjury.* Whatever lie my brother or his wife said against me, no matter how false, it would incriminate me."

I risked asking, "Do you still love your brother, Ethel?"

Chin up just a little. "Let's just say," she said, "I once had a love for my brother. A great love for him."

Was there the faintest tremor in her voice?

"And now?"

For the only time during the interview, her face went ice cold. "It would be pretty unnatural if that hadn't changed."

Down the hall, the matron rose from her love story magazine.

"I'm afraid our time is up, Ethel."

The hand darted out and back again. "Nathan, please see what you can do for us . . . till my time is *really* up."

"I will. Oh, and your husband sends his love."

"I'm sure he does." This time the smile was wistful, nothing at all flirtatious in it. "Do you know they let us see our children now and then?"

"Yes, Julius mentioned that."

"It's quite terrible."

She might have said, *Pass the salt.*

I said, "Oh?"

"We meet in the counsel room, on the other side of that steel door down there."

I nodded. "That's where your husband and I talked."

"Awful room. Such artificial conditions. I do my best. We sing songs, my boys and I. Growing boys. The first time they came, after we'd been separated for so very long, they wondered how it was possible that I'd gotten so short."

Her chin crinkled under a pursed goodbye kiss of a smile.

The matron was there.

Ethel and I exchanged nods, and she returned to her cot and *Saint Joan.*

The matron walked me down the corridor.

I said to her, "She's strong."

The matron's face was impassive but her eyes betrayed humanity. "During the day. Cries herself to sleep at night, though. Every single night."

And she unlocked the gray metal door.

CHAPTER 6

My cell—at the Waldorf Astoria—was better appointed than Ethel Rosenberg's; but then I was on Drew Pearson's tab, not Uncle Sam's. I had asked at the desk if there was a preferred suite that Pearson booked when he was in town—wouldn't be fair to outdo the boss— and it seemed there was.

And what do you know—turned out the columnist liked to live well.

The suite was modern yet lush, all corals and light greens. At right—through the entryway and into a long narrow marble-floored living room, nestled on a fluffy white rug—a pair of lime leather couches faced each other over a glass coffee table near a marble fireplace with a bronze-framed mirror over its mantel. Down at left, a dining room yawned behind French doors; at the far end, a picture window with drawn drapes of a geometric pattern looked onto the city, while beyond the fireplace sitting area was a closed bedroom door. I wondered if anybody as famous as the Honeymoon Killers had ever slept there.

The Rosenberg material was piled on the dining room table—a small but complete kitchen nearby—but I mostly camped out by the fireplace, going over the stuff and taking notes. That's where I was right now, checking back over things I'd discussed with Julius and Ethel.

I'd intended to stop by the A-1 office in the Empire State Building and talk to Robert Hasty, who I'd stolen from Bradford Investigations in D.C. to head up my Manhattan branch. We'd only opened shop a few months ago. But it was early evening by the time I got back from Ossining, so that was out.

The Copa had Sinatra headlining—maybe I could pull strings for a table and possibly snag a date with a Copa Girl, as the beauties in the club's chorus line were called. But seated on the edge of my bed— after hauling a phone book from a nightstand drawer and nearly getting a hernia—I decided to take a flier, and looked up Natalie Ash.

Luckily there was only one listing by that name, though there were several listings for "N. Ash" and two more for "N. Ashe." And 65 Morton Street meant Greenwich Village, not Knickerbocker.

I tried the number anyway.

No answer.

Shrugging, I called the Copacabana, asked for manager Jack Entratter, got him after a little name-dropping ("I do jobs for Frank— *ask* him"), and wangled a table for 9 p.m. They served till ten and the show started at eleven. Nothing ringside available, even for a name-dropper, but I'd get backstage later and Frank would fix me up. He spilled more girls than most guys ever caught.

I showered and shaved and then, in a what-the-hell moment, sat back down on the bed in my boxers and black socks and tried Natalie Ash again. This time somebody answered. Somebody female.

"Hello," a husky alto said. No attitude of any perceptible kind, no identification either.

"Miss Ash? Natalie Ash?"

"Who's asking?"

"Nathan Heller. I'm an investigator working on the Rosenberg case. Are you the Natalie Ash who was their neighbor at Knickerbocker Village?"

A pause. "You're a little late to the party, aren't you?"

There was a lilt in her voice that emboldened me.

I said, "If you mean the Communist Party, I'm strictly a capitalist. But I am trying to save those two crazy kids, even if it is for money."

Her laugh was easy and sultry. I wondered if something as attractive as that voice was attached to it.

"Heller, is it? Jewish, right?"

"That depends."

"On what?"

"On whether that's a plus or a minus."

A throaty laugh. "It's a plus where I come from," she said. "Look, I just got in from work, but I was about to head out for a bite. I'm not meeting anyone or anything. What are you after, just to interview me? Talk to me?"

"That's right. Ask a few questions."

I could almost hear her narrowing her eyes as she asked, "So who pointed you in my direction?"

"Julius Rosenberg. I visited him at the death house this afternoon. Talked to Ethel, too, but your name didn't come up."

This time the pause was longer.

"Sounds like you're for real, Mr. Heller." And a short pause. "I guess it's early enough that we could get together tonight, if you like."

"I would like that very much, Miss Ash. Maybe we could meet for that bite you were going out for. My treat. Might take the sting out if any of the memories I stir up are unpleasant."

"Well . . . I guess that would be all right."

"Or you could come to me. I'm at the Waldorf."

No pause at all: "No kidding? You really *aren't* a Communist. You'd buy me supper there?"

"Why not? I'm on expense account."

"That's inviting. But I don't have anything to wear suitable for the Starlight Roof, I'm afraid."

If she was a Red, she was one familiar with the Waldorf.

"We could meet in the lobby," I suggested. "Just outside the Tony Sarg Oasis? Come by cab and I'll square it with you later."

"How will I know you, Mr. Heller?"

"I'll be the handsome devil with reddish brown hair and silver at the temples. In Botany 500."

"No carnation?"

"None. How will I know you?"

"I'll be the good-looking light-brunette looking for a handsome devil with—"

"Reddish brown hair? Check. Shall we say nine?"

"Nine is fine."

*So much for Sinatra*, I thought, but I was smiling as I hung up. Who needed a Copa Girl, anyway? I was meeting a real woman for a late supper and a promising interview.


She was tall, in that sharply slender Lauren Bacall way, hair falling to her shoulders with a confident bounce and an uncaring arrogance as to whether it was dark blond or a golden brown. Everyone in that part of the lobby gawked at her because she was both stunning and (for the Waldorf anyway) oddly dressed—a fashion-model beauty in an oversize black turtleneck sweater, ash-gray slacks, and white-laced black oxfords, carrying a small black purse.

She saw me standing near the restaurant entry and came to a sudden stop to beam at me like we were old friends, displaying a nicely toothy smile. Then she came quickly over and held out a hand to me: no rings, no jewelry, of any kind.

"You must be Nathan Heller," she said.

Her big wide-set eyes were a chocolate brown under thick well-shaped brows, her nose suspiciously well carved, her cheekbones so sharp you might get cut on them. The only makeup, besides maybe some light face power, was bright red lipstick. Disturbingly, it was the same color as Ethel's.

Taking her hand but not shaking it, I said, "And you're obviously Natalie Ash. But I'll just call you Natalie. 'Obviously Natalie' sounds too formal."

She laughed a little, giving that just about what it deserved, then put the smile away like a prop she was finished with to allow me to take her arm in a surprisingly familiar fashion. We went in.

The Tony Sarg Oasis, named for the late cartoonist who'd designed the first Macy's Parade balloon animals, was as much cocktail lounge as restaurant. Its curving walls were home to a lively mural of Disney-style animals, though Mickey and Donald and crew weren't usually tossing down drinks like this comic menagerie.

I wondered if there'd be any objection to her wardrobe, but we were immediately seated, if off to one side and in a corner, which was fine with me since it gave us some privacy. Also, we were well away from the small bandstand, where violinists and cellists played corny Hungarian rhapsodies.

We had cocktails first, a Rob Roy for her and a daiquiri for me. But the drinks hadn't come yet when she turned those big eyes loose on me and that wide mouth made half a smile that was worth more than most any whole one.

"I *knew* I'd heard of you," she said.

"You did? You have?"

She nodded and the golden brown hair bounced; no dandruff on her black sweater. Some of her was bony under there; some of her was not.

"After I hung up," she said, "I went over to a stack of *Life* magazines. Took ten minutes but I found you. You're that 'Private Eye to the Stars,' aren't you?"

"Guilty. Of being the subject of that article, anyway."

Her head tilted, ready to be attentive. "So how does a Chicago boy get to be a Hollywood detective?"

"I'm not really. Not in any sense of the phrase. I handled some big cases—"

"Lindbergh, Huey Long, Sir Harry Oakes . . . all before my time of course."

She was thirty-five anyway, so that was debatable.

"Big cases," I continued, with a sheepish smile, "that enabled my agency to open up a branch office out West."

"You don't mean Death Valley, though. You mean Hollywood."

"I mean Hollywood. And just recently we opened up a branch here in Manhattan."

The cocktails came.

She sipped her Rob Roy, then ate the cherry, plucking the stem. "That's why you're in the city? This new branch office?"

"No," I said, and I told her briefly about the anonymous group funding the eleventh-hour investigation.

"Is this pro bono?" she asked. The eyes were wide but I detected something wary in them.

"No. I mentioned I was on expense account, remember? No, I'm on the clock."

"Right now?"

"Right now. And I'm working my tail off, can't you tell? Listen, if you like goulash, it's very good here. The specialty."

We both ordered that.

The conversation through the meal focused on her background. She was from upstate New York—Ithaca. Her father was a retired history professor at the college there. Her mother was a teacher, too—high school sociology—but would be retiring soon.

Then she dropped a minor bomb, between forkfuls of goulash: "Die-hard Communists since forever, Mom and Dad. I was raised that way. And I didn't disappoint."

Hungarian fiddles were fiddling. Rome wasn't burning, but somebody's baked Alaska was.

As casual as possible, I said, "You're a Communist?"

She nodded. "But I keep that to myself." Though she certainly didn't seem to be. "It's gotten very passé in the Village, you know. Very much last decade."

"Some people consider it current," I said. "You've heard of Joe McCarthy, I take it."

She made a face, shook her head, and all that hair went along for the ride. "He is *so* late to the game. There *used* to be a lot of left-ies in the State Department, but they were flushed out *years* ago. Why is it a surprise that in the Depression so many smart people were socialists?"

"Short memories," I said. "McCarthy was a New Dealer."

"What about you, Nate? It's okay I call you Nate?"

"Wish you would, Natalie."

I gave her the brief rundown, from my unionist old man to me voting for FDR in three presidential elections, but omitted the part where my father committed suicide with my gun. Not appropriate supper conversation under a mural of a tipsy tiger.

"You know," she said, after the plates had been cleared away and we were on our second Rob Roy and daiquiri respectively, "I think you're perfect for this job. You're not a zealot. Just a guy who votes right, or actually left, who can keep an open mind."

"Thanks."

"Why do you think Julie gave you *my* name?"

I explained that my interviews with the Rosenbergs had almost certainly been recorded.

"If Julius answered any of my questions," I said, "that he'd refused to answer in court, citing the Fifth? Well, the feds would have it on him. Same with Ethel."

"Isn't electrocuting them enough?"

"You'd think. But if there were ever a new trial, the government would have that to use." I sipped my drink. "I wonder if they really will kill that little woman."

"Ethel."

"Ethel. Looks like the worst thing she may have done was type up some notes. Even if her husband *was* up to something and she had a certain awareness of it . . . the chair? It's literal overkill."

"They're just trying to make Julie talk."

I nodded again. "Running a bluff."

"Oh, they *may* kill her, all right."

"You think so, huh?"

Her expression was matter-of-fact. "They don't give a damn about Ethel Rosenberg. She's just another Commie to them."

"What *is* she, really? What is she to you?"

"A friend. A mother down the hall who couldn't keep a handle on her rambunctious older boy . . . a little full of herself sometimes . . . but a friend."

"Ah."

"Also, a Communist."

How could something so unsurprising sound so shocking spoken out loud?

"Julie, too, of course," she said. "It's not like the government hasn't known that from Day One."

"Which is why it's just the kind of thing Julius and Ethel couldn't tell me." I took another sip. Just the right amount of rum. "So—how active with the Party were they?"

"Very. Meetings, organizing, protests. Well . . . not Ethel. Not after she had the first boy. But a lot of that City College crowd—and I was friends with plenty of them, they stayed close to Julie—were real activists. Young Communist League."

"Who graduated to card-carrying members of the Communist Party USA?"

"Well, we haven't carried cards for a long time. That would be kind of a stupid thing to do, don't you think, Nate? In this country right now?"

"Right." I drained the daiquiri. "So. The Greenglasses were active in the Party, too? David and Ruth—true believers, were they?"

Natalie nodded. Finished her drink. We ordered another round. While we waited, she got some cigarettes from her purse, Fatimas, and offered me one.

"No thanks."

"No bad habits, Nathan?" she asked cheerfully, lighting up.

"Not that one. I smoked during the war. Haven't since."

The new round arrived.

She dragged her cherry around in her cocktail, then said, "And that's what it's all about, I think. Where it really started."

"Where what started?"

She leaned in conspiratorially. "Julie recruited Davey into the Party. I think Ethel encouraged Davey too . . . *and* Ruth. You know, it's like any enthusiasm. If you have a stamp-collecting club, and you have a friend who's interested in stamps . . . what do you do?"

"Invite them to join."

She nodded a bunch of times. She was getting looped. And of

course that was fine with me, as long as I could keep pace with her without getting as looped as she was.

"So from Davey's vantage point," she said, slurring just a little, "*all* of this is Julie's fault."

"How so?"

"If Julie hadn't invited him into the CP—the Party—then Davey wouldn't have gone down this road."

"What road?"

She gestured with the Fatima. "The road to Los Alamos and so many other things. Word among those who know . . . who *know* . . . is that Davey was willing to do just about *anything* for the Soviets."

"Because he was a true believer?"

"He talked like one. But also they paid him. He was in it for the money as much as the cause. I don't believe Julie had any part of it, but I can tell you this much—there's no way Julie would've taken money for doing what he thought was right. No damn way at all."

"So somebody other than Julie enlisted Davey to steal secrets at Los Alamos."

More nods. "You bet. Probably that Gold guy. He's a creep."

"You know him?"

"No. I was in court that day. Gave me the willies just looking at the slob. See, I was in court for a lot of it. Lots of Julie's friends from the Party were there."

"Show of support?"

"Subpoenas. Unfriendly witnesses, half a dozen of us. Those jerks Saypol and Cohn didn't have the nerve to call any of us. Not one."

Well, they hadn't needed to, had they?

Another round.

"You're saying that Davey was the atom spy," I said. "That when he got cornered, he pinned it on Julie, who he blamed for getting him into this mess in the first place."

"That's what I'm saying." Then she leaned in again, smoke drifting between us. "And here's how I know—Davey quit the Party right about when he would've started playing spy. But Julie stayed in—a member of the CP to the end. Right up till they hauled him away."

"I don't catch the significance."

She let smoke out her mouth. "Well, what people in the Party were saying back then—this was, what, eight, ten years ago—was that whenever some good comrade suddenly dropped out, it meant Russian agents were recruiting American Party members."

"To do what?"

"What do you think?" She put the cigarette out in an Oasis tray. "Their bidding. And the first thing those recruits had to do was quit the Party."

"To keep a low profile."

"Keep a low profile."

We needed another drink. We got one.

"Listen," she said, overenunciating a little, "what's your plan? How are you going about this?"

"Hoping to gather new evidence. Start by trying to track down that famous console table."

"The spy table! From Macy's! What a laugh."

A Tony Sarg elephant danced on the wall nearby.

"Other witnesses would be helpful, too," I said. "If any of those friends you mentioned who got dragged to court knew anything . . ."

"No. No, they won't get involved. . . . Anyway, three or four have flown the coop. Parts unknown."

"But some are still around?"

"Sure. But first, they may not know anything, which is likely why they haven't skipped. Second, they don't want to be asked on the stand if they are or ever were . . ." She raised a shush finger to her lips, then mouthed: R-E-D-S.

"So I'm out of luck then?"

"Not necessarily," she said, hitting all five syllables of that last word. "What you need is civilians who maybe saw something. Saw Davey putting the pressure on Julie for that money. Neighbors at Knickerbocker, maybe."

"I was thinking the same thing. You used to live there. You know people at Knickerbocker Village."

"I do. I could help you. Knock on doors with you."

"Would you do that, Natalie?"

"Nathan! You're the private eye to the stars. You were in *Life* magazine. What *wouldn't* I do for you?"

I grinned at her. "I'd like to know." Okay, maybe I was getting high, too.

I paid the check and we walked out, having to work at it some.

She leaned on me in the lobby. "Look. Honey. Can I come upstairs a while? That's where your room is, right?"

"It's not in the basement," I said.

We both had a good old laugh over that one.

She said, "I just need to lay down a while . . . lie down a while . . . is it 'lie'? Or 'lay'?"

"I'm going with 'lay,' " I said.

"Don't get cocky."

We held each other up as we laughed at how funny we were.

The uniformed elevator boy, who was about sixty, took us up on a surprisingly unsteady elevator. We made it down the hall to the white door I was currently living behind and I somehow got the door key in and turned it and opened up and showed her inside.

On seeing my marble-floored digs, she whistled, or tried to. "You *are* a capitalist, baby! Wow. So this is how the other half lives!"

"How the other half when he's on an expense account," I said, "lives."

"You have anything to drink?"

"Do you think we need it?"

"Need? What's that?"

There was liquor in the kitchen, but I said, "No. We've had enough."

"Spoilsport."

I walked her to the couch. There was only one light on, a floor lamp across the room. We sat.

She said, "I was glad you could get that key in that lock."

"Why?"

"Because I want you to fuck me."

I thought about that.

"Okay," I said.

She stood. She was a little wobbly but she made it. She pulled off the big loose sweater and tossed it dramatically. It went about a foot and half. She had a black bra on and it took her a while to undo it. I was just about to offer my help when she got it unhooked and dropped it to the floor.

It was a surprise that breasts like that had been hiding under that big sweater on this slender girl. They would have kept her from making it as fashion model, that was for sure—large and conical and dark-tipped with erect nipples that scolded me for what I was thinking.

She had to do a little dance that was more funny than sexy, getting out of the slacks, but I was so hard by now it didn't matter. Her panties were semi-sheer and the bush beneath wasn't kidding. When she climbed out of them, the dark thicket, unhampered by fabric, sprang out a little.

"Help me," she said, kicking off her oxfords. She wanted to move the coffee table off the throw rug.

I helped her. We set the thing aside and we smiled at each other in our accomplishment. It occurred to me that I should take my clothes off, too. So I did, tossing them here and there. Meanwhile, she was getting something out of her little purse—a Trojan in its wrapper. Maybe she'd been a Girl Scout, assuming they also were prepared. This saved me a trip into the bedroom where I had some in the nightstand. Trojans, I mean. What a woman.

I sat on the couch and then she was on her knees sucking me for the longest time. When I felt like she was about to get more than she bargained for, I said, "Floor," and went down there. I took a throw pillow from the couch and put it under her. She smiled at me. Impossibly long legs parted wide, knees pointing in opposite directions yet beckoning me between them. Pink smiled sideways through the thicket. I knelt and reciprocated for a while, then got the Trojan wrapper off somehow, but she took it from me and slipped it over me, like she wasn't drunk at all. Nimble as hell.

Then I climbed on top of the little Commie and drilled her like a bad tooth.

# CHAPTER 7

In my dream it was a rainstorm, but when I crawled up into cotton-mouthed wakefulness, I realized it was the sound of the shower in the nearby bathroom. I was naked under sweaty sheets and consumed with a tiredness that seemed to say I needed sleep when I'd already had something like nine hours. A headache, not blazing or anything, was the only other evidence of a hangover.

I had to piss like a racehorse, so there was no question of niceties when I invaded the bathroom during my guest's shower. Her form behind the textured translucent glass, moving gracefully in the downpour only made my condition more desperate.

That condition was acerbated—and there's no delicate way to put this—by what uncouth males refer to as a piss hard-on. If there's a medical term for it—like erectile urination syndrome—I haven't heard it, though down South I understand such stiff dicks are referred to as "morning glories." Nothing glorious about having to pee with one. It's like trying to paint a picture with a fire hose.

The upshot was, just after I'd finished and used Kleenex to mop up the mess, she stepped dripping from the shower, and after I handed her a towel, she got her face dry enough to see me standing there at naked attention.

"We have to stop meeting like this," she said.

89

"Sorry." I shrugged. "When you gotta go . . ."

"Well, let's not waste it."

Still dripping, she grabbed me by it and led me into the other room. She shoved me onto the bed, then stood there in all that pearled skin toweling off her hair, leaving damp gypsy tendrils, the tips of the full breasts perked with cold. I did my part, getting a Trojan out of the nightstand. Soon she was on top of me, moving slow and rhythmic, head back and forward and back and forward, pelting me pleasantly with moisture. It was slow and sweet, until it got hot and heavy, and when she collapsed into my arms, I whispered, "Good morning. What was your name again?"

That made her laugh, and then she got off of me and jiggled into the bathroom. This time I let her have her privacy for a while. When she exited in a terry-cloth hotel robe, I took my turn— shower, shave, and so on. She had her gray slacks on and was getting back into the oversize black turtleneck when I came out like Tarzan in a towel.

"You want breakfast?" I asked. "We can call for room service or there's the coffee shop."

She shuddered. "It's all I can do to keep last night's goulash at bay. How hungover are you?"

"Not bad. I did have a dull headache but you got rid of it better than Bayer."

She paused and assessed herself. "Other than a little nausea, I seem to be okay."

"All women get nauseous after screwing me. Nothing to worry about."

She laughed some more. "I *could* use coffee."

"Well, I have a kitchen for that kind of thing." I gestured in that direction.

"A kitchen in your hotel room?"

"Sure. Doesn't everybody?"

"You are a true enemy of the people, aren't you, Nate?"

"Right. A capitalist dog. Or is that pig? But we've established we're both decadent, so we have that common ground. Shall I put the coffee on?"

Before long we were sitting at the little kitchen table in the little kitchen like an old married couple or maybe a young one. The coffee tasted swell and the company was fine. With no lipstick and not a hint of makeup, her hair a mass of unattended curls, she was just lovely.

"So what do you do?" I asked, peering over a coffee cup brim.

"Apparently I pick up older men and have my way with them." She arched an eyebrow to go with her arch tone. "I still need that cab fare, by the way. Don't be generous or I'll feel cheap."

"You're embarrassing me. I don't usually kiss on the first date, either. I meant—what do you *do*? Last night when I called, you said you just got home from work."

She shrugged, coffee cup at half-mast. "I manage an art gallery in the Village. A group of artists got together and rented space that used to be an antique shop, and hired me to run it."

"Modern art?"

She nodded, sipped the coffee. "Some top talent in the New York School—Reinhardt, Motherwell, Mitchell, Hartigan, Leslie."

These names had been rattled off with obvious pride. I'd heard of none of them.

"Pollock was invited," she said, with a smirky shrug, "but he's too famous now. He's like you."

"What? How?"

"*Life* did a piece on him and made him rich and famous. He isn't paying off grocery bills with paintings anymore." She gave me a pixie smile that was very winning from such a worldly girl. "You'll have to come down and check out my gallery."

"Now that you've seen my etchings, you mean?" I set my cup down. "Listen, Natalie—do you remember offering to help me out at Knickerbocker Village?"

"To look for new witnesses to help Julie and Ethel? Sure. Just say when. I have help that can cover for me at the gallery."

"You also mentioned friends from their circle—others Julius and his wife knew in the Movement. Some you said have skipped, but maybe a few are still around."

"You could get background from them," she allowed, with a thoughtful nod. "They won't come forward, though. Just too damn dangerous."

"I get that."

She shrugged. "These are people I haven't talked to in some time. Like I said last night, when somebody gets recruited from our ranks to get . . . you know . . . *really* involved? They drop out of the Party."

"Understood. But would you see what you can do?"

She nodded. "Give me a day or two."

I gave her five bucks' cab fare.


For all its fame, the Empire State Building remained something of a flop.

The monumental limestone-and-steel building, tallest in the world and a terrible place for a giant gorilla to hide, remained the epitome of the 1920s boom years, its 1931 opening tactfully delaying the availability of the highest windows in Manhattan to jump out of.

As a tourist attraction, the Empire State was literally tops; as an office building, it was a bargain for businessmen. Eighty-six floors were home to mostly small shops—watchmakers, diamond merchants, barbers, low-end wholesalers—and, until the last few years, it was so underoccupied, its nickname was the Empty State Building.

The A-1 Manhattan branch had wound up here because we'd taken over the James S. Bolan Detective Agency—the boss, an ex–New York City police commissioner, had died last year with no one from the firm picking up the reins. We were happy to. It got us a client list, suitable space, and reasonable rent.

I survived the swift ride to the forty-sixth floor and clip-clopped down a dim marble corridor past smoky glass doors, stopping at ours, which read:

## A-1 DETECTIVE AGENCY
### (FORMERLY BOLAN)
### Nathan S. Heller, President
### Robert J. Hasty, Vice President
### NEW YORK, CHICAGO, LOS ANGELES

The atmosphere was perfect for a private detective agency, like something right out of Hammett's world and the black-and-white movies they spawned. But maybe not ideal for changing times. That would come.

Entering into our optimistically large waiting room—devoid of clients and with no receptionist—I had an immediate sense of what a small start we were making here. The place managed to be both relentlessly modern and a bit dingy—a drop ceiling with fluorescent light panels supplemented by metal nose-cone light fixtures; wall-hugging faux-leather armless chairs (mostly dark green with an occasional yellow); smooth medium brown walls; and a corner table where a droopy potted philodendron seemed to be surrendering to a selection of last year's magazines.

A door at right said "EXECUTIVE OFFICES" and a big window revealed the desk of what should have been a secretary's post, where instead big round-faced Bob Hasty sat. Right now this was a one-man operation and that window let him keep tabs on any clients who materialized.

He heard me come in and glanced up from the stack of mail he was going through and grinned over at me. Not quite forty, Bob had the stocky build of a high school tackle, hair light brown, eyes dark blue, nose a lump, lips thick, grin infectious. He looked like the happy drunk he'd once been till he went AA; but he'd seen more than his share of unhappiness when he'd worked homicide in both D.C. and Manhattan.

I went in and he got to his feet for the handshake ritual, then sat back down as I took the client chair opposite. I tossed my hat on his desk.

Nodding at the mail, I said, "Is that strictly money going out, or is some coming in?"

"A wash at the moment." He was in a brown gabardine with a brown-and-white bow tie. Behind him were two doors, one to his office, which for now he only used for consultations, and the other to mine, which I'd not yet used at all.

"I'd say you look good, Nate," he said cheerfully, "but you got Dracula eyes. Tie one on last night?"

"I got a female liquored up to make her talk," I said, "and then she took advantage of me."

"Life can be cruel sometimes," he said with a chuckle. He gestured vaguely. "I got coffee. . . ."

"No, I'm fine. I won't be here long. I have an appointment with Manny Bloch in about an hour."

"Rosenberg's lawyer," he said with a nod.

I'd briefed Bob by phone on the job the other day.

"I wish I could pitch in," he said with a shrug. "But till we get some people hired, I'm holding down the fort, and strictly using freelancers."

We had adjacent space next door for an eventual bullpen of half a dozen operatives.

I filled him in about my interviews with Julius and Ethel Rosenberg, emphasizing the need to find our only potential physical evidence—that console table.

"Send a man over to Macy's," I said, "and another to the junk shop the table was sold to. I don't have the name yet, but I'll be getting it from Bloch this morning. In the meantime, I hope to talk to Harry Gold and David Greenglass in prison."

"Where are they?"

"Lewisburg. And that female I mentioned is going to help me track down new witnesses."

Bob's face was expressionless, which was as close as he came to a frown, unless he was beating on someone. "Some of these bigger junk shops sell to smaller secondhand stores, you know. We may need to put two or three men on that. That furniture could be any-where on the Lower East Side."

"Fine. Do that."

His eyes narrowed. "You didn't say how much we're getting for this job."

He wasn't out of line asking. Like Fred Rubinski in L.A., Bob was a vice president with the A-1.

"A flat three grand," I said. "But I'm laying all expenses off on Pearson."

"Would that include the tab we run on the freelance boys?"

"Probably not. I'm already sticking it to that old cheapskate by staying at the Waldorf."

That made him grin, but just momentarily. "That's a respectable fee, but chasing a phantom table around town like that, I don't know. It's a lot of hours. And this thing may run right up to the night of the execution—when is that?"

"June sometime," I said. "And I may need more men to chase down various leads. I want to find handwriting samples from David Greenglass, for one thing. Nice legible extended ones."

I explained.

After listening patiently, Bob said, "Nate, we can run through that three grand without trying, hiring all these freelancers . . . and *your* time is the most valuable the A-1 has."

"Nice of you to say, Bob."

"And now you want to trot off to Pennsylvania to talk to a couple of unfriendly witnesses, and run down possible new ones here on turf you're not familiar with? I don't know."

"Bob, there are certain things it's going to take to make a going concern of this expanded business of mine. Of ours. *You* could start by, oh, maybe watering that fucking plant in the other room? Or possibly getting the carpet cleaned?"

"Go to hell, Nate," he said pleasantly.

"Now, what could *I* do to help the situation? Let me think. How about I can go out and try to clear the Rosenbergs, and get us the kind of headline publicity the A-1 hasn't seen in a while?"

"You pull this off," he said, shaking his head, "and you'll make a lot of Republicans unhappy."

"Just the crazy ones," I said. I grabbed my hat and put it on, getting to my feet. "And that still leaves all those Democrats. . . ."


Manny Bloch's modest office was in a building near the U.S. Federal Courthouse on Foley Square. The walls were home to framed diplomas and black-and-white photos of leftist political figures posed with the attorney; half a dozen ancient dark-wood filing cabinets listened in on our conversation.

Behind a big beat-up chunk of a desk piled with papers and file folders, Bloch rocked gently in his swivel chair as we spoke. He was of medium height and build, looking older than his fifty-some years, thanks to short-cropped kinky white hair and deep-set eyes with dark bags, the latter emphasized by dark slashes of eyebrow. His gray suit was rumpled and off-the-rack, his tie a black-and-white striped number that reminded me of old prison uniforms.

Seated across from him, I'd already filled him in on my plan of action, plus asked for and gotten the name and address of the junk dealer who purchased the Rosenberg's furniture.

"I have to admit I'm outright astonished," Bloch said, in a fluid court-schooled baritone. "I figured that damn table was gone forever. But if we find it, can we *authenticate* it?"

"I'm working on the Macy's end," I said. "That should give us a damn good shot."

If I was expecting handstands of joy and appreciation out of Bloch, I'd come to the wrong place.

With what was a perpetual doleful expression, he said, "The handwriting angle seems worth pursuing, too. I should have thought of that. I'll request any letters of David Greenglass's that might be in the government's hands."

I frowned. "You really think they'll turn them over?"

"No. But they have a responsibility to. So we'll try, and then get their refusal on the record. Anyway, just because they act in bad faith doesn't mean we have to."

It was bite-my-tongue time.

I knew Bloch had made two massive blunders in the trial. First, he'd passed on cross-examining Harry Gold, a notoriously inconsistent witness; and second, he'd requested that the government impound David Greenglass's sketches supposedly giving away atomic bomb secrets. By bending over backward to show patriotic concern for national security, Bloch had only given credence to the government's claim that the material in question was significant.

"Looking for new witnesses," Bloch said, nodding, "who might be able to substantiate the money trouble between David and Julius? That also strikes me as worth doing. But might I make a suggestion, Mr. Heller?"

"Of course."

"Try to eliminate anyone who might have a background in the Communist Party. Not just people from Julius' personal history, who you should avoid in any case . . . but any casual acquaintances, neighbors, who might themselves turn out to have pink skeletons in the closet."

Courtroom blunders or not, Bloch was no novice in this area. He downplayed himself to the press as just an "obscure people's lawyer." But he'd been in some high-profile political cases over the last decade, including both the Willie McGee rape and the Trenton Six murder.

"But I have to caution you, Mr. Heller, that though I continue to make my best effort, my confidence in the judicial system doing the right thing in this case is . . . well, let's say, badly frayed."

"You don't think we can get a new trial, with new evidence?"

"Possibly. Right now we're putting together an appeal based on that passport photographer's perjury. So we haven't given up."

"Nice to hear."

The woeful face took on a smile that was fairly ghastly. "Mr. Heller, may I make the assumption that you're Jewish?"

Everybody was asking me that.

"My old man was an apostate Jew," I said. "My mother was Irish Catholic. I'm not anything at all, except a businessman."

The smile widened into something less depressing. "Well, that sounds fairly Jewish, at that."

I smiled back at him. "Why would that be an issue, Mr. Bloch?"

"Well, let me ask you this." Like all lawyers, he mostly answered questions with other questions. "Do you think it was pure coincidence that the defendants were Jewish, and that the chief prosecutors and judge were also Jewish?"

I shrugged. "They're also all New Yorkers. Hardly remarkable that they're all Jewish, too. There's a lot of delis around this town, or haven't you noticed?"

Shrugging back, he said, "Yes, about a third of New York City *is* Jewish. But in the Rosenberg trial, not one *juror* was."

"You think there was an anti-Semitic factor here."

The black slashes of eyebrow rose and fell. "Jews like prosecutors Saypol and Cohn and Judge Kaufmann might be anxious to prove they're good Americans . . ." His voice dripped sarcasm. ". . . unlike these Jews the FBI says are traitors and spies."

I didn't know what to say to that. He might have had a point, but what was there to do about it?

"Of course," Bloch said, "Saypol and Cohn are gone—to the New York Supreme Court and Joe McCarthy's staff respectively."

Not sure I should comment, I did anyway: "I don't know if Cohn is gone, exactly. He's still keeping an eye on the case. A fairly close one."

He frowned. "You're sure of this?"

"That's all I'm going to say on the subject, Mr. Bloch. Listen, I have one more request of you."

"I'll do my best to comply."

"I want to interview Harry Gold and David Greenglass. Ruth Greenglass, too. Ruth I can track down, but I don't know how to go about getting permission for the two in prison. Obviously, they may not be anxious to talk to me. And the government may not be so anxious to have me do that, either."

He was already shaking his head. "I'm afraid I can't be of help to you there. Oh, I'll make a call to John Rogge—David's lawyer. But he'll almost certainly turn me down. I'll do the same with Jack Hamilton, Gold's counsel. And I expect the same result."

"Well, please try. You can reach me at my New York office . . ." I gave him one of our newly minted cards. ". . . or at the Waldorf."

One dark eyebrow went up. "The Hammett committee must be paying you well."

"Not particularly. But I'm not in this case for the money. My old man was a dedicated union man."

He liked hearing that, as I thought he would.

"I *will* try," he said. "But about the only way you could get to David and Gold is if you had an in with somebody on the government side. And that's not likely."

"Maybe I should ask Roy Cohn," I said, with a grin.

"Or his boss McCarthy," Bloch said, followed by a horse laugh. "They're in town, you know." He gestured with a pointing finger. "Over at the Federal Courthouse. Easy walk from here. Doing some kind of press conference."

"Yeah," I said. "I believe I read about that in the paper."


The press conference was held at 1 p.m. in Room 110 in the courthouse, open to the public and televised. Burnished oak walls and floors and even furniture gave the good-size chamber an air of significance. I was toward the back of a gallery of spectators numbering around one hundred as McCarthy—with young Robert Kennedy at his side—announced that he had personally made an agreement with Greek cargo vessel owners to break off trade with Red Chinese and Soviet bloc ports.

Dressed for the occasion in one of his dark blue slept-in-looking ready-made suits, McCarthy said he was making this announcement outside of Washington and in New York because the latter was the USA's shipping center.

"I've negotiated this deal *personally*," McCarthy said in his familiar herky-jerky cadence, "because I didn't want any *interference* by *anyone*."

The effect on Red China's seagoing commerce would be damaging enough, he claimed, to hasten a prompt and victorious conclusion to the Korean War.

"I'm *sure*," McCarthy said, "that President *Eisenhower* and Secretary *Dulles* will be proud."

I doubted that McCarthy's interference in foreign policy would go down smooth with anybody but his most devoted acolytes. But what did I know? To me politics was being able to get a parking ticket fixed.

Cohn craned around from his seat in the front row, looking in a foul mood as the public and press filed out and the camera crews tore down. McCarthy's favorite weasel could not have liked seeing Kennedy, the architect of the shipping deal, at the senator's side basking in the glow of publicity.

"Nate Heller," McCarthy said, with a big smile. "Good—you got my message at your hotel, I see."

"I did. Is there somewhere we can talk? I have a brief report and I also need some help."

McCarthy nodded and turned his hooded-eye gaze on Kennedy. "Wait for us out front, would you, Bob? *Roy!*"

Cohn popped up, then stepped up, his eyes gleaming, his smile small yet triumphant. Kennedy's expression of accomplishment faded and he nodded and went out, filing in behind some reporters.

McCarthy led us into a small adjacent room where tall windows let in the overcast afternoon. For some reason that kind of cloud-filtered sunlight made me squint worse than the brightest day. We sat at one end of a table suited for six.

"We do have to make this brief, Nate," McCarthy said pleasantly, his thick blunt hands folded on the table. "We're flying back to D.C. this afternoon."

Cohn was sitting opposite me, his suit dark blue like his boss's but hardly ready-made. He was studying me with the expression of a sadistic kid looking through a magnifying glass at the ant he was roasting.

I gave them a report on the meetings with Julius and Ethel Rosenberg. I left nothing out but played down the console table somewhat, saying that finding it seemed a long shot.

"And if we do," I lied offhandedly, "I doubt it's enough to get a new trial."

McCarthy was nodding, but Cohn snapped, "What else?"

"Have I done, you mean? I've made contact with a former neighbor of the Rosenbergs, who used to live down the hall from them at Knickerbocker Village. Natalie Ash."

"Commie," Cohn said like he was coughing up phlegm.

"At one time," I said with a shrug. "I don't know if she's still active. She was on your witness list, wasn't she, Roy? Why didn't you call her?"

"Didn't trust her to tell the truth," Cohn said. "She's one of half a dozen 'friends' of the Rosenbergs who we suspected of being Soviet agents. *Still* suspect them. Some have taken a powder."

That shopworn tough-guy phrase made me smile. "You mean Russian agents, or Americans who deal secrets to the Soviets?"

Small sneer. "What's the difference?"

"Plenty. You'd get way more traction finding an actual Russian spy on our soil . . . right, Joe?"

McCarthy nodded emphatically. "If we had one of those, that would be fucking Christmas."

"See what I can do," I said brightly. "Miss Ash is taking me on a tour of the Rosenbergs' building at Knickerbocker Village, to see if there are any neighbors who witnessed David and Julius arguing over money and that failed business of theirs. Or heard or saw anything suspicious."

Cohn said, "Good. That's a dead end. You'll never get a new trial that way."

Several strong witnesses and that console table very likely could, in my opinion, but I didn't say so.

Still, there was something I did need to say.

Pointedly directing my words to McCarthy, I said, "Joe, if I should happen to find new evidence—particularly evidence that seemed to clear the Rosenbergs or at least cast doubt on their conviction—I'll have to come forward with it. You do understand that, right?"

Nostrils flaring, Cohn said, "Who the hell are you working for?"

McCarthy was frowning but said nothing.

Now I looked at Cohn. His face was red and a scar on his nose was white.

I said, "Granted I'm a double agent of sorts. But I'm accepting money from the Hammett committee. And you haven't asked me to turn that money over to you."

The hoods on Cohn's eyes actually rolled back some. "You're taking *our* money, too!"

"Not yours personally. Uncle Sugar's—as we called him in the service." I gave Cohn my nastiest smile. "I signed on to your committee as a consulting investigator. Well, I've been investigating and now I'm consulting. Got it?"

His upper lip curled back over feral teeth. "You have a goddamn attitude problem, Heller."

"I get that a lot." I turned to McCarthy. "Listen, Joe, I know your pet monkey here has a hard-on against the Rosenbergs. After all, he went to a lot of trouble helping frame them."

Cohn was on his feet, veins standing out in bas relief on his forehead. "You son of a bitch!"

I smiled at McCarthy like a friendly priest. "I mean, more power to the little guy. He and that Saypol character, who's a judge himself now I understand, got Ethel Rosenberg a cell on Death Row because she did a little typing. *Maybe* did some typing." I transferred my gaze to Cohn. "Not bad, Roy. Not bad."

"Listen to me, you smug bastard," Cohn said, a barking bulldog. "I didn't frame that goddamn traitor Rosenberg, and his wife was in it up to her fat neck. He was spying for the Soviets. The FBI told me all kinds of things I couldn't use in court, so I worked with what I had."

McCarthy said, "Sit down, Roy. . . . What's your point, Heller?"

It had been "Nate" before.

"My point is this. As a private investigator licensed in three states, one of which we're in right now, I am an officer of the court. And as an officer of the court, I am reminding you, a senator of the United States, that I cannot and will not withhold evidence. Joe, I can't imagine that you'd want me to."

"Of course I wouldn't!" McCarthy said, leaning back in his chair like somebody had opened a furnace door on him.

Cohn's tiny hands were clenched. "Fire him, Senator. Fire his ass."

"No," McCarthy said. "He's doing what I asked him to—he's reporting back his findings." With a strained smile, he said, "Just continue to let us know what you uncover."

"If anything," I said with a shrug. Then I leaned forward and gave the senator an earnest look. "But I need your help, Joe. Can you pave the way for me to talk to Gold and Greenglass at Lewisburg penitentiary?"

Cohn yapped, "Why talk to *them*?"

"The Hammett committee expects it of me," I said, fabricating just a little. "They believe Gold and Davey boy were lying." I turned to Cohn. "More than that, Roy, they think you coached those two and fed them lies like candy when their own stories came up short."

The veins were standing out again. "Now you're accusing me of suborning perjury!"

"I'm not. The lefties are. Is that a surprise?"

Cohn, breathing hard, just glared at me.

McCarthy said, "But as Roy says . . . why talk to them at all? Just tell Hammett and crew that the prisoners refused to talk to you."

"We could do that," I said. "But if I go down there and they stay consistent with what they said in court, it'll undercut any effort to get a new trial."

McCarthy and Cohn exchanged raised-eyebrow looks.

"And why in hell would they change their stories?" I said with a casual shrug. "They probably suspect—and are probably right— that the visitation room will be wired for sound. And they won't say anything they don't want the government to hear . . . since they are hoping for early release on good behavior one of these days."

McCarthy was waiting for Cohn's reaction, which after a few seconds of contemplation was a curt nod.

"I can smooth the way," McCarthy said. "I'll attend to it first thing tomorrow."

"Thanks, Joe."

The senator, smiling to where his blue jowls might burst, rose and offered his hand. I shook it. Cohn and I just ignored each other.

Outside the meeting room, a clutch of reporters awaited Mc-Carthy and he stopped to chat informally with them, Cohn staying close, anxious to soak up some of the attention denied him earlier when Kennedy was getting it.

As if summoned by my thoughts, the young assistant counsel appeared at my side.

"I've, uh, been waiting for you, Nate. Step outside with me, would you? We don't have much time."

We didn't even have enough time for me to ask, *For what?*

Instead I just followed the tousled-haired kid, who was in a dark brown suit with no topcoat. I wore a Burberry because there was a chill now to go along with the threatening sky. A breeze with some teeth in it was at us till we stepped behind one of the Grecian columns flanking the entry.

"There are a few things you need to know, Nate," he said. It was cold enough for his breath to smoke. "When I was over at Justice, it was, uh, common belief that Roy Cohn invented that Jell-O box yarn."

"Really?"

"Really. And then put it in the mouths of his, uh, witnesses. Like medicine they had to take."

"Rumor or fact, Bob?"

"I thought it was rumor at first. Then I checked the files—they weren't sealed—and read Harry Gold's first FBI interview." His light blue eyes held me. "When Gold describes his meeting with the Greenglasses in Albuquerque, he makes no mention of the Jell-O box."

"Hell you say."

Using two pieces of jagged Jell-O box, cut up in the Rosenberg kitchen, had been such a vivid, unifying detail in the testimonies of Gold, David, and Ruth.

"Or," Kennedy went on with a bitter little bucktoothed smile, "that 'Julius' sent him. What Gold first tells the agents is he *thinks* his password was 'Benny or Joe or somebody sent me.'"

I grunted a laugh. "But somehow, over time, his memory got jogged."

"Somehow it did, yes. And Cohn likes to brag around the office that he, uh, personally prepped Gold and the Greenglasses. No details, of course . . . just a wink and a grin."

I pulled the Burberry collar up; it was getting colder. "How about when the FBI first interviewed the Greenglasses? Did you get a look at that?"

He nodded. "David barely mentions Julius in his initial interview. Neither does Ruth."

"Cohn again?"

Another nod. "He's a ruthless little prick, Nate. He railroaded those two. I'm not saying the Rosenbergs didn't do what they were accused of—there was some talk around Justice that they were getting what they deserved, but—"

"Nothing more specific?"

He shook his head. "I *can* tell you for a fact that the, uh, FBI interviews with all three witnesses have almost no mention at all of the Rosenbergs. At that point Cohn and his U.S. attorney boss Saypol take over, and, uh, suddenly the Rosenbergs are the bad guys and the story gets rich with all this Eric Ambler spy melodrama."

I mulled that momentarily. "Eventually Gold did come around to telling the same tale as the Greenglasses. You think that's strictly Cohn's coaching?"

"Call it encouragement. The government housed both Gold and David Greenglass at the Tombs, on the, uh, eleventh floor—the 'Songbird' wing where 'cooperative' witnesses get preferential treatment."

"Next you'll be telling me they shared a cell."

He smirked. "Not quite, but they did see each other on a daily basis—played chess together . . . and very likely got their stories straight. Follow? *This* is what you're up against."

I put a hand on his arm. "Thank you for this."

He smiled that disarmingly shy smile of his. "One friend to another, Nate. I can't give you anything on the record. This is just for you to know what you're dealing with."

"I appreciate it, Bob. But it's not like we're close friends."

"If you can find a way to make Roy Cohn look bad," he said, with an expression as ruthless as anything his rival had to offer, "we will be."

And he slipped away.

CHAPTER 8

I spent much of the tedious train ride to Lewisburg, Pennsylvania, going over the transcripts of Harry Gold's and David Greenglass's testimony, as well as various newspaper clippings and magazine articles, and some off-the-record information culled from Justice Department sources by Pearson's man Jack Anderson.

Particularly interesting was the FBI's assessment that their star witness Harry Gold was a pathological liar. There had been considerable federal nervousness about how Gold might conduct himself on the stand. I could have told them they needn't worry—nobody testifies more believably than a pathological liar.

Harry Gold, the son of poor Russian Jewish immigrants, grew up in a rough section of Philadelphia, a bookworm picked on by schoolmates and imbued with the socialism of his Depression-battered parents. After earning a college degree in chemical engineering, the young man found getting work difficult until a Communist pal, also a chemist, arranged a position in return for some industrial espionage. The recipient of Gold's criminal toil was Soviet Russia, his justification that he was "helping them along the road to industrial strength" (while pocketing a few dollars).

Eased over the next several years into actual espionage, Gold claimed he wanted to quit, but feared his handlers would either expose or eliminate him. During the Second World War, the nondescript, pudgy, stoop-shouldered spy became the courier of atomic secrets obtained by British physicist Klaus Fuchs, who was working on the Manhattan Project at Los Alamos. With Russia now an ally, Gold claimed he was only giving the Soviet Union "information that I thought it was entitled to."

As he rose in spy ranks, Gold began spinning elaborate tales to his contacts about a nonexistent family life, including a wife and kids (he was a bachelor). Drinking heavily now, he got increasingly careless in his spycraft, almost as if he wanted to be caught. He'd even been given several days' warning that the FBI was closing in, but didn't begin removing incriminating evidence from the house he shared with his brother and father until his time had all but run out. Soon he was confessing to the FBI.

Maybe I didn't consider myself a Jew, but I could recognize a schlemiel when I came across one, and Harry Gold seemed to fit the bill. That didn't make him any less a skilled liar, particularly considering he'd fooled all the spies he was working with into thinking he was somebody he was not.

Lewisburg, population 5,268, might have fallen off the cover of *The Saturday Evening Post* or *Collier's*, an idyllic community of shaded lanes, brick houses, and well-tended lawns—perfect for the university there and well suited to be the commercial center of such rich surrounding farm country. Maybe that was why the former Northeastern Federal Penitentiary—the cab took me a mile and a half from town out State 404—looked more like a university, or maybe a monastery.

Possibly it was the Italian Renaissance–influenced architecture, utilizing rough-kiln bricks, concrete blocks, and cast stone. More likely it was the massive-walled facility's red-tile roof standing out against rolling green hills. But this was a prison, all right, its endless gray concrete wall with red-brick guard towers enclosing twenty-six acres where red-brick buildings sprawled and a massive smokestack made a break for the sky.

In the administration building of what had been declared "the most advanced penal institution in the world," I was told by Deputy Warden Franklin Baxter that the two prisoners—one at a time, of course—would be brought to me in one of the attorney/client meeting rooms.

"Would it be easier for you," I asked innocently, "if I just visit them at their cells?"

I was playing a long shot—if the meeting rooms were bugged, maybe this assistant warden wasn't in on it. Wiring the cells would be far less likely.

"Actually that *would* work out well," he said. Slender, weak-chinned, about forty, he was bald on top and dark on the sides, with earnest brown eyes behind black-rim glasses. "Less manpower involved."

A guard escorted me to Gold's cell through what was indeed an unconventional, modern facility. The seven-hundred-foot main corridor fed a series of three-story cell blocks alternating with administrative units—chow halls, gyms, clinics.

Gold was in a one-man cell, six by ten with a metal bed, chair, and toilet. The guard had informed me that this was a cell block for "hardened criminals," but Gold was here in controlled isolation for his own protection. Apparently spies were about as popular as pedophiles within these walls.

In a darker gray uniform than Sing Sing style, Gold was seated on the green-blanketed bed with his back to the wall, reading Irving Stone's *Lust for Life.* At first I thought this was the wrong cell because he wasn't the pudgy character whose picture I'd seen or who had been described by Ethel as a "fat slob." He must have dropped sixty or seventy pounds inside, though his face retained a round-ness and a peculiar lopsidedness, as if he'd had a stroke. His hair was dark, his forehead high.

No cell was opposite us, just a wall against which a guard stood sentry, down a ways to give us a semblance of privacy. The cells on either side of Gold were vacant, possibly to further iso-late him. He came over and stood facing me through the bars. He was about five eight. I didn't offer a hand to shake—I'd been told no physical contact with the prisoner—and Gold knew not to, either.

"I wasn't expecting you here at my cell," he said. His voice was soft, a second tenor; he reminded me a little of Elmer Fudd without the lisp. Or the shotgun. "You *are* Mr. Heller, right?"

"Right. Pull up that chair and sit if you like."

"And make myself at home?" He shrugged. "If you're standing, I'll stand. I do enough sitting."

"Whatever you say."

Droopy eyes fixed on me. "I admit I'm a little confused. As I understand it, you represent a group trying to get the Rosenbergs a new trial. Private investigator from Chicago, right? Yet word's come down that I'm to cooperate."

"Word from the FBI, you mean."

"Well, from *on high*, anyway." His eyes were dark and, droopy or not, had an alert intelligence at odds with his unimpressive veneer. "Let me guess. You asked at the last second to see me at my cell, figuring the counsel room was bugged."

I had to grin. "Nicely reasoned, Mr. Gold. How about your cell? Anybody but God listening in?"

He shook his head. "It's not wired. I've looked and looked, and there's just no possible way, unless a G-man's hiding down in that stool. That'd be shitty duty, huh?"

And he returned *my* grin.

Another prisoner who'd maintained a sense of humor. Which would seem necessary, to maintain sanity, too. Not that Jack Benny had anything to worry about.

"So," Gold said, not loud, "what am supposed to tell you?"

"The truth."

"What truth is that?"

"Whatever truth you're comfortable sharing."

He scratched an ear. His tongue poked inside a cheek. The eyes tightened. "Unless I know who I'm talking to and why, Mr. Heller, I'm not comfortable at all."

"Well, like you said, I'm Mr. Heller—Nathan—hired to take a

last-ditch shot at clearing the Rosenbergs. Anyway, if we're not wired for sound, what does it matter what I ask, and what you say?"

He winced in thought. Maybe five seconds later, he said, "So ask."

"Okay. Part of what I'm up to is looking for new physical evidence."

"Not much of that in this case."

"Hardly any. But there's been some controversy about whether you really went to New Mexico to see David and Ruth Greenglass at all. You *have* been known to tell stories."

His expression was slackly innocent. "Have I?"

"Well, you invented a whole family for yourself."

He shook his head quickly. "That was a cover story. I was only a liar on the job. That's what spies *do*, Mr. Heller—lie every day they're out there spying. I did it for sixteen years and I'm glad that part of my life's over."

"Was the New Mexico trip a lie? The hotel registration card the prosecution produced was a photostat, not the original. Wasn't properly initialed and dated when the FBI agents checked it in. And the time-date stamp is off by a day."

He smirked. "So what story does that tell you?"

"No story at all. But it is suggestive."

"Of what?"

"The government needing to establish your presence in Albuquerque for the Greenglass document exchange. That hotel registration card could be an FBI forgery."

He had started shaking his head halfway through that. "Look, I got to Santa Fe on Saturday and went looking for the contact address, second-floor apartment on High Street. Nobody was home. So I went looking for a bed but all the hotels were booked. Finally I got floor space at a rooming house to sack out on. Knowing some lowlife might roll me and accidentally take what I had on me . . . documents from *Fuchs*, you know? . . . I didn't sleep a wink. Morning comes, I drag my ass to the Hilton and get breakfast. Nice crowded place to disappear in, the Hilton. I registered under my own name, and got some real sleep before going back out to make contact with the Greenglasses. Which I did. That explain it, Mr. Heller?"

"It does."

"And if that dope Manny Bloch had bothered to cross-examine me, it would've come out at the time."

He had a point.

"Mr. Gold—"

"Make it Harry, would you? You know, I think I will sit down."

I turned to ask the guard if I could have a chair. He nodded and went off to get me one.

"I'm Nate," I said, and now we shook hands. His grip was a little moist but not limp or show-offy, either.

He was studying me, head to one side. "What master are you serving, Nate?"

"Why, I'm a double agent, Harry. You must know about them, right?"

He made a wry face. "I do, but they're always really working for one side or the other. Which side are you?"

My expression was pleasant. "I got in to see you, didn't I, Harry?"

He nodded three times. Was I supposed to nod back five times and whistle "Kalinka" and identify myself as a fellow Soviet agent? Maybe not.

The guard was back with my chair. I sat.

I asked, "Had you ever dealt with Julius Rosenberg before?"

He shook his head. "No. Not in my circle—didn't know him from Adam. I'd just been told to say that Julius sent me."

"But don't Soviet spies use code names?"

He waved that off. "This wasn't a code-name situation. I guess that name was given to me because it would ring true with the Greenglass couple. Because Julius was their relative."

"But you didn't know that then."

"No. I mean, it became clear, but . . . no."

"I heard you originally said 'Benny sent me' . . . or was it 'Joe'?"

He eyed me warily. "What am I supposed to say?"

"I just wondered why that changed over time."

Anxiety flickered in his eyes. "When the FBI interviews you, it gets real in-depth, really intense. Things come back to you."

"Interesting. Because this particular thing that came back to you was important. It's really all that links Julius Rosenberg to those atomic bomb documents. Everything else comes from his brother- and sister-in-law, who he was on the outs with."

He was frowning. "Mr. Heller, I think maybe we're through here."

"Mr. Gold, if certain FBI files got out, you could be in serious trouble over these inconsistencies. If it got out that Roy Cohn gave you the idea to substitute 'Julius' for 'Ben' or 'Joe,' then—"

"Then what, I'd be in *trouble*? I'm doing thirty years for chris-sake! And don't bad-mouth Roy Cohn to me—he's working at get-ting me a reduced sentence."

"I'll tell you what you'll get, Harry. If the Rosenbergs go to the electric chair, and your perjury comes out? You'll be an accessory to murder. You might even get the chair yourself."

"It doesn't work like that. I'm not a fool."

And he wasn't.

I said, "Of course, maybe Cohn didn't feed that to you. Maybe you and David Greenglass got your stories together at the Tombs." I gave him a wistful sigh. "Bet you wish you were back there, Harry, in one of those Songbird suites. I hear the guards pass out cigars in the afternoon."

He lifted the weak chin. "It's not so bad in here—mornings in the hospital, afternoons in the library. And a damn *good* library."

"I'm glad you're happy, Harry."

For such a soft-looking man, he could summon a hard gaze. "Look. I don't know who you're really working for. But I will tell you this much. I did something bad, really goddamn bad, some-thing I got manipulated into doing because I was confused, and misguided. But just the same, I'm ready to do my time."

*Was the "something bad" handing over atomic secrets to the Russians? Or was it helping frame Julius and Ethel Rosenberg?*

He got up, pushing back the chair, which grated on the cement floor. "We *are* done."

I remained seated, leaning back, arms folded. "Thirty fucking years, Harry. Why did you settle for such a lousy deal?"

He was almost to his cot; he turned and coldness stared back at me. "Because it's better than Death Row."

So that was it—he'd committed treason, a capital crime, and they had him cold. Thirty years alive was better than forever dead.

"Ethel Rosenberg is no spy," I said. "She's a housewife, Harry. You're really okay with her dying so you can keep breathing, even in a concrete box?"

Tiny sneer of a smile. "You tell me, Heller. Would *you* give *your* life for that dumpy dame? Not goddamn likely!" His shrug was dismissive. "Anyway, they won't kill her. They're just using her to get Rosenberg to talk, and I bet he's got plenty to talk about."

*That's what he* bet, *but he wasn't sure. . . .*

I stood and crooked a summoning finger.

He frowned, staying where he was.

"Come on, Harry. No, really. Come over here."

Very tentatively, Harry Gold returned to the bars of his cell, but standing back a ways, so I couldn't reach in for him.

I whispered, "You did fine, Harry."

And I winked at him.

His head reared back and he blinked. Thought about it. And then he smiled and winked back.

I was just moving away from the cell when he said, "You gonna talk to Davey Greenglass while you're here?"

I halted and turned back to him. "I am."

"I don't talk to that S.O.B. anymore."

"You fellas have a falling-out?"

"I got sick of him at the Tombs. All he does is feel sorry for himself. You got to make the best of it when you're inside. Anyway, I got the word not to talk to him in here."

"From on high?"

"No. Down low. Right here in this star-spangled hellhole. Everybody's shunning him, and if I do the same, I don't get shunned so bad. They hate his fat ass."

"Because he sold out his country?"

He shook his head. "Because he sold out his sister."

Born in 1922, David Greenglass grew up in poverty on Manhattan's Lower East Side. He learned the trade of machinist at Manhattan Haaren High School and, after graduation, briefly attended Brooklyn Polytechnic Institute, where he flunked every subject he took. The future spy—who would supposedly memorize intricate atomic bomb plans and diagrams—had no further higher education.

He did pursue an interest in Communism—both he and his future wife, Ruth Printz (they met in their teens), became members of the Young Communist League, encouraged to participate by David's sister Ethel and her husband Julius.

When he was twenty and she was eighteen, David and Ruth were married, and, soon after, in 1943, David joined the U.S. Army, where within a year he rose to the rank of sergeant. He was assigned to the top-secret Manhattan Project, stationed first at the massive uranium enrichment facility at Oak Ridge, Tennessee, then reassigned to the Los Alamos laboratory in New Mexico, where he claimed to have slept through the first atomic bomb test.

Greenglass was in an adjacent wing that also segregated hardened criminals. His cell was identical to Gold's, down to a folded-open hardcover on the green-blanketed metal bed, in this case *A Dog's Head* by Jean Dutourd, a book and author I'd never heard of. When I arrived at his cell door, he was stretched out, propped by a thin pillow. He got up and went over to where he'd already positioned a chair facing the bars.

He was easily my six feet but twenty or thirty pounds heavier—prison life hadn't dropped the pounds off him the way it had Gold—with enough bulk to look imposing, only he didn't. There was a softness to him, a layer of baby fat diminishing any threat, and a smirky baby face centered on the front of a bucket head on top of which sat a Medusa-like nest of black wavy curls.

This time the guard had brought a chair along for me. Greenglass and I nodded at each other, since a handshake was out, and we both sat. Why was he smiling? Nervousness? Some private joke? Seemed to me the joke was on him, since I was the one on the right side of these bars.

"I'm Nathan Heller," I said. "You were obviously expecting me."

"Obviously." His voice was higher-pitched than you'd expect from a man his size. Suddenly I thought of Curly Howard. But whose stooge was he?

"You understand," I said, "that I represent a committee of citizens who have asked me to look into the Rosenberg case."

"Sobell, too?"

"I have an associate in California who's arranged to visit Morton Sobell at Alcatraz, yes." My L.A. partner, Fred Rubinski, was handling that. "But Sobell's not the focus of my investigation."

The smirky smile in the baby face pursed to a near kiss. "Morty claims he barely knows Julie. A lie."

Testimony from an expert witness.

"You understand," I said, "the *real* significance of my being here."

He winked at me. "Oh, I got the word. You wanna be able to report back the same old stuff to your clients."

"Right. But, also, Mr. Greenglass—"

" 'Davey,' " he said, and waved a plump hand magnanimously. "Everyone calls me 'Davey.' " Little grin. "Well, back on the Lower East Side, it was 'Doovey,' but I won't inflict that on you."

"Thanks. And I'm Nate." I got out my notebook and ballpoint. "What we'll go over is, as you indicate, very old news. But I've only been on this job for a little over a week, so it'll be helpful for me to hear the, uh . . ."

"Party line?" he said with a pixie smile.

Maybe if you're a guy who'd dodged the electric chair, and helped your wife avoid any charges at all, you had a right to be cheerful. But even when it took sending your sister to Death Row?

Still, I stayed pleasant. I told him that I'd avoided a counsel room to be in a bug-free environment. He accepted that reasoning. Then I fed him questions and his answers were almost exactly what

I'd read in the trial transcripts. It had been a while since he'd last performed this comedy, but he still remembered his lines.

He folded his arms, leaned back in the metal chair. The infantile features were framed between bars.

He said, "My wife visited me in Albuquerque on November 29, 1944. I can pull that date out of the air 'cause it was our second wedding anniversary. Ruth said that back in New York, Julie had asked her over for supper. He told her that I was working on the atomic bomb project, and that the people he worked for wanted me to get them inside dope for the Russians."

I frowned. "Ruth didn't *know* you were working on the atom bomb? You'd never told her?"

"No. She got it from Julie. I'd kept it to myself—it was top-secret. Anyway, I told Ruth I wouldn't do it. Wanted no part of it. But she said Julie told her Russia was an ally and deserved to have the same information as we did . . . that is, as America did."

"What did you say to that?"

"Nothing at first. But I thought about it and it made sense to me. You know, the war was going on! The Russians were on our side, but here we were holding things back from 'em."

"What were you asked to do?"

He shrugged. "Julie instructed Ruth to tell me that he wanted the general layout of the Los Alamos project—buildings, number of people, things like that. Also any names of scientists working there. That was the first thing I put together, a list of Oppenheimer and Urey and a few others. I was just a machinist—I didn't know them all and anyway some were using fake names."

"On your next furlough," I said, "in January '45, you gave Rosenberg written information on the atom bomb?"

The big bucket head nodded. "I did. That little list of scientists, and some sketches of flat-type lens molds—that's sort of what makes the bomb tick . . . although it doesn't *really* tick, of course." He flashed a silly little smile. "Also, another list of some possible recruits among my fellow soldiers. Anybody sympathetic to the cause. The Communist cause, I mean."

"Those sketches, Davey—they weren't available to the prosecution, so you did your best to re-create them, right?"

More nods. "Facsimiles, yeah."

Hardly "best evidence"—drawings made years later by this expert with a high school education.

I said, "So you went to the Rosenbergs while you were on furlough, and somebody came up with a recognition device for a courier to use, calling on you back in New Mexico."

This subject seemed almost to bore him. "Yeah, yeah, the Jell-O box thing."

I managed to keep a polite expression going. "Yes. The Jell-O box thing. Go over that."

His smirk turned humorless. "Julie, Ethel, and Ruth go into the kitchen," he said, a schoolkid reciting a poem he'd been made to memorize, "while I stay in the living room. Five minutes or so later, they come back with one side of a Jell-O box, cut in two. Julie has one piece and Ruth has the other. Then he showed me how the pieces would fit together, like a puzzle, if a courier came around in Albuquerque. I said, 'That's clever,' and Julie said, 'The simplest things are the cleverest.'"

"And eventually back in Albuquerque, Gold came calling."

"Yeah, in June 1945. A Sunday. I'd never seen him before. He says, 'Julius sent me,' and gets the piece of Jell-O box out of his wallet, and it matches up."

"Then you gave him the latest pilfered information."

"Sure, a packet of stuff. Sketches relating to the project, one showing the face of the flat lens mold."

"Which you drew up again for the prosecution, years later."

Tiny smile. "That's what I did."

"You cut up a Jell-O box for them, too."

"You bet. To show what it was like."

I was looking at the guy who had fabricated all of the prosecution's (secondhand) physical evidence.

I jotted a few notes, then said, "Let's jump to 1950."

"Okay."

"Your brother-in-law came to your apartment . . . ?"

"Yes, yeah, Julie told me the guy who'd come to our flat in Albuquerque was about to get arrested, and that I should leave the country. I told Julie I needed money to pay my back debts, and of course he owed me from the machine-shop business. He'd said he'd get me some money."

"Who from?"

"His Russian pals. Eventually Julie said he'd get me five thousand dollars so I could settle my debts and then skip to Mexico. He told me I'd need a tourist card and a letter to avoid inoculations at the border. He'd fixed that up with a doctor. Plus, I needed to get passport pictures of Ruth and me and my family."

"Those were the pictures introduced at the trial?"

"Right, those were the ones."

Only they weren't passport pictures—they were typical family portrait–style pictures, David and Ruth and their two children, one a babe in arms.

"Did Julius get you that five thousand?"

"He did. One thousand to settle some personal debts, another four to skip to Mexico."

"Were you usually paid for your spying?"

A shrug. "I got money for my services. Such as Gold giving me five hundred dollars. Not that much, considering the risk."

Atom bomb for five Cs—hell of a bargain.

I checked my notes, then said, "Okay, that's good, Davey. That's fine."

He gave me a tiny grin. "Get what you needed, Nate?"

I nodded, slipping the notebook away. "Got what I needed. Thanks."

For a guy in stir, he seemed awfully amused. "You just have to show your client, that committee, that you talked to me, huh?"

"Right." I sat forward, lowering my voice, darkening my expression. "But, Davey . . . for my *other* client? There's some things I need to go over."

119

The grin faded. "Well, I gave you everything. I'm not supposed to say any more."

"This is off-record." I leaned close to the bars and almost whispered. "Davey, we have a problem. There's at least one leak in the Justice Department. I need to ask you a few questions, just between us, so that I know what I might be up against."

His tiny eyes flared. "Christ, I haven't heard anything *about* this. . . ."

"What could an FBI agent or some U.S. Attorney's Office whistleblower know?"

Fat hands made fat fists. "Shit. They'd know I didn't mention Julie or Ethel or the Jell-O box or any of that stuff till way into the interviews with Cohn. I didn't *want* to involve Julie. Well, not so much Julie as my sister. I didn't mention her *at all* for the longest time."

"Why not?"

"Are you kidding? Why involve my sister if I didn't have to? But they didn't have *anything* on her. I don't know how they got away with arresting her. Hell, we were two weeks out from the trial before Cohn comes to me and says, 'Ruth tells me your sister was there, that Ethel typed up the atom bomb notes.' So *I* said that, too."

"*Did* Ethel type the notes?"

He shook his head, and the nest of black snakes on top stirred. "I don't honestly remember. But probably Ruth typed them. She's a professional typist, you know. I'm not sure Ethel was even in the room."

"What role *did* Ethel play?"

"Well, she's married to Julie. She knew what he was doing with his life. She'd have to, right? I *tried* to protect Ethel, but when it came right down to it . . . Look, the feds had Gold and were pulling other people in, too, including Julie. First guy who says he'll cooperate, who says he'll talk, is in the best of the bad spots. I told them, 'I'll give you the story, but my wife has to be completely out of this.' " He shrugged. "And they stuck to that bargain."

"The leaker says when you were first interviewed, you implicated Ruth—said she was in the room when Gold came to your apartment to pick up documents. But in court you said she wasn't around."

"That's right. Cohn let me change that. The FBI was easy about it, too. They had *me*. Why did they need Ruth?"

I'd gotten a little loose with my questioning, so I shifted into the mode he would expect, saying, "You're not going to weaken, are you, Davey?"

"No! Hell, no." He snorted derisively. "But, shit. They're not going to kill Ethel. No way in hell. Both she and Julie can clear themselves, if they just cooperate."

"And if they don't?" I asked. "Are you man enough to sit by and watch your sister die?"

But I was thinking, *Are you worm enough?*

"What," he said, his smirk back in full force, "I'm going to come forward and call my *wife* a liar? It's not my sister I have sex with, Nate."

So he did have standards.

"There's more to it than sex," he clarified, maybe sensing how that had sounded. "I mean, my wife is more important to me than my sister. Or my mother and my father, okay? She's the mother of my children. Like Ethel is the mother of *her* children, and she and Julie should put those kids ahead of anything else. If Julie and Ethel want to be martyrs, that's up to them. Me, I just want to get out of here as soon as possible and be with my family. Find a job and disappear into a normal life. American dream, right, Nate?"

"Some people would say that's pretty cold, Davey."

"Maybe. But handing over my sister is hardly the worst thing I ever did."

"No?"

He smiled bigger than before, but this time with not a trace of amusement or smugness, either. "I helped build that bomb, didn't I? The one killing over a hundred thousand people? If I'm gonna lose sleep, *that's* what it'll be about."

But somehow I thought that—even in here—this guy would sleep just fine tonight and any night.

Like the big baby he resembled.

CHAPTER 9

For a full morning well into early afternoon, Natalie Ash—looking much the Bohemian beauty in a loose peasant blouse, black skirt, black tights, and sandals—helped me conduct a canvass at Knickerbocker Village, where until a year or so ago she had lived.

Like a massive brick oasis in the midst of crumbling tenements and pushcart commerce, Knickerbocker Village covered an entire city block at Cherry and Catherine Streets. Two twelve-story buildings, each with a courtyard whose greenery shimmered on this sunny April day, offered up an impressive sixteen hundred apartments, one of which had been occupied by the Rosenbergs at the time of their arrests.

As we went up in a self-service elevator, Natalie said, "Back in the thirties, they tore down tenements to put this place up, in the name of a housing project, then chased out the former tenants with their high rent."

"How high?"

"In today's money, fifty bucks a month for a three-room, one-bedroom apartment."

"Not bad for Manhattan."

"Sky-high for *this* area." She shrugged, her dark hair bouncing on her shoulders; she had on hoop earrings that gave her a gypsy cast. "At least it's given some lower-end white-collar workers a decent place to live. Nursery school, playground, elevators, laundry facilities, steam heat, electricity."

"Why did you leave?"

She gave me that nice wide grin; again her only makeup was bright red lipstick and a little face powder. "Well, it wasn't because of a shortage of socialists to talk politics with! Place is crawling with them."

But her tone said that she felt they'd sold out. *Did she include the Rosenbergs?* I wondered.

Natalie shrugged, continuing, "The art gallery had apartment space above. Went with the job. Anyway, another thing this place has is hot-and-cold-running kiddies."

She wasn't exaggerating. We mostly talked to mothers in their twenties and thirties who wore head scarfs like bandages, with little ones in arm and/or toddlers toddling. Glimpses of the apartments revealed fairly nice digs—parquet floors, small modern kitchens that we were sometimes invited into, and tiled bathrooms, a couple of which I sampled on this long tour of a blandly modern apartment building that was just beginning to show some age.

"She was stuck-up, that Ethel Rosenberg," one young mom said, a cigarette dangling like Bogart in one of his early pictures. "Snooty. If she didn't already know you, she wouldn't speak. And them stupid hats with feathers! Lousy taste, that woman. And them brats of hers, particularly the older boy! She let that little monster get away with murder!"

A slightly older female resident said bitterly, "The *trouble* those Rosenbergs caused around here! We had FBI in our hair for weeks. And now there's a black mark on this place. Some places got a plaque that says, 'George Washington slept here.' We ought to have 'Julius and Ethel Rosenberg sold their country down the river here.'"

Those women, like a baker's dozen of others with similar views about their former neighbors, were not (Natalie assured me) among the many socialists and outright Communists who lived in Knickerbocker Village.

"Definitely two breeds here," she said, lifting a well-shaped eyebrow as we walked to our next doorway. "The more conservative types kind of keep to themselves, or a close circle of friends. Lefties like to organize hobby groups—fencing, photography, singing. What can I say? Socialists like to socialize."

"Ethel was active in the singing group, I assume."

"She was. But like I said before, for your purposes, Nate, we need civilians—not anybody whose pink-hued background will either endanger them or make them easily dismissed."

Not all reports were negative about Ethel and Julius. Though not outright friendly, Julius always said hello, according to some, and Ethel would at least nod. A mom in her mid-thirties with boys around the same age as the Rosenbergs' considered Ethel an enormously patient parent, even if she "overdid it with the Dr. Spock and *Parents* magazine stuff."

"When my Andrew was young," another woman in her thirties said, speaking with the temporary serenity of a mother during school hours, "all us moms would sit together in the courtyard tending our tykes, and smoke and talk, or maybe go for walks around here, pushing strollers and baby carriages. Mrs. Rosenberg tried to fit in, she really did, but that boy of hers was a crier, real darn fussy. You couldn't carry on a conversation! So she'd roll him away, kind of embarrassed. And as he got older, he was a *real* pill. Ethel never learned to do like in that one Bugs Bunny cartoon, remember? Use that Dr. Spock book as a paddle?"

The Rosenbergs had lived on the eleventh floor. Natalie and I hit not only that floor but the one above and below. No one reported seeing the Rosenbergs with either of the Greenglasses, much less having overheard an argument; in fact, few would have known David or Ruth by sight. The Rosenbergs were loners—despite what Natalie had said, these socialists didn't seem to have socialized much.

"Maybe we should come back in the evening," Natalie said with a sigh as we left the building, "and talk to the men of the house."

I shook my head. "With the Rosenbergs' notoriety, and all the stuff in the papers about the Greenglasses selling them out? There isn't a husband on the planet who wouldn't have told his wife about something interesting he witnessed between Julius and David."

By mid-afternoon, we were in a very different sort of village—Greenwich. Different not just from the twelve-story Knickerbocker but just about anywhere else in New York City. No endless avenues cutting through skyscraper cliffs—you could see the sky in the Village—rather, meandering streets lined with comfy-looking brick or frame houses, cozy residences jammed together on side streets, and of course (surrounding and spilling over Washington Square) bars, boîtes, coffee houses. Some tourist traps, others genuine Bohemian haunts.

Natalie and I had burgers and fries at a small table by a window in the barely lit, publike White Horse on Hudson Street. I had a good view of the artistic types wandering by: long-haired women with no makeup, men in beards and boots. The view across the table was even better—this girl was a free spirit, as her peasant blouse proclaimed, braless breasts fighting under there like kittens trying to claw out of a burlap bag.

"I wish the morning had been more productive for you," she said, after a sip of beer.

"Me, too. But that's the way my business works. You ask one hundred questions for every answer worth hearing. You knew or know Ruth Greenglass, right?"

She nodded, then took time for another sip before saying, "We were . . . you know, comrades. Haven't seen her in some while. Don't even know if she's living where she was at the time."

My turn for a sip. "My understanding is she hasn't moved."

"Same cold-water flat?"

"What I hear. Her husband's in stir, and a government snitch gets benefits but the pay stinks."

She was smiling.

"What?" I asked.

"It's funny," she said, "how you sometimes talk like a detective."

"Well, I am a detective. Maybe that's why."

"I mean a detective out of Dashiell Hammett or Mickey Spillane."

Now I was smiling. "Well, I do try to avoid it, because it can sound kind of silly. On the other hand, some women seem to like it."

Her throaty voice turned sultry—kidding-on-the-Washington-Square sultry. "You don't have to try hard with me, Nate. We're already . . ."

"Comrades?"

That rated a chuckle. "Maybe we can have a little cell meeting tonight, just the two of us. You haven't seen the gallery yet, or my apartment."

"That sounds like a nice way to end the evening. But there's more work to be done. Private eyes get their best work done after night-fall, you know."

"Such as what?"

I finished my beer. "Well, I think we're finished at Knickerbocker Village, don't you?"

"We are if you don't want to go back to talk to the men, or maybe hit the other floors."

"I don't. Any other ideas, honey?"

That also made her smile. "I'm your honey now?"

"If I call you 'baby,' you'll say I'm trying too hard. And anyway, I like 'honey' better than 'comrade.'" I leaned in and gave her what I like to think of as my wicked smile. "But that doesn't mean I won't come to your apartment later to go over your manifesto."

She laughed till beer snorted out her nose. I smiled to myself. *You've still got it, Heller,* I thought.

Her laughter dissolved into giggles as she touched a napkin to her face and held a hand up for me to pause the conversation.

Then: "Nate, did you ever consider that maybe Julie and Ethel don't *want* to be saved?"

"Well, of course they want to be saved. Who doesn't want to be saved?"

She shrugged. "True believers."

"Even when they leave two little boys behind? I don't buy it."

"Maybe you've never believed in anything."

"Sure I do."

"Like what?"

"Survival. Doing a job well. Living good. Baby, zealotry pays even worse than snitching."

She smiled a little. "You're doing it again."

"Talking like a detective?"

She nodded. "And here you don't even carry a gun."

"Not when I'm interviewing mommies at housing projects, I don't." I leaned forward, speaking just loud enough to be heard over the bar clatter. "Listen, Natalie—I appreciate you helping me, I really do, but you don't have to. I can fend for myself."

She thought about that, then said, with a little eyebrow shrug, "You might want to talk to Mrs. Rosenberg. Sophie Rosenberg. Julie's mom? She may have seen or overheard something."

"Think that's worth doing?"

"I do. I know her well enough to set that in motion. Sophie's in Washington Heights." She gestured to a pay phone on the wall back by the restrooms. "Should I try her now?"

I shook my head as I checked my wristwatch. "No, I have to get back to the hotel. I have a long-distance call to make in about an hour. Could you meet me at my room around six-thirty? Then we'll take a cab to Mrs. Rosenberg and then maybe catch a bite back down here somewhere. El Chico, maybe?"

That was fine with her—a little touristy but "good chow."

She said, "We can catch the subway to Washington Heights near the Waldorf."

I shook my head again. "No, cab is fine. I'm on an expense account, remember?"

The toothy smile flashed. "You *are* decadent, Nathan Heller."

"Think you're the first one to notice?"

On the sidewalk she headed toward her art gallery with a wave, and I paused to watch the nice rear view for a few seconds, then hailed a cab, thinking, *If I must go Bohemian, let it be with a Bohemian dish like that.*

. . .

Morton Sobell—another Lower East Side boy raised by leftist parents—claimed to have known Julius Rosenberg only slightly when they'd attended City College. An electrical engineer, Sobell and his friend/roommate Max Elitcher worked for the U.S. Navy's Bureau of Ordnance during the war, including design work on radar and advanced electronic devices. By 1947, he was working at Reeves Instrument in Manhattan on a computer for evaluating airplane and guided-missile designs.

When David Greenglass was arrested by the FBI, Sobell walked away from that high-paying job and took his family on an impromptu vacation to Mexico. Reports of Julius' arrest prompted Sobell to use false names as he made purchases and moved from hotel to hotel around Veracruz and Tampico. Finally he was delivered by Mexican police to the FBI just across the Texas border. He was charged with five counts of conspiring with the Rosenbergs to provide defense secrets to Russia, but the only evidence against him was the un-corroborated testimony of his "old friend" Elitcher, who claimed he and Sobell were members of a Rosenberg-led espionage ring.

As a codefendant, Sobell chose not to testify in his own defense. Currently he resided at Alcatraz, the federal penitentiary designed to house America's most hardened, hard-to-control, and notorious criminals. Mild-mannered, bespectacled mad professor Sobell fit only the "notorious" part. He was almost certainly incarcerated at the Rock in hopes he would crack and exchange information for a reduced sentence or parole.

I had arranged through Manny Bloch for my California partner Fred Rubinski to visit Sobell, who'd agreed to the visit, which had taken place earlier today. Fred, who'd gone by train up from L.A., was checked in at the St. Francis, and that's where I called him, on the nightstand phone in my Waldorf suite, as I sat on the edge of the bed.

"My God what a place," he said, the connection good, hardly a crackle.

"You mean your hotel?" I said, needling him.

"No, that fucking prison!" Fred, best described as a slightly better-looking Edgar G. Robinson, had a husky voice courtesy of his God-knew-how-many-cigars-a-day habit. "Boat ride, bus ride, walk here, walk there . . . do you know they make you go through a damn *metal* detector before you enter the visitation area?"

"Well, at least you made a return trip," I said, "which is more than Sobell can say. What did you get out of him?"

Heavy coast-to-coast sigh. "It was a bust. I figure Sobell only agreed to see me to relieve his boredom. And right off the bat, he comes out and says he figures I'm visiting for the feds, that the Hammett committee is a sham."

"I didn't expect much out of him. He probably figures everything is recorded there."

"Right. It's a phone system, so they're probably routinely doing that. You're both facing bulletproof glass through a little hole cut in a common wall about, oh, a foot thick. It was like looking into a damn tunnel."

"You didn't talk long?"

"Oh, we talked for the whole hour."

"Well, Fred, what the hell did Sobell say then?"

"That he was innocent. That the only thing close to spying he'd ever done was industrial. That he barely knew Julius Rosenberg. That Max Elitcher was a rat bastard who got himself in a corner and had to give somebody's name and just picked his old pal's out of a hat. That the FBI arranged with the Mexican cops, when Sobell and his family were cooling off down there, to bust him on a bogus bank robbery charge. That the Mexican cops in the middle of the night burst in and beat him senseless with blackjacks, then heavily armed Mexies drove him and his family in two cars across the border to the waiting feds. That he made a mistake not testifying but that his attorney said he should just keep mum because the prosecution's case was so damn weak, he'd surely walk. Now the guy's doing thirty years at Alcatraz, Nate. If you were him, would you pay the lawyer bill?"

"He's paying now," I said. "For a trip that was a bust, you sure got a shit-pot out of him."

Fred sent me a Bronx cheer all the way from California. "Nothing that helps. He was talking for the hidden tape recorder. Just wanted the government to know how pissed off he was at the way he was railroaded. He says he hardly knows Julius and doesn't know Ethel at all."

"Listen, Fred, thanks. I appreciate this."

"I hope we're getting a good payday."

"Fair to middlin'. But I'm sticking Drew Pearson with all the expenses, which will be more than we make and then some."

That made Fred laugh, and we signed off.

It was almost two hours before I was due to meet Natalie, so I drew the drapes, took off my suit coat and tie, kicked off my shoes, and sacked out on the bed. As the president of the A-1, I wasn't used to the kind of legwork I'd put in this morning, and I was beat.


The suite was so fancy it had a doorbell, and that was what woke me. I'd been out for a while, down deep, judging by my grogginess and the film in my mouth. The bell rang again and I checked my watch on the nightstand: just before six. She was early.

I padded out into the living room and crossed to the entry area, slipping in my socks a little on the marble floor. I was preparing something witty to say to Natalie when I opened the door and it wasn't her.

Instead, I found two characters with the kind of lumpy faces that come from beatings that healed wrong. They came barreling in, wearing scowls and tailored suits and hundred-dollar hats, the one in front shoving me back, the one behind him slamming the door shut. I'd never seen them before but they seemed to dislike me anyway.

The one in front was tall and bullnecked and the one in back was taller and bullnecked. They shared olive complexions, dark eyes, dark well-oiled hair, cauliflower ears, and a scattering of facial scars. They could be told apart chiefly by the one in front having scar tissue over his right eye that made it droopy, while the other one didn't. Maybe they were brothers.

"Get dressed, Heller," the front man said, his voice conveying all the music of furniture scraping. "You're coming with us."

A statement to that effect usually is followed by the display of a badge, but no badge was in sight, and anyway the ex-boxer or maybe ex-wrestler look of the pair made them as muscle. Cheap hoods in expensive suits, as we Hammett-type detectives say, and I kneed the spokesman in the balls.

He bowed to me, graciously, hat flying, the bigger guy moving forward, reaching into his coat probably not to scratch himself, eyes big and indignant, and I lurched toward him, throwing my forearm into what little throat he had, slamming with bone and force, and he went down on his back, gurgling, hands at his neck as if trying to strangle himself. The spokesman was still bending forward, his ass in the air. I kicked it and sent him sliding across the marble floor into the living room. The bigger one, hatless now, had his legs up like a bug on its back, gasping for air, clawing for the gun under his arm, but I got to it first, yanking it free from its holster, a .38 Colt Police Positive with a five-inch barrel.

The spokesman, whose slide had stopped just before the two facing fireplace couches, turned over and was getting a gun out himself from under a shoulder, but I kicked the piece out of his fumbling grasp and he looked up at me with fear in both eyes, droopy one included, a schoolyard bully with the tables turned. His gun hit the marble floor just right to spin like a top. Cute. With my left hand, I grabbed up the weapon—also a .38, a Smith & Wesson Chief's Special—and went over and sat on the couch facing where my guests lay on the floor. My hands full of their guns, I crossed my legs and waited for them to recover.

The smaller one, or I should say the less large one, got to his feet first, unsteadily, as befitting a guy who just got kneed in the nuts and kicked in the ass. He looked at me like he didn't know whether to rush me or cry, then did neither, just stood there with his arms at his side, open palms toward me in reluctant surrender.

I waved to the couch opposite and nodded for him to sit down. We said nothing to each other. What the hell did we have to talk about? We hadn't even met.

The bigger guy finally got off his back and to his feet with the fluid awkwardness of a film running backward. He had no expression at all but his face was very red, flushed crimson with either shame or rage or maybe a cocktail of both.

I waved with his partner's gun for him to come join us. Then they were both sitting across from me, glass coffee table between us, and I had their two weapons, one pointed at each, which struck me as comical. I was in my mid-forties and had hardly broken a sweat. Wasn't breathing hard, either. Maybe I *was* a detective out of Hammett.

"Where were we going," I asked cheerfully, "before I decided not to?"

The droopy-eyed slightly smaller one had composed himself, to some degree anyway. His hands were on his knees. The bigger guy, blood in his face fading, had fists in his lap. Big as this pair were, they might well charge me, confiscated .38s or not. And I hadn't patted them down, so they might have further weapons.

But I didn't think so.

"Listen, Heller," the droopy-eyed prick said, but I raised a hand to halt him.

"Make it 'Mr. Heller.' But I don't want your names. I don't want to dignify you assholes by using your names. I'll ask again. Where were we going?"

"To the barbershop," he said.

"You forgot 'hippity hop.'"

"No. Really. Mr. Costello is down there, waiting to talk to you. Also, getting his hair cut and a shave. Mr. Costello likes to double up on things."

"Frank Costello," I said.

The spokesman nodded, then the other guy did, too. Delayed reaction.

"Mr. Costello just wants," the spokesman continued, "to talk to you, Mr. Heller. Public place. No muss or fuss."

There had already been a fuss, and they both looked mussed. But I didn't feel the need to rub it in.

Besides, for the first time, I was a little bit scared. Scratch that. I was very damn scared. Frank Costello was the top mobster in New York. And New York was a fairly big town.

"Just to talk," I said.

"Just to talk," the spokesman said.

"Then why did you two come in like Gang Busters?"

"Because Mr. Costello said we should."

"Why did he say that?"

"He said we should rattle you a little. Put the fear of God in you. Then bring you downstairs for a talk."

"I don't get rattled that easy, and I don't believe in God. So get the fuck out of here."

Now they looked at each other. And then at me.

The spokesman said, "It's a friendly invitation, Mr. Heller. A public place."

"You said that, and as invitations go, this one hasn't struck me as all that friendly. Get out."

"Mr. Heller . . ."

"Maybe I'll be down in a few minutes. I'll give you your guns back then."

The spokesman looked troubled. He looked like a guy trying hard not to fart.

"What?" I asked.

"Could you not tell Mr. Costello about this?"

"That I took you girls to the woodshed? Why shouldn't I?"

The bigger one growled. Actually growled.

The spokesman said, "Let's agree to call this a misunderstanding. It won't do none of us no good with Mr. Costello, he hears about this—makes us look bad, makes you look uncooperative. Then nobody here has to have a grudge against nobody else. What say, Mr. Heller?"

He squeezed a smile out like the metaphorical fart he'd been suppressing.

The bigger one didn't manage a smile, but at least his face was flesh-colored again, except for random white scar tissue. He was nodding a little, agreeing with his partner's assessment.

One at a time, I emptied the bullets from the two revolvers onto the coffee table, making brittle rain. Then I motioned to the door and they got up slowly and walked in that direction, with me following. This was dangerous, since they could turn on me, now that the weapons were unloaded. But I believed they really had come to summon me, not thrash me or kill my ass.

On their way, they picked up their respective hats where they'd been knocked off and put them back on. The bigger guy opened the door for the spokesman, who stepped into the hall; then the bigger one followed, and they both looked back at me like dogs expecting a treat. I handed them their empty guns.

"See you downstairs in five minutes," I said.

The spokesman nodded, the bigger one frowning but in nothing more than stupidity, and I shut the door on them.

Okay, *now* I was breathing hard.

Fucking Frank Costello.

I went into the bedroom, got the nine-millimeter Browning from my suitcase, the shoulder holster too, and put them on. Tie snugged back on, in my suit coat and shoes and everything, I returned to the entryway, gun in hand, carefully opened the door, and found the hallway empty.

Time to go to the barbershop.

Hippity hop.

CHAPTER

The Waldorf barbershop was like something out of a Busby Berkeley musical circa 1934, all chrome and marble and green and black, with endless rows of black-leather-padded porcelain chairs facing each other in generous space made infinite by backing mirrors. You half-expected the white-uniformed barbers to start tap-dancing with the pretty green-uniformed girls manning (so to speak) the manicure booths at the far right. Maybe, if I waited long enough, an overhead view would have the girls forming a big pair of scissors around the boys as a giant head.

The prettiest manicurist, a redhead, was in the last booth. That's where Frank Costello, the so-called Prime Minister of the Underworld, was getting his nails done. Funny I hadn't noticed those nails looking particularly nice when—during Senator Kefauver's televised Crime Committee hearings—the focus was on the gangster's nervous hands after Costello objected to being on camera.

Otherwise Frank Costello had never conveyed public nervousness in his life, sporting the same cool demeanor and slicked-back good grooming of movie star George Raft, whose older, not-quite-as-handsome brother he might be. Costello's apparel was Hollywood gangster, too—dark blue pin-striped suit more expensive than a week at this hotel, light blue shirt, blue-and-white striped tie, jeweled silver cuff links. I couldn't see them, but it was a safe bet that his shoes had a mirror shine.

He kept a suite here, or anyway his mistress did, and whether he slept here or in his apartment on Central Park, he came to the Waldorf barbershop for a daily haircut and sometimes manicure; the place was his second office. The man he replaced in the mob hierarchy, the deported Lucky Luciano, had lived at the Waldorf, too. So had my late friend Benny Siegel of don't-call-him-Bugsy infamy. Of course, lately Costello had lived in various federal pens, due to contempt of Congress and tax charges.

But at the moment, he sat in a booth at his beloved Waldorf tonsorial palace.

"Nathan Heller," he said, his voice a mellow baritone with some edges that could use sanding. There was a warmth conveying an old friendship about to be renewed. We'd met a few times over the years, but nothing to rate that.

"Mr. Costello," I said with a nod and a smile. "I understand you wanted to see me."

Costello nodded and said to the manicurist, "Shoo, sweetie, while I soak. My friend and me need to speak."

She seemed used to this kind of thing and her smile was sunny as she swayed off to cool her pretty heels.

I said, "Be right with you, Mr. Costello."

His two boys were seated on a bench against the rear wall, as if waiting their turn. With my back to their boss, I handed the spokesman a white Waldorf stationery envelope as lumpy as his face. He gave me a wary look.

I nodded to his confederate, who was concentrating on whether to shit or go blind. "Split 'em with Chuckles here. And remember that *this* is the way I sent them back to you."

The spokesman felt the .38 slugs through the paper and nodded, then slipped the envelope in his suit coat pocket. He managed a smile for me and even winked with the droopy eye, which was creepy but appreciated.

Back at the booth, I slid in across from the mob boss as if I was the new manicurist and said amiably, "Mr. Costello, you had your boys throw a little scare my way. Was that really necessary?"

He shrugged shoulders that had no real need for the suit coat's padding. "I was trying to make a point, Nate. Hope they didn't overdo. And it's 'Frank,' please. Come on. How long have we known each other?"

We didn't really know each other at all.

"Way back," I said with half a smile. "I believe Frank Nitti introduced us."

Melancholy made a momentary visit to Costello's face. "He was a good man, Nitti. Wish he was still around. Chicago could use him. They say you two was tight. Father and son, almost."

"An exaggeration. What point, Frank?"

"What's that?"

"You said you were making a point."

It was frankly absurd seeing New York's most powerful gangster with his fingers dipped in two little clear-glass finger bowls. But somehow I managed not to laugh.

"Yeah, right, I was," he said, nodding. "And the point I was making is that you could get yourself in hot water, Nate, if you don't watch yourself."

This is where Sam Spade on the radio would say, *Seems to me you're already in hot water, Frank—your fingers, anyway.*

I said, "Why's that?"

He drew a breath. He had the kind of big chest that drawing a breath made huge. Then he exhaled and it was merely big again. "Somebody asked me to *really* make a point, Nate. Beat you within an inch, dump you on a side road, to think things over."

"What kind of things?"

Naturally arching eyebrows arched farther. "You're looking into this Rosenberg deal. Trying to find new evidence, new witnesses."

"I suppose I could ask you how you know that, Frank. But what I really want to know is . . . why do you care?"

"I don't give two runny shits whether those Commies live or die. Fine with me if they go to the chair, though I admit I'm not much for frying females. Call me a sentimental slob."

"Well, you did say 'somebody' asked you to hand me my ass. So it's obviously not your idea. Why didn't you?"

"You said it yourself, Nate. We go way back."

I had to say it. "We don't know each other all that well, Frank. I respect you. You run things like Nitti did, like a business executive—and you don't sell poison." Narcotics trafficking was out under Costello. "And maybe you respect me, too. But is that enough to give me a pass?"

He drew another chest-expanding breath, a natty gorilla with his pinkies soaking. "The somebody who made this request of me is a good friend of somebody else, who I *do* respect."

I actually could follow that. "But you don't respect the party who *asked* you to get my attention."

Costello frowned in thought. "Well, I do and I don't. He's young. He's smart as a goddamn whip. And mean as a damn snake. Has the makings of a top mouthpiece, kind we can always use in my business. But he's reckless, this slimy little cocksucker. And the idea that somehow I owe *him* enough that this little shit can come to me with a demand like this?" He sighed deep enough to make the water in the tiny dishes ripple. "Truth is, Nate, this person who imposed on me? Is the one I'd like to dump on a side road with a swolled-up head and something to think about."

"Whereas you're giving me a free ride?"

He raised a hand from a bowl and pointed a dripping finger. "What I'm giving you, Nate, is free advice. There is nothing, no fucking thing, this sleazy little smart-ass kike won't do. . . . Excuse me, that was out of line. You're of the Hebrew persuasion yourself, right?"

"Nobody persuaded me," I said with a smile. "I just got my old man's name hung on me. Thank God for my mother's Irish mug, huh?"

He found that amusing and laughed. Unless that was a cough.

"The thing is," Costello said, "this certain smart-ass kike is well connected. In my world, sure, but also Uncle Sam's, plus in this city generally. He was the right hand of a guy I helped rise to a high position which is useful to me. Do you know what two guys I'm talking about?"

Roy Cohn had been U.S. Attorney Irving Saypol's second-in-command, and not just at the Rosenberg trial. Saypol, of course, now sat on the New York State Supreme Court. You couldn't get that kind of appointment in this state without Costello's nod.

"I know who you're talking about," I said.

He pointed a dripping forefinger again. "This smart-ass kid is concerned that you might actually clear that Commie couple."

"Still a long shot."

"I'm a good American and I hate Commies like the clap, but this is your business, so I won't interfere."

"Other than to get my attention short of a ride in the country."

He beamed at me, at the moment reminding me more of Bela Lugosi than George Raft. "That's right, Nate. I can see why that other Frank liked you. You have brains. Try to hold on to them. . . . Okay, honey!"

That last wasn't for me—he was summoning the manicurist, who was seated off in a corner, using an emery board on her own nails. The redhead looked up brightly and padded over, all lipstick and curves. A month's worth of her tips from just Costello would likely finance a few nights at the Waldorf, too.

"Before you go," he said to me (I'd already slid out of the booth), "be my pleasure to stake you to a haircut and shave."

This is where Sam Spade would say, *No thanks, Frank. I've had enough close shaves for one day already.*

Checking my watch, I said, "Rain check, thanks. In about five minutes, I'm meeting a girl almost as cute as Mildred here."

I'd deduced the redhead's name by checking out the plastic name tag on her left breast. I'm a professional detective.

"Well, then, make yourself an appointment on the way out," he said magnanimously, as the girl withdrew his right hand from the water, "and tell them to put it on my tab."

"Thanks, Frank," I said.

And I did.

. . .

Washington Heights, extending from 155th Street to Dyckman Street, was bordered on the west and east by two rivers, the Hudson and Harlem respectively. Built upon a series of bluffs and cliffs, the immigrant neighborhood—with its steep concrete staircases connecting different areas—had seen an influx of European Jews fleeing Nazism in the 1930s and '40s.

Approaching by cab in the early evening, I watched block after block of apartment buildings appear against the sky like battlements of long-ago European villages. The ten-floor hillside apartment house where Natalie and I were dropped wasn't far from City College, where Sophie Rosenberg's boy Julius had once gone, though at the time she'd lived nowhere near.

Mrs. Rosenberg sat across from us on her wine-colored flocked sofa in her modest living room with its busy wallpaper clashing with busier drapes. She wore a black dress—in advance mourning?—with a floral brooch and round, wire-rimmed glasses a bit too large for a face reminiscent of her son's. Her dark hair, up in a bun, had heavily grayed and her eyebrows seemed raised in perpetual bewilderment, bony hands with parchment skin clasped in her lap. In her early seventies, she looked at least that, the many lines in her face like deep cuts, her short compact frame having once supported a rather stout body whose flesh had been whittled by grief.

She insisted on getting us coffee and cookies, a tray of which rested on a small drop-leaf table by a street-side window, over to our left as we sat on a pair of mismatched English armchairs about as comfortable as what awaited her son and daughter-in-law.

I had traded in my latest Botony 500 for a custom charcoal number from Richard Bennett Custom Tailors in the Loop, a nice and smooth fit despite the nine-millimeter under my left arm. Natalie was all in black—sweater, skirt, tights, sandals.

"This much space I don't need," Sophie Rosenberg said with a dismissive shrug. I had complimented her on her tidy apartment.

"Four rooms is too much. But I have the boys with me at first, you know, before they get too much for me."

Her grandchildren, she meant.

She'd recognized Natalie as a friend of her son's, but when I questioned her about her in-laws, David and Ruth Greenglass, she had little to say.

"Ethel's family, they don't have much to do with us," she said. "Tessie—Ethel's mama—not a nice woman. She brings Ethel up too strict, David too soft. Ethel, she tries to do better. That's why the boys, they such wild ones. You spoil a boy, you know, and later they go wrong sometimes."

The irony of that was unintended, of course. I doubted she'd know irony if she tripped over it.

"Oh, Doovey and Ruth? Always talk kind to me. My heart, it breaks thinking about what they do to Julie and Ethel. You think you *know* people."

She was vaguely aware of the business disagreements between Julie and "Doovey" at their machine shop, but never overheard any real arguments.

"I so wish I could help, Mr. Heller. But this, it is hard for me. A educated woman, I'm not. I don't follow this sad story in the papers. I turn off the radio. I don't go to the court for the trial, not one day. Nobody in the family goes. Just too hard. Too sad. Too tragedy. Visit Julie, this much I can do. Mr. Bloch drives me over, kind man. . . . Drink your tea, Mr. Heller. Natalie, you too, eat some cookies. Help yourself. I make them this afternoon."

I went over to the table for a macaroon. Looking past the tablecloth, I noticed the wood was mahogany, the style spare and modern, nicer than anything else in this place, with its older furniture, probably sometimes secondhand.

*No,* I thought. *Not possible. . . .*

I refilled my tea and collected another macaroon and returned to my uncomfy chair, trying not to indicate any excitement. "Delicious, Mrs. Rosenberg."

"Trick is the coconut. Always at Passover, I make dozens and dozens."

*Was this Passover?* A question that revealed just how Jewish I was . . .

"That's a nice table, Mrs. Rosenberg," I said offhandedly, between nibbles. "Where did you get it?"

"Oh, that table belongs Julie and Ethel. If . . . *when* they get out, back it goes."

Natalie's big brown eyes swung to me.

I said, "I understand all the furniture in the Knickerbocker Village apartment was sold to a junk man."

"Yes, this I handle personal. Those things, they bring five dollars."

"Was that *all* of Julie and Ethel's things . . . ?"

Her tiny shrug seemed to require big effort. "All but this and that, like toys and bicycles and some chest drawers for the boys' bedroom—not here now, boys *or* chests—and that table. It's a very nice one. From Macy's, it is."

I turned to Natalie, her eyes wide, her mouth poised in mid-macaroon bite.

"Mrs. Rosenberg," I said gently, "are you aware of a console table that your son owned that was—"

"Right *there*," she said, frowning and pointing to it. *Was her guest crazy? We were just talking about that!*

I tried again. "Didn't you know that the table in your son's apartment was said to be a special one used for microfilming?"

Small dark eyes blinked behind big round lenses. "Your what?"

"You didn't know that anyone was looking for that table?"

She shook her head. "Nice enough, that table. But who would make a fuss finding?"

"You mind if I take a closer look?"

"Be my guest."

I rose. "Could I impose on you to clear it? Move the tray to the kitchen?"

Rising quickly, Natalie said, "I can do that," and Mrs. Rosenberg just looked on as if wondering whether she'd admitted two luna-tics to her apartment.

The table was a small, ordinary drop-leaf affair designed to rest against a wall. Nothing rigged for spying or anything else. No ornamentation. On the underside were grease-pencil numbers—1997—possibly indicating its price, $19.97. With tax, that would add up to just about what Julius said he'd paid Macy's for it.

I was trembling a little. I admit it. You work very hard to bring thorough established procedure to an investigation, and the only part of my training that I'd applied this evening was noticing something right in front of me. So that didn't make me Sherlock Holmes, but it also didn't make this discovery any less exciting.

Natalie was crouching down and getting a good look herself.

"It fits the way Julie described it in court," she said, "and with none of the special spy attributes Ruth reported it having."

I raised a waist-high hand and gave Natalie a look that said, *Calm cool collected, now.*

We returned to our armchairs.

I asked, "Other members of your family come visit you here, I assume?"

"Oh, yes."

"You have . . . two daughters, is that right?"

"I do. Lena and Ethel—the other 'Ethel' in the family." She smiled. "Sometimes at family gatherings, things they get confusing, two Ethels." The smile faded.

"Have either of your daughters commented on the table?"

"Oh yes."

"What have they said?"

"Nice table!"

"You said the members of your family didn't go to the court-house to attend the trial."

"Too hard. Too painful."

*Was it possible none of the Rosenberg family, beyond Julius and Ethel, knew of the significance of the missing console table?*

"Forgive me, Mrs. Rosenberg," I said, "but . . . do you read and write?"

She paused, clearly embarrassed. "Not English."

"But your daughters do?"

"Certainly!"

"Did *they* follow the trial in the papers?"

"No, no, no. Too upsetting. Why put yourself through this kind pain?"

"Did they visit their brother where he was being held?"

"Yes. Good sisters."

"Did they keep up with the court proceedings in that way, do you think? Getting reports from Julius?"

"Oh no! They speak of personal things. Family things. Why talk about sadness? Why get more *shroyft*?"

Right. Why get more *shroyft*?

I said, "You mentioned your son's attorney, Manny Bloch."

"Nice man. Lovely person."

"He's been in this apartment?"

"Yes, he would come to take the boys to see their mama and papa at . . . where they stay."

She couldn't bring herself to say "prison."

"So Mr. Bloch didn't linger?"

"Didn't what?"

"Didn't stay long?"

"No. Not long."

"You said he picks you up to take you to visit your son."

"He does this. Very nice."

"You never had him here for a meal, say."

"No. Do you think I should have?"

"So he never mentioned your nice table, said anything about it."

"Why would he?"

I sat forward. "Mrs. Rosenberg, I think that nice table of yours may be a key missing piece of evidence."

"Piece of what?"

"A clue. Something to help your son and his wife."

"This is possible how?"

"It just is. If I'm right, I'll explain further, in as much detail as you like. For now, I'd just like your permission to take some pictures of the table tomorrow. And possibly—and this is important—to take it away and keep it somewhere safe."

She had been quietly nodding all through that, even as she looked ever more bewildered. "All right, Mr. Heller. If that would help Julius. But if it does?"

"Yes, Mrs. Rosenberg?"

"You have to give it back to him and Ethel. It *is* their table."

We excused ourselves and Natalie and I had a quick powwow near our discovery.

"What now?" she asked.

"I'll call my local man at the A-1 branch office," I said, "first thing tomorrow. Honey, this is really heating up."

She nodded, excitement dancing in the dark eyes. Then she frowned in thought, and gave a finger snap. "There's something else we can try. I know it's been a long day, but if you're up for it . . ."

"What?"

She raised a cautionary hand. "Let me just see first, before I get you all excited."

I grinned at her. "And you know how easy it is for you to get me all excited."

She gave me a crinkled-chin smile in return, then called out to our hostess, asking if there was a phone in the apartment. There was, in the kitchen, and Natalie went off to use it.

I helped myself to another macaroon and some tea, then returned to my armchair and told Mrs. Rosenberg that we'd call her before coming by tomorrow morning, and that I would probably not be alone for the visit. I explained that Bob Hasty ran my local branch office and that he would likely accompany me and possibly bring a professional photographer.

Five minutes or so later, Natalie returned, golden-brown hair bouncing on her shoulders; she wore a small, self-satisfied smile. She gestured to me to rejoin her at the drop-leaf table and I excused myself to Mrs. Rosenberg and went.

"So excite me," I said.

"What's this do for you? Ruth Greenglass has agreed to talk to us."

"You're kidding."

"Not a bit." Natalie reached in her small purse and withdrew a tiny address book. "I just called her. She's still at the same number on the Lower East Side. Thought she might have changed it after all the publicity, but no."

"When can we see her?"

"Right now."

# CHAPTER 11

Natalie had said Ruth Greenglass would see us "right now," but getting from Washington Heights to the Lower East Side took forty-five minutes. When no cab had availed itself, Natalie and I made the trek by subway, where in my Dobbs hat and tailored suit I must have been an invitation to dine to prospective muggers. With the nine-millimeter under my arm, however, I felt I could risk it.

The ground floor of the shabby Rivington Street tenement—with its mask of fire escapes and checkerboard of lit and unlit windows—was home to an electrician's shop and a neighborhood grocery. Both were closed at this time of night—it was going on nine-thirty—though nearby bars provided the street with some rowdy milling color. Natalie commented idly that David's mother lived around the corner on Sheriff Street and Ruth's father's dry-goods store was just down the block.

Four creaking flights of barely lighted stairs took us to the spongy landing where Ruth's door awaited, but it took only two knocks to summon her. And she was something of a surprise, considering the surroundings.

Ruth Greenglass had taken the opportunity to spruce up, knowing how long the trip from the Heights would take. Her deftly applied makeup included bright red lipstick, not unlike Natalie's, and she wore a long-sleeve filmy white rhinestone-buttoned blouse (slip peeking through), a black patent-leather belt, and a black-and-white horizontally striped skirt, presumably an unintentional echo of old-fashioned prison uniforms.

I'd expected a dowdy housewife, but this was a good-looking woman, buxom but petite, nearly pretty in an Andrews Sisters kind of way; her dark hair was fashionably styled, upswept waves in front, rolled bun in back. Her smile was surprisingly warm as she offered me a regal hand, which I clasped briefly, though for a fraction of a second I considered a half bow.

She raised a red-nailed finger to her full red lips and whispered, "Little angels are sleeping."

She opened the door for us and we stepped into a living room that seemed ill-suited for such a nicely dressed, well-groomed hostess. The secondhand furnishings in this dismal, paint-peeling space made Sophie Rosenberg's apartment, with or without a drop-leaf table, look palatial. The narrow kitchen she walked us to was primitive at best: exposed pipes, bare sink, ancient stove, and a claw-foot bathtub. Having grown up on the West Side of Chicago, I knew in a cold-water flat the proximity of the tub to a hot-water source was a necessity.

The smell of coffee greeted us. She led us to a small scarred table—one of its sides snug to the wall—covered by a simple white cloth with red trim; an ashtray, book of matches, and pack of Chesterfields served as a centerpiece. No door separated us from the hallway, so we kept the volume low. Kiddies were sleeping, and the youngest one—a girl—probably wasn't school age yet.

The small attractive woman stood between Natalie and me where she'd seated us and rested a friendly hand on our nearest shoulders.

"You're Mr. Heller," she said pleasantly, her voice a low timbre.

I said I was and nodded.

To Natalie she said, "A surprise hearing from you, dear, after all this time." Not chilly but not warm, either.

"I'm sorry to be such a stranger," Natalie said with a nervous smile. "I bet those two of yours have grown."

"Like weeds. Something David is missing out on, I'm afraid." She swung her dark-eyed gaze around. "Coffee, anyone?"

We were all in favor of that and she served us up. I put sugar and milk in mine, Natalie the same, our hostess taking it black. She finally sat, offering us a smoke that both Natalie and I turned down. Our hostess lit up a Chesterfield, inhaled deep, held it, then thoughtfully exhaled a gray-blue cloud away from the table.

"It's generous of you, Mrs. Greenglass," I said, "to see us at such short notice, and at this late hour."

"Actually this is better than earlier," she said. "Barbara and Steve can be handfuls, and Stevie has homework while Barbie has to be kept amused. Being a parent is a full-time job, and I *already* have another one."

Natalie said, "You're working?"

She exhaled smoke through the teeth. "Typist in a secretarial pool. Somebody has to support the family."

That was the opening I was hoping for. "Must have been a terrible shock," I said, and sipped the coffee.

"Excuse me?"

"When they sentenced your husband to fifteen years." I gave my head a single sympathetic shake.

Her pleasant expression hardened at the thought of the injustice of that. "I didn't expect it, I admit," she said. "Fifteen fucking years— Steven will be twenty, Barbara sixteen! So unfair. So very unfair."

*But maybe not*, I thought, *as unfair as railroading your sister-in-law into the Sing Sing death house.*

I said, "It may not be that bad. There's always parole."

Her glistening red upper lip curled in contempt. "Our attorney told us that if we told them what we knew, and fully cooperated? Then David would get a suspended sentence. If the judge was in a bad mood, he said, the worst we could expect was David getting maybe three years."

"No question about it," I said with a small matter-of-fact shrug and sigh. "You were double-crossed."

"But what can I do about it?" she asked, the hardness gone.

She *was* attractive. I could see why she was apparently the only person on the planet that David Greenglass gave a damn about, besides himself and maybe those slumbering kids down the hall.

"Well, Ruth," I began, then stopped as if afraid I'd overstepped. "May I call you Ruth?"

She tamped cigarette ash into the tray. She made her smile go pleasant again. "Please. And do you prefer 'Nathan' or 'Nate'?"

"Nate's fine." We'd keep it casual. Another sip. "Did Natalie tell you why I wanted to chat?"

Ruth nodded. "She said you're a private investigator working for a group trying to get clemency for Ethel."

"That's not *exactly* right. I'm looking for new evidence, new witnesses."

She turned sharply to Natalie. "*You* said that—"

"Please," I said, holding up a hand. "I'm not here to cause any difficulty. I think you might want to consider coming forward, but—"

The dark eyes flared. "Coming forward!"

"Just listen." I was as soothing and folksy as Arthur Godfrey on the radio. "All I ask is one cup of coffee worth of your time."

Her expression grew guarded. ". . . All right. I'll listen. One cup only."

I smiled with all the warmth I could dredge up. "Understood. No question about it—the government went back on their deal with you and David. You played ball, all the way. And, yes, you got immunity. But your husband sure as hell didn't get any favors. How close do you and David stay in contact?"

"He writes twice a week. I'm frankly not as good about it as he is—maybe once. There's just nothing much to say. I leave the kids with Mother and go to Lewisburg by train once a month. Why do you ask?"

I flipped a hand. "I just wondered if he might have mentioned me. But it must be too soon. You see, I visited him at his cell recently."

The full lips twitched a bitter half smile. "And did you ask *him* to come forward? And come forward about *what*, I might ask?"

Natalie's gaze was going from Ruth to me and back again, as if watching a leisurely but intense tennis match.

I had another sip of coffee. "No, my approach to your husband was different. I'm afraid I used an old investigative technique to get him to talk freely with me."

"What technique is that, Mr. Heller?"

"Please. 'Nate.'"

"What technique is *that*, Nate?"

"I lied to him. No, that's too harsh. I led him to believe that I was working undercover for an interested party in the federal government."

Of course, I hadn't really lied to David about that—at least not where Senator McCarthy was concerned. But I couldn't cop to that in front of Natalie, now could I?

Ruth stabbed her cigarette out in the ashtray. Her pretty face hardened into something significantly less attractive. I could tell she wanted to toss my ass out right now, but she needed to know what David had spilled.

I told her. Told her that he'd admitted that neither he nor she had mentioned the Rosenbergs in their first statements to the FBI. That he had no memory of Ethel typing up the atom bomb notes, and that in fact he thought Ruth had done it. That she and David had pretty much said whatever Saypol and Cohn told them to.

Finally I said, "That Jell-O box yarn was cooked up by Roy boy, wasn't it? It didn't exist till two weeks before the trial."

She stared at me stonily. "Was it recorded, your little talk with my husband?"

I shook my head. "Strictly off-the-record. I like to know things. It tells me what evidence to look for. Hell, I know your husband isn't going to change his story at this point . . . at least not unless *you* do. You have nice legs, Ruth, but I guess we all know who wears the pants."

She could have exploded at me for that, but she just lighted up another cigarette, turning sideways in the chair and crossing one of those nice legs, attractively set off by her prisoner-print skirt.

"You think I should come forward," she said flatly. "And let everybody know what words were put in my mouth and by whom. Is that what you think, Nate? Mr. Heller?"

"You have immunity, don't you?"

She laughed and there was some cigarette rasp in it. "Not from perjury! What kind of chump do you think you're talking to?"

Not the kind of chump she married, certainly.

"No," I said, "but you'll get immunity again, if you expose what the FBI and Saypol and Cohn talked you into doing in exchange for a deal they didn't keep."

She laughed smoke. "There's the crux, Nate. You have no idea who and what I'd be dealing with, coming forward. What deal do you think those sons of bitches will make and break next?"

"They won't dare."

She laughed again. "Really? You're a little old to be in the Boy Scouts, aren't you, Nate?"

"I'm no Boy Scout. I'm from Chicago. But I have connections in the press—big ones. . . . The name 'Drew Pearson' mean anything to you? If you come forward—teary-eyed wanting to tell the truth—and spring your sister-in-law from Death Row, you'll be a heroine. You'll be famous and probably rich, when you sell your story to the tabloids. No more cold-water flats for Ruth Greenglass. That blouse is pretty, but it's nylon, right? Don't you think you deserve silk?"

She sat staring at the tub, smoke in, smoke out. Natalie gave me a sideways glance and I shrugged. I wasn't stringing this woman—I really did think she could turn this whole case upside down, or more like right side up. There would be a new trial, Julius would get maybe the fifteen years David got, David would get a reduced sentence or early parole, and Ethel would walk out of the death house and back into the arms of her boys in a nicer apartment than this one.

Finally Ruth said, "I won't say it's not tempting, Chicago. You're smart and you're convincing. But I don't feel like bucking the U.S.

Attorney's Office and the FBI, either. J. Edgar doesn't strike me as anybody inclined to make deals, in his great big atomic spy case."

I leaned toward her. "Ruth . . . it won't even seem self-serving—you can say you couldn't stand to see your innocent sister-in-law go to the chair."

She smirked. "Ethel's not going to the chair. It's a bluff."

"But what if it isn't? By the way, that console table that you described as a secret spy device given to Julie and Ethel? I found it. And it doesn't match up with what you said under oath. At all."

The dark eyes narrowed, the sticky red upper lip curled just a tad.

"Not too late for you, Ruth," I said. "To help yourself and maybe David, too."

She shook her head, and a dark tendril escaped from her hairdo and tickled her forehead. "I don't intend to do anything to antagonize Uncle Sam, get me? My fate—David's fate, my *family's* fate—that's all in the hands of the prosecution and prison officials and parole boards."

"Ruth, I think you're being shortsighted. You can change history."

"I already made history and it was no damn fun. That's your cup of coffee, Nate. Nice seeing you again, Natalie. I'll show you out."

She did.


A quick cab ride took us from the Lower East Side to Natalie's address in the Village. Along the block at street level were a corner grocery (closed), a cleaner's (also closed), a bar bleeding bebop, and a blacked-out display window with "VILLAGE ARTISTS" lettered in a drippy indifferent free hand.

I was helping Natalie out of the back of the cab when she said, "Here's your chance to see the gallery."

"Let's do it tomorrow. I'm pretty beat."

"It's not that late. Anyway, there's my apartment right here, if you need to lie down. Or is it 'lay'?"

I didn't need any more invitation than that. I paid the cabbie off and joined her where she was unlocking the front door.

"An art gallery," I said, "with the window painted black? Some kind of arty statement?"

She flashed a grin over her shoulder. "More like a peacekeeping effort. This is the cooperative venture of a bunch of egotistical, half-mad artists. You think they want anybody else to get showcased out front?"

She had a point.

Inside, she locked the door behind her, then hit several light switches, revealing a long narrow space that would have been as white as the window was black if there had been any overhead lighting. The walls of the former antique shop were painted out white and so was the ceiling—only the ancient floor, which hadn't seen varnish in decades, had been spared the white brush. Each wall was hung with unframed canvases, mostly very large, each getting spotlight-like attention from carefully aimed track lighting. Spillover into the wide aisle between walls created a dusk effect that Natalie, all in black, practically disappeared into, but for the ghostly cameo of her pale face with its scarlet mouth.

She slipped her arm in mine. "What do you think? Does this kind of thing do anything for you?"

"I like it as design. Nice splashes of color for a bachelor pad."

"But . . . ?"

"But nothing. It's fine."

The bright smile in the dim room turned sideways. "Come on, Nathan. You won't hurt my feelings. But you'd be smart to pick up a painting or two. These are going to be going for a lot of money before long. Pollocks are in the thousands already."

"You don't have any of those."

She shrugged. "Lee Krasner is part of our group."

"Who's she?"

"Pollock's wife."

We were walking slowly down the center of the room, with her pointing out the sights left and right like a tour guide, telling me the names of the painters behind the work.

"*That's* Krasner, there. . . ."

A horizontal canvas of shades of green, yellow, and blue, an abstraction labeled a "still life," though on closer look a bowl of fruit did seem to be trying to claw its way out.

"That's Reinhardt right there. . . ."

Geometric shapes, red, blue, white.

". . . and Mitchell, another of our woman painters . . ."

Bold colorful dabs, yellows and pinks and blues, like a van Gogh that got smudged before it became a picture.

". . . Alfred Leslie . . ."

A canvas broken into square and rectangular shapes of smeary gray and occasional heavy green outlining. A gifted five-year-old finger painter.

". . . another of our women, one of my favorites, Grace Hartigan . . ."

Semi-abstract, pink and red and white, with childish images discernible.

". . . and that's a Larry Rivers."

Naked half-finished figures floated.

We were at the far end of the gallery, where several small black tables with black chairs were arrayed.

She drew away and faced me, hands on hips, like Superman or maybe Wonder Woman. "Not to your taste, Nathan?"

"I'm a Varga and Petty man, I'm afraid."

To her credit, she chuckled in a way that said she recognized the artists I'd cited.

Still, something about the work displayed here resonated with me, however vaguely. Something that related to this so-called Atomic Age of ours, where bombs reduced us to smears and ashes and indistinguishable body parts. There was movement in this art, if nothing moving, and in its way reflected the postwar world more accurately than Norman Rockwell ever could. Not in a world where nobody sat still long enough to be painted anymore, unless they were very, very rich and really damn dull. Life went by now in a blur, never quite forming.

Natalie sat at one of the tiny tables. I sat across from her.

She got a Fatima out of her purse and lighted it with a small silver Zippo. "I admit I'm a little disappointed in you, Nathan."

"Well, sooner or later I disappoint any woman who gets to know me." I gestured toward the facing walls of paintings. "Anyway, I'm not your audience. Smarter, hipper people are. I know parts of Chicago where this stuff would sell through the roof. Crazy, man, crazy."

Her smile pursed into a kind of kiss out of which she let smoke seep. "Now you're just being kind."

"No. Not patronizing either. If this were a bar or a club, I'd dig it just fine."

She smiled a little at the middle-aged man saying "dig." Brightly, she said, "Why don't I play waitress, then? And get us some beers? I have a fridge in the storeroom."

"Why not?"

She left the Fatima behind in a little black ashtray as she fetched the beers. In her absence, I sat gazing around the gallery, with its pools of light showcasing each abstract canvas, like lighthouses in a sea of ignorance.

She brought back two cold bottles of Pabst. She sipped hers, I sipped mine.

Brow furrowed, she said, "Nathan, there's something I want to ask if you'd do for me."

"Sure. What wouldn't Nick do for Nora?"

Something bittersweet touched her smile. "*The Thin Man*. I haven't thought of those movies in years. Loved them as a kid."

"Of course you did. Comrade Hammett's work."

She tried to get comfortable in the hard chair, not an easy trick. "You're not FBI, are you?"

I about did a spit-take. "No. *Hell* no. J. Edgar has a file on me thicker than the Manhattan phone book. I told him to go fuck himself once upon a time."

That got a laugh out of her. "You know, I wouldn't be surprised if that were true." She retrieved the Fatima from the ashtray, took a drag. Set it free. "It's just . . . I'm trying to figure out where you're coming from in this . . . inquiry of yours."

Another sip of beer. "What you see is what you get, kiddo."

She was studying me. "You're not FBI. And you're not a socialist or Communist."

"Hell, I'm barely a Democrat. Look, I do jobs for money. I try not to sell out my clients, but I like to keep an open mind."

Working very hard at it, she made her words sound matter-of-fact: "How much would it take for you to walk away?"

". . . From what?"

"This. Investigation. This effort to clear the Rosenbergs."

I squinted at her through drifting cigarette smoke. "Wait a minute. Are *you* FBI?"

She managed a halfhearted smile. "No, Nathan. What you see is what you get, me too. I'm a Communist. As advertised."

I shifted in the hard chair. "Then why the hell would you want me to walk away? Julie and Ethel are friends of yours. They're comrades, right? Julie, anyway."

"Ethel, too. She's no spy, but . . . Nathan, I'm going to level with you. I was one of Julius' ring."

I frowned at her.

She was frowning just a little, a woman telling her man she's been cheating on him but hopes he won't mind too much.

"Julius is who I reported to, Nathan. I know of seven others, but there could be any number more. This went on all through the war." She gestured with the Fatima, a brushstroke worthy of the surrounding artists. "We didn't all work together, you see, although many of us knew Julie and Ethel socially, and a lot of us went back to City College days, though not me."

I sat there absorbing her revelation. "Julius Rosenberg ran a major espionage ring. During the war. For the Soviets."

She nodded. "Yes. He's guilty of that."

"What about David and Ruth?"

"Oh yes. But they were mostly part of a different, bigger ring. They *really* know the secrets." She smiled as if she'd just told me she wasn't a virgin and hoped I wouldn't care. "So, Nathan—how much?"

I reached for her cigarettes and lighted one up; she took that in quizzically, but said nothing.

I said, "I think you've misjudged me, Natalie. I'm not the most ethical guy on the planet, but I'm not necessarily for sale to the highest bidder. You're making my head spin, honey. You're a Commie? Well, I knew that. You helped Julius Rosenberg feed inside dope to the Soviets? Okay, nobody's perfect. Makes it tougher to look the other way, but let's say I can. Let's say I can *dig* that maybe you thought America shouldn't be keeping things from an ally like Russia."

Her chin came up just a little. "That's a true, valid motivation."

"Yeah, yeah. Just enlighten me, because I don't get this modern art. Why would you want *not* to clear the Rosenbergs? Certainly it's not because Julie's been guilty all along, and clearing him would be wrong. *Why*, Natalie? Explain it to a square who just isn't hip enough to get it."

She touched a breast. "Nathan, I hate the idea of Julius and Ethel going . . . going to their deaths like criminals. I don't really think it will come to that—the government knows that they don't really have anything on Ethel."

"Don't make any big bets. The feds don't run a bluff like that in public. What the hell is really going on here, Natalie?"

She put the Fatima out, got another one going, her eyes moving fast with thought.

Then she said, "I don't have to tell you that the government is using Ethel as a lever to get Julius to talk. But what you may not know is the specific information they're after—the names of his ring."

"His spy network."

She nodded. "Some of us have flown, Nathan, but others are still here . . . hiding in plain sight. If Julius dies in the electric chair, as a good party member in his position would do, all of the rest of us are safe."

I goggled at her. " 'Safe'? You can't believe that. The feds probably already have your name—*all* the names. They just want confirmation, and nice juicy details. If I can't clear the Rosenbergs, how do you know the government's tactic won't work? That at the last minute Julius will spill?"

She shook her head, the dark golden hair bouncing off her shoulders. "No. Never."

"But if I deliver new evidence and witnesses for Julius and Ethel, and they get a new trial—"

"The investigation starts all over again."

The Fatima was fuming; me, too.

"You know," I said, "I can be a little dim sometimes. And I have an Achilles' heel, which can be accessed by somebody like you through my fly. You weren't Nora to my Nick, honey—you were Mata to my very stupid Harry. A spy all the way."

She shook her head again, something like embarrassment coloring her expression. "Just keeping an eye on you, that's all."

"No, it was more than that. You were sending me on wild-goose chases. You knew those Knickerbocker Village interviews were a waste of time. You knew that poor nice illiterate lady who gave birth to Julius Rosenberg didn't know a goddamn fucking thing. We'd just sit there eating macaroons, keeping me occupied. Boy, you must have soiled your panties when that console table turned up."

"Stop it."

"What did you have lined up for me next? Grant's Tomb? A day trip to the Statue of Liberty? And what, shove me out a hole in Lady Liberty's crown like in a Hitchcock picture?"

"We can give you ten thousand dollars."

"Try fifty thousand."

She drew in smoke slowly, let it out the same way. "I'll have to talk to some people, but I think that can be arranged."

"So then you're tied to the Soviets," I said, thinking out loud. "You're not just the American Communist Party, you're out of the

Russian branch office. Doing Moscow's bidding. It's a cinch you and the other small-time spies couldn't raise fifty grand. Not when fucking David Greenglass sells atomic secrets for five hundred bucks!"

She stayed in business mode. "Do you accept the offer, assuming I can—"

"You and your comrades, here and abroad, want the Rosenbergs dead, all right," I said, talking as quickly as it was coming together in my head. "But not just to protect the rest of his espionage ring, no. You and your comrades, and Moscow, too, need to keep secret the direct ties between the American Communist Party and the Soviets. Think of the red meat you'd be throwing McCarthy and the other Commie hunters and haters if they learned that for *years* the Russians have recruited their U.S. spies from *your* ranks. That's called treason, honey. And all they got the Rosenbergs on was conspiracy. And look where they sit. And where they're *going* to sit."

Her expression was cold but the dark eyes had hurt in them. "Do you care, Nathan? Really care? About anything but money?"

"I care about my son. Yes, I have a son, and an ex-wife, and fifty grand would cover a lot of alimony. But if I were Julius Rosenberg, I would have sold out all of you well-meaning idiots for my kid. A long time ago."

Her eyebrows went up. "I believe fifty thousand *is* possible. That's of course tax-free. You would make a report to the Hammett committee on anything you like . . . with the exception of tonight's discovery."

I stabbed out the cigarette and grinned at her through the smoke. "That's what brought you out from behind your mask, isn't it, Natalie? That little table could change everything. Including lead to a new trial and the investigation that would come with it. But tell me, honey—why arrange a meeting for me with Ruth Greenglass?"

She said nothing.

"Maybe you figured I'd find my way to Ruth on my own," I said, thinking out loud again, "and you preferred being there when I talked to her, sitting right between us, reminding her with your presence that there are other comrades around who wouldn't want her cooperating with me in any fashion."

One eyebrow went up. "So your answer is 'no,' then?"

"Hell. The kicker just came to me."

"Really."

I got to my feet. "Two brave martyrs, one a helpless housewife— what mileage international Communism could get out of that! The movement is better off with the Rosenbergs dead."

"Don't go!" she said. Louder than seemed necessary.

I heard the door open and I was backing away from the table as they came out from the storeroom.

Three of them, skinny, scrawny, bearded, in dark sweaters and dungarees and sandals, and maybe that was to fit in with the Bohemian crowd or possibly they really were part of that bunch. They were positioned side by side like a modest firing squad, tallest at left, shortest at right, a stair-step effect that was almost funny.

But there in that underlit part of the gallery they also displayed something decidedly unfunny—the kind of glittery glowing eyes that come out of the dark at you when you walk down the wrong alley. Little eyes that go with gnashing teeth and claws.

The short one said, "You come with us now. Not gonna be any trouble."

Why was the smaller one always the spokesman?

All three stair-step comrades were pointing guns at me. Dark compact automatics. Wouldn't you know it? Makarovs. Russian pistols in American hands.

Now I knew why Natalie had taken me to see Ruth. At Sophie Rosenberg's, she'd called for backup to meet us at the gallery. To wait in the storeroom till she'd made her pitch to my baser instincts.

My head was spinning now. Had the bitch put something in the beer? But I'd only had a sip or two. Not poison—she wouldn't want me to die here; just sedate me, so I could be more easily moved.

"Go on and take him," she said softly, unhappily. "He doesn't carry a gun."

So it surprised her and them when I dove into a patch of darkness between spotlighted paintings and got the nine-millimeter out from under my arm and orange and blue blossomed in an abstract image but in a very concrete way put a bullet in the short one's forehead. The guy in the middle, getting more than he bargained for, turned and went running toward the door in back and I shot him the same way. In the back. He arched as if someone were throwing him roses from a box seat, then fell forward with a floor-rattling thud.

The tall one was already running at me, charging and yelling his wordless war cry, shooting as he came; how many future masterpieces he ruined, I won't hazard a guess, but I rolled across the aisle and into another strip of darkness and when he adjusted his footing, slowing to face me, two bullets punched him in the face, sending a splattery spontaneous spray of red and white and gray and green dripping onto the wall.

"There's your Pollock," I said to her.

I must have sounded a little crazy because she went running toward the back, then sudden-stopped at the fallen man, dead from his own doomed break for it, and she was down there snatching the gun out of his hand when I said, "*Don't,* Natalie!"

But she had the gun now and thrust its nose my way, her eyes big and wild in a face white with only that splash of red across her mouth and she fucking made me do it, crouched as she was I couldn't go for a leg and I was no damn trick shot, anyway. The two slugs caught her in the chest, shook her like the naughty child she was, and she fell over her comrade, draped there like a flag dropped in battle.

# CHAPTER 12

The men in dark suits and dark hats came in quickly, three of them, with guns in one hand and identification wallets open in the other.

*"Mr. Heller, put your weapon down! Government agents!"*

This came from the one in front, a blandly handsome man about thirty, his cheeks flushed.

Their guns appeared to be nine-millimeters, similar to my own, which I lowered. The odds were against me and anyway I knew feds when I saw them.

He continued coming quickly my way, as if following his gun and ID, while the other two were at the door, one talking to the other, a Negro, issuing him instructions I couldn't hear, then getting a nod in return as the colored agent slipped outside, I guessed to stand guard. Then the fed walked toward us, I thought to join us, but instead began checking the bodies.

"Are you all right, Mr. Heller?" the man in charge asked. For a change he was the tallest of three. His eyes were blue and his rosy cheeks enlivened a very Caucasian complexion. He looked like he'd be as comfortable on a surfboard as in a business suit. When did feds get so young?

My ears were ringing from the close-quarters gunfire and my nose rebelled at the smell of cordite mixed with the sewer stench of bodies voiding their bladders and bowels at death. I was dizzy and the abstract paintings were moving, coming to life, swimming in their spotlights.

"I'm fine," I said unconvincingly. "They gave me a drugged beer, but I only had a few sips. Some kind of sedative, but the adrenaline's fighting it off."

"I don't need you to tell me what happened here. Just wait a moment."

"Okay."

He called to the one who'd been checking the bodies. "Fatalities?"

"All four, sir," he called, kneeling over Natalie's remains. He was even younger, though his features had a sharpness his bland-faced superior's didn't.

I said to the man in charge, "Could I have a better look at that ID of yours?"

"Certainly."

He held it up but didn't hand it to me.

I don't think I could recover his name under hypnosis, because my eyes went directly to the bold "CENTRAL INTELLIGENCE AGENCY" over the curving "UNITED STATES OF AMERICA" superimposed under the agency's bald-eagle seal. The face on the ID matched that of the agent patiently dealing with me.

"All right?" he asked pleasantly.

"Fine," I said.

He took my gun from a hand that was barely hanging on to it. "You'll get this back. We need it for matching up bullets and various forensics concerns. Do you know where the Waldorf is?"

"I'm . . . I'm staying there."

"Not the hotel. The restaurant."

I said I'd been there but I was a little turned around. He reminded me that it was just off the intersection of Eighth Street and Sixth Avenue. It would be a short cab ride or half an hour if I felt like walking it. I was to take a table in a corner if possible, and wait.

"For what?"

"My superior," he said. "Listen, you need to go. We have to deal with this scene and do some cleanup."

Maybe you think you would have asked why they were helping me like this. Trust me—you wouldn't have.

"Fine. What about the cops?"

"In this situation, we are the cops. You're clear, just do as I say."

As he said. Not as he asked.

He said, "My superior is Agent Edward Shepherd. Got that?"

"Edward Shepherd. How I will know him?"

"He won't be a Bohemian. You may have to wait an hour or even more. Understood?"

"Yeah."

As I went out into the cool night, I passed the Negro agent who was dealing with two irritated uniformed cops, one quite a bit older than the other. The cops weren't happy when I ignored them and walked away from the gallery, but the agent held them back and, as promised, dealt with them.

No one knew why, some years ago, a respectable chain of cafeterias decided to set up shop in the Bohemian heart of Greenwich Village. And for almost as long, the Waldorf had been better known as the Waxworks, thanks to fluorescent lighting that cast a yellow pall on its patrons, echoed by peeling yellow wallpaper. The darker yellow tile floors, ironically enough, had not seen wax in memory.

The clientele this time of night was mostly drinking coffee, and a good number were drunk, some extravagantly so as artists and poets and musicians sang their own praises and bemoaned the shortcomings of their lessers. These were self-defined outcasts, their attire at once striking and shabby, drab and outlandish. The clatter of dishes and the ding of the cash register tried unsuccessfully to make music of it all, but the effect was that any private conversation here could stay that way.

Like everybody else, I had coffee, which entitled me to my own little piece of real estate for as long as I could make it last—refills were a nickel, a tactic designed to encourage customer turnover that didn't seem to be working.

Perhaps I looked more respectable than other potential table hogs because the cashier, a pleasant if hard-looking fortyish brunette in a hairnet, let me in on a secret: If I needed the restroom, I should ignore the "Out of Order" sign. That was just there to keep bums and drunks from wandering in and using the facilities. The way to tell the bums and drunks from the rest of the clientele, apparently, was that they weren't drinking coffee.

The tables were small square slabs of something pretending to be wood. I found one in a corner, as directed. I had walked here. Or more like sleepwalked, a numb shell-shocked soldier who had paused at an all-night drugstore to buy some smokes, having left the Fatimas behind with Natalie.

I was halfway through my third Lucky Strike when the taste turned foul and I lost the impulse. The combat mood had faded, replaced by a sick feeling that made even the coffee hard to take. I had killed four people tonight. Three men whose names I didn't even know. A beautiful young woman I'd taken to bed and for whom I had a certain affection. I began to weep.

Apparently this was typical behavior at the Waldorf Cafeteria, because no one seemed to notice, much less care. And I got hold of myself quickly before the rough paper napkins sanded my face off.

He came in like an apparition of normalcy, someone who'd wandered off Wall Street and stumbled into Cairo. His suit was gray sharkskin, his tie a darker gray, his hat darker yet with a jaunty green feather. He was one of those medium men—medium height, build, weight—but he lacked the anonymity of features that so many CIA and FBI agents wore like camouflage. Boyish with a twinkle in his dark blue eyes, he smiled a dimpled gap-toothed greeting as if this were a reunion of two fraternity brothers.

He leaned in and presented a hand for me to shake. I did. Like in *The Three Bears*, not too hard, not too soft, just right.

"I'm getting myself coffee," he said, some Southern drawl in it, "and you seem to be out. Shall I refresh your cup?"

"No thanks," I said.

He returned with coffee and a slice of apple pie with some cheese on it. "Hope you don't mind—I've been up a while, and could use a little boost of sugar."

"Not at all."

"Like a piece yourself? Happy to fetch it. My treat."

"No. Thank you."

He sat and doctored his coffee with cream and sugar.

"Name is Edward Shepherd," he said. "But I hope you'll call me 'Shep.' I'm hopeful we'll be friends, or at least friendly. May I call you 'Nate'?"

"Sure."

He leaned forward in familiarity. "Do you mind if I don't display my credentials here in public? There are likely individuals among us who would recoil at the sight of what appeared to be any kind of police identification."

"I believe you're who you say you are."

He had a bite of pie and waited till he'd chewed and swallowed it down before speaking again. "I apologize for the wait. You've had ninety minutes, nearly, to assess the situation yourself. Would you like to give me your thoughts, or shall I fill you in?"

I leaned back in my hard chair, folded my arms. "Why don't you eat your pie and I'll take a crack at it."

The gap-toothed smile flashed. "You're very generous, Nate. Please. Tell me what you've gathered."

He was keeping his voice down, so I did the same. But the loud talk and laughter of the boisterous regulars here gave us plenty of cover.

"You've had that art gallery under surveillance for some time," I said. "Wired for sound?"

A nod as he chewed apple pie.

"But you weren't in the car or van yourself. Those three who burst in just a little too late, like the cavalry in a western movie . . . *they* were the surveillance team."

Another nod, another bite of pie.

"You're either local or happened to be in town and are some kind of security chief. You were called, came right down, and while I cooled my tail here, you've been reviewing the playback of what turned an art gallery into a shooting gallery."

He sipped his coffee, said, "Nicely thought through. Well put, too. Anything else?"

"You may have been following me during my inquiry into the Rosenberg matter. I'd like to think not, because it would mean I've been shadowed for several weeks and didn't catch it. Embarrassing."

He chuckled as he forked another bite of pie.

"How about it, Shep? Care to confirm or deny any of that?"

"No," he said. "What does it matter? We're here to help you out of a spot, and clean up that mess. I don't say *your* mess, Nate, because I kind of feel like that mess was imposed upon you."

"What will become of the, uh . . . others?"

A shrug. "That hasn't been decided yet. Probably they're just not gonna be around anymore. The assumption'll be that they've fled behind the Iron Curtain. Several of the Rosenberg ring already have done so, as the late Miss Ash indicated."

"Then Julius Rosenberg *was* the linchpin of an espionage ring feeding the Soviets information."

He pushed the empty plate aside. "Durin' the war, yes. That I can confirm. I can tell you quite a bit more, but off-the-record, with no way for you to verify. You just have to take my word. And I would deny it all, naturally."

"Why tell me *anything*, Shep?"

He only gave me half the grin this time. "You're a hell of an investigator, Nate. I think you have a right to know what is really going on in this business . . . at least as the Agency sees it."

"And what's your agenda? Yours and/or the Agency's?"

"You mean, what do I hope to convince you to do? Well, that's up to you. I think you may want to walk away from this endeavor, at this point, but possibly not. Possibly not."

"No agenda. That's tough to buy, Shep."

He shrugged, sipped more coffee, shrugged again. "Let's talk a while before you decide."

"All right. But first let me ask you something."

"Shoot. Sorry. Poor choice of words."

I frowned at him; his lightness about all this was starting to grate. "Very poor. I took four lives tonight. Three were strangers but that doesn't help much. One was a woman I liked and trusted."

He made a noise in his cheek. "That kind of thing can shake a fella."

"Yes it can."

"Of course, from what I read in official files, you've dispatched rather more than your share of troublemakers in your time. And I'm guessing not all of the scores you've settled have made it into the official files."

"Let's say you're guessing right, Shep. But before this conversation proceeds, tell me. What are you boys doing, working a case on U.S. soil? Isn't that J. Edgar's purview?"

His closed-mouth smile plumped his cheeks. "Well, now isn't that just precious, comin' from somebody as worldly as Nathan Heller."

"*Why*, Shep?"

He flipped a hand. "First, the Russian threat isn't domestic, it's international, and that means we need to keep an eye on things and a hand in. Second, I wouldn't trust the FBI with finding out whether my gardener is drinkin' the beer out of the cooler I keep on the back porch."

That actually got a smile out of me; not much of one, but a smile. "Where does the U.S. Attorney's Office come in on that list, Shep?"

He drank some coffee and said offhandedly, "Well, let's say the FBI feels about them the way I feel about the FBI, and with some justification. Saypol and that yappin' terrier Cohn screwed this thing up royal."

"How so?"

This smile was sly. "I believe you already know—you've been investigating. But let's start with them suborning perjury, and wind

up with railroadin' a little Jewish mother into the death house. . . .
Sure you won't have some pie?"

"No. But I'll get myself some more coffee."

I did.

I returned.

We resumed.

I said, "If you know a miscarriage of justice was perpetrated by
the U.S. Attorney's Office, why the hell don't you do something
about it?"

"What was that word you used? 'Purview.' I like that. Not our
purview. And anyway, I understand that the government comin'
down heavy on the Rosenbergs—not to mention their own damn
witnesses, Harry Gold and David Greenglass—might just serve as
a deterrent. You know, to homegrown Commies who look up to
Russia and want to help the 'Movement.' "

"A deterrent in that small sense," I said, "but stupid in a bigger
one. How does giving Gold and Greenglass stiff sentences encourage other reformed Reds to come forward?"

"Well, of course it doesn't, and you're exactly right. Hell, even
ol' J. Edgar himself is against the death sentence for Ethel."

I blinked at that one. "Not for humanitarian reasons, surely."

"Oh, my no! Not hardly. But Mr. Hoover knew from the start
how the winds of public opinion can change. A wife and mother,
no previous criminal record, sentenced to die? And now, after a passage of time, there's a considerable call for clemency."

"I don't give a rat's ass what spying Julius may have done during
the war," I said. "He and his wife were convicted on fabricated evidence. Under the law, that makes them not guilty."

"You don't know how right you are, Nate." He gestured with
open hands. "And that's why I'm here. To tell you a few things that
even the trial prosecutors didn't know."

"Why didn't they?"

He sighed. "Because the source of these things must be protected. And all I can tell you, Nate, is it's not a source in the sense
of a snitch or a whistle-blower. No. This is solid intelligence data."

*Now who was dealing in secrets?*

I said, "I'm listening."

"The Ash woman wasn't lyin' to you, Nate. Julius Rosenberg operated a large espionage network during the war, handling recruitment of agents for himself and another, larger ring operating out of New York. He handled the data those agents collected—on jet planes, radar, all sorts of technical and scientific data."

"What about Ethel?"

"Maybe she *did* do some typing. But is a brain surgeon's wife automatically a doctor? Is a concert pianist's wife necessarily a virtuoso musician? Still, she was probably at least, you know, *vaguely* aware of what her hubby was up to."

"But not enough to put her on Death Row. It took her brother to put her there."

The CIA agent chuckled; the strangest things amused him. "David and Ruth—particularly Ruth—played those prosecutors like con men workin' marks. You know that sketch of Davey's that Cohn told the jury was of 'the atom bomb itself'? The one that Manny Bloch stupidly requested be kept out of the trial?"

"To make the defense look patriotic?"

He nodded matter-of-factly. "That's the one. Well, our science boys say it was worthless. Imprecise, confused, garbled. Turns out, guess what? A high school graduate machinist wasn't capable of condensin' into a single diagram a two-billion-dollar development effort by the top technological minds. And the lens mold sketches Greenglass passed to Harry Gold in Albuquerque? Or anyway the facsimiles he made from memory? They were rough, rudimentary, worthless crap."

Even after all I'd learned, this staggered me. "So the atomic bomb spies didn't really have the goods?"

"No, and I assume you refer to the Greenglasses, not the Rosenbergs. Oh, Julius was a Soviet spy, no question, which makes it tough for even the likes of Nathan Heller to conduct an investigation that will clear him and his wife. You might get them a new trial, but as Miss Ash pointed out, that'll only reopen the investigation."

I grunted a nonlaugh. "And if it comes out that Julius was a turn-coat American who spied for the Soviets . . . well, he'll be back on Death Row."

Shepherd's eyebrows went up. "Maybe."

"Why maybe?"

"Well, start with Ethel. She was involved with the Communist Party before her two boys came along, and she was probably some-what aware of what Julius was up to."

"So she might deserve five years." I shook my head. "But, Jesus—not the chair."

"And as for what sentence Julius really deserves? Fifteen years is as far as I'd go. Because the man had little or nothing to do with passin' atomic secrets to the Soviets."

"You sound sure of that."

"Well, consider that the crucial family get-together of September 5, 1945—David's delivery of secrets, the Jell-O box vaudeville, Ethel typing up the notes, all of it—is said to have happened *after* the Soviets fired Julius."

"*What?*"

Shepherd allowed himself a smug smile. "You're gonna love this, Nate. Seems in mid-February '45, Julius Rosenberg got his ass fired by the Soviets. When the crimes he was convicted of took place, he wasn't a spy anymore. . . . I'm having another piece of pie. Plenty more to tell you, Nate."

I went with him to the cafeteria counter and selected a shim-mering red dish of Jell-O. Cherry. Seemed fitting somehow.


Two days later, Julius Rosenberg and I sat at the same small square scarred-up wooden table in the counsel room at Sing Sing. The light above cast the kind of jaundiced glow you got at the Waldorf Cafe-teria. Again, he was in his prison grays with his left hand cuffed to a metal ring screwed into the table, his ankles shackled as well. He looked thinner and the circles under his eyes were a dark blue, not unlike the memory of a mustache that stood out in his five o'clock shadow.

"I'm confident, Mr. Rosenberg," I said, "that we're not being recorded today."

He frowned a little, clearly skeptical, and pushed his wire-rim glasses higher on the bridge of his nose. "Why would that be the case?"

"I'm here in part as an emissary of a federal agency."

"Really?"

"Not in their employ, mind you. Just passing along a kind of offer. It touches on aspects of the case that the government would not like to have recorded."

"I'm intrigued, Mr. Heller."

"I'm going to save that offer for last," I said, "on the off-chance that someone might be listening in, ready to hit a switch once I've passed that offer along."

A small smile. "You have an admirable shrewdness, Mr. Heller. I take it there's more to talk about than this mysterious entreaty."

I nodded. I told him about the console table and its discovery in plain sight. He shook his head at the bad luck that had kept it out of the trial, and bemoaned not having thought to suggest looking in his mother's place himself. I told him that a furniture buyer at Macy's had identified the markings on the underside of the table as the store's, and identified the model number as a drop-leaf sold for approximately $20 plus sales tax. No sales slip tying it to the Rosenbergs existed, however, as the store's sales and delivery records for 1944 and '45 had been routinely destroyed. But the table's evidentiary value seemed clear.

In addition (I told him), exemplars of David Greenglass's entirely legible handwriting had been procured. And while I had no new witnesses to bring forward, I'd learned from various interviews facts that suggested other avenues of appeal.

For example, I'd suggested to attorney Bloch that affidavits be taken from prominent scientists as to their opinion of David's capacity to sketch and describe an atom bomb from things he'd overheard as a machinist on the project.

"David swore on the witness stand," I said, "that at the time of his arrest, he disclosed all major espionage incidents involving you and Ethel. That strikes me as easily proven perjury. His story and Ruth's just got richer and richer as time went by."

"Other than his own name," Rosenberg said, "everything that came out of David's mouth was perjury."

"There are other lines of inquiry," I said, tossing a hand, "that your attorney can pursue, and I've suggested a few more, including some not entirely kosher. But as for me? I'm at the end of the line."

"You've done well, Mr. Heller. But why stop now?"

"Well, I've earned the fee the Hammett committee put up and then some. The A-1 is not a charitable institution. So that's part of it."

"There's another part?"

I nodded. "I've learned that you were the head of a spy ring for the Soviets. That you are—in that sense, at least—guilty."

He said nothing.

Either he had no response or he suspected we were being recorded despite my assurance otherwise.

"But," I said, "I also know that if you had any role in the passing of atomic secrets, it was minor. Hell, man, Russia laid you off before all that atomic shinola really got going!"

His eyes jumped behind the round lenses. "You . . . you *know* about that?"

"Sure. Like I know that those so-called atomic secrets were worthless, were just ridiculously oversold to the jury at your trial."

He squinted at me, trying to bring me into focus. "I don't understand, Mr. Heller. . . ."

"Really nothing else to understand, Mr. Rosenberg. The government has known much of this all along. They have been prepared from the start to let Ethel walk and give you a relative slap on the wrist, just for your cooperation. And you've known that all along."

He didn't deny it.

I leaned forward and gave him a chummy smile. "Listen, I get it. This all started back in college for you, an idealistic lark, and when a few years later you got into the spy game, it was for what seemed like a good cause. And naturally when you went to assemble your network of industrious little Commies, you went to friends and even relatives. Selling these people out is anathema to you. I get that. But any of your people whose past actions would *really* put them in danger have already fled. Most are behind the Iron Curtain right now. The rest are prepared to take their chances."

"So you're just like McCarthy," he said, quietly bitter, upper lip curling back like the keyed lid of a sardine can. "McCarthy and HUAC and Nathan Heller. You'd have me name names, too. Betray friends. Family. You'd have me be no better than Greenglass and his shrew."

"In this case, I would, yeah."

His chin tilted up, Joan of Arc waiting for the first match. "Well, Mr. Heller, I'm not made that way. It disappoints me that you are."

"My feelings are hurt but I may get over it. Do you want to hear that offer? It's from the CIA. A spook-to-spook proposal."

He shrugged, his lidded-eyed expression oozing contempt.

"The good folks at the CIA would like you to talk to a council of rabbis, reps of various Jewish organizations, and some former Communists. They'll share with you evidence that the Soviet Union is anti-Semitic and intent on wiping out the Jews within their borders. You and your wife would receive clemency for speaking out to Jews worldwide, and for inviting them to leave the Communist movement, as you've done, and to join with you to destroy it."

"My," Rosenberg said.

"The international Communist movement has built you and your wife up as heroes and martyrs, making it impossible to discredit you with any plausibility. Take it as a compliment, Mr. Rosenberg. It's an acknowledgment that—whatever else anybody might think—you and Ethel have displayed immeasurable courage."

"I see."

"This council will also share with you evidence of Russian slave camps, where all kinds of daily horrors take place, and give you a full tour of Stalin's bloody purges. Plus the inside dope on the Slanksy show trials, and the public hangings that followed. What do you think?"

"I think the CIA has lost its collective mind," he said. He was frowning so deep, his eyes barely showed. "Do they really think my Ethel and I might be so easily manipulated? That we would *shill* for them in exchange for our lives? Can they *imagine* that we haven't already heard these ridiculous charges against Mother Russia, which are just so much capitalist propaganda?"

"Yeah, that's what I thought you'd say," I said. "But I owed this particular Agency guy a favor, so . . . anyway, I think that wraps it up for us, Mr. Rosenberg."

He nodded, quickly regaining his composure. "I do thank you for your efforts, Mr. Heller. It does sound like you might get us a new trial."

"For better or worse," I said with a shrug. "But as a father myself, what I don't get is how you can put politics above your two boys . . . and the life of your wife."

"I don't believe they will kill Ethel."

"Oh I think they probably will. And you'll go first. They'll sit you down and hope at the last second, if it comes to that, you'll say you'll cooperate if they spare the mother of your children. But if you stay mute, Mr. Rosenberg, remember—you've boxed them in. She'll have to go."

He was studying me in horrified fascination. "*You* would name names, Mr. Heller?"

"For my son? For a woman I love? You're goddamn right."

"Then you're as bad as David and Ruth."

"Maybe. I don't think I'd sell out a sister for my boy. I'd find some other way. Of course, I don't have a sister, so it's a tough call. But I think we can agree that, as in-laws go, those two are the rat-bastard bottom."

I got up to knock on the door and let the guard know I was finished here. Rosenberg sat there staring at me, trying to understand me. He apparently hadn't met anybody from Chicago before.

# CHAPTER 13

Dashiell Hammett's apartment on West Tenth in the Village was a duplex, and I was let in up seven stairs by an attractive colored housekeeper who walked me across a large yet cozy area that was both living room and bedroom, with a fireplace and a view on a small garden. We stopped at the mouth of a wrought-iron spiral staircase.

"Mr. Hammett," she called down, "your guest is here."

Hammett's voice came up: "Nate, join me."

I corkscrewed down to where he was sitting in an office that was as spare and cold as the upstairs had been warm. No framed celebrity photos, book jackets, or movie posters, just brick walls. There was something of a cell about it—a few wooden file cabinets, a cot, and a dark-wood desk, where he sat at a typewriter with a blank sheet of paper rolled in it. On the left of the typewriter were a dictionary and thesaurus, and a cup of pencils a blind beggar might have forgotten there; on the right were a box of white paper and an overflowing ashtray near a book of Stork Club matches and a pack of Camels. He had already swiveled so that his back was to his work, though there was no sign of any going on, and rose to shake hands.

His grip was firm, particularly for a man so frail-looking, his mostly white shock of hair swept back, his posture casual, though the eyes behind the plastic-rimmed glasses were sharp. His skeletal frame swam in a short-sleeved pale yellow shirt and brown pants.

He got me a hard chair from somewhere. Then I sat facing him, filling him in on the discovery of the console table as well as much of what I'd learned. Natalie Ash and her anonymous friends from the art gallery I edited out.

When all that was done, I said, "I was able to tap into some federal sources. I'm afraid I may have let certain parties in the government think I was working undercover for them."

"Oh dear," Hammett said with half a smile, letting out a stream of smoke.

"I can let you know what I learned," I said, "but only if I have your word that none of it goes any further."

He nodded.

From this man, that nod was all I needed.

So I gave him all the rest of it, including most of what Shep Shepherd had shared last night. The writer listened quietly, with cool intensity, reacting not at all to the revelation that Julius Rosenberg had been a spymaster of sorts. He was halfway through another Camel before he finally interrupted.

"Julius Rosenberg was *fired* by the Soviets?" His dark eyebrows had climbed, making his hair seem to stand up, like a comedian's in a haunted-house movie.

I doled out a nod. "Once Rosenberg was fired from his civilian job with the Signal Corps, and didn't have the access to secrets he'd had, he was of little use . . . and since he'd been fired for denying he'd been a Communist Party member, that put a spotlight on him."

"And his Russian handlers couldn't have that."

I turned a hand over. "Keep in mind Rosenberg had stayed active with the Party—kept up his dues, socialized with other party members, maintained friendships with those he'd recruited for spying . . . *all* against Soviet protocol."

Hammett shook his head. "So far in over his head, the poor bastard. Meaning well is just not good enough. Did Rosenberg have *anything* to do with the passing of atomic secrets?"

"Very damn little. He wouldn't have been David Greenglass's handler at all if it hadn't been for the accident of David getting assigned to Los Alamos."

"I doubt that was an accident," Hammett said. "That's the lead I would have followed if I were J. Edgar Hoover. Disgusting though that thought is."

I shrugged. "Well, as far we know, it was an accident. Either way, Rosenberg was David's handler for maybe a month. That might involve the first batch of information that the world's worst brother-in-law delivered on furlough—the names of a few scientists, the general layout of the Los Alamos facility."

"And from that," Hammett said coldly, "Cohn and his boss Saypol tell the jury that Julius and Ethel gave the Soviets the atomic bomb."

"A slight exaggeration for effect."

His eyes narrowed. "Can any of what you learned from government sources be brought to light in a new trial?"

"Possibly, but not all of it is helpful to the Rosenbergs."

"How so?"

"For example," I said, "the console table may be a moot point in a new trial. Seems an apartment on Morton Street here in the Village, above an art galley, was used for years by Rosenberg and his ring to do exactly the kind of microfilming of filched documents that the missing table was thought to be designed for."

Hammett frowned through a wreath of smoke. "Why didn't the government bring any of this out at the trial?"

"I frankly don't know. Exposing the real facts must in some way compromise agents still in the field, or possibly represents code-breaking that needs to stay secret."

He gave a slow nod of agreement; the man was a seasoned investigator and didn't need spoon-feeding.

I slapped my thighs like a department store Santa summoning the next brat. "Dash, I'm done here. I've provided that attorney, Bloch, with the evidence he needs to seek a new trial. Nothing more I can do. Frankly, nothing more I *want* to do."

"Why is that, Nate?" His eyes tightened. "What if I went back to the committee for another round of financing?"

"Thank you, but no. Julius and Ethel are committed to their cause—so much so that they probably *should* be committed."

"You did talk to them both," Hammett granted.

"They're fucking zealots. Anyway, Julius is. On the one hand, he's convinced himself they'll free Ethel at the last minute. On the other, he . . . and maybe she . . . are ready to become heroes to the Movement. Martyrs. You can't help a would-be martyr."

"They don't want to name names," Hammett said, with an elaborate shrug. "I understand that."

"It's more than naming names, Dash. Julius knows the darkest secret of all—that the Soviets recruited their U.S. agents from, and with the help of, the American Communist Party."

Hammett wasn't smiling now; what little blood had lurked behind the parchment flesh of his face drained out. "If that's true, I knew nothing of it."

"I'm not accusing you. But do I have to tell you what might result if Rosenberg *did* trade that secret for his life, or Ethel's?"

He sighed Camel smoke. Shook his head. His eyes had a ragged look. "That would fuel this Red scare hysteria into something unimaginable. Mass pickups of tens of thousands of Communists and leftists. Prisons full of people whose crime is the wrong politics. Jails or concentration camps."

"So much for it can't happen here."

Hammett shuddered. "Browder would be the next to check in at Death Row."

He was referring to Earl Browder, who had been the head of the Party during the war.

"And who knows?" I said. "We might just wind up with a President McCarthy running the shots in this country."

The writer sat there looking down, thinking, smoking. Then his eyes lifted to meet mine. "Nate, I agree with you. Time to close up shop."

"No question the Rosenbergs were railroaded, Dash. But I don't know if I've done them or anybody a favor, making a path to a new trial. Clemency is their best hope."

"I believe you're right."

He walked me to the door here on the basement level.

"You know," I said, pausing at the sill, "what it really gets down to is a very old story—a couple of big-shot criminals lay off their crimes on a couple of small-time Charlies. The Greenglasses held a grudge that made Julius and Ethel the perfect patsies."

"If you keep talking like Sam Spade," he said, grinning like a skull as he put his left hand on my shoulder, "I'm going to have to charge you royalties."

That hand on the shoulder seemed an uncommonly warm gesture for this self-contained man.

I said, "David Greenglass is a creep and he's married to Lady Macbeth. But I admitted to Rosenberg, at Sing Sing, that in their place? . . . I would probably have named names, too. If it meant my wife's life and the welfare of my kid."

"Naming names wasn't their sin," he said with a shrug, his latest Camel bobbling. "Lying was. Selling your own family out, that's the crime."

This coming from a guy who'd gone to jail rather than name names.

He read my expression.

"That surprises you, Nate?" Another of his eloquent shrugs. "Some people can take that kind of harassment, some can't. Hell, Nate, if I'd been tortured, I'd have talked. But a little jail time? I can do that standing on my head."

Drew Pearson sat on the couch by the fireplace in the Waldorf suite, where two of Frank Costello's bully boys had been not long ago. In a gray pin-striped suit almost as nice as the Prime Minister of the Underworld's, he stretched his arms out along the back of the couch, potentate-style, and looked around the living room like a prospective buyer.

"So *this* is why my regular suite wasn't available," he said, a sneering smile echoed by his well-waxed tie-her-to-the-train-tracks mustache.

As luck would have it—good or bad, I wasn't sure—Pearson was in town for an Associated Press luncheon. He'd called my room about two-thirty and invited himself over for an update.

I delivered him a Scotch on the rocks; I'd supplied myself with a few fingers of Bacardi, neat. I sat across from him.

"I knew you'd want me to be comfortable," I said, and sipped a little rum. "Anyway, I'm almost out of here. You wanted an update, but I can give you a final briefing."

He frowned. "You're wrapping it up?"

"I am. And I have an exclusive for you so big, you won't even whine about taking care of my expense account."

I told him about the discovery of the console table, and Macy's confirming it as theirs (just as the Rosenbergs had claimed), plus the implications that all meant for a new trial. I also mentioned the David Greenglass handwriting exemplars and the possibility of perjury as another basis of appeal.

"There's plenty more," I said, "and I can give you the gist, but there's nothing you can use. Everything I got was either off-the-record or from parties who will deny what they shared with me."

"Understood. What did you learn, man?"

I shook a scolding finger at him. "You can get sued and lose, Drew, if you put any of it in your column. Don't make a confidential unnamed source out of me."

He nodded once, curtly, and reached for his Scotch, which he sipped several times as I told him that Rosenberg had run a Soviet spy ring during the war; that Cohn had manufactured evidence, putting words in the mouths of David and Ruth Greenglass; and that while Julius was guilty of passing nonatomic secrets to the Soviets, the government had nothing on Ethel.

Swirling ice in what remained of his Scotch, Pearson asked, "Will Rosenberg talk, to save her?"

"No. He's a true believer. I think she is, too."

"Well, we know they'll kill *him* if he stays mute. But will they kill her?"

I shrugged a shoulder. "I think they'll have to, Drew. The feds have backed themselves into a corner. Anyway, guys like Cohn don't give a damn. He just likes being famous for catching atomic bomb spies."

"He's a shit," Pearson said.

As rarely as this Quaker swore, that was an astonishing observation, despite being rather obvious.

"What," he asked, "are you going to tell McCarthy?"

"Haven't got that far yet," I said. "He thought I was going to sabotage the investigation. I have made a few highly selective reports along the way. This much I know—ol' Tail-Gunner Joe won't love me for finding that missing table."

Pearson finished his Scotch. "Well, do your best to stay on his good side."

"Why?"

His eyebrows rose. "McCarthy is as dangerous as his boy Roy Cohn is ruthless. And they're out there right now making America safe from Communists. That's a category that includes every Democrat in the country except the Southern ones, Nathan. So I'd like you to remain in his good graces. Perhaps he'll hire you on for something else."

I grunted a laugh. "Why would I want to work for that loon again, assuming he even wants me to?"

His light blue eyes bore into me. "You're as close as I have to someone on the inside, Nathan. We need to take this man down."

"Give it time. He'll probably do it himself."

"Well, you might be needed to give him a push. So don't burn the bridge. Get something really damaging on him, and you'll learn that underneath it all, I'm generous at heart."

I managed not to waste any rum on a spit-take. "If you say so, Drew. But in a day or two, I'll be back in Chicago, where the closest thing to political policy is the daily number."

He rewarded that witticism with his ingratiating toothy smile, rose, and shook hands with me across the coffee table. I got him his hat and the London Fog raincoat he'd arrived in and gave them to him at the door.

Halfway out, he said, "I've got a flight to catch or I'd suggest we have supper. Next time. We'll make it the Empire Room."

I'm still waiting.

Since Pearson would break the console table story in his column tomorrow, I needed to talk to McCarthy today. I didn't expect to get right through to him, but I did. Or almost—the first staffer I spoke to on the phone sent me over to Joe's lovely right-hand "man," Jean Kerr.

"Nathan," she said, in a lilting second soprano that seemed suited to both her red hair and Irish heritage, "I can put you through to Joe in just a few minutes. He's in his office visiting with Senator Taft."

This was an example of the mountain going to Mohammed— Robert Taft was the Senate Majority leader and the papers whispered that he was trying to rein McCarthy in.

I said, "I can call back in half an hour, Jean."

"No, it shouldn't be long. Gives me a chance to say how much we appreciate the work you're doing for us."

That implied she knew of my undercover mission for McCarthy on the Hammett committee, which indicated just how trusted this woman was in the inner circle.

"Actually I'm just tying a bow on it," I said. "This will be my final report, unless Joe asks me to come to D.C. for a really detailed briefing."

"If he does," she said, with that mild flirtatiousness that charmed every male with whom she came into contact, "you'll have to go out to dinner with us. You're married, aren't you, Nate?"

"No, that ship sailed. If you have a sister who looks like you, it's a date."

She laughed musically. "Not an available sister at the moment, but a very attractive young staffer who likes older men."

"Ouch."

"Well, she's very young, Nate. I hope that isn't a problem."

"I'll struggle past it."

More musical laughter. "I thought you might. . . . Oh, there goes Senator Taft. Doesn't look terribly happy. I'll put you through."

"Thanks, Jean."

Then McCarthy's voice came roaring on, in hail-fellow-well-met mode. "Nate! Just getting worried about you, boy. What do you have for me?"

"My work for the Hammett committee is over," I said. "I ran through their fee doing mostly a bunch of spinning-my-wheels interviews."

"I have no trouble with you wasting the money of a bunch of goddamn pinkos."

"Didn't think you would. But in the process of that, I did stumble onto a piece of new evidence. The one I warned you about."

I told him about the console table.

I could almost hear his heavy dark eyebrows meet in conference. "You think that'll be enough to get the Rosenbergs a new trial?"

"Maybe. Your boy Cohn and his boss made a big damn deal about that table in the court, including saying that Macy's had no tables like it in the twenty-dollar price range. Claimed you had to give R. H. Macy at least eighty-five bucks for one. Shows possible prosecutorial misrepresentation, or as we say in Chicago, fuckin' lying. Certainly bad faith."

His voice bristled with irritation. "Saypol was damn sloppy. That case was won by *Roy*, not his employer."

"Is Roy with you there right now?"

"No, he's out of the office. Why?"

"Because I know for a fact that he fabricated evidence and suborned perjury. How much of that will make it into an appeal, I can't say. Quite a bit of what I heard came from federal sources talking off-the-record."

"*Traitors.*"

"Or patriots. You say 'tomato,' I say 'tomahto.' Joe, I've walked the ends-justify-the-means line plenty of times. But that Howdy Doody you use for a majority counsel dances all over it. Friendly advice—don't go hitching your wagon to that star, 'cause one of these days it's gonna fall so fast you won't even get a wish."

"He's very smart, Roy, and bold . . . but I do admit impulsive."

I told him about the prick siccing Costello on me.

McCarthy's voice was uncharacteristically hushed. His words came quick: "I knew nothing of that. Hell, that's terrible. I will talk to him. Goddamnit, that's over the edge. I will fucking *talk* to him, Nate."

"I'd rather you fire him. But if you're thinking about slapping his wrists, skip it. I'll get him alone one of these days and knock him on his ass. Then when he gets up, I'll knock him on his ass again, and that may go on for some while."

His voice went weirdly pitiful. "I'm sorry. I really am. I consider you a friend, and that kind of thing just can't be condoned."

"I appreciate that, Joe. I just hope you hear me when I say Cohn is a loose damn cannon. And I apologize to you, for finding that table."

Of course I wasn't sorry about that at all.

Surprisingly, he wasn't upset or even a little concerned. "Oh, that's not gonna go anywhere. That Bloch character will never get an appeal through, no matter what they find or think they have."

"Why?"

A casual confidence oozed from him. "Nate, they have to present their appeal to Judge Kaufman, who despises the Rosenbergs and would send them to the chair a thousand times if he could. Bloch and anyone else who tries won't get anywhere. And if they get to the Supreme Court with it, that'll be a dead end, too. The only court they have any chance with is the court of public opinion, and so far the government's winning that battle, too. A split decision, maybe, but winning it."

"Well, Joe, we'll see if you're right. In the meantime, I'm going back to Chicago. Sorry if I was a disappointment."

"No," he said, "I'm very satisfied with your performance. And I may have something else for you, before too very long."

"Oh?"

That odd, oddly compelling public cadence came into play. "We're gearing up for our *investigation* into the CIA. And we have tons of *documents* reflecting many months of preliminary *inquiry*.

There's indications of KGB *agents* infiltrating that esteemed agency. Did you know that Acheson's son-in-law contributed four hundred *dollars* to the Alger Hiss *Defense* Fund?"

Dean Acheson had been Truman's secretary of state, and had been a foe of Joe's for years—the symbol of the hated State Department.

"No," I said, "I missed that one somehow."

Now a chummy, excited tone replaced the cadence. "Nate, you'll want to be involved in this one. I don't think an investigation has ever interested me more."

I couldn't have been less interested, but I said, "You know where to find me."

Sometimes being a capitalist isn't easy.


McCarthy had been right about Judge Kaufman, and the Supreme Court as well.

Kaufman rejected the console table appeal, saying the table had been a minor part of the prosecution's case, when of course the opposite was true. Over the weeks and finally months, he batted away several more appeals, pushing lawyer Bloch into switching his emphasis onto clemency, chiefly in the hope that President Eisenhower might change his mind and step in.

That didn't happen. What did happen was Ike making disparaging remarks about Ethel, declaring her (on the basis of absolutely nothing) a mastermind spy who had worn the pants in a despicable marriage of spies—an accurate statement, if he meant David and Ruth Greenglass.

Supreme Court justice Harold Burton—who as Cleveland mayor years ago had been my friend Eliot Ness's boss—had been swayed enough to ask for a three-week stay of execution, so that additional arguments might be heard. He was one of four justices who thought that way; five others didn't.

The Rosenbergs were scheduled to die on Friday, June 19, 1953—their wedding anniversary—at 11 p.m. Bloch's last-ditch effort was to try to milk another twenty-four hours out of Judge Kaufman by reminding him that the Rosenbergs were scheduled to die on the Jewish Sabbath.

In what at first seemed a rare act of compassion, Kaufman agreed that this was inappropriate. Hours later came the Jewish jurist's anniversary gift: He was moving the execution *up* to 8 p.m.—before sunset.

Still hoping for Julius to break down and cooperate, the FBI set up a command post at Sing Sing with two direct lines to the FBI's New York office. In the counsel room on the second floor of the death house—where I'd first met with Julius—FBI agents were prepared for an anticipated interrogation of one or both Rosenbergs. The ability to halt the executions at any moment had been painstakingly gone over with the warden—"even after they are strapped into the chair." Maybe Hoover thought Ethel would be sitting on her husband's lap.

Julius Rosenberg had no change of heart. Following standard procedure, the warden signaled guards to fasten the leather helmet over the condemned's face—it was already rough enough on the observers. Why subject them to the nasty sight of death convulsions and ruptured eyes?

Julius went quick.

Ethel didn't.

After the standard three jolts, one short, two long, she was still alive. Two more shocks were required. It took her four minutes and fifty seconds to die.

In Chicago, outside city hall, crowds celebrated, and upraised placards pronounced "DEATH TO THE COMMIE RATS" and other stirring sentiments. According to the papers, similar anti-Rosenberg demonstrators mobbed the sidewalks outside the White House, and in cities and towns coast to coast, including liberal California, where pro-Rosenberg picketers were chased from the streets and beaten.

Like a last-minute confession from Julius or Ethel, a public outcry over the injustice done them just didn't happen. Instead, the court of public opinion handed them another guilty verdict, endorsing a show trial worthy of Old Joe Stalin himself.

# – BOOK TWO –

## DEEP CREEK

# CHAPTER 14

In lacy black two-piece lingerie, the beautiful girl was sprawled on her back on the floor, her long black hair flowing around her chin-tilted head in a terrible blossom, her eyebrows high over slits of terror, a ball gag in her mouth, her shapely black-seamed silk-stockinged legs up in the air, wrists tied behind her upraised thighs keeping the uplifted limbs in place, ankles cinched by rope that angled past impossible high heels to the mercy of an unseen captor.

I flipped to the next 8-by-10.

The same beauty was in the out-of-doors now, tied between two trees, legs spread apart, dressed only in a leopard-skin bikini and thigh-high hose. Here her hair was a perfect shoulder-length pageboy, but her eyes again showed fear approaching tears, the ball gag strapped once more into her mouth.

I flipped to the next photo. An almost attractive blonde in bra, panties, and hose had a paddle raised above the very shapely bottom of our same black-haired beauty, also in bra and panties and hose, tied facedown into a barber's chair with clothesline, glancing back at us in pretty distress. Next: the beauty on her back in black bikini lingerie and stockings and heels with wrists and ankles tied to the legs of an ottoman, mouth wide in a silent scream, eyes wide in horror. Then: leopard bikini, heels, sheer black stockings, wrists and ankles hooked up to a pulley contraption that seemed intent on drawing and quartering the beauty, her eyes showing lots of white in wide-open terror.

"I sense a theme," I said.

I was sitting in my seldom-used, barely furnished office at the A-1 Detective Agency's Manhattan branch on the forty-sixth floor of the Empire State Building. Out the window was a mid-November morning, with a very gray fall out there clawing into winter. This was my first day in the big town for at least a week of interviewing prospective A-1 operatives to fill the desks and the office next door that we'd taken over.

Moon-faced, bow-tied Bob Hasty, sitting across from me in the client's chair, said, "They're called bondage photos."

"I've seen this kind of thing," I said with a shrug. "Not a kink that draws me in, but I know there's an underground market for the stuff."

"Recognize the girl?"

"The doll with the pageboy? Yeah. She's in all the girlie magazines. Bettie Page."

A smile blossomed between pink cheeks. "Ah, so you're a fan."

"No, she's got a pageboy and her name is Page and it kind of sticks."

He pawed the air. "You don't have to make excuses for me, Nate. I know it gets lonely on the road."

I grinned at him. "Fuck you, Bob. What does this have to do with hiring operatives? Not that she wouldn't be ideal for under-cover work."

Too easy, but I said it.

He sat forward and got serious. "She needs help. The government's been on her ass, not that I blame them. But the guy who takes these bondage photos is a client of Mendelson's."

Mendelson of Mendelson, Mendelson, and Mendelson. Remember the old joke? "May I speak to Mendelson?" "Mr. Mendelson has retired." "Then may I speak to Mendelson?" "Mr. Mendelson is in court today." "Then can you put me through to Mendelson?" "Speaking." Anyway, the youngest Mendelson was an attorney here in the building who did criminal defense. The A-1 was handling his investigations.

"Don't tell me," I said. "The government's after Bondage Boy for using the U.S. mails to distribute pornography."

Bob looked hurt. "Nate, this stuff isn't pornographic."

"Of course it isn't, but tell it to the bluenose judge. So—what are we supposed to do for Miss Page?"

"Like I say, we're doing this for Mendelson, who represents the bondage photographer guy, whose name is Irving Klaw."

"Sure it is."

"As far as I know," Bob said, turning up both palms, neither of which was hairy, "that's his real name. Klaw's had a movie-photo and book store for years on Fourteenth Street in the Village. Stumbled onto this bondage racket when his male clients kept buying movie stills that showed actresses tied up. Didn't matter whether they were stars or nobodies, just so they were female and gagged or bound or whatever. So Klaw starts shooting his own photos, some of it made-to-order for his clients. His mail-order business takes off. And, Nate, this stuff with Bettie and the other girls, it really *isn't* pornographic—no nudity, no men in the shots. This is outright harassment."

"Well," I said, "remember—the government has a responsibility to keep its citizens from having any fun. If you haven't been paying attention, Bob, sex these days is strictly for making babies."

He smirked at me. "I'll write that down. Anyway, she'll be here in ten minutes."

"Who will?"

"Bettie Page! I'm going to let her fill you in on the details."

"The details of what? Look, I appreciate you trying to fix me up with pinup girls, Bob, but—"

"Nate, for months you have been more like a monk than the poon hound we all know and love."

I winced. "I can't believe I actually hired a guy to represent my agency in the big city who says 'poon hound.'"

"Do I lie?"

Really, he didn't. Since that business with Natalie Ash, I had been uncharacteristically chaste, doing no chasing, and had been accused by my Chicago partner, Lou Sapperstein, of becoming "dour," which I had to look up.

So I agreed to take the meeting, and when Bettie Page was shown in to my office by a smiling, twinkly-eyed Bob Hasty, I found myself staring, and not at him. Not hardly.

The beauty with the shoulder-brushing black hair in the page-boy cut was both exactly what I expected and not at all. Her face was perfectly framed by black locks, her make-up surprisingly light though the dark red lipstick brought Natalie Ash unsettlingly to mind.

But this was no Bohemian, nor a wicked girl into sadomasochistic fun and games. Her quality was more girl-next-door, if you were that lucky a bastard, with a wholesomeness and a winning personality that leapt at you like a friendly tiger. She wore a pink short-sleeved sweater tight enough that the white bra beneath bled through, with a dark brown leather belt cinching a wasp waist above a tan skirt that hit just under her knees. Her nylons were beige, not dark black, and her high heels were low-slung, not sky-high. Subtracting the heels, I made her as five foot five, and despite a towering personality, she seemed almost petite. The scent of Ivory soap wafted.

I stood behind the desk, while I could still risk it, and offered my hand. "Miss Page. I'm Nathan Heller."

"Oh, Mis-tuh Heller," she said, and smiled like a cheerleader, her Southern accent honeying her sultry second soprano, "ah would know you *anywhere*. Ah've seen you in the magazines."

Wasn't that *my* line?

Bob held her chair for her and she sat and he went out, grinning like a goofus, shutting us in.

"There was that nice spread in *Lawf*," she said, meaning *Life*, moving her head just enough for the black tresses to swing a little, "and so many stories in the detective magazines. Ah've posed for a few covers of those mah-*self*, you know . . . not of any with stories about *you*, but . . ." She noted the photos spread out on my desktop like a bizarre hand of cards. ". . . they like to tie you up for *those* shots, too."

"I'm familiar with your work, Miss Page."

"You're a Chicago boy," she reminded me. "Well, ah've been there and done some sessions. Maybe you saw me in *Modern Man* or *Figure*?"

"I try to support local publishing," I said.

She had a little black purse in her lap, both hands clasping it, like a fig leaf that might slip. "Ah'm a little *embarrassed* comin' to the Private Eye to the Stars with such a piddly little problem."

"Not at all."

"You know," she said, with a raised eyebrow and a confidential air, "ah had a screen test mah-self once. Way back in '44."

I'd figured her for mid-twenties, but studying her, and doing the math, thirty seemed more like it.

"Ah was so *turr*-ible," she said, and shivered. "They did my hair up like Joan Crawford, up off this high forehead of mine? And this Southern accent that ah simply cannot *shake*, no matter how many classes ah take, well . . . it did *not* go over good, and so, here ah am."

"You're a very popular model, Miss Page."

"Yes, of a certain type. You know, when ah first come to town, ah went to Eileen Ford? And she threw me out on mah fanny. Mah hips were too darn big, she said, and ah was *way* too short. But Mr. Klaw, oh a wonderful man, *he's* put me in a movie. Ah just fini-shed shootin' it. *Striporama*—keep an eye out. So maybe ah do have a right to your attention."

Did she always rattle on so? Or did she know how charming she was, and what an effect she might have on a miserable pile of male protoplasm like Nathan Heller?

"You have it, Miss Page," I said. "My attention, I mean. But first, let me guess—Mr. Klaw is in trouble with the United States Postal Service, and because you're his top model . . . Again, I'm guessing, but you are?"

She nodded, still clasping her purse.

"Because you're his top model, you're afraid it might come back on you."

She made a limp-wristed gesture. "Oh, but it already *has,* sugar. . . . Sorry. Mis-tuh Heller. It's just that . . . ah just feel so very . . . *comfortable* with you."

"Call me Nate then."

"Ah will if you'll call me Bettie, or Betts. Some of my friends prefer the latter."

"I'll stick with Bettie. You said it's already come back on you, the photos Mr. Klaw sells?"

She nodded and the bangs bounced. "Two investigators came to see me last week. Knocked right on my apartment door. They had credentials but not any badges. They weren't FBI or Treasury or anything. They had private investigator licenses, though, and they were from Washington, D.C., all right."

I frowned. "Well, sometimes congressional committees use private investigators. I've been hired that way myself. What did they want?"

"They said ah could get a clean bill of health if ah'd just testify against Mr. Klaw. Ah said ah didn't have anything bad to say about Mr. Klaw, and they said, don't worry about that, sweetie—*sweetie,* they call me!—we'll let you *know* what to say."

"Were you told to report anywhere? Here or in D.C.?"

She shook her head, tossing her tresses. "No, *sir.* They just said ah'd be hearin' from 'em, and not to leave the country. Ah've never even *been* out of the country! Well, Mexico. Does that count?"

"Bettie," I said, "what would you like me to do?"

Her red mouth pursed into a kissy smile. Her eyes were a blue I hadn't seen since the ocean in Nassau. "Sugah, ah haven't been just entirely forthcomin'. Ah know that you're an important man and don't take on just any ol' case. Like ah said, ah read about you in *Life* and *True Detective.*"

"Okay," I said.

"Wasn't too long ago, was it, that you did some investigatin' yourself for Senator Kefauver? Right there in Chicago? Helped the man expose some of the mobsters and gangsters and such that are so prevalent in your community?"

Now I followed. This was seduction, and I was the seductee—only not in the fun way I might hope.

I said, "The investigators from Washington who called on you . . . they were working for the Kefauver Committee?"

"Yes, sir, the committee lookin' into juvenile delinquency and comic books and dirty magazines and how the last two are responsible for the first. And isn't that just about the *dumbest* thing you ever heard?"

"Just about," I admitted.

She sat forward; the breasts in that pink sweater came right along with her. She and they stared at me.

"Mr. Heller . . . Nathan . . . sugah . . . ah'm a Tennessee gal myself. Why, when ah go back home, ah'm one of the senator's constituents! Couldn't you go and talk to him a little bit for me? Convince the man to give a hometown girl a pass on this silliness? Ah wouldn't hurt Mr. Klaw for the world."

"I couldn't guarantee anything, Miss Page. Bettie."

"Well, your partner, Mis-tuh Hasty?" she said, reminding me who my partner was, in case her pink sweater had given me amnesia. "When we first talked last week, he happened to mention that you're headin' to Washington later this week, on other business? Couldn't you just work this in for me? Drop in on Senator Kefauver, your old boss man? Maybe he owes you for helpin' him out in Chicago."

"I'll try," I said.

She frowned. She could do that without wrinkling her face. It was the goddamnest thing.

"Nate," she said, "there is one *other* little thing."

"Yes?"

"Ah'm not a rich girl. Ah understand the per-day rate around here is one hundred fifty dollars, but ah'm guessing you as the big chief must get more than the little injuns. Could we work somethin' out?"

There was absolutely no hint of sexual favors in her tone or her expression. I swear to you. No kidding.

But a man can hope.

"Bettie, let's see first if I can accomplish anything for you. Since I *am* heading to D.C. anyway, there's no harm in me trying. Then we'll talk remuneration."

That smile dazzled. "Sounds fair, sugah. But either way, when you get back to town? Ah'd like to take you out to dinner. Mah treat. Some real fun spots down in the Village."

"That's where you live?"

She nodded. "You familiar with that part of town?"

"Somewhat," I said.

After the televised organized crime hearings made its committee chair a household name, Senator Estes Kefauver seemed a shoo-in for the 1952 Democratic presidential nomination. His New Hampshire primary win shoved sitting President Truman out of the race, with the Tennessee lawmaker going on to win all but three primaries. Campaigning in a coonskin hat and oozing folksiness, Kefauver seemed to have the nod in the bag . . . until the smoking-room boys chose Adlai Stevenson instead.

There was always 1956, and toward that end the publicity-seeking senator had gone the committee route again, his target this time not crime but juvenile delinquency, which was caused (or so the specious assumption went) by violent TV and movies, comic books, and pornography.

Kefauver's walls in his inner sanctum at the Senate Office Building were as full of framed celebrity photos, awards, proclamations, magazine covers, and newspaper headlines as Joe McCarthy's were vacant. Like McCarthy, however, the senator sat behind a big standard-issue government desk, which was stacked with papers and file folders. In white shirtsleeves, red suspenders, and red-and-white striped tie, this modern-day Ichabod Crane had sharp eyes that lurked behind round-framed tortoiseshell glasses, his beaky nose giving him a hawklike visage.

The busy man did not rise to his full six four, merely stuck his hand out for me to reach across the desk and shake, which I did. I'd been told the senator would only have a few minutes for me, but that was all I'd need. This would work or it wouldn't.

"Nathan," he said, in an easy, soft-spoken drawl, "it's been some while. I see from the press that your business is flourishing. Coast to coast now. My congratulations. How can I be of help?"

I gave him half a smile with just the right hint of smart-ass in it, and in my tone. "I understand you've moved on from grown-up crime to the juvenile variety."

A hint of irritation tensed the eyes.

"Our research indicates," he said with a hint of archness, "that juvenile offenders often grow up to be full-fledged adult law-breakers."

I put in more than a hint of archness. "So then you're looking into improving the reform school system, to nip this kind of thing in the bud."

He leaned back and chuckled. "I think you know what we're looking into."

I opened my hands, as if showing I had no weapon. "Juvenile delinquency—it's all the rage. But you're going after the root cause—funny books and under-the-counter brown-wrapper smut. And supposedly movies and TV, but Hollywood polices that themselves pretty thoroughly. That's a twin-bed world, and the bullets never make you bleed."

"Nathan—I made time for you today. Don't make me sorry."

I sat forward. "Senator, you don't *really* believe you can prove a cause-and-effect relationship between cheap entertainment and juvenile delinquency."

"It's doubtful," he admitted, "but we'll listen to the testimony and examine the evidence."

"You mean a parade of witnesses will come in, experts with

their b.s. and scared-shitless publishers and creative types. Some defensive, others apologetic, some both. Along the way, you'll showcase all kinds of racy, tasteless exhibits and you'll be all over the TV again. More power to you."

He sighed, tossing his glasses on the desk, rubbing the bridge of his nose. "Nathan, I know you're a cynic, and as worldly as they come. You know damn well, as do I, that my crime committee didn't put any gangsters away. But we lifted the rock and showed America the squirmy things down under there. I hope to do the same thing this time around. Expose this trash so popular with youngsters. Warn parents and educators. Juvenile delinquency is just a symptom of a greater weakness in our land, in our whole moral and social fabric."

"I can wait while you jot that down, Senator. Or is that something you've already committed to memory?"

He might have snarled and thrown me out on my ass; but he knew me too well from when I worked for his crime committee in its Chicago phase.

"What are you here for, Nathan? You want something. Everybody in this town wants something. Like the bartenders say, what's yours?"

I smiled. "First, Senator, I want to remind you that you have made no secret of your distaste and even disgust for Senator McCarthy's tactics. Second, I have a specific request about a constituent of yours on your witness list who you are poised to destroy in the reckless McCarthy manner."

"I'm listening."

I told him how Bettie Page, "a good Tennessee gal who makes her living by showing off the nice figure God gave her," had been hassled by two investigators claiming to represent him. That they had suggested they would help her with her testimony against publisher Irving Klaw in a manner that suggested suborning perjury. Further, that she was a dangerous witness because she had the kind of Southern-fried charm and brains that could backfire on the committee in a public interrogation.

"Remember when Virginia Hill testified? Usually she has the biggest boobs in the room. But going toe-to-toe with you boys, she made bigger boobs out of the lot of you."

He sighed. "You want this woman—Bettie Page—scratched from the prospective witness list."

"Yes. Talk to her as a resource if you have to, but don't put her on display where she'll become some kind of grotesque fallen woman for American housewives to rip apart. Also, this guy Klaw has been good to her and she doesn't want to finger him—not that he's broken any laws."

His eyes and nostrils flared. "You've *seen* the filth he puts out?"

"It's a dumb fantasy where men dominate women and sometimes women dominate men. Whips and ropes and leather union suits and what have you. The national audience for that stuff would fit in this office."

He put his glasses back on. Sighed again, but smaller. "Okay. I'm somewhat in debt to you, so . . . okay. Consider her scratched from this race. Anything else, Nathan?"

I grinned. "No, sir. Not unless you can put the fix in for me with the income tax boys."

He grinned back at me. "Just pay the man, Nathan."

His phone rang, he answered it, and I was gone from his mind before I'd even cleared the chair.

I had another appointment here in the Senate Office Building.

# CHAPTER 15

In one of his standard dark blue ready-made suits with a shades-of-blue striped tie just waiting to be stained, Joe McCarthy was hunkered over his mashed potatoes, green beans, meat loaf, and coffee, with apple pie chaser. I was having the same, substituting iced tea for the drink. We were in the Senate Office Building cafeteria, on the basement level, and at just past noon the place was bustling. Strange knowing that all around me were famous people, while the only faces I recognized besides McCarthy's belonged to Senator Taft (a newsreel and front-page frequenter) and Jack Kennedy, who I'd once gotten out of a marital jam.

The cafeteria, which might have been in a school or hospital with its white walls and colored help, and institutional food quality to match, took up several interconnecting rooms. A few luncheon conference meetings were under way where two or three or four of the square Formica-topped wooden tables were pushed together.

The senator and I were at a single such table in a quiet corner, where my host sat with his back to the wall, like an Old West gunfighter. The corner was quiet in the sense that the clatter of dishes and the Babel-like conversations surrounding provided the same kind of eye-of-the-storm privacy to be had at that other cafeteria, the Waldorf.

We chatted socially through the meal, him asking about how my boy Sam was doing, me congratulating him on his recent marriage to Jean Kerr. All very friendly, even frothy. Whenever one of his colleagues walked by, he would beam them a squinty-eyed smile and, whether friend or foe, address them loudly by name; in either case, their response would be a strained smile and polite nod.

Then halfway through the apple pie, I said, "I'm a little surprised your mascot isn't along."

He knew who I meant.

"I invited Roy," he said, with that familiar tightening of his mouth that was half smile, half grimace, "but he declined, and sends his regrets."

"Declined why?"

"Well, he has a full docket right now. Dave Schine, his right-hand man, just got drafted, and we're trying to make arrangements so we don't lose an, uh, valuable asset."

"Schine—that's the hotel heir? Cohn's book-burning buddy from the European jaunt?"

McCarthy's frown suggested hurt more than displeasure. "That's not fair, Nate." He sighed heavily. "Frankly, Roy's absence at this lunch meeting of ours has more to do with him being . . . *embarrassed* . . . than anything else. And I assure you the boy doesn't embarrass easily. . . . *Bob, hello!* . . . Generally, Roy doesn't seem to care what people think about him. So take it as a compliment."

"Is that right."

The big shoulders shrugged as a bite of pie stalled halfway to home. "He only cares what a person thinks of him if he *respects* that person."

Or needed that person to get ahead.

"Joe, Cohn doesn't like me because he knows I see through him. He's a conniving little shyster."

The overgrown eyebrows grew together in a frown. "That's overly harsh. He's the smartest boy I ever ran across. I told you before, he's a bit on the excitable side, and can be *rash* at times—"

"Like sending Frank Costello's goons to rough me up."

His face reddened under and around the blue shadow of his

most recent shave. "I talked to Roy about that, as promised. Scolded him severely. . . . *Jack, how's tricks? . . .* That's the primary reason he's embarrassed, you ask me. He knows he misjudged you. You came through for us. I could have told him you would."

And I could have told McCarthy that I considered Roy Cohn the murderer of Ethel Rosenberg. Instead I forked another bite of apple pie.

He read my silence as the accusation of his absent lapdog that it was. "This Rosenberg case isn't over yet, Nate. Not by a long damn shot."

"Well, they're both dead. That's pretty over."

He shook his head somberly. "What they set in motion is alive and well. Remember, some months ago, I mentioned an army base in New Jersey we were looking into?"

"Vaguely."

"Base in question is Fort Monmouth, where Julius Rosenberg worked as a civilian for the Signal Corps . . . and set up his wartime spy ring—his fellow Commie Sobell was a part of it. . . . *Bill, how are you doin', pal? . . .* Two scientists from the base, who took some kind of long-distance powder, were key suspects in the ring. And Roy's investigation has already connected *seventeen* current civilian employees at the base to Rosenberg and Sobell."

I had another bite of pie, followed by a sip of iced tea.

He was ranting in full nasal speechifying mode now: "We have in our pocket an East German *defector* who has seen fresh information on guided *missile* systems and radar *networks*. This extremely dangerous espionage rocks the very *foundation* of our defense against atomic attack. . . . *Wayne, sorry I missed that vote! Did fine without me, son! . . .* This house of *spies* is still in operation and allowed to flourish thanks to the Army's benign *neglect* . . . and to subversives within their very ranks."

"So you're taking the Army on, as promised."

The heavy eyebrows rose, the sleepy eyelids forcing themselves wider. "The generals have to take responsibility for their actions, like anybody else. Their *inactions*, too."

"I thought you were gearing up to take on the CIA," I said, just to goad him.

But he shot right back: "As soon as we're finished with the Army, those birds are next. Actually, that investigation is concurrent and ongoing. . . . *Mark, you look well, fella!* . . . If the CIA had done its damn job, this nest of Reds in New Jersey would have been eradicated during the war."

I could just imagine how much the administration and many of his fellow senators might relish Tail-Gunner Joe traipsing through CIA intelligence files and personnel records.

I raised a palm as if being sworn in. "This isn't anything I want to be involved in."

"I'm not asking you to. Not . . . precisely."

"Well, what are you imprecisely asking, Joe?"

He lips peeled back and his eyes narrowed in a particularly ghastly smile. "You may be sitting there thinking I'm naive to have the gall to imagine I can take on the Central Intelligence Agency. Even *Dick Nixon* has discouraged me, and there are few more vociferous foes of the Commie rats than him. But I say that even the *CIA* is not immune to *inquiry.* Should they be allowed to conduct themselves as they please, under a blanket of *secrecy*?"

"That's how spying works."

He shrugged. "Well, I do understand that need . . . and I certainly wouldn't call out any active agent except in executive session, and put their operations or even their lives at risk. But this is *our* country's baby, and *our* dirty diapers, and we have *got* to wash them . . . and I'm in favor of washing them in public as much as possible."

"Dangerous line to walk, Joe."

The nasal public speaking mode was in full sway again: "Nate, the CIA is riddled with *Commies* and security *risks.* Right now we know of a homosexual forced to *resign* from the State Department who is currently a *top-salaried* man with the CIA. We have so many *normal* people, so many competent Americans, must we employ so many . . . *unusual* men . . . in government service?"

I made this as gentle as I could. "Joe . . . meaning no disre-spect . . . but you have been accused of being 'unusual' yourself, and so has Roy Cohn. Not that I give a damn, but I think Cohn is queer as a three-dollar bill. But that's not the reason you'd be wise to get rid of him."

He was shaking his head as if flies were buzzing around it. "Ludicrous. He's all *man*, our Roy. I can't believe you'd make such an unfounded, scurrilous accusation."

Said the king of unfounded, scurrilous accusations.

"But," he said, "that kind of thing does relate to why I asked you to stop by."

I wasn't "stopping by." I had been hired, at double my day rate, to fly at McCarthy's expense to D.C., where I was being put up at the Mayflower.

"Why *did* I stop by?" I asked.

The small mouth sneered. "These CIA spooks are ruthless bas-tards who will stop at nothing. They assemble secret files on people to buy their silence and cooperation. They're a lousy damn pack of blackmailers."

"I hear J. Edgar does the same thing."

"Hoover is not my concern. It's come to me secondhand that the Agency has a file on me, if you can believe that. . . . *Ernie, great to see you!* . . . with information of a, uh, damaging nature. Don't ask me what's in the file, and whether it's true or not—I don't know. Just get your hands on that goddamn file, Nate. I can't go into a full-scale investigation of the CIA without knowing what they . . . what they *think* they have."

"Joe, I don't exactly have a horde of snitches in the Central Intelligence Agency."

I didn't mention that I had a fairly high-up contact in the form of Edward "Shep" Shepherd, since that was none of McCarthy's busi-ness, and anyway, I wouldn't dream of approaching Shepherd about this.

"Nor do we, Nate. They're a closed-ranks bunch. But I have a good solid lead that I'd like you to check out—an unhappy civilian

scientist at an army base, working for the Agency. He's a constituent and a supporter of mine from back home."

"I'm to go to Wisconsin for this?"

"No. He's an hour from here, in Frederick, Maryland. You can
take a train or rent a car. . . . *Lyndon, we need to talk later!* . . . All on
expense account. My office can set up a meeting, probably tonight.
If he's not available this evening, you'll stay over a day or two till
he is. I'll write you out a check upstairs for a thousand-dollar non-
returnable retainer."

"You've talked to this scientist?"

"Twice on the phone. Briefly. He appears to have a lot to report
on the Agency's misbehavior, and you should gather that information, of course. But also pursue him as a source for getting your
hands on that file. I can't go forward in confidence against these
people unless I know where I stand."

"Why me?"

"I'm shorthanded with Schine drafted. Anyway, Nate, I need
someone who's not from D.C. circles to do this thing."

This sounded straightforward enough. Turning the senator
down might make an enemy out of him, particularly considering
how Cohn and I didn't get along. And I preferred McCarthy thinking we were friends.

"All right," I said, getting out my notepad. "What's the scientist's
name?"


Dr. Frank Olson lived in a new-looking ranch-style house on a quiet
wooded lot outside Frederick, Maryland, nestled in the foothills of
the Appalachians, a little over an hour's drive southwest of D.C.
I arrived, as arranged, at around 7 p.m., pulling my rental Ford into
the driveway behind a nonrental Ford, then crossed the lawn to the
front door of a cozy nest worthy of TV's Ozzie and Harriet. I was
met at the door by a tall, slender woman in her late thirties, her
dark hair in a short perm; she bore a strong, pleasant resemblance
to actress Patricia Neal. The smell of a recent meal of liver and

onions combined with the warmth of inside came out on the stoop to greet me.

"Mr. Haller?" she asked, her smile wide, her eyes kind. She wore a navy housedress with white trim.

"It's 'Heller,' ma'am," I said, returning the smile, taking off my hat. I had a Burberry trench coat on over my Botany 500.

She gestured graciously. "Well, please come in. Frank's in the den. I'll get him for you."

I stepped directly into a living room furnished in atomic-age modern, my presence of no interest to three children—a boy nine or ten, a girl eight or so, a boy maybe five—sitting like Indians with their backs to me before a video hearth just to one side of an unlit flagstone fireplace. *Mr. Wizard* was on.

The Olsons seemed to be getting a jump on Christmas—Thanksgiving wasn't here yet, but in front of the picture window, a tree with twinkling lights stood guard over an array of brightly wrapped presents.

"*Mr. Heller!*" a mid-range male voice called. "Frank Olson."

From a hallway came a medium-size suburbanite with a ready smile and an outstretched hand. His dark blond hair was thinning, which conspired with a weak chin to emphasize the elongated-egg shape of his head; but his pale green eyes were sharp in slitted settings, his nose long and somewhat flattened, as if he'd been a boxer in his youth. He was in the off-the-rack brown suit he'd likely worn to work, but the collar was loose, no tie in sight.

We shook hands. I was still just inside the door and Olson's wife came up alongside him and said, "There's coffee in the kitchen," but her husband shook his head, his full-lipped smile fading.

"I think Mr. Heller and I will take a walk, dear," he said.

"Oh. Well, all right." She seemed surprised. I was, too—it was a chilly evening. She beamed at me and said, "Then I'll have coffee for you when you get back. I'm Alice, by the way."

"Alice," I said, shaking the hand she stretched out to me. "And I'm Nate. That coffee will be welcome."

Olson had slipped away to get a topcoat from the front closet.

He stuffed a hat on his head in a half-crushed Jimmy Durante manner and gestured for me to step back out. His smile had returned, though on the porch he whispered, "You never know who's listening, inside."

We didn't walk far, just to a stand of high trees on the lot, the night clear but dark with a slice of moon fingering through mostly bare branches. We stood between cedars and he offered me a cigar from a steel case. I said thank you, no. He lighted up with a match, turning his face orange in the darkness, and puffed till it really got going. The evening was cold enough that you didn't need a cigar to make smoke, though, your breath doing that just fine.

His smile was winning and wide; he looked a little goofy with that jammed-on hat. "I'm really kind of tickled to meet you. When Mrs. McCarthy called and said you'd be coming, that you were representing the senator? Well, I recognized your name right away."

"That's flattering." Not really surprising that McCarthy had used his wife among his office staff to make the call.

He wet his lips. "Saw you in *Life* and a bunch of other places. Which is why I didn't ask to check your ID; I mean, why bother? Brother, have *you* met everybody and his duck. His *Donald* Duck!"

"I suppose I have."

"You know, you might think that scientists are a bunch of stuffed shirts, Nate, but you'd be wrong. Take me—I'm known around the lab for practical jokes. It's okay I call you 'Nate,' right?"

"Right," I said, hoping this wasn't one of his jokes. "And you're Frank."

"I'm Frank. The one and only. Guys I work with at Fort Detrick, they're real cards. Wild men. I always kid 'em, saying, 'You're all just a bunch of thespians!' A 'thespian' is an actor. It's different from 'lesbian.'"

"Sometimes."

He grinned. In the jammed-on hat he might have been a burlesque comic. "That's a good one! It's just kind of funny, you know . . . 'thespian,' 'lesbian.' You grab any laugh you can in my kind of work." His smile became strained. "Because it's not all fun and games, believe me."

His life-of-the-party manner did a poor job of hiding his anxiety.

"I'm going to guess, Frank, that a lot of what you deal with is classified."

"Oh, yeah. A-Number-One classified. Top-secret all the way."

"And yet you got in touch with Senator McCarthy because you've become disturbed by some things you've seen. Is that right? Am I close?"

The smile turned terrible, the eyes squeezed almost tight. He was a clown who gave somebody a hot foot but to his horror burned their toes off.

"Nate," he said, the full wet lips forming a very sickly smile, "you have no idea."

He leaned against the tree behind him. He puffed at the cigar as if it were oxygen he needed. His smile was still there but his eyes were focused down.

The life went out of his voice. "I've had ulcers for years. Sometimes I think the damn things will kill me. I'd like to quit my fucking job, become a dentist or something, but . . ."

"They won't let you?"

"They *say* they will. They say they will." His eyes found mine and were haunted. "But do you know what we've been looking at lately, over at the lab?"

"No."

"Ways to alter the memory of personnel who know too much. With drugs, hypnosis, electroshock, brainwashing. And if none of that works?" He swallowed, shivered. "Nate, I'm a biochemist and I know my stuff."

"I'm sure you do."

"Well, I'm here to tell you the CIA has more varieties of toxins to kill you untraceably dead than Heinz has soups or Carter has pills."

The cigar had gone out and he set another lighted match to the tip, puffing it back to life.

"Listen, I hate the Commie bastards as much as the next guy," he said, eyes glistening, voice strong again. "That's why I turned to Senator McCarthy. But I like to think my efforts for America are *defensive*—the Japs had a biological warfare program, so we needed one, too, right? For a long time I concentrated on counterbiological warfare—vaccines and specially treated apparel, to protect against attack."

"So you were already at this during the war." My hands were in my Burberry pockets.

He nodded. "Oh, yes. I've been with the SOD—the Special Operations Division—from the very beginning, back in '43 when Defense Secretary Forrestal started it."

Something cold went up my spine, and it wasn't the night air. "Forrestal?"

"Yes, and frankly I've always wondered if that jump he took from a high window at the nuthouse wasn't a put-up job. Just another way to get rid of somebody who *really* knew too much."

*Olson didn't know how right he was. Jim Forrestal had been a client and a friend, and I was one of the handful alive who knew he'd been murdered.*

"But more and more," Olson said, "we've been developing poisons and germ strains." He grabbed his belly, as if struck by a sudden cramp.

"You okay, Frank?"

He nodded several times, still clutching his midsection. "I started really getting twisted up inside over all this about . . . three years ago, I guess it was. A strain of live bacteria I helped develop was released from planes above San Francisco. The hospitals there got rushed with 'flu' patients, and a number died. Died! More and more it's become standard operating procedure to perform experiments on people without their consent or even knowledge."

I frowned skeptically. "A biological warfare experiment, carried out right here in the good ol' US of A?"

He nodded, puffing nervously on the cigar. *Say the secret word and you'll win a prize.* "For a certain type of militaristic mind, Nate, biological warfare is the best thing to come along since sliced bread. With atomic warfare, there's complete destruction of private property. But with bacteriological weapons? Only *people* get destroyed."

"Which is a plus."

"Some see it that way, yes. And anyway, it's incredibly cheap, bacteriological attack—the poor man's atomic bomb. With the right virus, you can kill every living human being over a one-square-mile area for about fifty bucks."

I frowned. "Frank, if the Soviets have biological warfare programs . . ."

"Oh, they do!"

". . . we probably need them, too. Right?"

He held up a hand and waved it, like a kid in the back of class trying to get recognized. "I'd be the last guy to object to research, Nate, although targeting unwitting human guinea pigs goes over the line. Sometimes . . . sometimes . . ." He leaned against the tree again. ". . . *way* over."

Then he threw up.

I let him finish, took him gently by the arm, and said, "Frank, are you okay?"

"Don't tell Alice. The liver and onions were my idea."

"Mum's the word. Let's, uh . . . move upwind."

We did, finding a fresh pair of cedars to stand between.

"Why don't you tell me," I said, "just how far over the line they've gone."

He nodded. He'd lost his cigar in the vomiting episode and got another out and started it up. I let him puff a while.

Finally he said, "They have me developing delivery systems for biological agents like anthrax and botulism."

"By 'delivery systems,' you mean . . . ?"

"Assassination devices. Terrible. Then . . . then I got pulled in on a program dealing with . . . advanced interrogation techniques."

"Torture."

He nodded again. Puffed some more. "We're talking mind

control—hypnosis, electroshock, drugs, the usual suspects . . . but also marijuana, morphine, Benzedrine, lysergic acid diethylamide. You might not have heard of that one—it's a hallucinogenic. Sensory depravation, brainwashing, lobotomies . . . everything was on the menu. Test subjects were 'volunteered' who couldn't object—prisoners, mental patients, coloreds."

"This happened *here*?"

"Well, no. Most of it was conducted overseas. If you saw my passport, you'd think I've been having a whirlwind world tour—England, France, Scandinavia, Germany. Nate, I've . . . I'm a *scientist*, I'm used to seeing lethal experiments done on animals. It's sad but necessary. But on *human* guinea pigs? And crap like what they did in San Francisco? That has to stop. These people I've worked for, they have to be *stopped*."

"Who exactly were these human guinea pigs?"

He shrugged. "German SS prisoners, Norwegian collaborators, all sorts of forgotten souls from jails and detention centers."

His cigar had gone out again but he kept puffing.

I asked, "Are you willing to come forward, Frank?"

"Nate, that's just it. I don't think I can. Not unless the senator can get me a presidential pardon for breaching security. But I *could* be a source. I can point McCarthy in the right direction. Or, if once I go public, maybe that would mean I'd be safe—a hero, and maybe nobody would dare touch me . . . ?"

I couldn't lie to him. "How many toxins was it you said the CIA had on hand?"

He closed his eyes. Opened them. "Right. Right. Accidents can happen."

I put a hand on his shoulder. "But if McCarthy puts the top CIA brass in the hot seat at one of his hearings, he can ask all sorts of embarrassing questions that could put an end to this kind of medieval bullshit forever."

"That's my hope," he admitted. "That really is my hope. I mean, are we America or the Spanish fucking Inquisition?"

I would have to get back to him on that.

"Listen, Frank, there's one potential problem—the CIA's rumored to have a file on McCarthy. I don't know what's in it. . . . I'm not even sure it exists. But if it does, it's certain to be embarrassing. Do you have any friends in the Agency who might be able to leak it to you?"

His eyebrows rose almost to the pulled-down hat. "Oh, Nate . . . I don't know. That's a tough one. That's dangerous."

"More dangerous than filling a stranger like me in on all these juicy CIA horrors?"

He smiled and grunted a laugh. "Not really. I'll do some careful poking."

"Don't get yourself in a jam over it. Find some innocent way to get a look. Maybe you can tell some spook buddy of yours that you can't stand McCarthy and you're just sure as hell that he's a hypocrite. What does the file say, anyway? Something like that."

"Might work." He was nodding. Puffing, at the cigar. "Might."

"Good. I'll fill the senator in. When can we talk next?"

He mulled it momentarily. "I start a work retreat tomorrow. Goes through the weekend. Might be able to put some feelers out for that file then. How about I call you when I get back?"

"Perfect." I gave him one of my cards with the New York office info on it.

Then we came in from the cold and had coffee in the Olson family's bright shiny new kitchen.

The three kids were watching *Beat the Clock*.

# CHAPTER 16

El Chico in the Village was in a triangular cellar at 80 Grove Street where Sheridan Square and Seventh Avenue met. The restaurant served up food and music right out of Spain, Cuba, and Mexico, in a Moorish setting replete with stucco walls, Spanish artwork, hand-wrought grillwork, heavy dark carved furniture, ornate carriage lamps, and an occasional wall-displayed bullfighter's cape, all overseen by a mounted bull's head and an aging parrot named Señor.

Bettie Page had insisted on paying my $150 fee for handling the Kefauver matter, and I had insisted on reciprocating by taking her out for dinner.

As we studied our menus, she said, "Ah so *appreciate* what you did for me, Nate. Havin' a congressional committee goin' after me—thought by itself scares me silly. He's a *horrible* man, that Kefauver."

I shrugged. "He's just another politician."

"Ol' Estes wants to be president so bad he can taste it. He doesn't care if it takes tramplin' over innocent folks. Like a sweet man like Irving Klaw."

"Or a sweet girl like Bettie Page."

She shuddered behind the menu. "Ah wouldn't cotton to havin' my face and however else much of me the newspapers might see fit to print splashed around the country where my mama and sisters and brother and everybody ah was raised near could think the worst of me. Ah *owe* you, Nate."

The azure eyes peered at me seriously over the top edge of the menu.

I said, "I'm not looking for any kind of payoff except your company this evening," wanting to get her in bed as bad as Kefauver wanted to be president.

"Well, that's good, because when ah say ah 'owe' you, ah don't mean a tit-for-tat kind of thing—"

"I know you don't." When she said "tit," something twitched in my trousers. "But you're kind of famous, and I'm kind of famous, and kind-of-famous people ought to stick together."

She lowered the menu and gave me that wide, naughty-girl grin. "Because they have so much in *common*, you mean?"

"Something like that. We understand that people are always after something from us, and all we're after is a little pleasant company."

"Gracious yes."

"Unless you wanted to get next to me for my Hollywood connections," I teased. "Another screen test maybe?"

"Heavens no!" She cocked her head, narrowed her eyes. She whispered, the flicker of our table candle's flame licking her pretty face, "Or did you do me a favor, Nate Hellah, just to try 'n' get into my lacy little panties?"

"Naw, they'd just rip at the seams."

That made her laugh. It was a nice, rolling, musical laugh.

Scant conversation followed, just a lot of exchanged smiles and eye contact as we ate dinner (arroz con pollo for her, paella Valenciana for me). The lack of talk wasn't due to running out of things to say, rather the noise level of flamenco foot stomping and guitar strumming.

With her well-brushed black hair bouncing on her shoulders, Bettie would have made a pretty gypsy herself, although her blue eyes and creamy complexion gave her away as an all-American girl. Her dress was the color of her eyes with a wide black patent-leather belt that hugged her tiny waist and a blue-and-yellow scarf knotted at her neck.

By the time we were having flan and espresso, the entertainers were on a break.

"You know we're barely putting a dent in that hundred-and-fifty," I said.

"Afraid ah'm a pretty cheap date, sugah," she said almost apologetically. "Ah'm not a drinkin' gal, so that keeps the tab way down."

"So then we'll just have to do this again. Maybe tomorrow night."

A half smile dimpled a cheek. "You don't waste any time, do you, Nathan Hellah?"

"Well, I'll only be in the city into mid-next-week. We should have all our hiring done by then. Of course, we still haven't found a secretary."

She shrugged. "Ah have excellent secretarial skills myself, Nate. But ah don't suppose you and Mistuh Hasty could afford me."

"Oh?"

She nodded, spooning some flan between red lips. She tasted, swallowed, said, "Ah was a secretary for a real-estate man and then a lawyer when ah first came to town. But now ah get more for one modelin' session than ah did for a week of secretarial work."

I sipped espresso. "How'd you get started modeling? Of course, I imagine many a man over the years has told you you'd make a good model. . . ."

"Oh, yes, that ol' wheeze of a come-on . . . but ah used to take these long walks, when ah first came to town. Sort of in a reflective mood. About this time of year, three years ago, ah'm strollin' down the beach at Coney Island and it's all deserted, but ah see this beautiful colored man stripped down to his trunks and doin' exercises. Body right outa Michelangelo. Ah just watched for, oh, maybe half an hour. Then he comes up to me and says, 'You know you'd make a good pinup model.' And before you know it, ah'm up at his studio makin' my first portfolio."

"Why did you trust him over anybody else?"

"Oh, ah forgot to mention. He was a policeman. A Brooklyn cop. Showed me his badge and everything. He was the one who advised me to cut my hair in bangs, you know, and that's mah trademark now. My first pics were published in Harlem magazines. Then the phone just started to ring."

She was a chatterbox, but with the words flowing out in such a musical way, honeyed by that Southern-belle drawl of hers, the result was pure charm. Didn't hurt that she radiated beauty like the steam off our espresso.

We went to the Village Vanguard next, where we caught Professor Irwin Corey, that wild-haired zany expert on everything ("Wherever you go, there you are!"), but Bettie didn't care for the cloud of cigarette smoke, so when the shabby-tux-wearing madman finished his set, we departed.

It was going on eleven as, we walked arm-in-arm toward her apartment. The Village is about as blasé a place as I've ever been, but still she turned heads. Whether they recognized her (and in this part of the city they might) or were simply stunned by her natural beauty, I couldn't say; but short-haired females and long-haired males alike took a gawking gander.

"Sorry to be a party pooper," she said. "Ah just can't abide cigarette smoke. And almost everywhere you go in this town, to have a little fun? There's just a *fog* of the nasty stuff! . . . You don't smoke, do you, Nate?"

"I did in the service," I said. "They kind of pushed it on you— free packs handed out on bases and at USOs. Stateside, I seldom have the urge."

"Sometimes you still do, though?"

I nodded. "If things get tense. Something that feels like combat."

"What feels like combat in civilian life?"

*People shooting at you.*

"Oh, various things," I said. "So what do you like to do for fun, Bettie? Where can you go in Manhattan for a good time that's not a smoke-filled room?"

A big smile blossomed. "Oh, ah *love* to dance. Ah just love it to death, and a nice big ballroom, so open and airy and well ventilated . . . that's mah idea of a good time in the big city. . . . Here we are. This is my brownstone."

We stopped at the steps. "Well," I said, "how about dancing with me tomorrow night? At the Starlight Roof?"

"The Waldorf! Oh, that would be wonderful! But that's so *expensive*."

"I'm determined to give you that hundred-and-fifty back, and we're barely started."

"You are a doll, Nathan Heller." She got on tiptoes—low heels again—and gave me a kiss on the mouth. A brief one, but nice, and kind of lipstick-sticky, somewhere between a peck and the real thing.

"I'll send a cab," I said. "Around seven."

She nodded, touched my cheek, kissed the air, then went quickly up the stairs, her bottom working under the blue dress as if powered by pistons.

I was staying at the Waldorf again, in a regular room this time, not a suite (my own dime not Pearson's). I was in my underwear and socks on the bed, pillows propped up behind me, reading *The Caine Mutiny* in paperback. Good as that story was, my mind kept wandering.

Initially it was the lovely girl I'd spent the evening with. Somehow it was a shock that the queen of the bondage photos was such a sweet, smart kid—no drinking, no smoking, just dancing.

There were other thoughts cutting into the Herman Wouk novel, interrupting even my rhapsodizing about Miss Page. The nightmare stuff that Frank Olson had shared with me Tuesday evening lingered like a foul taste. Olson seemed like a good guy, like all of us who'd gone to war, figuring we were fighting a battle that needed fighting. That deserved to be fought. That required winning. Now, in peacetime, the idealistic roots of it were rotting and twisting into something grotesque.

I hadn't shared any of Olson's revelations with McCarthy. All I'd done, before flying back to Manhattan on Wednesday morning, was call him at his Senate office and tell him that I'd spoken to "the individual in question," that the scientist indeed seemed to have dirt, and that he was willing to try to get access to "that certain file." On an unsecured phone line, vagueness was the better part of valor.

"He's going off on some kind of work retreat," I'd told McCarthy. "He'll be back in touch with me when he gets home."

Paperback folded open on the nightstand, bedside lamp switched off, I climbed under the cool covers and closed my eyes, hoping these tumbling thoughts wouldn't keep sleep from coming. It came, and then the phone rang.

The shrillness made me sit bolt upright as if from a bad dream. Phone calls after midnight are never good news. And few people knew I could be reached here, so it must be serious.

"Hello?" I said. Yes, it was a question.

"Mr. Heller," a quavering mid-range male voice said. I didn't recognize it. "Nate? It's Frank."

*Frank the fuck who?* I thought, sleep-bleary.

"Yes, Frank," I said, playing along.

"I just got home from the retreat. Sorry to call so late. I felt I had to. Needed to."

*Frank Olson.*

I reached over and clicked the lamp back on. "No, that's okay, Frank. What's up? Is everything all right?"

"No, I . . . I'm sorry, I shouldn't have called. Should have waited."

He sounded bad—flustered, upset, though not drunk or anything.

"Frank? You still there?"

"Yes. Nate. Mr. Heller. I'm so sorry, but I . . . I made a terrible mistake."

"Mistake? What kind of mistake?"

"Really shouldn't have talked to you. Really shouldn't have got you involved. Can you just forget it?"

"Forget it?"
"Everything we talked about? Thanks."
And he hung up.


The Starlight Roof, accessed by special elevators, perched on the top floor of the Waldorf, overlooking Park Avenue. Under a grill-like ceiling blinking with electric stars, the immense supper club had welcomed princes and presidents, sheiks and movie stars, high society and low celebrities. The bandstand had seen the likes of Glenn Miller, Eddie Duchin, Count Basie, and Duke Ellington, but most often (like tonight) Xavier Cugat, whose Latin-themed orchestra was striking in royal-blue jackets, Cugat himself in a white dinner jacket. This was a world of Grecian columns and pilasters, stair railings with flower boxes, antique gold mirrors, and an ocean of a dance floor where couples in evening dress were doing the rhumba, a dance first introduced in Manhattan at El Chico, though no parrot or mounted bull's head was in sight.

I was in a black sharkskin suit and Bettie wore a simple elegant-looking white dress with one shoulder bare. Her heels were white and so was her purse, a virginal look undercut by her curves and the shocking black of her shoulder-brushing hair.

We sat up a level from the dance floor and we talked over Chateaubriand and Cabernet Sauvignon (wine she was not averse to). She learned of my failed marriage and my son Sam, who would be spending his Christmas break with me in Chicago. I learned of her rough upbringing in a broken home where poverty led to a two-year "sentence" at an orphanage with her sister.

"My daddy was a sex maniac," she said casually, sipping wine. "He was screwin' my sister all along, and he messed with me but ah never let him inside of me."

I managed not to choke on the wine. "That's awful. Bettie, I'm so sorry."

"You didn't have anything to do with it, sugah. Look, ah know some gals get messed up, when they get taken advantage of. Ah got lured into a car and gang-banged when ah first came to the city. Well, not exactly gang-banged—ah told 'em ah was in my period and those dirty bastards forced me to blow 'em, each and every one."

We were secluded between pillars so I assume no one else heard this frank talk.

"Ah had a husband once, who tried to rape and kill me, not necessarily in that order. So if anybody has a right to be loco in the *cabeza* over sex, honey, it's me. But you know what? None of that's sex. And it sure isn't love. It's sick, sick, sick, and ah don't let a few bumps in the road ruin the rest of the ride."

"That's a remarkable attitude you got there, Bettie."

"Enough talk. Let's dance."

We did the rhumba and she was nicely fluid at it, and a lot of wide eyes and smiling faces took her in. She wasn't exactly graceful, but she so enjoyed herself, that lovely face bursting with joy, that you couldn't help but watch her with almost as much pleasure as she was giving herself. On the slow numbers, she molded herself to me in a dreamy, cuddly way that Kefauver would no doubt have found obscene. Of course, Estes was a serial adulterer, so who was he to talk? I didn't recognize her perfume and asked her what it was. She said Max Factor's Hypnotique and I felt hypnotized all right.

She did the rhumba for me in my room, too, pulling the white dress off as I sat watching on the foot of the bed with just my suit coat and tie off. Underneath there was no fancy lingerie out of Frederick's of Hollywood—just a white bra and white panties and pale thigh-high nylons that needed no garter belt. But for her white heels and the sheer stockings, she took everything off, doing the rhumba all the while to the memory of Cugat. She kicked off the heels, glancing girlishly over a shoulder at me, and then tugged down the panties. Her bottom was full and round and dimpled, the effect magnified by the startlingly narrow waist, the globes rising and falling individually with the rhumba rhythm. She caught the panties with a toe, then flicked them away, and swung dramatically toward me. Her muff was as black as spilled ink, full, luxuriant, her breasts neither large nor small but beautifully shaped and given perfect display by her prominent rib cage. I must have been gaping like a fool, taking this all in, because she was grinning, eyes flashing, giggling a little.

She danced some more, and then knelt before me.

"See, honey?" she said. "No sick bastard can ruin this for me. Ah *like* sex."

Then she unzipped me, unleashed me, and began to suck and suckle the hardness she'd made. Time suspended as the sweet warmth of her mouth went up and down and now and then stopped to suck, for minutes or forever, and she sensed I was close, so close, and drew away with a naughty smile to shake a no-no-no finger at me.

"You don't get off that easy, sugah," she said. "Undress. Right now."

For an eyeblink the naked woman was the dominatrix in leather with whip in hand.

I undressed.

Right now.

My clothes were scattered like shipwreck wardrobe washed on shore. Now she sat on the foot of the bed, watching me. Her eyebrows lifted as I stepped out of my boxers and she smiled wickedly, then slid to the floor and turned her back to me again, kneeling over and leaning against the bed, presenting her dimpled bottom like a gift.

I knelt behind her and bounced again and again against the fullness of that magnificent rump, producing moans of pleasure from us both. Then we moved hand in hand to the bed for some man-on-top action, her head back, the lovely face swimming in a sea of black tresses, eyes rolling back. But once again, right before I came, she squirmed giggling out from under, and turned me onto my back and took over, riding me, riding me, riding me, as if she had a crop in hand, those breasts bobbling in my face and her lush grinding bottom filling my hands, as I plunged again and again into the tight heavenly warmth and wetness of a real woman, not a pinup at all.

. . .

Over the next several days, I wondered if I had botched it with
Dr. Frank Olson. Had I pressed too hard for information in the first
interview? Had asking for his help getting the file on McCarthy been
too soon, or too much? Had I gotten him in a jam because of it? I
didn't call McCarthy's office to inform him that Olson had bailed
out on us, because I feared I'd screwed the thing up, and hoped to
remedy the situation.

Toward that end, I tried to call Olson, but that was limited to the
evening, since I didn't know how to reach him at work and wouldn't
have tried him there in any case. Those evening calls I got his wife,
Alice, who said Frank couldn't come to the phone; I kept leaving my
number and she kept taking it, but nothing. I read a strain in her
voice and wondered if her husband was in a fix because of me.

Shit.

In the meantime, Bob Hasty and I were close to assembling a
staff for the A-1 Manhattan branch, including a secretary/reception-
ist. My work here would soon be done, Chicago beckoning.

I took Bettie out several more times, most memorably to the
Stork Club, a place she'd never been, and frankly she was disappointed: "Kind of like sex for the first go, sugah—not quite as advertised, but maybe next time."

The nightspot, on Fifty-third Street in spitting distance of Fifth
Avenue, had never been a favorite of mine, its reputation built as it
was on its famous clientele. I was in my sharkskin suit again, Bettie
in a baby-blue satin dress that draped her like lucky liquid, as we
were allowed past the gold-chain version of a velvet rope and into
the small lobby with checkroom and telephone booths, to move by
seventy feet of mirrored barroom into the care of a maître d', who
showed us into the main room with its softly flattering lights and
mirrored walls.

Despite the good-looking younger upper-class types, the obviously wealthy couples with their jewels and Rolexes, and assorted
out-of-towners trying to act like they fit, famous faces belonging

to movie stars and Broadway names—the key elements—were conspicuous in their absence.

The only face that was anything approaching famous—other than our own nearly famous ones—belonged to a hooded-eyed, narrow-faced, deeply tanned weasel in a dark suit.

Roy Cohn and a big blonde in a bare-shouldered gown, most likely an upper-tier call girl, sat in a banquette for four. She looked more like his stepmother than a date, as if daddy had gone off to the john and left sonny boy with his new showgirl mommy. A more famous face, Walter Winchell, who was working the room, leaned in and talked chummily with Cohn. I had met Winchell several times but always had to reintroduce myself; Chicago celebrities just didn't count.

The orchestra was a glorified combo and only passable, but we enjoyed ourselves on the postage-stamp dance floor, or anyway Bettie did. The food, at least, lived up to its rep—filet of sole Almondine for her, shad roe with bacon for me, followed by Baked Alaska.

I had just finished my portion of the dessert when I noticed, across the way, Roy Cohn sliding out of his booth, the bosomy blonde barely noticing. I watched him head out.

"Excuse me," I said, rising at our small table.

"Take your time, sugah," Bettie said, still working on her Baked Alaska.

The famous owner of the Stork, Sherman Billingsley, had relegated the men's room to the third floor, with only a small restroom with a handful of urinals and zero stalls off the main-floor bar. Billingsley, in pursuit of elegance, didn't want customers stinking up the joint.

Roy had the sparkling white-and-black room to himself. No attendant was present in the relatively small space. I waited till Cohn finished, and he was still zipping up when he turned to me. His eyes flared momentarily.

"This isn't my office, Heller," he said, with sleepy contempt. He moved to the sinks and washed his hands.

"I heard different."

"Did you."

"The blonde's a little obvious, Roy. You're trying too hard."

He dried himself with a paper towel, tossed it in the trash, then bared his teeth in an ugly smile. "Go fuck yourself."

I slapped him.

The eyes opened wide and a hand flew to his face, but didn't land, fluttering like a butterfly over where I'd smacked him.

"I suppose," he said, softly, "I had that coming."

"For siccing Costello's boys on me."

He nodded.

I sucker-punched him and he went down like a matchstick castle.

"That's just a *taste* of what you have coming, Roy. And we haven't even gotten to the Jewish housewife you framed into the chair."

"You're fucking nuts," he said, mouth and jaw trembling. He hadn't gotten up. His expression looking up at me was that of a whipped dog trying to summon the courage to bite back.

I kicked him in the stomach and he puked his Cornish hen a la Winchell. Then he was just a contorted, crying fetus in a tailored suit.

I counted on my fingers. "I've slapped you. Slugged you. Kicked you. What do you suppose will come next? Stay away from me, Roy. Stay out of my life, and maybe this won't end with me killing your ass."

He nodded a bunch of times, still down there. I straightened my tie in the mirror and went out.

Time to head back to Chicago.

Bettie stayed over at the Waldorf. Before we'd gone out, she'd dropped off an overnight bag at my room, because tomorrow was Thanksgiving, and we'd made plans for what the weatherman claimed would be a crisp fall day, no snow or outright cold. On the docket was making it over to Macy's to watch the parade wind up, then taking in *Kiss Me, Kate* at Radio City Music Hall, where the live Christmas show had just debuted. The Empire Room would be open in the evening, to accommodate hotel guests, serving up a turkey dinner with all the trimmings, including postdessert dancing to the Mischa Borr Orchestra, a Waldorf mainstay.

The day began, however, with spontaneous half-awake cuddling that quickly got serious, starting with me in charge till suddenly Bettie was riding me again—in a slow, grinding, romantic fashion that would be the only thing about Manhattan I would really miss— and then the phone rang. Make that the goddamn phone. Still mounted, she paused like a rider taking a moment to take in a western vista while I reached for the nightstand and answered the thing.

"Hello?" I said. Again, a question.

"Mr. Heller?" a female voice said. Vaguely familiar. "I think Frank's in trouble."

Alice Olson.

"They took him Monday and he was supposed to be home yesterday, and now it's Thanksgiving and no word, no sign."

"Maybe I can help," I said.

# 17

CHAPTER

I sat at a small round Formica-topped table in the modest modern kitchen of the Olsons' ranch-style home, with Alice Olson across from me, the aromas of a Thanksgiving dinner hanging pleasantly in the air. On the kitchen counter were two pies—pumpkin and (her husband's favorite, she told me) apple, each with a few pieces missing. Dishes were piled in the sink, the carcass of a turkey on its tray. Sounds of television and children's laughter came from the living room, where Bettie was keeping the kids company. The Olson kids loved her; she was good with them, a smiling angelic vision in a pink sweater, interested in anything they had to say; for once, she was up against somebody as chatty as she was. Three such somebodies.

I'd seen no harm and some possible benefit in bringing Bettie along. I'd promised to spend Thanksgiving with her and she was game for an adventure. At Penn Station, we'd taken an 11 a.m. to Washington, D.C.—tickets were no problem, travel on the holiday itself running light—arriving around four, and renting a car for the less-than-an-hour ride to Frederick, Maryland.

We got there just before five. Alice met us at the door in a cream-color apron and brown-and-gold leaf-patterned-print housedress, saying we were just in time, and we sat down in their little dining room for a Thanksgiving meal where I was the only man at the table, not counting nine-year-old Eric and five-year-old Nils.

Alice told us she hadn't heard from her husband yet today and had waited the meal as long as she could. That was all she said about it in front of the children, the conversation at the table taken up mostly by questions (and answers) about Bettie and me and our respective families. Bettie spoke fondly of her siblings and her mother (her abusive father notably absent), and I played proud papa relating the extraordinary accomplishments of my five year-old son, who I'd talked to earlier today, long-distance.

The food was typically hearty holiday fare and just fine, the stuffing particularly, but Alice had said, "I'm afraid I can't offer you second helpings. Have to save some for Frank. He might show up any moment, you know."

The undercurrent of strain was almost imperceptible, but it was there all right, and now that Alice and I were alone at the little table, under a single hanging lamp, dusk darkening to night out the windows over the sink, the haggardness and worry were all too clear in the long, attractive face.

"You're very kind to come all this way," she said, after pouring cups of coffee for us, "and spoil what must have been a lovely day you two had planned."

"Happy to help," I said. "To *try* to, anyway."

"The business card I found that you gave Frank—do you mind my asking? You're not a part of his work, are you? Not someone attached to that in any way?"

"That's right, I'm not."

"You're a private investigator."

"I am. From Chicago, with a Manhattan branch."

She was sizing me up and I didn't blame her. "The other night . . . did Frank hire you to do something for him? To look into something? I'm just wondering if it has anything to do with . . . with the *strangeness* of these past few days."

"Alice . . . if may?"

"Certainly."

"And make it 'Nate' or 'Nathan.' What Frank approached me about must stay confidential, at least for now. But if there is a connection between the 'strangeness' you've experienced, and what he and I discussed, know that any efforts I make will be in his . . . and your . . . best interests."

Her smile was thin but better than a frown. "I guess I'll just have to take you at your word, then. It does seem as though an investigator is exactly what I need right now."

I sipped the coffee. Out in the other room Bettie and the kids were laughing.

"Tell me about this 'strangeness,' Alice. When did it start?"

She nodded, sipped, gathered her thoughts.

"Frank got back from the retreat in time for dinner, Friday evening," she said, glancing at me occasionally, but mostly staring into her recollection. "I knew something was wrong, right away. He seemed stiff, withdrawn . . . and he's usually so outgoing."

"Where was this retreat?"

"A lodge with some cabins at Deep Creek Lake. Just sixty miles or so from here. It's not unusual for Frank to go out of town for a meeting, anywhere around the country in fact, even overseas. But this time it was close to home."

"Is this lodge a place you're familiar with, Alice?"

She shook her head. "No. I just happened to see the directions he'd been given . . . for the 'Deep Creek Rendezvous.' The slip of paper was right here on the kitchen table." She pointed between us.

"Any sign that this meeting, this retreat, was in any way out of the ordinary?"

"Nothing at all. Vin Ruwet, Frank's division chief, swung by for him Wednesday morning, honked his horn. Frank gave me a nice big kiss and said he'd see me in a couple of days. I helped him on with his coat and he said, 'Tell the kids be good and I love them.' "

"You didn't hear from Frank while he was gone?"

She shook her head. "No. But that's not unusual. Things didn't get unusual until we were having dinner the night he got back. He seemed so . . . mechanical, so cold. He hardly ate a thing, hardly said a word. The kids were all over him with questions and news about school but he'd just give a faint smile and nod, and finally they stopped trying, just talked among themselves. After they ran off chattering to watch TV, I said to Frank, 'Well, at least the children in this family can still communicate.' Then he looked up at me and smiled. . . ." She swallowed, and her eyes were moist. ". . . Just his normal self, you know? And he said, 'We'll talk later, after they go to bed.'"

"*Did* you talk?"

She sighed. "Not really. When I'd tucked all the kids in, and the house was quiet, I came in the living room and he'd turned the TV off, and was just sitting on the couch, staring out the window. At nothing. I asked him what was wrong and he said, 'You don't need to know.' Not nasty or anything. Just . . . I didn't need to know. This was *his* problem. But I knew it was our problem, and I pressed."

"Were you able to get anything out of him?"

"Just one thing. He said, 'I've made a terrible mistake.'"

*Was I the mistake he'd made? Breaching security by talking to Mc-Carthy's man? Had someone discovered that?*

She said, "I asked him, 'What could possibly be that terrible? You're here with us, you're fine, what *is* it?' But all he would say, and he said it several times, was, 'I've made an awful mistake.'"

"What was his manner?"

"Withdrawn. But not so cold now. Not cold at all. I made a fire in the fireplace and sat next to him and . . . and he reached his hand out for mine, held it tight. We just sat there holding hands and not saying a word for what had to be an hour, and then, suddenly, he said, 'I have to resign Monday morning.'"

I shifted in the kitchen chair. "Did he say why?"

She shook her head. "No, and I asked him several times, begged him to tell me, but he just wouldn't say. Sunday he moped around, not mean or angry . . . sort of sullen. Finally I figured I just needed to get him out of here, so I said, 'Let's go to the movies.' He didn't object. So I piled the kids into the car and we all went downtown to the theater. But I think that was a bad idea."

"Why?"

"Well, the movie playing was really gloomy and downbeat—*Martin Luther.*"

Not exactly *Kiss Me, Kate.*

"The kids fidgeted and misbehaved," she said, "and Frank just ignored it. After it was over, Frank didn't say a word. And when Monday morning came, he said again he was going to resign and I said he should do whatever he thought was right."

"*Did* Frank resign, Alice?"

"Apparently he tried. He called about two hours later and said he'd talked to Vin and that Vin had talked him out of it and everything was fine. That he hadn't made a mistake, after all. And that evening? A little withdrawn, but pretty much his old self."

"Back to normal."

"Yes," she said, her eyebrows going up, "but not for long. Tuesday, he came home from work just before noon with his boss Vin along. Frank walked me right here into this kitchen and sat me down at this table where I am now and said, 'Vin wants me to see a psychiatrist.' I knew he'd been upset and acting a little odd, but that had never crossed my mind! I didn't know what to say, particularly in front of Vin, and Frank sensed as much, and said, 'Vin came along because he was afraid I might try to hurt you.'"

"*Hurt* you?"

"That was my reaction! Frank hurt *me*? That made no sense! And I said something to that effect, and Frank said, 'I'm sorry, but they're afraid I might do you and the kids bodily harm.'"

Bodily harm. Oddly formal phrase.

"This Ruwet," I said, "where was he during all this?"

"Sitting where you are. Frank was here." She pointed to the empty chair between us. "Vin's a family friend, and I said to him, 'What's this all about, anyway?' And Vin said, 'It's going to be all right.' And I said something like, 'All right! It's *not* all right! I don't understand *any* of this!'"

Alice was shaking. I reached across and touched her hand. She swallowed, forced another thin smile, then slipped her hand out from under mine, got up wordlessly, and refilled our coffee cups.

She sat, sipped, resumed. "Frank and Vin went into the den and talked for maybe half an hour. I just stayed out here, trying to make sense of things, feeling like a truck hit me. Then Frank came in quickly and said, 'We're going back to Fort Detrick. They're making arrangements for me to see a shrink.'"

"Did Frank seem all right with that?"

"He did, in a shell-shocked kind of way. I said, 'Who besides Vin says you need a psychiatrist?' And he said, 'They think it's best.' And I said, 'Who the hell are *they*?' But all he said was, 'It's going to be fine.' I've always stayed out of Frank's business. You have to understand that we never talked about his work—I've never even been inside the building where he works. So I don't know where I got the gumption to say it, but I did—I said, 'I'm coming with you.'"

"Good for you. How did his boss react?"

"Vin stayed low-key. He said we could all ride to Washington together. A car from the base came to pick us up. Vin was in uniform—he's a lieutenant colonel—and we stopped by his house so he could change into civilian clothes. There was a military driver but he was in civvies, too."

Interesting.

I said, "How was Frank doing?"

"At that point, when we were just setting out, Frank got anxious, and wanted to know where we were going. Vin said, 'Washington, D.C., and on by air to New York.' I asked why New York, and Vin said, 'To get Frank the medical attention he needs.'"

"He couldn't get that in D.C.?"

She shrugged. "That's all the answer Vin gave me, and I was kind of reeling at that point. Anyway, I ask, 'How long are you going to be there?' And Frank says, 'Not long,' and I say, 'But *how* long? Thanksgiving is the day after tomorrow!' And Frank says, 'I'll be home for Thanksgiving, honey. Don't worry. I promise.'"

She began to cry.

I'd been anticipating this and came around with a handkerchief. Then I settled into the nearer chair, her husband's. From the living room, Bettie—on the floor with the little girl, playing dolls near the premature Christmas tree—glanced toward us with a sympathetic frown.

When she was able, Alice said, "We stopped for lunch on the way, at the Hot Shoppe, a little restaurant we know. But Frank seemed even more anxious, looking around the restaurant like it was . . . strange and threatening. When his food came, he pushed it away. I said, 'Dear, you have to eat,' and he said, 'You don't understand, Alice—they can put anything they want in your food.'"

"'They,'" I said.

"They. And I asked him *again* who 'they' was, and he said, 'Forget it,' and waved it off. In Washington we went to a military-looking building near the Reflecting Pool."

CIA headquarters.

"Vin left us in the car with the driver and went in. In the backseat, I held Frank's hand and asked him to promise to be home for Thanksgiving. He said he would. Then Vin was back, and Frank squeezed my hand and slid out of the car. 'See you in a couple of days,' he said. And that's the last I've heard from him, Nate."

They were keeping him under wraps for some reason. Likely they knew he had become a security risk.

They.

I sipped my coffee. "So he's likely in New York, or possibly in D.C. Do you have names I can follow up on? People Frank works with who are situated in Manhattan? I don't suppose your friend Vin gave you the name of the shrink he was taken to."

Her expression was woefully apologetic. "I'm afraid I don't have anything like that at all for you. And with Frank working for the government, in such sensitive areas, this may be impossible for you to look into. Now that I see it in front of me . . . and hear myself go through the story . . . I'm afraid I've wasted your time."

I leaned forward, patted her hand. "Is there anyone at Fort Detrick who might talk to me? Someone who works with Frank, who Frank trusts, who might have seen things or heard things about this episode, over these past few days?"

Her eyes came alive. "Yes. Yes, there is! Norman Cournoyer—

I should've thought of him right away! He's a biochemist at the lab who's very close to Frank. We socialize. I could call him—maybe he'd be willing to be bothered, even though it is a holiday."

"Let's try," I said.

In the living room, the children laughed.

"I'll go give Norm a call," she said, getting up. "Have another piece of pie while you're waiting, please. Just . . . not the apple."


The cocktail lounge of the Francis Scott Key Hotel in downtown Frederick was not hopping. Right now, it was a bartender fighting boredom, a couple at the bar getting chummy in a way that said they were either old friends or had just met, and two two-fisted drinkers who were acquainted and conversing but keeping a respectful stool between them.

"Place was packed this afternoon," the only waitress reported, delivering beers to me and my guest. She was short and blond and cute in a white blouse and black skirt.

"Oh?" I said, summoning interest.

She nodded. "The Packers-Lions game. DuMont Network had it . . . and *we* had the only TV."

It was on right now, over the bar, a 17-inch screen playing *You Bet Your Life*.

"Green Bay led at the half," Norman Cournoyer said, "but the Lions took it." His voice was a second tenor with some rasp.

"I'll run a tab," she said, leaving two pilsners.

"That's why DuMont is the also-ran network," I said. "Who wants to watch football on the head of a pin?"

"Well," Cournoyer said with a shrug, "you may be right, Mr. Heller—but every male in-law of mine was crowded around my TV like it was a damn campfire."

Tall, slender but solidly built, with close-cropped black hair and heavy black eyebrows, Frank Olson's best friend at Camp Detrick somehow conveyed both an intellectual air and a man's man's bearing. He was Superman in Clark Kent mode: sharp dark eyes behind plastic-rimmed glasses, strong nose, cleft chin, olive complexion smudged with McCarthy-esque five o'clock shadow. He wore a long-sleeve yellow sportshirt with brown trim on the pockets and collar and cuffs, top button buttoned.

"Funny to be in a bar with so little smoke," he said, glancing at the minuscule crowd. "Are you a smoker, Mr. Heller?"

"No. Left that behind in the Pacific."

"I stopped when I started working in an area where you learned what you took into your lungs can kill you."

That was already a little more frank than I'd expected him to be.

His face maintained a deceptively bland expression. "Alice says she hasn't heard from Frank since Vin Ruwet dragged him off to D.C. to get his head shrunk."

"That's right."

A sip of beer. "She also says you're an old friend of Frank's who happens to be a private investigator, and you've offered to try to find him."

"Yeah. I'm starting with you. Have *you* heard from him, Mr. Cournoyer?"

He shook his head. "But if Frank told Alice he'd be home for Thanksgiving, and he didn't show? Then he's in it very damn deep, Mr. Heller. Very damn deep."

Now I had a sip. "Sounds like you know what you're talking about, Mr. Cournoyer."

He gave me the kind of smile you give a pal who just told a corny joke. "Well, let's start with this—you're a private investigator all right, but you're no old friend of Frank's. I've known him since the war and I think he'd have mentioned knowing someone as famous as you."

"I'm not so famous."

Thick black eyebrows lifted above the clear-rimmed glasses. "Famous enough. But let's skip the dance. You can't play the jukebox while the TV's on anyway, right? You're who McCarthy sent to talk to Frank."

I looked at him over the pilsner. "He told you that?"

"He tells me damn near everything. I'm his sounding board, and he's mine. Frank could tell you, for instance, that I'm about to put my resignation in as an army officer, and that I've arranged to stick around as head of food service at Transylvania. Which is what we call Camp Detrick."

I squinted at him, as if it might bring him into focus.

"You're resigning," I said, "because . . . ?"

A hand flip. "Same reasons why Frank tried to resign. He just didn't *handle* it very well. He's got a lot of good qualities, Frank, but subtlety ain't one of 'em. See, I knew enough to stay on at Detrick, in a harmless capacity . . . although considering the kind of biowarfare research I've done, you wouldn't think they'd want me handling their food, would you, Mr. Heller. Or do you like the tangy taste of anthrax?"

"When you're a man who knows too much," I said, "it makes sense to stay on the team. Even as water boy."

"Bingo."

"What have they done with Frank, Mr. Cournoyer?"

He made a toasting gesture with his glass. "We'll make it 'Norm' and 'Nate,' what say?"

"I say, Norm, isn't a guy who swapped germ warfare for serving up Salisbury steak taking a big risk talking to me?"

"I'm off their radar," he said, with a shrug, his expression blank. "I'm a team player, like you said. Frank never has been. He's always bucking authority, never shy about speaking his mind. That's why he resigned from the Army and signed back on as a civilian employee, in the SOD."

I grunted a laugh. "The fun-and-games biochemical lab. Not as safe as the kitchen, huh, Norm?"

His face had a softness, but the eyes behind the lenses were hard. "Not as safe as the kitchen. Of course you know what they say about if you can't stand the heat. . . . You already talked to Frank, right?"

"Did he tell you that?"

He shook his head. "Just that he was going to talk to somebody McCarthy sent. I'm assuming that's you."

"Sometimes it's safe to assume."

"Why don't I fill in some background, Nate, and if it's one you already heard, stop me." A frown fought through his defenses. "Less I have to talk about this shit, the better I like it."

"Please."

A sip of beer. Another. "Did Frank tell you about his European trips?"

"He touched on them."

Black eyebrows climbed. "Including that he witnessed radical information retrieval?"

"I don't know what that is."

His voice was casually informative, as if he were sharing a barbecue recipe. "Well, Nate, it's an interrogation method that involves drugs, torture, and electroshock, among other goodies. Guinea pigs were Soviet prisoners, former Nazis, security leaks. These methods frequently lead to death."

"Frank mentioned something like that."

". . . Did he mention Korea?"

"No."

The dark eyes flared a millisecond, and his voice, already not loud, became a near whisper. "Hell, man, that's the key. Frank knows that biological weapons have been used over there. By *our* side. And he's not happy about that. He says some of these radical interrogation techniques, utilizing his work, have been used on Americans."

*Had Alice Olson sent me to a kook?*

I asked, "Why in hell would Americans be subjected to that?"

His voice, no longer a whisper but still on the soft side, turned as bland as his expression. "For one, debriefings of military and civilian personnel, who witnessed or participated in biological warfare in Korea. This involves brainwashing, memory wipes, all kinds of extreme experimental techniques. Frank has been worked up about all of this for months. It's been building."

"How so?"

"Well, he asked me if I knew the name of a good journalist, for one."

*Maybe I should have pulled Pearson in on this. Maybe I still should.*

He smiled faintly. "I didn't have a reporter for him, but I did suggest McCarthy. Ol' Joe's a ham-handed son of a bitch, but he'd get the story out. So that's what Frank did." What there was of a smile faded. "And look what it got him."

"*What* did it get him, Norm?"

"I don't know what it's getting him right at this moment, Nate. I have an idea, and I don't mind sharing it with you. But first you have to hear about what went on at Deep Creek Lodge."

I frowned. "The work retreat he went on?"

Cournoyer held up two hands, palms out, as if in surrender. "Now, I wasn't there, Nate. I *was* at *other* retreats at Deep Creek, mind you—beautiful place, isolated, all wooded, water on three sides, Appalachians looming. Scattering of cabins and a central stone lodge, fireplace, moose heads, the works."

"Got it."

Another hand flip. "So, anyway, this is secondhand, but it's secondhand from Frank. All right?"

"All right."

The waitress brought us fresh beers. When she'd trotted off, Cournoyer pushed his pilsner to one side and folded his hands. He might have been Daddy saying grace.

"Frank didn't say much about what went on the first few days," he said. "There were ten scientists present, some from SOD and others from a CIA team. Both groups were working, separately, on different aspects of the same germ weaponry project, and this was a chance to compare notes, brainstorm—a regular skull session. They'd done the same thing the year before. Just a friendly, productive get-together."

*If you consider germ warfare productive*, I thought.

Cournoyer was saying, "Two top CIA scientists on the project were running the retreat—Gottlieb and Lashbrook. Gottlieb's a real brain but an oddball, high up in the Agency. He stutters and has a club foot but don't underestimate him. Only in his mid-thirties, but somebody to reckon with."

"First name?"

"Sidney. And Lashbrook's is Robert; he's Gottlieb's deputy. Gottlieb is a big believer in this LSD-25 stuff—considers it a real tongue loosener, a kind of truth serum, potentially a very powerful tool. He's run all sorts of tests on unsuspecting subjects, last year or so. You need to know that going in."

"Okay."

He gestured with an open hand, painting the picture. "For two days, they have group meetings in front of the roaring fire, then split off for smaller specialized meetings—typical retreat stuff. They relax and unwind in the evening. After dinner on Thursday night, everybody enjoys a glass of Cointreau—you know, the triple sec?"

I nodded.

"Served up by Gottlieb and Lashbrook from a couple of bottles. A nice gesture, huh? Twenty minutes later, Gottlieb gathers everybody by the fire and tells them they've just consumed a healthy dose of LSD-25."

"Jesus."

Cournoyer shook his head, grinning. "No, you don't understand, Nate. These scientists are fine with experiments like this. They dose everybody else, why not themselves?"

"Okay . . ."

"In fact, Frank says they laughed their asses off—joke's on *us* for a change. For a while they're loud and boisterous, then all sorts of philosophical discussions get going. But after a while Frank starts feeling paranoid, and when in the wee hours everybody goes off to bed, he can't sleep. Gottlieb and Lashbrook act concerned and walk him outside the main lodge to a cabin, so as not to disturb anybody. And here's the thing—Frank told me he isn't even sure what he said to those two. He remembered being talkative, and thought maybe he'd said too much. About his guilt, about his misgivings, over what he'd been doing. What they'd *all* been doing."

"He wasn't *sure* he'd spilled?"

"No. It was fuzzy. But he *suspected* he'd been given a dose of his own medicine—that some of the interrogation techniques he'd helped develop had been turned back on him. And he was afraid he'd made an awful mistake."

Neither of us said anything for a while.

"I only have two names for you," he said. "Two people in New York who may know where Frank is. If you still want them."

*Something had crept through the bland mask—what was it?*

"Please," I said.

*Fear.*

"Nate. Mr. Heller. Do you know what you might be getting yourself into?"

"I think so."

"I'm not sure you do. For example, imagine you were me. You might be a CIA asset right now, planning to pat me on the back as you leave, and pinprick me with a poison that Frank or some other genius concocted and I won't see Christmas. I won't see fucking Friday. Do you understand?"

"I'm starting to," I said.

# CHAPTER 18

Fog got turned into an ivory mist by a two-thirds moon as I followed the winding dirt road and pulled into the driveway of the Olson house, where I had left Bettie. The ranch-style was set back a good distance, surrounded by tall trees whose remaining leaves shivered, ghostly gnarled limbs ticking the rooftop. Lights glowed within the house but the place seemed nonetheless lost in shadow.

Alice met me at the door with a confused, even tortured expression, my lovely black-haired companion standing just behind her with eyes as big as they were blue. The two women led me into the living room, the kids already in bed.

"Something odd has happened," Alice said.

*No! Not something odd?*

"Tell me," I said.

We sat on the couch with me between them, branches scratching at the windows.

"Vin stopped by, not long after you left," Alice said, her hands folded in her lap as she sat forward. "Vin Ruwet, Frank's boss?"

I nodded. "What did he have to say?"

"He apologized for not getting here sooner. He said Frank had several sessions starting Tuesday evening with a Dr. Abramson."

*Dr. Harold Abramson—one of the two names Norman Cournoyer had given me just minutes before.*

"Go on," I said.

"Vin said Wednesday night they'd had dinner together and gone to a Broadway show. This morning Frank seemed better and after breakfast they checked out of the Statler Hotel, and went to LaGuardia for a morning flight to D.C., for a session with some other doctor. After that, Vin was driving Frank here when Frank made him pull over. Told Vin he wanted to go back to see Dr. Abramson, that he needed more help. That he was afraid . . . afraid of doing me and the children bodily harm."

*That phony phrase again—who says "bodily harm" outside of a police report?*

"So what's happening now?"

"Frank's getting more help. Vin says."

"Was Vin specific about what kind of help?"

She nodded. "They took a plane from D.C. back to New York, to go to Dr. Abramson's home on Long Island—the doctor 'generously' interrupting his family Thanksgiving. I asked where Frank is staying tonight, but Vin says he doesn't know—somewhere on Long Island, he supposes. Supposes! If this is all so . . . so *benign* . . . why hasn't Frank called me? Where is my *husband's* voice in all this?"

*Temporarily silenced. Or maybe not temporarily . . .*

I took her hand; she was trembling. "Alice, I have names from Mr. Cournoyer to follow up on in Manhattan. Should I still do that?"

"Do you think we'd be wrong to?"

I shook my head. "We'd be wrong *not* to, in my opinion. But it's not my call."

"You think Frank's in danger?"

*Goddamn right I do.*

"Possibly," I said.

She swallowed; lifted her chin. "Then please do see if you can find Frank. At least get him to call me. And if he *is* in trouble . . . help him, if you can."

I summoned a smile. "Do my best to deliver him tomorrow, and you can heat up that wonderful meal for him. Okay?"

She nodded bravely, chin crinkling but no tears.

With a gesture toward my beautiful companion in the pink sweater, I said to Alice, "How did you explain Bettie to Frank's boss?"

But it wasn't Alice who answered: "You mean *Aunt* Bettie, sugah?"

On the porch, with the skeletal trees doing their wind-driven dance around us, Alice asked, "Do you think you should go over to Vin's and just . . . *talk* to him about all this?"

"I've been considering that," I admitted. "But I don't think so, not right now. For a family friend, Vin hasn't been much help to you. He's doing somebody's bidding. That you haven't heard from Frank suggests they're keeping him under wraps for some reason. I'm better off checking out the Manhattan leads first."

Anyway, Vin Ruwet appeared to be a cog in this, though important enough to the wheel to make it unlikely I could shake anything out of him. Plus he was a military man, and I didn't have any radical interrogation techniques handy to make him talk.

"Whatever you think," Alice said. She reached out and squeezed Bettie's hand, then gave me a kiss on the cheek, and an impulsive hug, after which she moved away with an embarrassed smile, hiding behind her half-closed door.

She said, with a touch of embarrassment, "Thank you for this."

"It's early for thanks," I said, putting on my hat. "Let's see if I deserve any."

"You will," she said, trying to convince herself more than me, I think, then sealed herself within the house.

Fifteen minutes later, Mr. and Mrs. Nathan Heller checked into the Barbara Fritchie Cabins on the fringes of downtown Frederick. We'd both brought small overnight bags just in case, and when Bettie trotted out of the bathroom in a sheer black nightie, brushing all that black hair, I finally had something to be thankful for this Thanksgiving.

The little cabin barely had room for the canopy bed, and the handful of other furnishings were also of an overtly Early American style, the wallpaper pink with tiny faded Liberty Bells, in a Fourth of July theme that was getting as threadbare as the comforter.

What had once been a top tourist court would soon belong to illicit lovers not particular about patriotic decor.

Not that we should talk, although our fucking was so sweet and warm it deserved a nicer word; it was as if we'd been together for years, but still found pleasure in each other. Wouldn't that be something? Married to Bettie Page. Maybe once a year she'd get out her leopard undies for me . . . I'd pass on the whips. . . .

She cuddled against me in the near dark, smelling of Ivory soap; some light from the street filtered in filmy curtains and threw a lace pattern over her.

"Ah feel so *bad* for that little family. The daddy's in a bunch of trouble, isn't he?"

"I believe he is. How much did you pick up?"

"He does secret government work, but he's had a kind of breakdown. Ah guess that makes him dangerous to some people."

"You're not wrong. And you knowing any more than that would be dangerous in itself." My arm was around her and I squeezed fondly. "Look, we'll catch a morning train in D.C. and be back in Manhattan by noon or so. I'm going to do some poking around that could get a little dicey."

She looked up at me, pretty, and pretty concerned. "How dicey, Nate? What kind of dicey?"

"Dicey enough that I'll be carrying a gun. I don't want you around that."

"Ah been around all *kinds* of people and all *kinds* of trouble. Don't you worry about little ol' Bettie."

"You haven't been around these kind of people and this kind of trouble. You should steer little ol' Nate a wide path for a few days."

"You're not headin' back to Chicago?"

"Not till I'm done with this thing. But after I am, we'll get back together for at least a night or two—all right?"

"No."

"No?"

"I'll stay in your room at the Waldorf till you go back to Chicago. Nobody's gonna bother either one of us there."

She was probably right.

"Ah'll just read and relax and order room service, and live in the lap of luxury. I mean, that room has a TV and everything! Doesn't that sound nice, Nate?"

"The lap part does," I admitted.

On this day after a holiday, midtown teemed with Christmas shoppers while the usual button-down worker bees seemed a scarce commodity. With no snow and a temperature in the early forties, fall appeared in no hurry to get out of winter's way, the sky overcast but only vaguely threatening. Under the Burberry, lining out, I was in the charcoal Richard Bennett number cut to conceal the nine-millimeter Browning under my left arm—with spooks in the mix, I would have felt naked otherwise.

The cab dropped me at 133 East Fifty-eighth Street, a thirteen-story brown-brick office building with its upper floors set back in an Art Moderne style that dated it to the early thirties. The modest lobby, with its five elevators, was underpopulated, though I did have to sign in. The directory put Dr. Harold A. Abramson on the eighth floor, but below his name was a surprise: "Allergist/Immunologist." Not "Psychiatrist"? Or even "Psychologist"?

Olson's pal Cournoyer, when he'd given me Abramson's name, had described the doctor on the q.t. as the CIA's top man using LSD-25 as a means of psychotherapeutic treatment. And doing it on staff at New York's prestigious Mount Sinai Hospital.

"In any case," Cournoyer had said, "it makes sense they'd take Frank to see Abramson—they're friends or anyway friendly acquaintances, going back to the war. And Abramson has all the right clearances."

Add to that Olson being dragged off almost bodily to see a "shrink" and I had naturally assumed that meant Abramson qualified. Down this rabbit hole, such assumptions were at your own risk.

The wood-paneled waiting room wasn't large but seemed bigger than it was, since it was empty of anything but chairs, old magazines, and a young receptionist. She had red hair, red lipstick, and green eyes behind black cat's-eye eyeglasses; not in nurse's whites, she wore a black suit with a white blouse, and looked up from *Look* magazine as if I'd caught her with her hand in the till.

"Dr. Abramson isn't seeing patients today," she said, defensive before I'd uttered a word.

I crossed over to her desk, Dobbs in hand, and said with a smile, "But he's in or you wouldn't be."

Her chin came up. "I might be here to answer the phone."

"You might, but there are services cheaper than you and, anyway, what you're doing is reading *Look* magazine. What do you think? *Are* the Commies infiltrating the Protestant Church?"

That was the story promised under a seemingly unrelated photo of a sultry Marilyn Monroe smoking a cigarette.

While she was trying to figure out whether I was flirting or making fun of her—I was doing both, of course—I handed her my business card and a brief signed letter of authorization from Alice. "Tell the doctor I'm representing Mrs. Frank Olson. He'll see me."

She had an intercom but she couldn't deliver the card and letter over it, so she went through the door to her left, between her desk and a low-slung table of more magazines.

While she was gone, I took one of Abramson's business cards from a little pedestal on her desk and slipped it into my suit coat pocket.

She returned and held the door open for me. "End of the hall," she said resentfully, handing me back the authorization letter, which I tucked away.

The hall didn't go anywhere much, with just a pair of facing doors on either side, offices and/or consultation rooms. The darkwood door with "DR. ABRAMSON" in gold was ajar at the dead end, left open as a courtesy, but my host wasn't feeling courteous enough to meet me there.

The office was nothing out of the ordinary, medium-size with framed diplomas on the walls and family pictures on the desk, a non-shrink-style brown corduroy couch along a wall. Blinds on windows over the couch were angled to let in a little of the gray day. The filing cabinets and the desk were a rich dark wood and whispered money, but nothing else did. Not even Abramson himself.

He was in his mid-fifties, in an off-the-fairly-expensive-rack light brown suit and a darker brown tie; sturdy-looking, pleasant features, bald, placid light blue eyes behind dark-rimmed glasses, strong nose, salt-and-pepper mustache, slightly jutting chin. He half-rose behind the desk and extended his hand for a handshake that gave nothing away. He might have been the principal of an Ohio high school.

"Mr. Heller," he said, in a mellow baritone that conveyed only minimal interest, "sit, please, and tell me how I can be of help to you. Or I should say of help to Mrs. Olson."

I took the waiting client chair, padded dark brown leather matching his own swivel version. I was happy not to be offered coffee or tea or anything at all really, since this guy's chief interest in life was LSD-25.

"Before we get to that, Dr. Abramson," I said, "I wonder if you might answer a basic question."

His smile barely qualified as one. "Ask it and we'll see how basic it is."

"Well, pretty basic. Mrs. Olson was told by Frank and his boss, Colonel Ruwet from Camp Detrick, that there was concern about her husband's mental state—after he came back from a recent work retreat. That Frank was suffering anxiety related to his job, which had him suddenly wanting to resign . . . but being encouraged *not* to by his boss, Ruwet. So he was taken here to New York to see a psychiatrist."

"That's all correct."

"Not really," I said, "since you aren't a psychiatrist—unless you're just too shy to list it on your door with your other accomplishments."

He gestured with a rather thick hand that made me glad he wasn't passing himself off as a surgeon, too. "I'm not a psychiatrist, Mr. Heller, or a psychologist, either. I have expertise in three fields—

immunology, allergy, and pediatrics, though currently I'm not actively practicing in the third. Why do you ask?"

"Oh, I don't know. An allergy doctor treating a mental patient is a little like going to a podiatrist for heart trouble, isn't it?"

This smile hardly rated as one at all. "That's rather an oversimplification and exaggeration. There are a number of reasons why, in this instance, I was the doctor selected to treat Frank Olson. But I frankly don't believe they're any business of yours, Mr. Heller."

"They're business of my client, Dr. Abramson—your patient's wife, and as far as you're concerned, I'm her."

"I do understand that."

"Good. Doctor, the circumstances here are very troubling. And if you—or someone you might refer me to for more satisfactory answers—can't explain why an allergist is treating Frank Olson for a supposed mental breakdown . . ."

"Mr. Heller—"

". . . *and why* Mrs. Olson hasn't heard from her husband for three days? My next stop will be the New York City Police for assistance in my inquiries, and I have some decent contacts there. And at the local FBI office, since this French farce has an unfortunate whiff of kidnapping."

For the most part, his face remained a bland mask; but a tightening around the eyes gave him away, that and a bristly look that his mustache got.

"Mr. Heller, I'm afraid we've gotten off on the wrong foot." He made his face smile. It was the way a dog seems to smile when it has peanut butter on the roof of its mouth. "Let's start over. . . . Could I get you some coffee, perhaps?"

"No!"

He blinked, taken aback by the vehemence of that. "Well. All right. I will do my best to respond. I have to be somewhat vague, because Dr. Olson's situation touches upon several classified areas."

"Why, are you a military man, Doctor?"

"No, but I am contracted to do work for the military and other government agencies. . . ."

"Including the CIA," I said.

The light blue eyes got wide behind the lenses, seeming not so placid now.

I said, "Yes, I know Frank Olson is involved in research for the CIA. No need to dance around it."

He shifted just a little in the leather chair. "But I'm afraid there is. I am limited as to what I can say. As a licensed investigator, you surely understand that."

"I do. But I can't let you hide behind it, Doctor."

He nodded slightly, then leaned back and folded his hands over the moderate paunch under his buttoned suit coat. "Mr. Heller, I assume you know that Dr. Olson works in biochemical research. He comes into contact with various dangerous chemicals in the course of that research, and we believe he became exposed to one such chemical that caused in him a psychotropic reaction."

I was supposed to picture a spilled test tube, not triple sec laced with a hallucinogenic mickey.

I said, "And you have an expertise where such reactions are concerned."

"That's right. As an allergist. Further, I am doing research into the reactions of patients in a clinical setting to a certain drug which Dr. Olson may have accidentally ingested."

That was closer to the truth, but still no cigar. On the other hand, I now had a clearer picture of the good doctor—so he was doing CIA-funded research into LSD-25. At Mount Sinai yet.

Staying deadpan, I said, "That's reassuring. I was afraid that he'd been brought to you because no in-house psychiatrists or psychologists had proper CIA clearance to handle a high-security patient like Frank Olson . . . and he'd have to settle for you. His old friend the allergist."

Some anger flared in the light blue eyes, though the face around them remained impassive. "That's an unwarranted assumption, and frankly insulting, sir."

"But you and Frank Olson do have a prior relationship."

This smile was more of a twitch. "I have known Frank for many years, yes. We worked on projects together during the war. He's a friend and I do think I have a certain ease with him. A certain ease with each other."

"And that level of comfort is obviously a positive thing." I needed to back off on needling him. "What kind of shape is Frank in, Doctor?"

He lifted a shoulder in a shrug. "I'm still evaluating that. I would say he alternates between seeming normal, very much himself, and . . . are you familiar with the term 'paranoia,' Mr. Heller?"

"Yeah. I'd say I have a pretty good handle on the paranoia concept."

"Well, on Tuesday we had a good long session right here in this office. Frank sat where you're sitting. And . . . You understand my remarks must be limited, due to patient confidentiality, and that I can only share with you what I would feel comfortable telling Mrs. Olson were she here in person."

"Sure," I said.

I had no doubt that there were confidentiality concerns in this, but I doubted Olson's rights as a patient was one of them.

"The serious nature of Frank's top-secret research and development," the allergist said, "has built an anxiety in him that is troubling. He feels guilty about some of the work he's done, and suffers from feelings of depression and inadequacy. These are feelings that appear to have been troubling him for some months, but this . . . chemical with which he came into contact has apparently brought it to the surface. That first session I felt . . . I *feel* . . . was a good one. Because we are old friends, we have a genuine rapport. Because I am in the same field that Frank is, he feels he need not be guarded with me."

"You mentioned paranoia."

He unlaced his hands and sat forward, then replaced them on the desktop. "I . . . Mr. Heller, I'm going over the line here, but I think Mrs. Olson has the right to know that there's a serious element in all this."

Who had said otherwise?

"All right," I said.

"Frank has been having trouble sleeping. With the kind of anxiety he's suffering, that's natural. But he believes that the CIA is putting stimulants in his coffee to prevent him from getting a good night's rest."

"Not caffeine, either."

"No. Specifically, Benzedrine. I don't believe I need to explain that that's the *last* thing the Agency would do to one of its top scientists. But talking to me, at length as we did, seemed to calm him. A logical, low-key examination of his concerns seemed to help. To get through."

"This was Tuesday afternoon?"

"Yes. That evening, I went to his hotel room, at the Statler, to check up on him. He was sharing a room with Lieutenant Colonel Ruwet, and Dr. Robert Lashbrook, another scientist, was next door, adjoining. Making sure Frank had proper support in this difficult hour."

"Keeping an eye on him."

Lashbrook was Dr. Sidney Gottlieb's right-hand man, but Abramson didn't need to know that I was aware of that.

"Call it that if you like, Mr. Heller. Lieutenant Colonel Ruwet called me and said Frank was getting agitated again. So, as I say, I went over there. Gave him something to settle him down, help him get to sleep."

"A house call, Doctor?"

"It was as much social as medical, Mr. Heller. We had several highballs, there in his room, and then I left him with a bottle of Nembutal capsules, and told him to take one . . . and that if he had any trouble sleeping, he should take another."

"Yellow Jackets and bourbon," I said numbly. "*That* was your prescription?"

I couldn't hide my disgust, but at least I didn't smack him—that kind of cocktail could give the nervous system a fatal one-two.

His chin came up. Funny how when people look down their nose at you, they present such a tempting target.

He said, "I'm told it worked, that he slept well. Then the next morning, Wednesday, I understand that Colonel Ruwet and Dr. Lashbrook took Frank to see a magician friend of his, just to cheer him up."

*John Mulholland, the well-known stage magician, was the other name Norman Cournoyer had shared with me.*

"You weren't along for that," I said.

"That's right. But Frank and I had a long session Wednesday afternoon—I canceled all my consultations to make room for him—and he seemed well on the road to recovery to me." He sighed. "You see, Mr. Heller, the question is whether we can get Frank back on his feet or if it will be necessary to admit him to a hospital for longer-term care."

"You mean commit him. Institutionalize him."

He raised a "stop" palm. "I would rather you not convey that to Mrs. Olson. That's what we're all hoping to avoid. No reason to alarm her."

"You don't think it's alarming, not hearing from her husband in three days?"

"Mr. Heller—"

"The possibility of committing him—is *that* why Frank hasn't been allowed to call Alice?"

Abramson was shaking his head. "No one has forbidden Frank to call his wife. That's his decision. He had the notion that he'd become dangerous to her and his children—no foundation for that, I assure you—and then in his better moments, he's embarrassed by all of this. He'll call her when he feels he's ready. Mrs. Olson has been kept apprised of her husband's situation. My understanding is that Lieutenant Colonel Ruwet spoke to her last evening."

"He did. After she'd had one hell of a miserable day."

"These things sometimes can't be helped. The reality is, yesterday, Thanksgiving, we had a setback. Frank was on his way home with Ruwet when he demanded he be turned around and taken back here, to work further through this with me. Of course, I wasn't in my office, but they brought him to me at my home on Long Island. I was only too glad to help."

"They?"

"Dr. Lashbrook and, uh, a colleague."

*Gottlieb?* I didn't press it. Anything I revealed would be assumed to be known by Alice Olson as well, and I didn't want to put her in harm's way.

Abramson was saying, "We worked for several productive hours, in the late afternoon and early evening. Dr. Lashbrook and Frank stayed in a hotel in Cold Spring Harbor, near me. I believe they had a pleasant Thanksgiving dinner at a local restaurant."

"That's nice," I said through my teeth. "Because Alice Olson's Thanksgiving wasn't so goddamn pleasant. Not when her husband failed to show and never called."

He opened a hand and shrugged. "It's a delicate, touchy situation. But we're making progress. This morning, first thing, I worked with Frank at the hotel in Cold Spring Harbor. Then we all drove into the city and I had a two-hour session here with Frank late this morning and afternoon."

I sat forward. "Are you saying I just *missed* him?"

Abramson said, "By about half an hour."

"And where is he now?"

"With Dr. Lashbrook, who's finding them a hotel to check into, I believe. I haven't heard from them, but should shortly. Where could I get in touch with you, Mr. Heller? The office number on your card?"

"You can leave word there, but I'm at the Waldorf. I would appreciate it if you'd let me know."

He gave me a patronizing smile. "I'll do that. But my feeling is that the situation, while in flux, is very hopeful. In a day or two, we should be able to return Frank Olson to his happy home. . . . Now, Mr. Heller, unless there's something else . . . ?"

"There *is* something else."

"Yes?"

I stood and put on my hat. "I appreciate everything you've shared with me, Doctor, but there are things about how this is being handled—shuttling a mental patient back and forth from D.C. to New York, with an allergist playing therapist, holding him at this hotel and that one, and all the while the patient is out of touch with his wife and family . . . it kind of smells, Doctor. Or maybe I'm just allergic to bullshit."

"This is *unnecessary* . . . un*called* for. . . ."

I leaned a hand on his desk and got damn near nose to nose with him. "So if Alice Olson doesn't hear from her husband some-time today—let's make it by midnight—I'm making good on my promise. I'm taking this to the cops or maybe to the FBI, and my understanding is the FBI and the CIA are *not* friendly rivals. Do you follow me, Doctor?"

He had turned a lovely shade of red with purple highlights. He pointed to the door as if I were his wayward daughter.

"You need to leave, Mr. Heller. *Right now.* I don't have to listen to such irresponsible, disrespectful, nauseating nonsense."

"Oh, you'll get over it. Take a couple of Nembutal, wash it down with bourbon, and call me in the morning."

When I went out, the receptionist was still reading *Look,* and the waiting room remained empty—not surprising, since the only pa-tient the doctor was seeing today was somewhere else.

# CHAPTER 19

The Bush Tower, just off Times Square at 130 West Forty-second Street, was the perfect setting for the office of a professional magician. With its thirty floors and fifty-foot width, the neo-Gothic razor blade of a building seemed impossibly tall despite much higher neighbors; back when it opened in 1917, it must have been a wonder.

John Mulholland had been a wonder in his day, too—a stage magician of some renown, author of best-selling magic books, editor of the professional magician's magazine, *The Sphinx*. We'd never met, but we'd been featured in issues of the same "true detective" rags, though I was nabbing murderers where he'd been exposing phony mediums.

Around 1940, I'd seen him perform at the Empire Room at the Palmer House back in Chicago. He was adept with cards, silk scarves, coins, and other small props—a live canary and its bird cage disappeared in midair—but could also set up large illusions like his famous "floating coffin." Mulholland's brand of tuxedo-clad conjurer was a bit of a wheeze these days, though there was always room for a magician on the bill, particularly with a beautiful female assistant in mesh stockings.

But what was he doing in the middle of Frank Olson's disappearing act?

The office door said—

## JOHN MULHOLLAND
### MAGICIAN      LECTURER

—and underneath it was a circular bronze plaque of a bas-relief rabbit under which curved the words: "The Art of Creating Illusions."

The door was unlocked, and I entered an apparent reception area whose side walls bulged with a series of four-shelf Art Nouveau dark-wood bookcases crammed with volumes on magic behind wood-and-glass triple doors, the top of each arrayed with statues, lamps, and artifacts of his craft. The only visitor chairs were to the left and right as you came in, where each wall had a massive framed colorful poster, Thurston contemplating a skull, Houdini helplessly handcuffed.

A large dark handsome work-stacked desk against the facing wall, with typewriter and banker's lamp, said this space was for more than reception. On the wall overlooking the desk was a row of smaller framed magician posters and above that signed 8-by-10s—Hollywood stars (Jean Harlow, Eddie Cantor, Jimmy Durante, Orson Welles) and famous magicians (Blackstone, Carter, Kellar, Karlini). Not a single Mulholland poster, though—could his love for the magical arts be bigger than his ego?

A slim male figure stepped through a doorway to the right of the desk, as if he had gone into a sarcophagus stage right only to emerge from another stage left. Despite the sudden theatricality of this entrance, I still had trouble making the lanky, jug-eared, thick-lipped, weak-chinned character be the famed John Mulholland.

No tux and top hat, gray hair combed neatly back, he wore wire-frame glasses and a gray suit with darker gray bow tie. Taller than me, he was slump-shouldered enough to seem shorter. He gave me a friendly if not effusive smile.

"May I be of service, sir? I'm afraid my secretary is away on Thanksgiving vacation."

"Mr. Mulholland," I said, taking off my hat as if about to pull a rabbit out of it, "I saw you at the Empire Room some years ago. I never saw a better magician."

The half smile was toothy and sincere, but he hadn't approached me yet. "That's kind of you. If you're here for a booking, I'm afraid I'm taking some time off from stage work."

I cut the distance between us by half but didn't press. "No, sir, I'm here to ask you a few questions about Dr. Frank Olson."

That froze him momentarily, then he said, "And you are . . . ?"

Now I went to him, holding out a business card. "Nathan Heller. President of the A-1 Detective Agency."

He studied the card. Before he'd come to any conclusion about it, I performed my own sleight-of-hand trick, handing him a second business card—Dr. Harold Abramson's.

"Dr. Abramson said you could be trusted to be discreet," I said. "I understand Dr. Olson was up here to see you earlier this week, and I wanted to get your impression."

A smile remained, but no teeth now, the sharp eyes in the near-goofy face very guarded. "What could I tell you that Dr. Abramson couldn't?"

I smiled. "Well, that's what I'm here to find out. If you're willing. I'm operating as an outside, impartial party, since everyone else involved in evaluating Dr. Olson so far has been a friend or a co-worker or both."

"I'm afraid I fall into that latter category, Mr. Heller." Now he seemed more at ease—he'd bought into my little trick. "Grab a chair, why don't you? I'll just sit here at Dorothy's desk."

But before he settled in, he went over, opened the door onto the hall and looked down right, and left, then locked it with a key. I pulled a straight-back chair over from under the Houdini poster and sat opposite him, where he was leaning back, lighting up a Philip Morris. The smell of cigarette smoke was strong in the office, unless that was the residue of some trick he was working up in the room behind him.

"You have a very impressive collection," I said, indicating the posters and crammed bookcases.

"Thanks, but those are just the tip of the iceberg." The resonant baritone of a veteran stage performer came through even in conversation. "I estimate I have thirty-thousand–some volumes on magic, and the largest collection of priceless magician posters in the world. Not to mention the props I've gathered from the biggest names in the profession. I started out as a lad, you know, with Houdini."

"That's very impressive," I said, meaning it. The "lad" was currently in his mid-fifties at least. "I hope you'll be able to get back to performing soon."

He exhaled smoke. "I will, when I've completed this current project. You're aware of that project, I assume?"

"Yes," I said. "Not in any detail, of course."

And now I had to run a bluff—based on who this man was and what the CIA might want with him. If I was wrong, I'd be out on my ass. If he called his handler, I might star in my own vanishing act.

"Just that it's obvious," I said, with a shrug, "that someone with your close-up magic skills would be ideal to help train agents to spike drinks and food and so on, without detection."

He nodded as casually as if I'd just complimented his handling of Chinese linking rings. "I admit it's proving a more difficult task than I anticipated, getting this all down into a sort of 'how to' book, making sure my techniques can be learned by an average person without exceptional manual dexterity."

I half-smiled. "Not just anybody has hands that are quicker than the eye."

"Yes, and there's so much more to it than that." He exhaled more smoke as if summoning a curtain to hide behind. "There's the psychological background of deception—setting the stage you might say, understanding who your 'audience' is. Distracting the subject's attention. And naturally we're dealing with small objects—paper matches, coins, stamps, a woman's compact—all used to deliver powders and liquids."

Nodding matter-of-factly, I said, "And those powders and liquids are drugs or chemical or biological agents?"

"Correct." He gestured with a fluid hand. "All this requires tiny pills, squirting gadgets, and concealed needles . . . and of course, the day before yesterday, when Frank Olson was here, I went over all of that with him."

Doing my best to stay a step ahead, I said, "Well, of course, because so many of the things Dr. Olson and his staff are developing require the kind of . . . delivery system . . . that you can contrive for him."

The smoke came out his nose this time, dragon-style. "Exactly. But I wasn't prepared for the shape Frank was in . . . and I have to say I object to not having been *alerted* to his condition, because I would have treated the situation with rather more care."

"What situation? What condition?"

His eyes tightened. "Well . . . you notice I refer to Dr. Olson as 'Frank.' That's because we've become friends over these last four or five months. We've met a number of times, both here in this office and at Camp Detrick. Of course, in those earlier meetings Frank took the lead."

I made a leap: "Because he was coming to you with the chemical and biological agents that required your expertise in delivery."

He sighed smoke, shook his head gently. "Yes, and perhaps it was all abstract to Frank, when we were talking biology and chemistry. But when I showed him various devices I'd come up with, things as simple as a pencil, it must have suddenly seemed terribly concrete to him."

"A pencil?"

He nodded, picking up a pencil from the desk and gesturing with it, as if it were an under-size wand. "You just remove the rubber eraser, hollow out the shaft a little, shave down the eraser, reinsert it, and *voilà*, you have a hiding place for loose solids."

"Loose solids?"

Another nod. "Chemicals in granular form, like salt . . . although we're obviously not talking about salt here. To disseminate the substance, you simply remove the eraser as if you're un-corking a vial."

"To slip it in a drink, for example."

"Yes, or food." He tossed the pencil back onto the desk. "For disseminating liquids, there's polyethylene tubing that can go up a sleeve, and, well . . . so many devices, so many methods. Simple but effective."

I leaned forward. "So when Dr. Lashbrook and Colonel Ruwet brought Frank around, you showed him what you've worked up for him lately."

"Correct. You see, right from the start, Frank and I really hit it off—he's a dyed-in-the-wool practical joker, you know, and usually when we get together, I give him some nice gags that he can play on his coworkers. Such a great smile, such a great laugh, that man. But this time . . . very different."

"How so?"

He gestured with the cigarette in hand and drew a smoky figure eight. "Well, when I told Frank I wanted to show him some of the new delivery systems, I asked Lashbrook and Ruwet to wait out here in the outer office. Frank and I went into my private area, which is as much a workshop as an office, and I showed him the gimmicks I'd devised."

"And Frank didn't react with his usual enthusiasm?"

The magician's eyebrows rose above his glasses, then descended. "Probably poor judgment on my part. There's a hell of a difference between some practical jokes to pull on your pals at work, and administering a dangerous drug to some unsuspecting party."

"How exactly did Frank react to these new toys?"

His eyes flared. "He got agitated. Worked up. He said to me, whispering, 'What's behind this? Give me the lowdown.' I didn't understand what he meant and said so. He grabbed my sleeve. 'Are they checking me for security? Do they want you to see if I'm a security risk?'"

"And what did you say?"

He held his left hand up in "stop" fashion. "That I knew nothing about it. That I was just a contract employee doing specific tasks, like writing my manual for them, and contriving the devices I was showing him. He grabbed my arm harder and said, 'They're all in a plot to get me. Are you part of it, too?' I said I knew nothing of any such plot! He seemed on the verge of tears. He asked, 'Why don't they just let me disappear?' I said nobody could disappear. When people disappear on stage, I reminded him, it's just an illusion. A trick. And he said I was wrong. That the people he works for could make *anybody* vanish."

He put out his cigarette. Fingered a new one out of the Philip Morris deck, thumbnailed a kitchen match to flame, and lit up.

I asked, "Did Frank stay agitated?"

"No. I was able to calm him down, rather quickly, and I took him back out here where the other two were waiting. Frank was sitting where you are, with the other two in chairs just behind him on either side. Lashbrook noted that Frank seemed awfully tense, and suggested I hypnotize him, to relax him."

"I don't remember you using hypnosis in your act."

He shook his head emphatically. "I don't. Too dangerous. Too unpredictable. Still, while I'm no expert, I'm generally able to hypnotize most subjects. But Frank said adamantly 'No,' refusing to let me try, and rushed out. Ruwet followed on his heels."

"Not Lashbrook?"

"He followed shortly, but first he paused to give me a check he'd brought for me—for travel expenses to a hypnosis seminar next month, ironically enough. In Chicago."

Ironically enough.

I said, just a throwaway, "I'm surprised Dr. Gottlieb didn't attend this meeting."

He shrugged, released another cloud of smoke. "Well, of course, that wasn't necessary, since Lashbrook is Sidney's deputy. His eyes and ears, you know. Anyway, I don't believe Sidney was in the city on Wednesday."

"Sidney, huh? Sounds like you and Dr. Gottlieb are friends, too."

His eyes lighted up. "Well, *friendly* certainly. I find him a *fascinating* character—the way he's overcome his stutter, largely, and of course his enormous intellect. He's a kind of spymaster, isn't he? And yet such a kind, humane individual."

Offhandedly, I said, "I've never met him. As I say, I've been brought in from the outside for a fresh read on Dr. Olson's status. But I admit I haven't heard anybody accuse Sidney Gottlieb of being 'humane.'"

Mulholland's smile was almost dreamy behind the wall of smoke. "Well, he's a Buddhist, for one thing. Lives with his wife in a log cabin on a fifteen-acre farm outside D.C., where they raise goats and grow Christmas trees—they sell them right there, on a roadside stand . . . busy time of year for him and his wife. They drink only goat's milk and make their own cheese."

Wait a minute—was he trying to hypnotize *me*?

I asked, fairly numbly, "Are we talking about the same Dr. Sidney Gottlieb?"

"Oh, yes. He's a scientist and a humanist, but he's also a patriot who is willing to do the tough things for his country."

Like spike the drinks of colleagues with LSD-25. "I'd like to talk to him about Frank Olson. You wouldn't happen to know where exactly that log cabin of his is?"

The horsey face lit up, smoke drifting out of his smile. "I do, but as it happens, he *is* in town right now. I spoke to him earlier today. I didn't ask him where he was staying, but I can almost guarantee you that you can find him this evening at the Village Barn."

I frowned. "In Greenwich Village? That cornball country joint?"

Mulholland nodded. "Yes. Sidney is a great enthusiast of square dancing, and any weekend night he's in town, he can be found there."

"For the square dancing?"

"That's right. That's the kind of man he is. Born with a club foot, but he dances the night away."

Convincing Bettie Page to go out dancing was not a difficult chore. What had to be negotiated was what kind.

"The country swing," I said, "I'm fine with. We can go out and cut a helluva rug. But for me, square dancing is strictly a spectator sport."

We were in my room at the Waldorf. She was getting dressed to go out, and the stage she was at—black bra, sheer black panties, garter belt with sheer black nylons—made negotiations touch and go.

"Oh, sugah, it's fun as a hayride," she said, all that black hair fluffy around her pink shoulders. "Ah can give you all the basics and you'll be just fine. Why, ah been square dancin' since ah was—"

"Please don't say 'knee-high to a grasshopper,' " I said. "I don't think I could stand it."

"Ah was gonna say 'frog,' if that helps."

She shimmied herself into a sheathlike pale yellow dress. I'm sure I've seen more remarkable sights, but I can't think of one.

I unpopped my eyes and asked, "You really think you can square dance in that?"

"No. We're gonna stop by mah apartment and ah'll put on somethin' more appropriate to the occasion. Are you gonna wear that suit, honey? Ah mean, it's nice but maybe a sports jacket—"

"Have to," I said. "It's the only one I have along that's cut to conceal this." I opened the suit coat to show her the nine-millimeter in the shoulder harness.

She came over and put her hand somewhere interesting. "Never show a Southern gal your gun, honey, unless you mean it."

"Stop it," I said, grinning. "I have serious business to do tonight, and you can help out by being my date. If I go single, I'll have women all over me."

"That's some big ego you got there, honey," she said, grinning back, working her hand.

"No, it's that the Barn is famous as a pickup joint. Stop that."

She stepped back and raised the yellow dress over the black nylons and I was done for.

We had just finished—she was still leaning over the foot of the bed with that glorious bottom in the air—when the phone rang. I checked my watch—ten-fifteen. Sitting on the edge of the bed with my pants still around my ankles, I answered it on the fifth ring.

"Mr. Heller," Alice Olson said, "Nate. I have good news."

I'd spoken to her earlier this evening, giving her a somewhat laundered report on my visits with Abramson and Mulholland, including that I'd delivered a kind of ultimatum—that if she didn't hear from Frank before midnight, I would go to the authorities.

Well, she'd heard from him, just fifteen minutes ago.

"Frank sounded good," she said, upbeat for the first time. "He said he felt much better. He said everything is going to be fine."

"That's wonderful to hear, Alice. Did he say when you'd see him next?"

"Tomorrow," she said. "He wasn't sure exactly when, but . . . tomorrow."

"Anything else?"

She laughed a little. Actually laughed. "Just that he had to wash his socks out in the sink."

"That sounds pretty normal to me. What hotel is he at, did he say?"

"Yes. He's back at the Statler. He's in Room 1018a."

I jotted that down. "Should I go over there now . . . ?"

"No. He was getting ready for bed. Maybe first thing tomorrow?"

"Sure. Did you mention me to him?"

"No, but you were working for him, so he shouldn't be surprised seeing you."

"Okay, Alice. But stay in touch. If anything happens at all, I want to know about it. No matter the hour. You have the number here at the hotel. Let me give you Bettie's—that's where I may be later."

I did that.

"Nate," she said warmly, "I think you really helped."

"I tried to apply just the right amount of pressure," I said. "But it's tricky."

We said our goodbyes, and I hung up, but this seemed too easy. Too pat. This wouldn't be over until I'd been face-to-face with Dr. Sidney Gottlieb, even if it took a fucking hoedown to do it.

. . .

The Village Barn was next door to El Chico (small world), at 52 West Eighth Street. Going strong since 1930, the place held no appeal for most Village dwellers and took aim at tourists, right down to a bus prowling Times Square to haul them back for "Three Shows Nightly" and supper for a buck. The music was mostly country and folk, usually with one mainstream act on the bill, but hillbilly comedy acts were the staple—Judy Canova, whose hayseed shtick made her a movie star, got discovered here by that well-known rustic, Rudy Vallee.

Bettie and I descended a steep set of stairs into a huge, high-ceilinged club that consumed the basement and first floor of the building, turning the space into the barn that its name threatened. The rough-wood walls bore homespun sayings ("Lord willin' and the creek don't rise!") as well as wagon wheels, saddles, rakes, scythes, and harnesses, with horse collars and milk cans hanging off the rafters.

A sea of tables for four with linen tablecloths to dress the place up surrounded the good-size dance floor, with a bandstand designed to suggest a hayloft. Bettie and I were guided by a cowgirl to a ringside table. A bar was off to the right, the bartenders looking like extras in a Roy Rogers picture.

Bettie had changed into a red dress trimmed white, the upper half hugging her, the lower a full skirt, though without petticoats. The boots she had on were black leather with heels that I had a hunch were not designed for square dancing. I remained in my nine-millimeter-friendly Richard Bennett charcoal number, also not designed for square dancing.

Right now Bob Wills and His Texas Playboys were playing "Deep Water," a nice slow number that we danced to while my eyes searched the packed house for Sidney Gottlieb.

I had no photo to go on, but the description given me by Norman Cournoyer was distinctive enough: tall, wiry, mid-thirties, prematurely white-haired, handsome ("kind of a Jewish Gregory Peck," Cournoyer had said). A major tell would be his slight but noticeable limp of the right foot, where he wore a built-up shoe due to his club foot.

We danced some more to Wills, and then got back to our table for some shoofly pie and coffee, and I was about to throw in the towel when Wills announced his band would now have "the pleasure of playing for any of you true-blue square dancers out there." He turned the microphone over to one "Piute Pete," self-proclaimed "Greatest Hog-Caller East of the Rockies." Despite his straw hat and overalls, Pete looked more like somebody working the west side of a deli counter.

Couples and some singles, too, rushed the dance floor. Bettie tried to tug me along, but I said no, and she ran out there with little chance of not finding someone eager to partner up with her. Half a dozen groups of the dancers did the hog-caller's bidding (*"Choose your partners!"*) as I sat suffering through hokey fiddle playing and wild cries from the bandstand (*"Forward and back!"*) while I sorted through hooked elbows and do-si-doing and partner swinging (*"Make a basket and kick the bottom out!"*) in search of a mad scientist who would probably just love to see what effect LSD-25 would have on an allemande left.

*Was that him?*

He fit all the particulars—tall, slender, white-haired, handsome, dark-eyed—though would the evil genius of Deep Creek Lake really be wearing a plaid shirt, blue jeans with rolled-up cuffs, and tooled-leather cowboy boots?

The calls and fiddling and dancing went on for a good half hour before a break sent Bettie rushing over flushed and smiling to settle in next to me.

"That Piute Pete knows how to call a Girl from Arkansas," the Girl from Tennessee said, apparently referring to a specific dance.

"You sure had a good time," I said pointlessly, my brain elsewhere. I was figuring out how to approach this guy. First, I would go over to the bar and ask a bartender if he knew Sidney Gottlieb, who was supposedly something of a regular here, and if so, point out my suspect. . . .

But then I glanced up and the white-haired handsome man in blue jeans was knifing straight toward us, wearing a big grin that struck me as slightly demented. And now that he wasn't dancing, his gait betrayed a slight limp of the right leg, and a built-up boot heel.

I unbuttoned my suit coat.

He stopped abruptly at our table, and tucked his hands behind his back so he could half-bow.

"Excuse me," he said in a rather musical baritone, "but aren't you Bettie Page?"

His speech was measured, with space between each word, as if English were his second language; but that wasn't it: This was how he battled back his stammer.

She went all Scarlett O'Hara on him. "Why, yes ah am. But ah hardly *evah* get recognized."

He half-bowed again, this time bringing a hand around to touch his plaid-clad chest. "I'm such an admirer of your artistry, Miss Page. My name is Sid Gottlieb. Could I join you for a moment? Perhaps buy you and your friend a drink?"

Bettie glanced at me. I'd not shared the name of the subject of my search with her—in fact, I hadn't even told her I was searching—and she probably just thought a fan was crashing the party.

"Please," I said.

All his attention was on her. "You really know how to square dance, Miss Page. I had no idea you were a country gal."

"That's 'cause you can't hear me talk in my photos, honey."

He beamed as he took the chair opposite us. "You know, I think we have a mutual friend—John Coutts?"

She frowned just a little, shook her head, and all that hair came along for the ride. "Ah don't believe so."

He twitched another smile, shrugged. "Well, his sobriquet is John Willie. I had assumed you knew him, because he has so frequently used you as a model."

"Oh, *that* character. Ah've never actually met him. He just puts me in his silly magazines and does those comic strips about me. He doesn't pay me a *dime*." She turned to me to explain. "This Willie's a customer of Irving's."

Gottlieb folded his hands on the table and leaned in confidentially. "I hope you don't mind talking to an enthusiast of your bondage photos. Mr. Klaw does such a *fine* job as a photographer. I mean, they're all in good fun, right?"

"It's just actin', sugah. And actually, it's Irving's sister Paula who's the shutterbug. But ah think it's dirty pool that your friend Willie uses me in his funny books without mah permission. Meanin' no offense."

"None taken. Really, Coutts is only an acquaintance. A friend of a friend who exposed me to your work. I would *love* to have an autograph."

"You bet, sugah. . . . What was your name again?"

"Sid. Gottlieb."

She signed a Village Barn napkin to him with, "See you at the next barn dance!" Then she gestured to me and said, "Mr. Gottlieb, this is my gentleman friend—"

"Oh, I know who he is," Gottlieb said with a snake-oil salesman's smile. "He's Nathan Heller. The famous private investigator." Now his attention was on me. And mine had never left him. "But isn't that rather counterproductive, Mr. Heller?"

I gave him the kind of smile generally reserved for in-laws. "How so, Mr. Gottlieb?"

His eyebrows flicked up and down. "Well, in your profession, don't you count on going unrecognized? So you can do undercover work?"

"I have a staff for that kind of thing. But I suppose you're right that it's counterproductive. Rather like being a famous spy."

A half smile tickled thin lips. "Well, a spy would not make his picture available to the press, whereas you're splashed all over various magazines. I would imagine you'd have a difficult time finding a photograph of a master spy. Of course, I'm just guessing."

The hog-caller was back at the microphone.

Bettie gave a little "ooh" of excitement, then asked our guest if he'd care to be her partner on this next round.

"No, thank you," he said. "I'm still catching my breath. Go ahead, please. I'll chat with your friend while you dance."

Bettie flounced out.

"Mr. Heller," he said, in his measured way, "I must confess I was expecting . . . hoping . . . you would be here tonight."

"Might be hard to believe," I said, "but this is my first square dance."

*"Hang up your coat and spit on the wall! Choose your partners and promenade all!"*

"Square dancing is a great passion of mine," he said. "Actually, folk dancing in general is. Whenever I travel, I come back with new steps. And I've been to some very interesting places. Margaret . . . my wife, she's not here tonight . . . is as much an enthusiast as I am."

"You spoke to Mulholland," I said, blowing past the bullshit, "and he told you he'd sent me here to find you."

A little shrug. "And you found me."

"And you found *me*."

He looked at the autographed napkin with a smile. "You did us a favor, talking to Mulholland."

"Oh?"

*"Meet that gal and hold her tight! Don't forget your date for Saturday night!"*

He folded the napkin and slipped it in his shirt pocket. "You obviously didn't have to work very hard to fool him into telling you anything you wanted to know."

"That assumes he was telling me the truth. He's a magician. Maybe he was manipulating me."

"A possibility."

I shifted in my chair. "I'm assuming you spoke to Dr. Abramson as well."

"I did. And your mission is obviously a noble one, and I frankly feel some of my . . . subordinates . . . have handled this matter badly."

"The Frank Olson 'matter,' you mean?"

*"Run across and don't get lost, and give your opposite lady a toss!"*

He nodded. "Not keeping Dr. Olson's wife more in the know was thoughtless and a mistake. All we've been trying to do is help Frank. He's a valued colleague."

"Do you normally spike the drink of valued colleagues with a dangerous drug? Oh, well, I guess you do, since Olson was only one of, what? Ten? Eleven, at the retreat?"

He flipped a hand. "We all experiment on ourselves. That's the nature of what we do."

"I would think the nature of what you do would include some scientific controls. To a layman, this all seems fairly freewheeling."

*"Around you go, just like a wheel—the faster you go, the better you feel!"*

"Mr. Heller, I can assure you that everything that's been done these past several days has been with Dr. Olson's best interests at heart. My understanding is that he's phoned his wife and will be going home tomorrow."

"That's mine as well."

"Good. Then I believe we've reached the conclusion of this episode—and of your investigation. . . . What a lovely girl, Miss Page. So shockingly wholesome. I suppose that's why those pictures she poses for have such appeal. Just look at those leather boots."

*"Salute your corner lady, salute your partners all—swing your corner lady and promenade the hall!"*

He rose, nodded, and threaded through the sea of tables toward the exit, the limp barely discernible.

CHAPTER

At around 2:30 a.m., the cabbie let me out on the Penn Station side of a nearly deserted Seventh Avenue, and I'd just paid him, and he'd rolled off, when I heard the cry of *"Jesus!"* from across the street.

My eyes shot to a guy in full doorman's regalia, hat and all, but not in front of the Statler Hotel, rather rounding the corner from Thirty-third Street, and looking up like he'd just spotted Superman. In a split second, I'd followed his upward-jutting chin and pointing finger to the blur of white, in midair, coming from well above.

I stood frozen in disbelief as the blur became a man who seemed to be diving, hands in front of him. Then he twisted and was suddenly coming down feet-first, as if only he could land that way everything would be all right, but his hands knew better, clawing at the air above him as if trying to grab onto it. With the sidewalk waiting to meet him, he hit a wooden partition covering some work on the entrance area of the hotel bar, then bounced off the plywood wall, landing feet-first on the sidewalk with a sound like the cracking of thick crisp celery stalks.

*I already knew.*

It was a big hotel, the Statler, probably a couple of thousand rooms, and this could have been any unhappy guest who'd decided in a dark moment that the best way out of the place was through a high window.

*But I knew it wasn't just any guest.*

The Village Barn always stayed open late, the 1:30 a.m. show well under way when Bettie and I had finally left and walked over to her apartment. She was on the fourth floor, a walk-up, and the place was nothing to write home about but she'd made it cute, painting the walls pink here or lilac there, the furnishings a mix of atomic-age modern and nice secondhand '30s Art Moderne. We sat in the kitchenette at a little wooden table and had some brandy and she told me what a wonderful evening she'd had.

"But half the time you were somewhere else, sugah," she'd said. "What's on your mind? What's troublin' you?"

"There's something . . . somebody . . . I should check up on."

"Well, it isn't dawn yet. We can go out again."

"No, this is business. I've been trying to track down a woman's husband, and before we left she called and said she heard from him, and he's fine. So my job is probably over. But something . . ."

She touched my hand. "Honey, you go on and check that out, if you need to. Ah can wait here for you, and we can go back out tomorrow. Ah mean, you're only gonna be in town a few more days. Don't wanna waste it."

I was on my feet, grabbing my hat. "I'll only be forty-five minutes or an hour at most. I'll come take you out for breakfast, and then we'll sleep all day."

"We'll do *some* sleepin'," she said, and winked.

When I left, she had propped herself up on her sparkly salmon couch, a couple of throw pillows behind her, a metal-legged atomic lamp glowing on an end table, as she read a paperback, *One Lonely Night*. Knees up, she was still in the red dress, hiked enough to show the sort of garter belt and sheer black stockings rarely found beneath square-dance togs, the leather boots still on.

Now I had Penn Station to my back and was running across a street so dead that ducking traffic wasn't an issue, my trench coat flapping in air chilly enough to make breathing visible. The gaping uniformed doorman was leaning over the apparent jumper, who was on his back, in a white undershirt and white boxers, one arm outstretched, fingers extended, reaching like David in the Sistine

Chapel, only God wasn't around. The fallen man's legs were together, twisted to one side, a pool of shimmering red spreading out from under him; a scattering of broken glass, like shaved ice in a cocktail, glittered with reflected light from the hotel's main entrance maybe forty feet away.

Frank Olson looked up at me, his pale green eyes filled with pain, his mouth filled with blood. The latter didn't stop him from trying to speak, though nothing came out but a gurgle.

The doorman, skinny, mustached, in his early twenties, had eyes wilder than Olson's; in the doorman livery, he looked like he'd wandered out of a high school production of *The Student Prince*.

He said, "I just slipped away for a drink. I didn't abandon my post or anything!"

Olson was groaning, gurgling, looking up at me.

"Never mind that," I said. What, did he think he might have reached out and caught the guy in his arms like an eloping bride from a bedroom window? "Go call for help, and get your night manager out here. *Now.*"

A few people had emerged from nearby bars and from the train station—not many yet, maybe five, six—and I said loudly, *"Police! Stay back!"*

They obeyed, to some degree anyway.

Olson was trying to speak again. His eyes cried blood and scarlet streamed from his nose and ears too; as he tried to speak, all he produced was frothy red bubbles.

I got a handkerchief out and gently wiped the foam away. "Hang on, Frank. Help's coming."

He didn't have a goddamn prayer, but he didn't need to hear it from me.

"Did you jump, Frank?" I whispered. "Or were you pushed?"

His only answer was a tortured expression that could have meant anything, including that nothing was registering but pain.

A dark stocky round-faced man in a dark blue Statler-crested blazer and light blue trousers knelt opposite me, his face taut with concern.

"Just hold on," he said to the bleeding sprawled figure. "You'll be okay."

He looked across at me, almost reaching his hand out for me to shake but thinking better of it. "Armand Pastore. Night manager. Someone said you're police. . . ."

"Nathan Heller," I said. "Ex-cop actually, but a licensed investigator. I thought somebody needed to take charge till the officers arrived."

He nodded his somber approval. His eyes and mouth were slits, his nose somewhat bulbous; but kindness lived in the blunt features.

I wondered if I should tell him that I knew this man; but in these circumstances, I figured I'd better play it tight.

The doorman came up behind the night manager. "Ambulance on the way, sir. I called the Fourteenth Precinct, too. What else?"

"This sidewalk is freezing," Pastore said, breath pluming. "Fetch him a blanket." Then, sotto voce, face turned to the boy, he added, "But, uh, call Saint Thomas Church first—see if anybody answers. Get a priest."

The kid nodded and ran off.

Pastore looked across at me again. "It's nearby, Saint Thomas. Stay with him, Mr., uh, Heller, is it?"

I nodded.

"Stay with him and I'll get these gawkers away." He got up and, in a voice much bigger than he was, ordered people to stay back. To make room for the ambulance that was on its way.

I was crouched there. The blood would have soaked my trousers if I'd knelt. I leaned in and again whispered.

"Frank—were you pushed?"

His eyes jumped, but that didn't mean *he* had. Sounds rose from his chest, his throat, but by the time they reached the bubbling mouth, what came out was incoherent mumbling.

"Did you jump, Frank?"

More frothy red mumbling.

"Blink once for yes, twice for no."

Gurgling.

"Were you pushed?"

He blinked four or five times, but that seemed to be just getting the blood out of his eyes as best he could. *Wasn't it?*

The doorman was back with a folded woolen blanket.

Pastore came over and took it from him.

"I don't know what's taking the ambulance so long," the night manager said.

I said, "It's only been a few minutes."

He and I covered Olson with the blanket, and the broken man groaned like a guy having a bad dream. I eased the blanket over where a section of shattered bone was poking out of his left arm.

A white-haired priest came rushing across Seventh Avenue, folded shawl and Bible in hand. Behind him were two uniformed officers. Pastore rose and so did I, as the priest slipped on his shawl and went to Olson's side and knelt, blood be damned, and began administering Last Rites.

The hotel man and I met the cops.

"Armand Pastore, night manager, Officers."

He shook their hands. One cop was in his mid-thirties, the other pushing fifty. The older one, as if asking the time, said, "Jumper?"

Pastore shrugged. "I guess so."

The seasoned cop turned to me. "Are you the house dick?"

"No," I said, and I got out my identification. "Nathan Heller. Private investigator, ex-cop, second on the scene after that doorman."

"We'll take it from here, Mr. Heller."

*Should I tell them why I had really come?*

I said, "Let me know if I can help."

The two cops immediately went into crowd-control mode. Maybe a dozen people had gathered by now and they got them well back.

That allowed me to return to Olson's side, where the priest had finished his work. I crouched where earlier Pastore had been.

"Hear that siren, Frank?" I asked. "Help's almost here. But before they get you to the medics, tell me—were you pushed?"

His right hand grabbed my arm, clutching; his head came up,

just slightly, lips moving, eyes wide with urgency, dripping blood
tears. I leaned closer. He took a deep bubbling breath, let it out, and
was gone.

I rose.

"Shit," I said to nobody.

*A man was dead. It was nothing new—people died all the time. But
Frank Olson had been my responsibility and somehow I'd let him, and his
wife, down. Whether LSD-25 had taken him through that window, or
Uncle Sam's minions had given him a push, this dead man was still my
responsibility. And I wouldn't let him down twice.*

I looked around. The two cops were dealing with a dozen people
now. The doorman was checking anybody who wanted to go inside
the hotel.

*Where had Pastore got to?*

Then I spotted the night man, across the street, standing on the
curb in front of Penn Station, facing his hotel. He was looking up,
slowly scanning the front of the big building. I jogged across, stopping for a moment for a lone cab to pass, then fell in beside him.

"He had to come from somewhere," the night manager said.

*Room 1018a*, I thought.

"That look on that poor bastard's face," he said, shaking his
head. "I'll never forget it. But I saw that before."

"Yeah?"

"During the war. Italy. France. That look that says a guy knows
that life is over for him."

". . . I saw it before too, Mr. Pastore."

"Where?"

"Guadalcanal. What's that?"

"What's what?"

I pointed. "There, that window shade. High up. Over to the
left. It's pulled way down, outside the window—watch the breeze
catch it."

"I see it!"

Then he raised a finger high as if testing the wind and began
counting to himself.

MAX ALLAN COLLINS —

"What are you up to?" I asked.

"I think I can figure out which room that is. . . ."

*1018a.*

The ambulance arrived with an unnecessary scream. Attendants clambered out and began dealing with what was now a corpse. The small crowd watched, and thinned, the two policeman maintaining order. No more cops had shown yet.

Pastore said, "I'm pretty sure it's 1018a. I'm going to get our security man to check it out."

"I'll go with you. But let me clear it with those two boys in blue first. I'll meet you at the front desk."

He nodded. "I'll see if any of our people have gotten calls from guests about jumpers. Maybe somebody saw something."

We moved across the street together, then Pastore rounded the front end of the ambulance to head into the hotel, while I went over and sought out the older cop. He had a bucket head and eyes that had seen everything twice.

I asked him, "Are plainclothes dicks coming over from the precinct?"

"Eventually."

"Well, the hotel manager thinks he may know which room belonged to the jumper. He wants to check it out. With your permission, I'll go with him."

"Might be better to wait, bud."

"It's Heller. And that night man can go where he likes in his hotel. As an investigator with a New York license, I'm an officer of the court. Maybe you'd feel more comfortable with me keeping an eye on him, till the detectives get here."

He thought about that, then nodded. "Yeah. Keep him out of trouble, Mr. Heller. Appreciate it."

I nodded back and headed in, the ambulance doors shutting with clanging finality as I passed.

As the vehicle pulled away without a siren, I went in and crossed the vast high-ceilinged ornate lobby to the endless front desk. Two clerks were on duty, giving the place a ghost-town feel. Out in front of the counter, Pastore was waiting for me with a pale slender guy in his late twenties, sharp-featured, also in a dark blue Statler-crested blazer and lighter blue slacks.

"This is my security man," Pastore said, "John Martin."

"Mr. Heller," the house dick said, extending a hand for me to shake, which I did.

I said, "Do I know you from somewhere, Mr. Martin?"

"Don't think so," he said with a mild smile on his knife-blade face. "But I worked hotels all over town. Say, I checked the rooftop doors. They're all locked. So our guest didn't jump from there."

Pastore started shaking his head halfway through that. "No, he came out the window of Room 1018a."

A frown formed on the security man's narrow face. "How do you know that?"

"I started with the window with that shade flapping, counted the number of windows above it, and then the adjoining ones toward the west end of the building. No question, it's Room 1018a."

"Nice work," I said. "But that flapping shade looked higher up to me than ten floors."

"It is," Pastore said. "It's really the thirteenth floor—we don't count the lower public floors."

Behind the check-in counter, a nice-looking brunette in the standard blue blazer spoke up: "Sir, here it is! The registration card for Room 1018a."

Pastore went over and she passed it across to him. "Thank you, Miss Stevens."

She wasn't through: "And as you asked, I checked with the switchboard girl—no one has called down to us from that room."

He said, "I'd better talk to her myself," and he disappeared behind the counter.

Maybe a minute and a half later, Pastore came back, reading aloud to us from the registration card: "Two names—Robert Lashbrook and Frank R. Olson. Lashbrook from Washington, D.C., Olson from Frederick, Maryland. No home telephone numbers listed. Registered about ten hours ago."

The security man said, "Let's check it out—I have my passkey."

"Good."

I brought up the rear as Pastore led the slender security man to the bank of elevators.

We got on and as we went up, the young man said to Pastore, "You don't really think the other guy's still in there, do you? I mean, if you were in a room and the person you were staying with went out the window . . . wouldn't *you* get out?"

"I don't know what to think," Pastore said, shaking his head.

"No one called down from that room," I reminded them.

At the tenth floor—or was it the thirteenth?—the night manager led the way, the security guy behind him with me once again trailing. At this time of night, actually morning, the floor was dead quiet. The carpeting was thick, the hallway wallpaper a bit dingy—the Statler, formerly the Pennsylvania, was one of those grand old hotels that maintained a lovely lobby while the rest of the place turned slowly shabby.

At 1018a, the stocky little night manager pressed an ear to the door and listened.

He drew back. "Nothing," he said softly.

He gave the door two rather soft knocks.

Nothing.

Two slightly louder ones, and still nothing.

Then he tried the door—locked.

Handing his boss the passkey, the security man whispered, "Sir, there won't be anybody in there."

Pastore stood poised to work the key in the lock, then his face seized up with thought and he backed away. He motioned and gathered us in a small group down the hall.

Quietly, he said, "If some son of a bitch went off his head and tossed his friend out the window, he could still be in there. Who *knows* what we're walking into? Let's wait for the police to come."

The security man said, "Good idea."

I stepped forward, drawing the nine-millimeter from under my suit coat. "Gentlemen, I *am* the police. Mr. Martin, take that key from Mr. Pastore and open that door for me."

The young man looked at his boss, who said, "No, I'll open it. You can go in first, Mr. Heller."

I shook my head. "You're right about the danger. I'm going in alone. Stay out here till I say otherwise."

The night manager accepted that, then unlocked the door and hopped quickly aside, and I pushed in.

But for spill-in light from the hall behind me, the room was dark, and chilly with outside air, the flapping of the window shade like lazy applause. In a few steps, to my right, light edged the nearly closed bathroom door.

Nine-millimeter ready, I nudged the door open with my foot.

Seated on the toilet, lid down, was a man wearing—like Frank Olson—a white T-shirt and white boxers. Lanky, mid-thirties, sandy-haired with a big cranium, straight nose, and bulb chin, the man sat slouched, head in his hands, as if lost in thought or maybe weeping. But when he looked up at me his eyes were not moist, not even red.

I said, "Robert Lashbrook?"

He reached for his glasses by the sink and put them on, but remained seated on the toilet. The small white bathroom had a jaundiced, unremodeled look; hanging over the shower rod were a pair of socks and an undershirt.

"Yes," he said in a controlled baritone. "You're with the police?"

If he recognized me from a photo any of his colleagues might have shared, it didn't show. I saw no reason to help him.

Still in the bathroom doorway, I nodded. "Didn't you hear us knocking out there?"

"No."

I put the nine-millimeter away, but left both the trench coat and suit coat unbuttoned.

I asked, "What happened here?"

"I heard a sound," he said. "I woke up and saw my friend, Frank

Olson, standing in the middle of the room. Then, at a dead run, he plunged through the window. Glass and all."

That had a hell of a rehearsed sound to me—maybe he'd been sitting in here cooking that up.

"You didn't call down to the desk," I said.

"No."

"You didn't go down to check on your friend?"

"I went over to the window. I leaned out and saw Frank lying there down on the sidewalk. What could I do? People were rushing toward him, from the train station and around. I could see he had help. So I waited for . . . for you people . . . and just stayed put."

"Well, keep doing that," I said.

I left him there and went to the light switch just inside the door, gesturing to Pastore to remain where he was. The security man was no longer around.

The switch triggered a nightstand lamp between two twin beds. Cold air continued to rush in. Against the right-side wall were a small portable television on a stand, a dresser with a mirror, and an armchair in the corner with a small reading table. The bed closer to the window had its covers on the floor, in a pile, as if a sleeper had woken and thrown them off.

Or had they been yanked off the sleeper and dumped there?

I returned to the john, where Lashbrook sat with his hands clasped between open legs. "Which bed is Olson's?"

"Nearest the window," he said, not looking at me.

I checked around and under and in the bed and found nothing that seemed of import. The nearby single window was gone but for a few random teeth of glass sticking from the frame. A radiator in front of the window showed no shattered glass on or behind it; no shards on the sill or carpet, either.

*Could Olson really have made a run for this window? If he was contemplating suicide, wouldn't he open it first? The window had been closed, the shade down. And in this small room, how could he have gotten up enough speed to make the "dead run" Lashbrook claimed he'd witnessed? And what about that radiator in the way?*

I went to the nightstand. The wallet there proved to be Lashbrook's, with various government IDs in it—Department of Defense, U.S. Army Chemical Center, and Central Intelligence Agency. Also in the wallet were individual slips with Abramson's office and home numbers and addresses; the same for magician John Mulholland; and another with no name but a phone number (Oregon 5-0257) and an address (81 Bedford Street, in Greenwich Village) but no name. There was also a key to a Yale lock with a "2B" etched on it. I slipped that in my pocket.

In the hall, I asked Pastore if he had a handkerchief. He gave me one. Mine had gotten bloody down on the sidewalk, dabbing Olson's mouth. Using the hanky, I did my best not to leave any of my prints or to smudge anyone else's as I gave the room a quick thorough search, primarily checking dresser and nightstand drawers, and also going through each man's lightly packed suitcase. Nothing meaningful turned up—to me, anyway.

Finally I checked the closet and found a hanger with a pair of dark dress slacks. I took them to Lashbrook, who was still sitting in the bathroom, and dangled them in front of him. "Are these yours?"

He shook his head. "Frank's."

"You wouldn't happen to know where your friend's wallet is? It's not in his pants or on the nightstand."

"I think he might have lost it a couple of nights ago."

"Why don't you elaborate."

He thought for a moment. "My friend was suffering from ulcers."

"Well, that explains it."

He tried again. "Frank's been having some mental problems. Wednesday night we went to a play—*Me and Juliet*, Rodgers and Hammerstein. It had some lighting effects that upset him. He rushed out at intermission, but I settled him down and we had something to eat and he seemed all right. But then he slipped out of our room during the night and threw his wallet with all his identification and money in it down a sewer grating. Or so he said."

*A man who wanted to disappear might well throw his identification away. A man who had visited a magician in the CIA's employ might have tossed his wallet, too, if he thought it or the money in it had gotten coated with something toxic.*

Lashbrook was saying, quite calmly, "In the morning, Frank wasn't in his bed. Thanksgiving morning. I found him sitting in the lobby with his hat and coat on. He had kind of a rough day after that."

"Mental problems, huh?"

"Yes."

"And you thought checking him into the tenth floor of a hotel was a good idea?"

He looked at me, harder. ". . . Who are you? What's your name?"

"I'll check my wallet and let you know. Just sit there."

With the door onto the hall standing open, I was able to hear the faint ding of the elevator, which probably meant the real cops had arrived.

As two seasoned-looking detectives came down the long dreary hall toward us, I asked Pastore, "You been a hotel man long?"

"All my working life."

"Ever hear of somebody getting up in the middle of the night, running across a room in his underwear, and diving into a closed window with the shade down?"

"Nothing like it," he said. He shivered. "Christ, at least when Murder Incorporated threw Kid Twist out that Coney Island hotel window, they *opened* the damn thing first."

I grinned at him. I liked him, and patted him on the shoulder.

"What kind of monster is this 'friend'?" he asked bitterly. "His buddy down there bleeding on the pavement. You know, he made a phone call, this Lashbrook. Or did I mention that already?"

"No. You didn't."

"I checked with the switchboard girl, to see if he called down."

"And he didn't. Yeah, you told us that."

"No, but he *did* make a *call*—out to Long Island."

Dr. Abramson.

I asked, "Your girl didn't happen to listen in?"

"Well, actually she did. Sometimes, when it's slow, they do that, these girls. Wasn't much of a conversation—just, 'He's gone,' this Lashbrook says. And the guy on the other end says, 'That's too bad.' And they both hung up."

I spent fifteen minutes with the dicks, left them my card, and got the hell out of there. I doubted they'd get any further with Lashbrook than I had. Out front, nobody was around and the doorman was glumly mopping up the blood. I caught a cab and when I got to Bettie's apartment, I hadn't even been gone an hour.

I knocked at her door but she didn't answer—it was ajar and my knocking swung the door open onto an empty apartment. That gave me a bad feeling, though there was no sign of any problem, much less a struggle—everything was pink and lilac and as pretty as the woman who lived here.

But who *wasn't* here.

I'd been looking around the place for any indication of a problem for maybe three minutes when the phone rang.

Smiling, thinking it was Bettie, I answered and quickly the smile went away.

"We've got your girl," a male voice said. "Don't do anything. Don't say anything to anybody. Stay right where you are. And maybe you'll get her back."

The line went dead.

As dead as Frank Olson.

As dead as some other people were going to be.

# 21
CHAPTER

Bedford Street in the Village was in a residential section where trees and narrow streets provided a contrast to the nightlife of nearby Sheridan Square. Structures told a scattered history of the city—here a remodeled farmhouse with twin gables, there an old three-story frame building, down the way a group of two-story-and-dormer houses from the nineteenth century. Number 81, on the corner of Bedford and Barrow, was a converted stable of ancient brick, now a small apartment house. The lower-floor windows were dark, but on the second floor, light smudged the glass like a threat of dawn.

At just after 4 a.m., I was alone on the street. The door to number 81 was at the left of the narrow-fronted building, wide enough for two windows below and three above. Up five steps to the stoop, a dead-bolt lock awaited me, but the key I'd pocketed from Lashbrook's wallet was a Yale. That was no great surprise—I'd figured that was an apartment key (2B)—so I got out my little sheath of lock picks from my wallet, selected the tension-wrench and short-hook picks, and started in.

With my back to the street, I presented a picture of a well-dressed man in a Burberry trench coat and Dobbs hat, having a little trouble working the key in his door—tipsy maybe?—as long as no one noticed the scarlet-brown edging along the coat's bottom, where Frank Olson's blood had touched it. But with not a single pedestrian and only a couple of cars to roll past, the risk was slight. I was out of practice at picking a lock, so it took almost twenty seconds.

Once inside, no vestibule awaited, only darkness. I got out the nine-millimeter. Minimal street light seeped in through a transom window and revealed, at right, a hallway that gave access to two side-by-side apartments in this boxcar of a building, while at left, a steep stairway yawned upward before me. This interior had been remodeled in recent years and had a bland newness at odds with the building's history.

The stairs were carpeted and I went up in silence, the automatic in my fist like a flashlight leading the way. The layout echoed the first floor, a hallway (hemmed by a railing that continued on from the banister) with two side-by-side apartments—2A, 2B. Light seeped under the door to 2A like spilt milk. I pressed my ear to the door and listened, the way Pastore had outside Olson's hotel room.

Conversation.

I couldn't discern any words—too muffled—but it was two men. They occasionally laughed. Some music was playing, a radio or a record player, instrumental, upbeat. Maybe Latin—"April in Portugal"? Somebody was having a good time tonight, even if it wasn't me. But who knew? Maybe after while things would turn around. . . .

My gun and I moved quietly down the hall. Had my key been to 2A, not 2B, life might have been simpler, although the click of the key opening the lock could signal my arrival and that might complicate things. Maybe I was better off this way.

Anyway, I had a feeling these two apartments connected—I made this as a CIA safe house, a facility where out-of-town agents could meet and even bunk in, where witnesses could stay under protection, where suspected bad guys could be questioned unofficially and possibly brutally.

No light escaped from under the door to 2B. Again, I leaned my ear to the wood, but heard nothing—not even a faint echo of the festivities in the apartment next door.

Using my left hand, I inserted the Lashbrook key in the lock and turned it till it clicked open. I turned the knob slowly, pushed the door open the same way, then closed it quietly behind me. A floor lamp with a zebra shade was on in a large living room with modern furnishings, walls painted red with white trim, off-white shag carpet, and bizarre sexually charged touches, from pinup-bottomed ashtrays to heart-shaped throw pillows, from bisque nude figurines to lamps with nude-girl bases.

Those red walls bore large elaborately gold-framed posters of racy French images—Toulouse-Lautrec can-can girls, a topless beaming wench opening a spurting bottle of Perrier champagne, a blonde leaning back with her graceful arms and hands above her, barely covered by a filmy black negligee ("Naughty Revue of 1952!").

Here and there, mounted on the wall, were exotic items that while not overtly sexual added to the general air of depravity—a Burmese spirit mask, a Tachi sword, a large hand-carved opium pipe. The right half of the wall on the street end was mirrored, with glass shelving holding a virtual library of booze behind a glass-brick ebony-topped bar with a handful of stools—leopard-skin seats and chromium stems.

*What the fuck was this place?*

It screamed high-end brothel, but wasn't set up to handle more than a john or two at most.

A door led to a bedroom, which was all but filled by a double bed with black silk sheets and a contemporary bookcase—headboard filled not with volumes but small pornographic Indian and Oriental statuettes of women demonstrating their acrobatic abilities and their potential to add new pages to the *Kama Sutra*.

Using Pastore's handkerchief (which was apparently mine now), I checked the nightstand drawers: more Trojans than had fought over Helen. Also various lubricants and tissues. The drawer below that offered handcuffs, a black blindfold, a black whip, a leather collar, leather ankle restraints, and a red ball gag.

On the wall facing the bed, over a low-slung dresser with a row of liquor bottles, was a big picture window of a mirror. Always a good whorehouse prop—many a man likes to see himself having his way with a beautiful naked woman.

*And I bet any men on the other side of that mirror also liked to watch . . . .*

A so-called two-way mirror is really just glass treated to be partly reflective and partly transparent—a brightly illuminated room on one side can be viewed on the other by watchers in the dark. That meant the johns lured here would be getting precious little mood lighting. Maybe their wives only liked it with the lights off and this made for a nice, bright change of pace. . . .

In the bathroom off the bedroom, a closet's fake rear wall was a door that easily nudged open onto a smallish room—with thick carpet on the floors, walls, and ceiling—that was set up to observe the bedroom I'd just examined and an identical one in the adjacent 2A. RCA reel-to-reel recorders were on the carpeted floor near each big window, by stacked tape boxes; and a pair of Kodak 16mm movie cameras were positioned facing in opposite directions to capture both rooms through their respective "mirrors."

Otherwise, this control booth was strictly Spartan—first Trojans, now Spartans—with decorations limited to thumbtacked black-and-white photographs on the carpeted walls of couples in those identical bedrooms doing what came naturally, and sometimes unnaturally. Four straight-backed wooden chairs were available for views on the proceedings. The only creature comfort was a small refrigerator stocked with bottles of beer. I wondered how often the DeMilles here had sneaked back into a bathroom to take a leak while a call girl and her john were covering the pissing sound with bed springs.

Okay. So a call girl helped get the goods on somebody in this setup—a politician? A Soviet spy who needed turning? Could be anything or anybody of that sort. And right now I didn't really give a damn.

What mattered was that two men were in that adjacent apartment, and Bettie was in there with them, as their unwilling guest.

That was my guess, anyway—and I was counting on being right, because I had nowhere else to look.

But they, and for that matter she, were not in either bedroom that the two-way mirrors revealed.

A small knob in the carpeted wall opened the hidden door that let me into the bathroom off the 2A bedroom, which was identical to 2B's—booze bottles lined up like soldiers on a dresser just in front of the mirror, a bed with its own black silk sheets and collection of obscene statuettes, and nightstand drawers again filled with rubbers and bondage gear.

The door here onto 2A's living room was slightly ajar, making the conversation of the two men audible. So was the music—sounded like the radio to me, Tony Bennett doing "Stranger in Paradise."

Nine-millimeter in hand, barrel up, I leaned ever so gently against the door and took advantage of the two-inch view it provided.

Not surprisingly, I was looking into another gaudy sexed-up living room with framed French posters and nude lamps and heart-shaped pillows. But this layout had something the other one didn't . . .

. . . *the one and only Queen of the Pinups, Bettie Page in the flesh, in black bra and panties with garter belt and sheer black stockings and leather high-heel boots, rope-tied at the ankles and wrists and elbows and above and below her breasts into a red vinyl open-arm armchair.*

All that separated this from an Irving Klaw photo shoot was the lack of a ball gag, but then they hadn't needed to gag her at all, at least not yet—she appeared dazed, groggy, the sky-blue eyes open but unfocused, her head lolling slightly, the black shoulder-brushing pageboy moving as if in slow motion.

*The bastards had drugged her—had they used that same LSD-25 junk? The stuff at Deep Creek Lake that had started the chain of events that led to Frank Olson's exit out a thirteenth-floor window?*

They were talking, over Tony Bennett's vocals, and one male voice, mid-register, said, "If we *do* that, you know what that means."

A raspy, lower-register male voice responded: "We're over the fuckin' line *already*, Johnny boy."

"Sid wouldn't like it." The voice on the phone from Bettie's. "He's *already* put out with us."

Bettie's eyelashes were fluttering like loopy butterflies as she gently rocked in the chair, apparently hearing none of it.

"What!" the raspy voice came back derisively. "You think the mad doc'll *really* give the bimbo back to Heller? And, what, let them two go skippin' off like Jack and Jill up the hill? Not before breakin' their fuckin' *crowns* he won't."

"Who can say? Not our call."

The voice on the phone walked past their woozy captive, who still showed no sign of any awareness. He headed toward what I figured was the apartment's bar setup, which should be over to my left, giving me a good look at him.

"Him" being John Martin, the security man at the Statler, still in his damn blue blazer with the hotel's crest, though his tie was off and the jacket hung open so that the .45 Colt stuffed in his waistband could be easily accessed.

*I knew I'd seen that sharp-featured punk somewhere!*

He'd been one of the CIA bunch who'd rushed into the Morton Street art gallery when the shit hit the fan. Not the blond guy in charge who I mostly dealt with, but the one who knelt over Natalie Ash's body, checking for signs of life that weren't there to be found.

Martin called from the bar, "Can I get you anything, Vince?"

And Vince, the raspy-voice guy, stepped past Bettie and into my line of vision . . .

*. . . and him I'd seen before, too!*

He was big and bullnecked with neatly slicked-back black hair and scar tissue over one eye that gave it a distinctive droop. In a white shirt with no tie, collar open, sleeves rolled to his elbows, and a pair of dark trousers, he clutched in his right fist a .38 Smith & Wesson that was probably the same gun I'd taken off him months ago at the Waldorf.

Vince had been the spokesman of the pair of thugs that Frank Costello had sent to my Waldorf suite at Roy Cohn's bidding, once upon a time. But what the hell could he be doing here? How could the CIA be in bed with the mob? What lunacy was this?

"What you can *get* me," Vince said, and his thick moist upper lip pulled back over big yellowish tobacco-stained teeth, "is some of them bedroom gimmicks—handcuffs and whips and shit. Come on, Johnny boy, it's been a rough night! Why not reward ourselves with a little fun?"

The Statler security man stepped back into view, a tumbler of amber liquid in his right hand, his back mostly to me.

"No," he said firmly. "We're already in Dutch with Sid. We play this straight. Anyway, hell—I'm not *about* to force myself on some helpless girl."

Revolver at his side, the thug stood near Bettie, who was still out of it, head hanging a little, eyes showing as much expression as golf balls.

"I mean, Johnny boy, *look* at what she had on under that dress," he rasped, waving the .38 at her, his mouth wet. "*This* ain't some innocent kid! She's beggin' for it! She's one sweet piece of ass and I mean to tear some off for myself."

I went in and he looked at me and I shot him in the head.

Bettie jerked a little, probably mostly at the ring of the gunshot, which slightly preceded the *glop* of brains and bone and blood splattering onto the glass of a framed Toulouse-Lautrec, where the stuff slid and streaked and dripped like lumpy cake batter.

The Statler kid dropped his drink and goggled at me but put his hands up, facing me now. He looked very young and very pale.

"Fuck," he said. "Heller."

Bettie raised her head a little, frowning like she was trying to make out an impossible eye chart.

"I knew I'd seen you," I said. "Are you going to make me kill you, kid? Not that I'd lose sleep."

Tony Bennett had passed the musical ball to Johnnie Ray, who was doing "Cry."

*Our* "Johnnie" swallowed. His lower lip was quivering. Maybe he'd cry, too. "Just take her and go, will you? I was against this anyway."

I grinned at him. "Well, that's nice to hear. But what about this dead hoodlum? Nice company you keep, John."

He was keeping those hands up nice and high. "Things got away from us tonight. Just spun out of control. You have to believe that."

"Oh, I believe it. I wasn't thinking everything had gone strictly to plan. Is Gottlieb coming?"

He swallowed thickly. "Who?"

I kept the nine-millimeter trained on him. "That's the 'Sid' you and the dead asshole were discussing."

Martin sucked in air, visibly trembling now. "I . . . I think Sid'll be along sometime. But maybe not till morning."

"This *is* morning, John."

He worked up the sickliest smile I ever saw. "Why don't you let me untie the girl, and you just take her. Just take her out of here. You said it before . . ."

He nodded toward Vince, who was on his back staring at the ceiling, mouth open, the yawn of a man permanently asleep.

". . . this is just a dead hoodlum. He'll be disposed of. Like you never did a thing here. But you do something to *me*, and that won't be so easy for the Agency to forgive."

"Oh, and I would *so* like the Agency's forgiveness. They seem to be so very understanding."

He ignored the sarcasm, bobbing his head toward Bettie, his expression hopeful. "So . . . should I? Untie her?"

"What did you give her? That LSD-25 crap?"

He shook his head. "No. Just a sedative to keep her quiet. She'll be fine. I swear!"

"Untie her then."

He nodded, swallowed again, and went over and knelt and undid the ropes that bound her ankles to the chair. She looked down at him, puzzled, as if she'd never seen a dog so big. He rose and, as he seemed about to begin work on untying her left wrist, he bolted around behind her and then the big automatic was in his hand.

And its snout in her neck.

The beauty in black lingerie raised her eyebrows as if she'd nodded off in class and the teacher had just called her name.

"All right, you son of a bitch," Martin said, a new edge in his voice, a nasty smile going, eyes tight and menacing. He suddenly didn't seem so young. "You just back your ass on out of here. Later, I may let her go, if Dr. Gottlieb approves it. If I were you, I'd head to your hotel—the Waldorf, isn't it?—and wait until someone contacts you. Personally, I don't think any harm will come to either you or the girl here. But it's not my place to decide."

She was seated there, oblivious, his pale face floating above hers like a seance trick, his chin almost touching the top of her head, the .45 dimpling her throat under her ear.

I said, "You're new at this, aren't you?"

"Fuck you, Heller. Get the hell out of here. *Now!*"

"I don't think you CIA boys get the training the FBI guys do. You're too collegiate. Too upper-crust."

"Shut up! Get out!"

"Were you absent that day?"

"What fucking day?"

"The day they taught you what happens with a head shot."

"Well, it fucking kills you."

"Yes. Immediately."

I fired and a third eye appeared in his forehead that did not signal enlightenment, rather a blankness that his other eyes mimicked, the bullet going through to spiderweb a Folies Bergère poster and spray lacy petticoats a glittering red. He lingered for a moment on his dead legs and feet, as if the Statler blazer were holding him up, though his arm with the gun fell at once to his side and the weapon tumbled with a thud from fingers no longer getting signals from the brain I'd shut off, and then as if every bone in his body had melted, he fell in a pile.

Bettie just sat there, numbly, like Ethel Rosenberg waiting for another jolt.

I came over, holstered the nine-millimeter, and untied her wrists and elbows and removed the ropes binding her to the chair. She began to come around, shaking her head, blinking, opening her eyes wide, and her mouth, as if trying to make sure everything still worked.

Her face swung toward me, and so did the black hair. "What . . . what *happened*? Nathan! Where *am* I? What's that awful . . . smell?"

"Death," I said.

The coppery tang of blood gave highlights to the foul bouquet of bodies evacuating waste.

I helped her onto her feet. Normally she was good in those exaggerated heels, but she was shaky now. She looked right. She looked left. She pointed at this body. She pointed at that one.

"Did you . . . ? *Those* are the two who came to mah place and . . . Are they *dead*?"

"Very," I said. "They tried to kill us both."

She blinked several times, as if fighting dizziness. "How . . . how did you *find* me?"

"Not important. Your dress is over in the corner. Put it on and let's get the hell out of here."

Her eyes went from corpse to corpse again. "Shouldn't we call the police?"

"No. Trust me on that. This never happened. What did they give you? They drugged you some way or another."

She swallowed, leaned on me. "They held a cloth near my nose and mouth. Must have been chloroform."

At least they hadn't held it to that pretty face, because it would have scarred her. As if this hadn't. . . .

I walked her to the red square-dance dress. Dazed though she was, she didn't need help slipping it on. For once, there was nothing erotic at all about it.

I said, "Did they make you drink anything?"

She shook her head, black hair brushing off her shoulders. "Didn't make me. Asked if ah was thirsty, after ah came around. . . ."

"Were you tied in the chair then?"

She nodded. "Yes. Ah said ah was *terrible* thirsty and they gave me some Coke Cola."

I grunted a sigh. "It may have been spiked with a drug. How are you feeling?"

"Better. Little off mah feed, but . . . better."

We were heading for the door when it opened and he stepped in—Dr. Sidney Gottlieb, a raincoat over his plaid shirt and blue jeans, to the top of his cowboy boots. He hadn't had a chance to change. The absurdity of it might have made me laugh, if we weren't sharing the living room with dead men.

"My God," he said, his eyes going from one corpse to another, shutting the door quietly behind him. "What have you *done*?"

"What have *you* done, Doctor?" I asked, getting the nine-millimeter out and pointing it at him, holding Bettie to me with an arm around her slender waist.

He raised his hands about chest-high, palms out. We were maybe six feet apart. "I have no weapon. I'm not a vuh-violent person."

I left Bettie to go over and pat him down. No gun. Of course, he might have a poisoned needle on his wedding ring or maybe a raincoat pocket full of poison pills. With this fucker, you never knew.

Returning to Bettie, keeping my gun trained on him, I slipped my free arm around her waist again and said, "Let's hear your story, Doc."

"No story," he said, hands still up, but something casual about it. His short hair gave him a Julius Caesar look. "These two foul-ups killed a man tonight, a man they were supposed to help."

"They were supposed to *help* Frank Olson?"

He nodded emphatically. "That's right. We had scheduled him to go into a hospital, Chestnut Lodge. Near Rockville, Maryland. Earlier in the evening, Dr. Olson had agreed to take treatment there, but he'd been so . . . vuh-*volatile* of late . . . we were afraid, come morning, he'd be, well, a handful. I arranged for our man at the Statler . . . the late Mr. Martin here . . . and another individual to handle, you might say, the rough stuff . . . the late Mr. Sarito there . . . to make the transfer in the middle of the night. We wished to avoid the embarrassment, for all concerned, of dragging Dr. Olson through a crowded lobby in daylight. And apparently he objected to being taken from his sleep to make this unexpected departure . . ."

"Apparently."

". . . and he put up a struggle, and, well, he wound up going out the window. Absolutely unintended."

"For the sake of argument, let's say I buy that. Why grab Miss Page here?"

He swallowed. "Your puh-presence at the Statler was most unfortunate and terribly upsetting. Dr. Lashbrook was beside himself when he realized whose questions he'd been answering. I suggested . . . I admit it came from me . . . that Miss Page be brought here as a way to leverage your cooperation. Perhaps not my best notion, or finest hour."

"Was it your idea to drug her?"

"Of course not! *Was* she drugged?"

"I think so. It may have been that LSD-25 of yours."

"If so, not my doing, nor my idea." He smiled at Bettie, who was clinging to me. "Dear, there's nothing to worry about. The substance has a tendency to muddle the thoughts, and occasionally there are heightened sensations. But you'll be yourself again soon, if you aren't already."

I said, "Not how it worked for Frank Olson, though, was it, Doc?"

He patted the air with his raised palms. "Let me suggest that you let me huh-handle this situation. Puh-personally. Obviously calling in the authorities would put all of us in awkward circumstances. You've killed two men, Mr. Heller . . . and I understand it isn't the *first* time you've wandered into a CIA operation and left bodies behind."

Bettie glanced at me.

"Killing me," Gottlieb said, "wouldn't do anyone any good."

"I might find it satisfying."

"Yes, but revenge is such a fleeting thing. Rescuing Miss Page is admirable—murdering me, in cold blood? . . . I doubt that's who you are."

I nodded around at the garish sex den. "What do you use this place for, Doc? This fraternity boy's idea of heaven? Blackmail?"

His eyes flared with indignation. "Heavens no! What do you take me for! I'm a *scientist*, Mr. Heller. And I like to think, in my way, a patriot. You won a Silver Star, I understand. Do I have to explain sacrifice?"

*And I knew.*

Just as I'd known that the figure falling from a high floor at the Statler had to be Frank Olson.

"You're *testing* that shit here," I said. "You bring men up here, visiting businessmen, poor bastards from Des Moines and Duluth, and then some prostie or maybe CIA femme fatale spikes a drink with your LSD-25 and gives it to her gentleman friend of the moment and you watch and record and film and . . . Jesus, you are a fucking monster. I really should kill your ass—if there's a God, He'll thank me."

Bettie squeezed my arm. "Let's go, Nate. Come on, sugah. *Please.*"

I looked down at her. Her eyes were wide and wild with fear—as they would have been when she was bound in that chair, if she'd known what the hell was going on.

"All right," I said to her. "But first help me with something. I think this is a job that will come fairly easy to you. . . ."

We tied Gottlieb into the chair where not long ago Bettie had sat. Maybe he was kinky enough to enjoy it, but I doubt it—I thought I saw real fear and discomfort in his eyes, much as I saw girlish pleasure in Bettie's as she cinched the final rings of rope around his upper torso. The finishing touch was mine—I fetched a ball gag from a nightstand drawer and Bettie giggled as she stuffed it in his mouth like a roasted hog and looped the strap around the back of his head.

And we left him there, in the den of government iniquity, in the stench of his killed colleagues, which was nearly as foul as the things he did to his unwitting human guinea pigs.

At Bettie's, with dawn at her windows, I took a card from my wallet and dialed a number. Early or late, I would get an answer, though not necessarily a direct line to the man I was calling.

And that proved to be the case—I had to leave my name and number. It took six whole minutes to hear back from him.

"Is Gottlieb yours, Shep?" I asked.

Edward Shepherd took a long pause and then said, "And if he is?"

"Is this a secure line?"

"Of course."

"Well, he's tied to a chair in that honeypot safe house on Bedford Street. With two dead men, who when they were still breathing kidnapped a friend of mine. One used to be your inside man at the Statler, the other is one of Costello's muscle boys."

"Thank you for the tip. Can we meet?"

"Well, you need time to put a little cleanup crew together, I suppose. How about in an hour at the Waldorf?"

"The hotel?"

"The cafeteria."

# CHAPTER 22

At six in the morning, the Waldorf Cafeteria—like any other respectable twenty-four-hour restaurant (not to suggest any respectability here)—was serving breakfast. At my side was Bettie, in a man's gray sweatshirt, blue jeans, and moccasins, wearing just a dab of lipstick but no other makeup, her hair back in a ponytail and jumpiness in the azure eyes. She'd said she didn't think she could sleep and didn't want to be alone, and frankly I didn't want to leave her alone.

Bettie understood that when my guest arrived, she would have to move to a table across the restaurant from us, while remaining in my sight. Surprisingly, we both felt like eating—not that it hadn't been an energetic evening, but after the Village Barn, nothing much about it had been what you'd call appetizing.

We'd got here a little early and had gone through the cafeteria line to gather orange juice, coffee, scrambled eggs, link sausage, silver-dollar pancakes, and other breakfast edibles about on a par with what I used to get at the mess hall at Marine boot camp in San Diego.

She ate slowly but spoke quickly. "Ah feel like ah *imagined* it all. Did ah imagine it all, sugah?"

"I'll let you know after I talk to my friend."

"Is he with the police, your friend?"

"The federal government."

Her big eyes grew bigger, and they could get very, very big. "Those were government men back there?"

"Bettie, don't think about it. I'm going to straighten this out for both of us."

"Are you bein' honest with me, honey?"

"I'm going to *try* to straighten it out. That's the truth-and-nothing-but version. But whatever I can put together will almost certainly include you getting amnesia about the last ten or twelve hours."

"Okay," she said, nodding, fine with that—such a pretty woman, ponytail bobbing. Nothing else bad today was going to happen to her, if I could help it. Big "if," maybe. . . .

When Shep Shepherd entered the cafeteria, pausing to hang up his fur-collared topcoat, he was uncharacteristically late—a good fifteen minutes. Bettie and I had been fifteen minutes early, so it felt longer.

But I wasn't surprised. First of all, I didn't know how far he'd had to come—I assumed somewhere in Manhattan, because if it had been Washington, D.C., he'd have asked for a later meeting. No, he'd had things to do. To organize. Like get that cleanup crew going. Even for an organization man, that takes time.

Yet there was nothing bedraggled about him, nothing to indicate he'd got a disturbing phone call that had drawn him from his comfortable bed just an hour and fifteen minutes ago. He looked clean-shaven and bright-eyed, if not quite bushy-tailed.

His hat (a Dobbs, I'd guess) was light blue with a dark blue band that matched his suit, which was a Botany 500, both right out of my wardrobe. His button-down-collar shirt was white, his tie a muted red with white stripes. My suit—the tailored charcoal number that concealed the nine-millimeter—wasn't as crisp and fresh-looking as his.

I'd been up longer.

Tucked under his arm was a fat, fastened manila envelope, which he flipped onto the table near where I'd set my hat. He nodded to Bettie, who quickly rose, smiling back nervously, taking her tray of eggs and such with her and heading across to another small table, the CIA security chief flashing her a friendly gap-toothed grin, but not overdoing it.

He tossed his hat on the chair next to him. I did not rise and we skipped the hand-shaking ritual as he bent a bit to ask if I minded if he went through the line and got himself some breakfast before we got started. He hadn't had a chance to catch a bite. I told him to go ahead.

Around us, the place was fairly empty. The clientele lacked the Bohemian spirit of the predawn-a.m. Village, those who'd endured long nights of booze and art talk having by now stumbled into a bed or a cot or a corner. A few shabby-looking drunks were hunkered over coffee and sometimes a roll, with bleary pissholes-in-the-snow eyes, men not looking much like they were contemplating the bright possibilities of the new day that lay ahead.

With a plate of biscuits and gravy, Shep returned and said in a Southern drawl much more understated than Bettie's, "That's a lovely gal you got there, Nate. You know, that's a rarity, that kind of figure, the old-fashioned hourglass variety. But she's got a pretty face, too."

"I'm glad you approve. She's from Tennessee. You two can get together sometime and talk about how downhill things have gone since the slaves were freed."

His quick laugh was about what that remark deserved. "Nate, would you mind if we start with you givin' me an account, in some detail, of your evening? As you see it, from when you arrived at the Statler—around two-thirty a.m., wasn't it?"

He ate his biscuits and gravy and I gave him all of it, leaving nothing out though identifying my client as Mrs. Frank Olson, with no mention of McCarthy. Biscuits and gravy are a sloppy dish, but he ate his with a certain grace, keeping some eye contact with me as I recounted the events. He'd nod now and then, to underscore that he was following.

When I was done, he was done, and he touched his mouth with a paper napkin, rose, and went over to dump his dishes in a plastic tub abandoned by a bored busboy, then got himself some more coffee. Just as he came back, a waitress was freshening mine. About a third of my breakfast was left, but cold as a stone by now. Across the room, Bettie had finished hers, and sat turned away from us, looking out the window at a street coming alive as dawn turned into day.

Shep and I had plenty of privacy—I'd taken the same rear table as our previous meeting—but the covering din of loud boasting musicians and writers and actors was absent. The handful of non-drunk patrons seemed to be shopkeepers who were having a quick breakfast before opening up. So our conversation was low-key, in volume if not content.

"For this exchange to carry any weight," he said with a lazy smile, getting out a pack of Chesterfields from a suit coat pocket, "we have to be honest with each other. So frankly, Nate, I don't appreciate you failin' to mention that your involvement with Frank Olson began with Senator McCarthy."

*How much did he know?*

Probably everything. So I said fine, and told him that McCarthy had wanted me to check Olson out as a possible source for dirt on the Agency, for an upcoming Senate investigation he hoped to mount; but that the incident at Deep Creek Lake had sent me in another direction, which was to help Alice Olson.

"What *about* Alice Olson, Shep? What am I to tell her?"

He had long since lighted up the Chesterfield, and had offered me one, too, which I declined, any combat mood having passed. An hour ago, I'd have grabbed for it.

He said, cool but with an edge, "You're not to tell Alice Olson *anything*. You're to stay away from the woman. Don't go to the funeral, either."

"Christ, man, she hired me to—"

"Oh, you'll call her, later today . . . but no mention of the Statler and the events that ensued. She's not to find out anything more about Deep Creek Lake than she already knows, especially the LSD-25 in her husband's after-dinner drink. Nate, that is strictly classified. Just give her your condolences and tell her you're sorry to have disappointed her." One eyebrow rose and the gap-toothed grin flashed. "Surely, you've disappointed women before, Nate."

"Amused by all this, are you?"

His expression turned somber. "Sorry. No offense meant, my friend. If you view all of this as a tragedy, I can certainly understand and commiserate."

He glanced at his Rolex.

His chin went up and he said, "In just a few minutes, Colonel Ruwet—Dr. Olson's immediate superior at Camp Detrick, with the family doctor along for support—will arrive at the Olson home and give Alice Olson the terrible news."

"What terrible news is that, Shep? You're going to need a better story than saying her husband ran through a closed hotel room window at about thirty miles an hour—a speed he'd worked up to in the space of maybe twelve feet."

"There is," Shep admitted, smoke seeping through the gap between front teeth, "some fine-tunin' that needs doing. For now, all that Mrs. Olson will learn—and this is what the press will get—is that her husband jumped or fell from a tenth-floor window at his Manhattan hotel."

"The press will want more."

He gestured with an open hand. "Of course, and they'll get the standard obituary material . . . *and* be told that Dr. Olson was in town to get medical treatment for his depression."

"You'll just leave out the part where he gets slipped an LSD-25 mickey, and that the 'shrink' he went to was an allergist."

Shep twitched a smile, tapped some cigarette ash on the floor. "Leave the details to us," he said, ignoring my sarcasm. "In fact, you need to leave it *all* to us. You'll be leavin' town as soon as possible."

I frowned. "You want me back in Chicago?"

"No, and not in L.A., either, not where you have offices and are well known. Take a break, Nate. Go someplace sunny and warm, and vacation for a week or two on the government's tab. Take the little doll along. Florida, maybe. She'll look swell in a bikini. By the way . . . do we need to worry about her, Nate?"

I shook my head, kept my voice calm. "No. She's confused about what happened anyway—I think they slipped her some of your LSD shit. I'll handle her."

His voice had a sudden hardness. "Good. You'll *need* to, because if she doesn't behave, we'll have to step in."

Emphatic now, I said, "There'll be *no* need. What about the, uh, men I . . . left back there at your safe house? They have friends, families—they can't just disappear, can they?"

He gave me a facial shrug. "You might be surprised. Anyway, it's our problem now, son. You're out of it. In the clear."

I shifted in the hard chair. "So then I just skip, and stay ahead of the cops? But what's my story when they catch up to me?"

He waved a dismissive hand. "They won't. Stay out of sight for a week, at least, and we'll have everything tidied up. You'll be the Little Man Who Wasn't There—you've been him *before*, right?"

I had.

"Of course," he said offhandedly, stubbing out his cigarette on the floor under his toe, "you may prefer to go to the police and tell them what *really* happened . . . includin' the two men you killed last night, or should I say this morning? . . . And then maybe you'll want to discuss with the authorities the woman and the three men you killed last April. . . . Or would you prefer that I continue to keep all of that mum?"

I said nothing as I watched him light up a second cigarette.

Then I said, "You can't put me on the spot, Shep, without incriminating the Agency."

Now he grinned big and smoke flowed out of his mouth like steam. "And who do you suppose is in a better position to deal with that kind of contingency—a private investigator or the Central Intelligence Agency?"

The pack of Chesterfields and his Zippo lighter were on the table between us. I helped myself to a smoke.

I lighted up, drew deep, held it, then sighed it out. "What's the score on the Statler guy? And what the hell was one of *Costello's* boys doing there?"

He shrugged. "Ex-Costello. My understandin' is that he and another like him got fired by the esteemed Prime Minister of the Underworld earlier this year . . . after they fucked up a simple visit to a hotel room to fetch somebody or other into their boss's presence. Vince—whose last name you don't need, 'less you keep track of your kills in a little book or somethin'—is . . . *was* . . . a Lucchese soldier for some while. We have dealings with these people here and abroad, you see. They can be handy people to know."

Somebody dropped a dish and it shattered.

I leaned closer. "You're saying the Agency's in bed with the mob?"

"I wouldn't say 'in bed.'" Another shrug, another smile. "Surely you've heard how Luciano helped us with the dockworker unions during the war, and how his people helped out with intelligence in Sicily. In our line of work, Nate, it pays to have friends in all sorts of places. As for the young man at the Statler, he's ours. *Was* ours. We placed him there because we've used the hotel for meetings and such, and havin' an inside man on staff's desirable. He served us well at several other hotels the last few years, too, usually as a bellman. But Mr. Martin was obviously in over his head in this particular exercise."

If my eyes got any wider, they might fall out and roll around on the table. "I'll keep that in mind, Shep—that in future, if I rub up against a hood or a bellboy, it might be one of your agents."

He leaned in, half-smiling. "Nate, you're rather overstatin' affairs. You see, the Agency has agents, certainly, and employees—Dr. Olson was one, as is Dr. Gottlieb. But we also have what we term 'Special Employees,' which is to say individuals who do undercover work for us in the course and context of their own separate employment . . . a security man at a hotel, say, or a federal narcotics agent, a doctor like Abramson, even a magician like Mulholland."

I grunted a laugh. "Handy people to know, like you said. Well, Shep, not to disappoint you, but I have no desire to join those ranks."

His eyebrows went up a little. "But Nate . . . you already *have*. Not a 'Special Employee,' no. What you are, Nate, is an asset. An asset is someone the Agency can call upon now and then for help. An asset is someone who can be relied upon for his discretion."

The back of my neck was prickling. "And if I don't *care* to be an asset, then I'm . . . a liability?"

He flicked ash on the floor again. "No one's forcing you to work for us. You can walk out of here right now. You can go to the police or Mr. Hoover's FBI and take your chances about those six people you killed in this city this year. All here in the Village. Pretty impressive box score, actually."

The thing on my face was only technically a smile. "Or I could always just tell you and your people to go fuck yourselves."

He nodded. "An option. A definite option. You can just keep it all to yourself and go about your business and we can go about ours, and possibly never the twain shall meet." Coldness came back into his voice. "Or maybe two years from today, somebody will hand you a drink with something lethal in it that Doc Gottlieb whipped up . . . or four years from Sunday, someone may brush by you on the street and that little pinprick you barely feel is a delayed gift of something fatal that Frank Olson cooked up in his lab, between practical jokes."

I took more smoke in. Let it out.

"You've made your point," I admitted. "But if I'm on the team— even if I prefer to warm the bench—what about Frank Olson? Are you really going to try to pass him off as a suicide?"

A big shrug this time, and more ashes on the floor. "Well, isn't he? Wasn't it suicidal of him—a scientist researching how security risks can be controlled or 'brainwashed' or disposed of—to approach Senator *McCarthy*? And then to talk to you, with your association with Drew Pearson, one of the few journalists who wouldn't be afraid to print anything he had on us. . . . Didn't Frank Olson spend every day after that retreat tellin' his superiors he wanted to walk away from his top-secret job? Sayin' that he just wanted to disappear? Well, now he has. Into history. As a suicidal scientist who cracked up."

I sipped my coffee but it had grown as cold as Shep's eyes and voice.

I said, "Was that Chestnut Lodge chestnut something you and Gottlieb came up with? Saying that Olson first said he'd go willingly, but fought back when your minions came for him in the middle of the night? Or were Martin and Vince *really* sent there in the wee hours to simply fling Frank Olson out a high window?"

"Does it matter?" His laugh had little humor in it. "Oh, there's a Chestnut Lodge all right, but Frank Olson knew it wasn't as benign as it sounded, because he knew of security risks who'd been sent there—for shock treatment, chemical therapy, even lobotomies."

My hands were fists. "What *really* happened, Shep?"

"Well, him bein' waked up by men who arrive unannounced to haul him off to Chestnut Lodge? And him *fightin'* them, not wantin' to make that trip? Why, that makes all the sense in the world. But then so does just throwin' him out a window—Agency's better off with him dead, after all."

"Shep—*what . . . really . . . happened?*"

"You choose, Nate. First way's manslaughter, second's murder. Either way, you killed the two men responsible, so whatever makes you warm at night, you just go with that."

"You're saying you don't know."

"I'm sayin' that's all you get."

"What about Gottlieb's man Lashbrook?"

"What about him?"

"He just sat back and watched this happen?"

A one-shoulder shrug. "Probably didn't watch. Probably tucked himself away in that bathroom and waited it out—*whichever* way it happened. You want more, Nate? I'm not givin' it to you. We're finished on this subject."

I pushed anyway. "What happens to Gottlieb?"

His frown evidenced mild irritation. "This got botched on the doc's watch, no question. To some degree, it was a comedy of errors—the man who *should* have been in charge of the Olson operation, a federal narcotics agent who looks after the Bedford Street safe house for us, well, he got called out of town. His mother died."

"Be sure to let me know where to send a sympathy card."

He ignored that. "John Martin and his Sicilian friend Vince were assigned the task, and that rests on Gottlieb's shoulders. I assure you, he'll be reprimanded."

"Reprimanded."

"Yes. And disciplined."

I leaned halfway across the table. "I should have 'reprimanded' *him* out a high window! And my guess is, he *likes* being disciplined, if it involves that sick shit in your safe house."

"That's uncalled for."

"Fuck you, Shep. Do you know the kinds of things your road-show Frankenstein is up to? That he's dosing unwitting subjects with this LSD-25 shit and God knows what else?"

He tossed a hand. "A necessary evil."

"Necessary! For Christ's sake, *how* can it be . . . ?"

His expression turned suddenly grave; any trace of folksiness was gone when he spoke: "The Russians are looking at LSD-25 and many other drugs, Nate, and they have no scruples about how they go about their research. They have a concentrated program of brain-conditioning able to make men confess to crimes they never committed, and capable of changing American patriots into mouthpieces for Commie propaganda."

"They're doing it, so we're doing it."

His eyes were tight. "We can't allow the Reds to get ahead of us, Nate, on this crucial battlefield of the mind—just because they don't hesitate to use unwilling human guinea pigs and we're too soft to do the same. Russia has mind control, and so *we* have to have it— just like the Bomb."

I shook my head, astounded. "So you align yourself with a twisted bastard like *Gottlieb*? I should have killed that son of a bitch when I had the chance."

He smiled faintly. "Nate . . . you want to be John Wayne. You want to be Mike Hammer. You don't want to settle for sending the small fry to hell, you want the man at the top. You want him to look down the barrel of your .45."

"It's a nine-millimeter."

Steel came into the drawl. "Okay, well then, use it. You've got it on you right now, don't you? Because if you want to remove the man at the top, you're lookin' at him—the big boy in this one is me, Nate. The CIA's Chemical Division is my baby. Shoot me right here in the Waldorf Cafeteria, and slip out the side door."

"Don't fucking tempt me."

He grinned. "Of course, I'm not the *tippy*-top of this operation— that would be *you*, Nate, and all your fellow citizens, the taxpayers who back the United States government . . . who rightly give the Agency their tacit blessing to do what is necessary to stop the Communist hordes."

"You make it sound like a war."

He leaned halfway across the table. "It *is* a war, my friend. It's the war on Communism."

I threw my hands up. "Jesus, Shep, you can't fight a war against an 'ism.' You can go to war with Red China or Russia, all right—if you care to risk the atomic consequences. But you can't fight an *idea* except with other ideas, even if all you've got is blustering bullshit like Tail-Gunner Joe's."

"Speaking of which . . ." He pushed the manila envelope toward me.

"What's this?"

"Payment for services rendered. Tonight—this mornin'—you handled two 'Special Employees' of ours who botched the Olson operation rather badly. Saved us the trouble of dealing with them."

I slid from the envelope a two-inch file folder labeled "McCARTHY—TOP SECRET" on its flap.

Shep said, "You were hired to find out what was in our file on Senator McCarthy. Well, there's the works, your own copy. Mostly it's sexual indiscretions, a lot of it involving bad boy Roy, but Joe's been . . . *adventurous* himself. Do what you will with it. Sell it to your pal Pearson and make out like a bandit. Or hand it over to Mc-Carthy, who is after all your client. Either way is fine."

I was flipping through, eyes landing on depositions from various individuals asserting various things, from homosexual encounters between McCarthy and Cohn to Caligula-like orgies at a beach house of the latter to accusations of pedophilia against the former.

And that was just a quick flip-through.

"You see, Nate, it doesn't matter what you do with it," Shep said with a sunny grin. "Either way, McCarthy will be finished. And if you don't give it to either of them, then we'll use the information in that file as suits our needs . . . if McCarthy really is foolhardy enough to make us the subject of his next witch hunt. Up to you, Nate. Really . . . from here on out . . . it's all up to you."

He collected his hat, his Chesterfields, his lighter, and gave me a pleasant smile and nod. "We'll stay in touch. We're going to be great friends, Nate, because none of this is personal. Hope you understand that."

He retrieved his topcoat and went out. The place was filling up, the cafeteria line crowded.

I had finished the cigarette a while ago. I had no urge for another. That had passed. What was left of my coffee and breakfast was cold. Bettie had her head on her folded elbows, like a student in class who'd finished her test and was taking a nap. She was facing the window.

I sat down opposite her.

She jerked up, ponytail swinging, those lovely blue eyes red, possibly from crying but probably from what she'd been through.

"What now, sugah?"

"Well, we'll get some sack time."

"Can we go to the Waldorf for that? The *other* Waldorf, I mean?"

"Sure. We'll pick up your toothbrush on the way."

"Then what?"

"You ever been to Florida?"

# CHAPTER 23

In mid-December, after two pleasant weeks in Miami with Bettie, I wound up back in Manhattan, where, at the Empire State Building, the A-1 branch was up and running, with a bullpen of operatives in the space adjacent to the executive offices. Bob Hasty knew nothing of the reasons for my sudden Florida vacation, but I was his boss and it was the right time of year, though the city had been unseasonably warm.

I sat in his office like a client and asked him if anybody interesting had come around looking for me.

"Interesting how?" Hasty asked. His moon face could take on an innocence helpful in an investigator. And his preference for bow ties didn't hurt.

"Interesting like cops or feds or hoods."

"Well, that's pretty interesting, I grant you, but no. I hope it doesn't break the heart of the A-1's celebrated prez, but nobody has come around looking for you at all."

"Good."

"Oh, there *was* a call yesterday from Senator McCarthy's office."

"In D.C.?"

"No. Temporary digs at the U.S. Courthouse. His subcommittee is holding hearings in town." He smirked. "Seems there are a bunch of Commies in the Army in New Jersey. How's a guy supposed to sleep at night?"

"When there's a Red under your bed," I advised, "sleep with a gun under your pillow."

McCarthy being in town saved me a trip to D.C., since what I had to tell him wouldn't do on the telephone. The office at Foley Square was small and spare, and—in his trademark blue off-the-rack suit and mildly food-spattered tie—the blue-jowled senator was too big for his little desk.

My chair across from him was hard and uncomfortable, but I wouldn't be in it long.

"Horseshit through and through," he said with a scowl, batting the air with a thick hand.

I had just given him a rundown on his CIA file, claiming not to have it—really it was in the A-1 New York branch safe, and would go back to Chicago with me—but saying I'd spent enough time with the thing to get more than the gist.

"It's poisonous stuff," I said, pulling no punches. "They've got you in public bathrooms blowing servicemen and vice versa, and diddling little boys and girls."

"Well, they should make up their mind," he said sneeringly. "Am I queer or not? It's ridiculous. Scurrilous lies."

"What they have on you is thinner than on your sidekick," I admitted. "Maybe you could weather it. But the Cohn stuff is devastating—the guy has had more sailors than the local recruiting office. Plus he's a hypocrite, chasing homos out of the State Department because they're security risks."

"Ridiculous! Roy Cohn is a man's man."

"My point exactly."

He shook a fist. "They're next, the dirty bastards. The things these CIA stuffed shirts do in the name of Americanism, it *sickens* me."

McCarthy was not long on self-reflection.

"No question they play rough," I said. "They're paid to. You need to back off this one, Joe. Look what happened to Olson."

He sneered with his whole upper lip. "Well, they obviously *killed* him. Because he was going to talk to *me*. We'll start there. These pricks don't scare me."

"They should. Start by firing Cohn. Repudiate the little son of a bitch, expose him as a pervert and fire his ass. It'll ruin him, which he deserves for plenty of better reasons, and then maybe you can shrug off the accusations that the Agency will unleash. Risky, but—"

"I won't be intimidated by lying accusations. Just because somebody makes outrageous unfounded charges against you, why should you fold?"

Not terribly self-reflective, no.

The CIA inquiry died on the vine, because McCarthy's pal Roy Cohn—to whom Joe remained mystifyingly loyal—had used the Fort Monmouth inquiry as a weapon to try to get his drafted buddy David Schine preferential treatment, browbeating Robert T. Stevens, the secretary of the Army himself. That was Cohn's bad judgment. McCarthy was riling the Army further by telling Brigadier General Ralph Zwicker in public that he was "not fit to wear that uniform" and didn't have "the brains of a five-year-old."

Out of this came the famous Army-McCarthy hearings, where McCarthy and Cohn—choosing to represent themselves—were the defendants in a hearing conducted by their own investigatory subcommittee. Two famous confrontations in the hearings, widely televised from April through June 1954, sealed their doom.

McCarthy, having been accused of cropping a photograph to change its meaning, was asked by his nemesis—folksy Boston lawyer Joseph Welch—if the original picture had come from a pixie. Joe, typically full of himself, snidely asked Welch, "Will counsel for my benefit *define*—I think he might be an *expert* on that—what a 'pixie' is?"

Welch, with a fatherly smile, said, "I should say, Mr. Senator, that a pixie is a close relative of a fairy. . . . Have I enlightened you?"

This of course got the much-rumored homosexual motive behind Cohn's efforts on Schine's behalf out in the open, if in a sideways, laughter-inducing manner.

Even more devastating had been McCarthy's attack on a young lawyer in Welch's firm, who was not directly involved in the proceedings, an instance of gratuitous cruelty on the senator's part that had unmasked him as a bully before millions of TV viewers.

McCarthy, possibly drunk with more than just power, launched an in absentia diatribe against the young attorney, who had once worked for the National Lawyers Guild, which the senator identified as "the bulwark of the Communist Party."

Welch responded eloquently and emotionally: "Until this moment, Senator, I think I never really gauged your cruelty or your recklessness." And when McCarthy blustered on, Welch, with some spine, said, "Let us not assassinate this lad further, Senator. You have done enough. Have you no sense of decency, sir, at long last? Have you no sense of decency?"

The door was open for McCarthy's many enemies, in both parties, to take him down. By the end of 1954, he had been censured by the Senate. He became a pariah to his own party and the White House, and his drinking accelerated, leading to frequent detox visits to hospitals. Finally he was put in a straitjacket and hauled to the sixteenth floor of Bethesda Naval Hospital, where he died in May 1957 of alcohol poisoning within feet of where his mentor, James Forrestal, had gone out the window to his death, a supposed suicide.

Jean Kerr McCarthy remarried in 1961 but protected her late first husband's legacy to the end. When she donated his personal papers to the archives of Marquette University, she restricted their use until 2050. She died of cancer in 1979.

Roy Cohn became one of Manhattan's most successful if controversial lawyers, with clients including Donald Trump, numerous mob figures, and the Catholic Archdiocese of New York. He never worked with David Schine again—the hotel heir married a former Miss Sweden, had six children, and produced films, including *The French Connection*, dying in a light-plane crash in 1968.

Cohn, meanwhile, lived with his mother in Manhattan and hobnobbed with the Studio 54 crowd, dating several women, including TV's Barbara Walters. He insisted he was not a homosexual even as he continued to throw wild gay parties. His legal career was marked by charges of misconduct, including perjury, witness tampering, and misappropriation of client funds; ultimately he was disbarred. He died at fifty-nine in 1986 of complications from AIDS.

I continued to do occasional jobs for Drew Pearson, whose power waned, in part because of McCarthy's attacks when both men were in their prime; but his muckraking style paved the way for modern investigative journalism. He died of a heart attack in 1969.

Dashiell Hammett never published another word, in part due to blacklisting but mostly because he held himself to so high a standard; he was working on an autobiographical novel, *Tulip*, at the time of his death in 1961. Hammett outlived his accomplishments, but his accomplishments outlived him. As a veteran of both world wars, the creator of Sam Spade, vilified as a "Commie," was buried at Arlington National Cemetery.

For decades, the Left considered the Rosenbergs martyrs, which I'm sure Julius and Ethel would have relished. But Julius must have known the truth would eventually come out about his espionage activities.

And it did, when in 1995 declassified documents—known as the Venona transcripts—revealed Julius' work for the Soviets. Now the Rosenbergs were bad guys, though nothing in the Venona files made Julius out as more than a minor figure in A-bomb spying, with Ethel shown to have no role at all.

The shameful railroading of these two minor figures by Cohn, his boss Saypol, and the FBI became painfully obvious—if you read past the headlines. But these days all anybody seems to know about the Rosenbergs is that they were guilty and really did deserve to die.

Well, hell, everybody dies. It's just that some people take longer getting around to it—like the Greenglasses, for instance.

After serving nine and a half years, David Greenglass joined his wife Ruth and their children to live under an assumed name in Queens. In 1979, David and Ruth participated in their only joint post-Rosenberg-execution interview. *The New Republic* interviewers characterized the couple's replies in the one-hour session as "so filled with contradiction, lapses of memory and apparent evasions" that it was doubtful the famous typing incident ever took place.

From 1960 forward, the Greenglasses lived a typical, even idyllic American life—Ruth a legal secretary, their son a doctor, their daughter a medical administrator. David again worked as a machinist and a sometime inventor, including coming up with a gadget that sold millions but got him only a $500 bonus—how unfair life can sometimes be. After Ruth's death in 2008, at eighty-three, David finally came forward and recanted, saying that to protect his wife, he'd lied under oath about his sister Ethel's involvement with Julius' espionage. He died at age ninety-two.

Harry Gold—who served just under half of his thirty-year sentence—only made it to sixty. He found work as a clinical chemist at a Philadelphia hospital, `where he fit in well, just as he had at Lewisburg Penitentiary.

Julius and Ethel's two boys, Michael and Robert, did not abandon their parents to history. The Meeropol brothers—they adopted the last name of their foster parents—fought for over three decades to prove the innocence of their parents, waging legal battles for the release of FBI files that eventually revealed the extent of the misconduct of Cohn and others. But when, at age ninety-one, Morton Sobell finally admitted in a *New York Times* interview that he'd spied for the Soviets, the two boys—an economics professor and a lawyer, respectively, and grandfathers now—did not challenge the confession, which implicated their father. But they still insisted, rightly, that their parents had been the victims of prosecutorial and judicial misconduct, and that the execution of their mother was a travesty of justice.

Out of my involvement in the Rosenberg case, one lasting friendship grew—Bobby Kennedy and I would work together on his Rackets Committee in just a few years.

Bettie Page had liked Florida; we'd had a great time there. Working with Miami photographer Bunny Yeager, Bettie posed for some of her most popular pinups, including a 1955 Christmas centerfold in *Playboy*, various fresh-air bikini shots, and a memorable photo layout in a wildlife park.

Back in New York, Kefauver kept his word and didn't make Bettie testify, but double-crossed us by issuing her a subpoena, so that she would have to sit waiting outside the hearing room, where Irving Klaw could see her and get rattled. Klaw was essentially ruined and dead by 1966. Kefauver's McCarthy-style attacks on crooks and comic books never got him to the White House, even as a vice president; he died shortly after suffering a heart attack on the floor of the Senate in 1963.

As she spent more time in Florida, I lost track of Bettie and last dated her around 1958. She said she was winding down her modeling—she'd begun late and feared she might start showing her age; she was wrong, but try to tell a good-looking woman that. Years later I learned she became a Born Again Christian when a neon cross glowed in the night and called to her.

This would have been around '59, but I didn't hear about it till much later, when the revival of interest in her pinups had made her a cult figure. My first thought, hearing about the glowing cross, was that she had probably been slipped LSD at the Bedford Street safe house. Enough time had passed that I knew about LSD flashbacks.

And when I learned that in her forties and fifties, this upbeat, smart, funny creature became occasionally violent—threatening her current husband with a knife and doing the same with a landlady—I again wondered about the impact of that acid trip and the violence she'd been in the middle of.

After all, in the 1970s, a number of stories about unwitting subjects that Gottlieb and his crew had dosed with LSD came to light, from a guy who just sat down at a table in Paris to chat with a fellow American (Gottlieb) and got a surprise in his coffee, to one of the doctor's coworker' wives, who got her dose in a glass of goat's milk. Bettie's experience didn't come out, but she fit the profile. Why else would someone like her suddenly have schizophrenia kick in, in her fifties?

Fortunately, after a decade in and out of mental facilities, a grounded Bettie Page emerged to learn she had become a pop-culture icon, sparked by cartoonist Dave Stevens having used her as a character in his *Rocketeer* comics. When he discovered Bettie was still alive, and living in Los Angeles, Stevens took her under his wing, doing everything from helping her buy groceries to reintroducing her to Hugh Hefner, who saw to it that an agent protected her rights. Her final years were happily prosperous.

As a friend of Hefner's from Chicago days, I got to get reacquainted with Bettie at the Playboy Mansion in the late '90s. I'd heard she refused to be photographed, preferring her fans remember her as she was. So I was thrilled to find she was still a beauty, with a pleasantly plump figure and her trademark black pageboy. We reminisced, but not about Bedford Street. She passed in 2008.

As for Edward "Shep" Shepherd, I was to encounter him a number of times, and as he predicted, we became friendly, even friends, though that might be pushing it. Often he would look me up in Chicago, and we'd have a nice meal, and he'd ask about my son and I'd ask about his son and daughter. Occasionally my status as an asset of the Agency—later called the Company—would come into play, notably with Operation Mongoose, which I've written about elsewhere.

Where Alice Olson was concerned, I did as Shep had instructed—she received a properly sympathetic call from me, and we never spoke again. Frank Olson's fall from a high window, and the good graces of the CIA, seemed to have found its crack in history to drop through.

As I write this, many of the players are gone.

On the rare occasions when he spoke to reporters or officials, Robert Lashbrook seemed always to change his story about what happened in Room 1018a at the Statler. Sometimes he saw Olson run toward the window, other times he was woken by the crash of glass. Gottlieb's deputy worked for the CIA for twelve years before leaving to teach high school science and math. He died in California in 2002.

Magician John Mulholland, who performed very little after

1953, continued to work for and with the CIA until his death in 1970. Once a major figure in his field, he is largely forgotten.

Dr. Harold Abramson continued working with the CIA on their mind control program, with an emphasis on LSD, which he continued to use on unwitting subjects. Seeking therapeutic uses for LSD, he continued his work at an insane asylum in Amityville, New York; he received national publicity when he fed LSD to fish. He died, at age eighty, in 1980.

Through the years, Colonel Vincent Ruwet—Frank Olson's boss, who I never met—often dropped by to see Alice Olson. Over drinks, he would lend a sympathetic ear as she described her difficulties raising three children alone. She was unaware that this family friend had been assigned by the CIA to "keep track of the wife." Ruwet died of a heart attack at church in November of 1996.

Ruwet's real role in Alice Olson's life was just one of many revelations that came out of the Rockefeller Commission, more formally known as the United States President's Commission on CIA Activities within the United States. The investigation arose from a *New York Times* article revealing that the CIA had been conducting illegal domestic activities since the 1950s, including opening the mail of citizens and surveillance of domestic dissidents.

Among its findings, reported in *The Washington Post* on June 11, 1975, was that an unnamed "U.S. Army scientist" had taken his own life after being dosed with LSD.

A month later, the Olson family—Alice, then fifty-nine; Eric, thirty; Lisa, twenty-nine; and Nils, twenty-six—held a press conference in the backyard of the ranch-style house I had visited twenty-two years before. They identified the "suicide" as Alice's husband, and their father, Frank Olson. Within two weeks, the family was in the Oval Office with President Gerald Ford, who offered them an official apology. A few days later, they met with CIA director William Colby in Langley, Virginia, for lunch and another apology. The family was given what was described as the CIA's complete file.

And in 1976 the Olsons received a financial settlement from

Congress of $750,000, on condition that all claims against the U.S. government in the death of Frank Olson be considered settled.

The official story now was that the CIA had slipped LSD into Frank Olson's after-dinner liqueur at a work retreat at Deep Creek Lake, to see how a scientist would behave on a mind-altering drug. Would he reveal secrets, and if so would the information be coherent? Did LSD work as a truth serum? But unfortunately Frank Olson had a bad trip and wound up taking a header out a high window.

Seeing this from some distance—I was semiretired from the A-1 now, my son Sam running the agency and its six branches— I smelled a cover-up. This was a classic "limited hangout," in CIA jargon, which is to say, *Tell just enough of the truth to get 'em off your back.* Some years later, I learned I was right—two of President Ford's aides had advised him to "contain the Olson matter" by apologizing and settling out of court, preventing any further demands or investigation. Give them a modest payoff and a photo op with the President, and they'll be happy.

The two aides were Richard Cheney and Donald Rumsfeld.

The presidential apology and the $750,000, which Alice divided among her children, was good enough for her. She had hit it off with the President; they had even laughed together, and she brought home a signed picture. She had never been eager to discuss her husband's death with her children, telling them, "You are never going to know what happened in that room." Now there was closure.

But the publicity generated by the CIA/LSD story had stirred the pot, and the Olsons began hearing from people with stories to tell. One was Armand Pastore, the night manager at the Statler, who shared his memories and doubts. And Frank's old friend Norm Cournoyer was another, among others from Camp Detrick and sometimes Deep Creek Lake.

It was Cournoyer who gave my name to Eric, who was actively investigating his father's death while putting his career as a clinical psychologist largely on hold. Eric tracked me down by phone in Boca Raton, where I was living with my second wife.

"Mr. Heller," he said, "this is Frank Olson's son, Eric."

The unnerving thing was that once he'd identified himself that way, the similarity of his voice to his father's put the latter's image in my mind, so that I felt in some fashion that I was talking to the father.

We spoke for some time, and I will admit that I was careful about what I said. I was impressed by how many pieces he had put together, and I was bursting to add missing ones. But there is no statute of limitations on murder, and five men and one woman had died under my gun in 1953 in Greenwich Village, some of it only vaguely self-defense. Also, I had a grown son and some grandchildren and a new wife I loved very much, and it's never too late to get killed by the spooks. Somebody could still pass me my last rum cocktail, or brush against me on the street for a fatal pinprick.

"This guy Gottlieb turns up everywhere!" Eric said at one point. "Is he the *only* person in the shop? Does he have to do *everything*?"

We both laughed at the dark humor of that.

And then he told me that, shortly before his mother died in 1993, he and she and his brother Nils (sister Lisa had died in a plane crash shortly after the President Ford meeting) had tracked down Sidney Gottlieb in the foothills of the Blue Ridge Mountains of Virginia. Gottlieb and his wife lived in a sprawling modern solar-heated home with a swimming pool at the end of Turkey Ridge Road, a dirt lane. Alice had arranged the visit by phone and Gottlieb answered their knock at once.

"He stood there, lean, wiry, reminding me very much of Paul Newman," Eric Olson said. "Right away he said, 'I am so relieved to see that you don't have a gun.'"

"What?" I said.

"My brother and mother and I were speechless. And then he said, 'I had a dream last night in which I opened this door and you pulled a gun and shot me.'"

"That must have knocked you back a ways."

"Mother was pale as a ghost. I said, 'We didn't come to harm you or anyone. We only want to talk with you and to ask you a few questions about my father.'"

"Gottlieb always has been a clever bastard."

"Right! Before we were even in the door, he'd disarmed us and taken control—we were already apologizing to *him*!"

Inside the house, Gottlieb's wife, Margaret, and Alice hit it right off, both having been the daughters of missionaries in Asia.

"But Mrs. Gottlieb seemed a little stressed by the whole occasion," Eric said. She excused herself, and the rest of the little group sat down in the living room. "Gottlieb proceeded to tell us his version of what happened at Deep Creek Lake."

The mad doc's take mirrored the official one, but when Eric and Nils pointed out the ways in which the government's story just didn't make sense, Gottlieb had said, "Look, if you don't believe me, there is no reason for you to be here. Your father and I went into this type of work because we were patriotic. We cared about our country and its survival in the face of Communism."

Eric said to me, "He was really good at painting himself as exactly like my father. But he overplayed his hand."

"How so?"

"He walked us to the door and looked right at me and said, 'You're obviously very troubled by your father's suicide. Have you ever considered getting into a therapy group?' "

I laughed. "You saw through his 'concern.' "

"I didn't realize it till later, but now I can see how much Gottlieb had at stake in defusing me. He played a hand in murdering my father, didn't he?"

I didn't answer right away. What flashed through my mind was every nasty fucking thing I knew about Gottlieb, who was like a James Bond villain who walked down off the screen. He had tried to kill Castro with poisoned cigars, fountain pens, and wet suits; attempted the assassination of Prime Minister Patrice Lumumba of the Congo via poisoned toothbrush; doctored an Iraqi general's handkerchief with botulism toxin; performed mind control experiments on captured Viet Cong; and burned all the MK-Ultra files when he finally retired from the CIA in 1972.

And so much more.

"Eric," I said. "I have advice for you but it isn't pretty. . . . You need to dig up your dad. Ever hear of a guy named James E. Starrs?"

I explained that in 1991—in part at my urging (I'd been involved with the original Huey Long case)—forensics expert Dr. James E. Starrs, of George Washington University in Washington D.C., had approached the family of Dr. Carl Weiss, Long's presumed assassin. Starrs felt an exhumation of Dr. Weiss's body might possibly lead to vindication for Weiss. The exhumation went forward and Starrs—with supportive evidence—presented his case for a bodyguard having killed Long. This Starrs did at the yearly meeting of the prestigious Academy of Forensic Sciences, to a positive response.

On June 2, 1994, in Frederick, Maryland, under the supervision of Dr. Starrs, a crane unearthed Frank Olson's concrete burial vault, from which the wooden coffin was removed and wrapped for transport to a nearby crime lab. The original autopsy report had described cuts and abrasions; the surprisingly well-preserved body showed none. But a major discovery soon followed: An unrecorded blow to Olson's left temple had caused major bleeding under otherwise unbroken skin.

Starrs and most of his team believed someone had sapped Olson and shoved him through the window—either in a struggle that got out of hand or as outright murder. The pathologist theorized either a hammer or the butt of a gun as the likely blunt object. Finally, he and his team concluded that the evidence from their examination—and a lengthy trip to the crime scene, utilizing computer reconstruction of the fall—was "rankly and starkly suggestive of homicide."

The findings of the Starrs autopsy spurred a new investigation by the New York public prosecutor, and many depositions were taken, with key players like Lashbrook and Gottlieb generating new information. Ultimately, however, the investigation did not lead to a new trial; nor have civil efforts by Eric and Nils proven successful thus far.

But on August 8, 2002, again in the backyard of the tree-surrounded 1950s ranch-style house, Eric and Nils Olson held a well-attended press conference to share findings based on years of investigation by the brothers, who—like the sons of the Rosenbergs— had given so much of their lives to this effort.

The death of Frank Olson on November 28, 1953, they said, was a murder, not a suicide; LSD experimentation was just the cover story created to handle a security risk; and a 1975 cover-up of the full facts surrounding their father's death was set in motion at the highest levels of the Ford administration.

To date, no one from the United States government has stepped forward to contradict any of the claims put forth by the Olson brothers.

But as the participants all slip into history and into the ground— Frank Olson's examined remains now in a different resting place, next to Alice—any sense of closure for the Olson brothers, or the rest of us, seems less and less likely. Armand Pastore, the best witness, died in 1999; so did the most obvious villain of the piece, Sidney Gottlieb. And while I have finally come forward, in the form of this memoir, even Nate Heller can't live forever.

Looking back on all of it—from the father and mother who died in the electric chair to the father who fell thirteen stories to his death—I can see that Joe McCarthy was right in a way. There *were* dangerous foes of democracy in our government.

They just weren't Commies.

## I OWE THEM ONE

Despite its extensive basis in history, this is a work of fiction, and liberties have been taken with the facts, though as few as possible—and any blame for historical inaccuracies is my own, mitigated by the limitations of conflicting source material.

Most of the characters in this novel are real and appear under their true names, although all depictions must be viewed as fictionalized. Whenever possible, interviews with subjects, or court and/or congressional committee appearances, have been used as the basis of dialogue scenes, although creative liberties have been taken.

Nathan Heller is, of course, fictional, as is his A-1 Detective Agency. In some cases, I have chosen not to use real names as an indication that either a surfeit of research is available on some minor historical figure or that significant fictionalization has occurred, such as a composite characterization. Natalie Ash is a fictional character with some basis in a number of female espionage agents involved in the Rosenberg case. Shep Shepherd is similarly fictional with roots in several real people.

For the most part, I have limited Heller to gathering information uncovered by investigators during the era depicted, although this has not been a hard-and-fast rule. Nonetheless, I at times omitted material that Heller could not have logically obtained in 1953. Nor did I attempt to cover every aspect and personality in the Rosenberg and Olson cases; part of my mission was reductive, to make complex events accessible, and perhaps encourage readers to sample some of the research material mentioned below.

As much as possible, I like to present Heller in a role occupied by a real person (or persons) in history. Joe McCarthy frequently hired private investigators in various parts of the country, and much of Heller's eleventh-hour inquiry into the Rosenberg case mirrors that of *National Guardian* reporters, including stumbling upon the missing console table.

The two intertwined cases examined in this novel are polar opposites in research terms. The fate of Julius and Ethel Rosenberg has been so much written about—and often from such biased extremes— that tackling the reading is daunting. I found indispensable two very different books, *The Rosenberg File* (second edition, 1983, 1997) by Ronald Radosh and Joyce Milton, and *Final Verdict: What Really Happened in the Rosenberg Case* (2010) by Walter and Miriam Schneir.

Radosh and Milton are dogged, thorough researchers who profess an objective viewpoint but are clearly in the anti-Rosenberg camp, if not rabidly so; in any case, their book is a treasure trove of data and detail. The second edition's introduction, however—which covers material updated since the first edition—absurdly assumes the reader is already familiar with the book being introduced. Read as an afterword, however, this poorly placed introduction is effective and illuminating.

Walter and Miriam Schneir—with their previous work, *Invitation to an Inquest* (1965, updated 1983)—became the premier advocates of the Rosenbergs as innocent victims of a government conspiracy. So striking was the difference between the Schneir view and the Radosh and Milton one that the two writing teams would appear together to debate the case in public.

The Schneirs, however, responded to post–Cold War revelations about the Rosenbergs by continuing their research and admitting in print that they'd been wrong. Their slender tome, *Final Verdict*, puts the pieces together in a convincing manner that is intelligently gray, as opposed to their own previous black-and-white reading of the case (and the opposing one of Radosh and Milton).

Also helpful was the very readable insider's look at the case, *Exoneration: The Trial of Julius & Ethel Rosenberg and Morton Sobell* (2010) by Emily Arnow-Alman and David Alman, cofounders and leaders of the National Committee to Secure Justice in the Rosenberg Case. Key, too, was *The Murder of the Rosenbergs* (1990) by Stanley Yalkowsky, which includes much of the trial transcript, annotated with the pro-Rosenberg slant its title indicates.

Other books consulted concentrate on individual figures in the case: the thoughtful, thorough *Ethel Rosenberg: Beyond the Myths* (1988) by Ilene Philipson; the first-rate *The Brother* (2001) by Sam Roberts, examining David Greenglass; the well-written if self-serving *On Doing Time* (1974, 2001), Morton Sobell's autobiography; and the well-researched, expertly crafted *The Invisible Harry Gold* (1982) by Allen M. Hornblum, which for all its merits is unconvincing in rehabilitating its subject's role in history.

Of the post–Cold War looks at Soviet espionage during the Stalin era, Allen Weinstein and Alexander Vassiliev's *The Haunted Wood* (1999), dealing with previously sealed KGB records, proved for me a dry and sleep-inducing read. Much better is *The Man Behind the Rosenbergs* (2001) by "KGB spymaster" Alexander Feklisov and Sergei Kostin, although the title is an exaggeration—Feklisov never met Ethel Rosenberg—and the book may be of questionable reliability.

The Frank Olson case has, to date, produced only one book, H. P. Albarelli Jr.'s painstakingly researched *A Terrible Mistake* (2009), a mammoth undertaking (for writer and reader alike) that covers not only the Olson death but CIA mind control efforts in general throughout the Cold War. Labeling *A Terrible Mistake* definitive is not premature, though it does suffer slightly from repetition and the lack of a sharp editorial hand. Nonetheless, I am indebted to the author for his scholarship and dedication, and this crucial book.

Other Olson research included chapters or major sections of *Dead Wrong* (2012), Richard Belzer and David Wayne; *The Magician,* (2008, 2010), Ben Robinson; *The Men Who Stare at Goats* (2004), Jon Ronson; *Raw Deal* (1998), Ken Smith; *The Search for the "Manchurian Candidate"* (1979), John Marks; and *A Voice for the Dead* (2005),

James E. Starrs with Katherine Ramsland. Also helpful was the documentary *Investigative Reports: Mind Control Murder* (1999), directed
by David Presswell and written by JoAnn Milivojevic. Finally, the
Olson family's Web site—the Frank Olson Legacy Project—brims
with information and numerous links to related articles (www
.franksolsonproject.org).

Among articles utilized are "The Olson File" (*London Mail*,
1998), Kevin Dowling and Phillip Knightly; "The Man Who Knew
Too Much" (2000, Gentlemen's Quarterly), Mary A. Fischer; and
"What Did the C.I.A. Do to Eric Olson's Father?" (2001, *New York
Times*), Michael Ignatieff.

Dashiell Hammett is one of four writers who inspired me at an
early age to write crime fiction, and who instructed me in how to
do it, in their very different ways. The others are Raymond Chan-
dler, James M. Cain, and Mickey Spillane. But first came Hammett,
whose *The Maltese Falcon* I consider the greatest private eye novel
ever written, unlikely to be surpassed.

So I came to this project having already read a lot about
Hammett—everything I could get my hands on, really—but I
can't point to one book on his life as the definitive one. All of the
following are worthwhile, and each provided material for my
characterization of Hammett: *Dashiell Hammett: A Casebook* (1969),
William F. Nolan; *Dashiell Hammett: A Life* (1983), Diane John-
son; *Dashiell Hammett: Man of Mystery* (2014), Sally Cline; *Shadow
Man: The Life of Dashiell Hammett* (1981), Richard Layman; *Hellman
and Hammett* (1996), Joan Mellen; and *Selected Letters of Dashiell
Hammett* (2001), edited by Richard Layman with Julie M. Rivett.

Hammett never headed up a committee like the one that hires
Heller here, but he was a vocal Rosenberg supporter, as were those
I appointed to his fictional committee, and he was involved with
many such leftist causes and groups—interesting, because if ever
a man seemed more an individualist and less a joiner, Hammett
was it.

Two strikingly different looks at the life of Roy Cohn are *The*

*Autobiography of Roy Cohn* (1988) by Sidney Zion and *Citizen Cohn* (1988) by Nicholas von Hoffman. Drew Pearson references include *Confessions of a Muckraker* (1979) by Jack Anderson with James Boyd; *Drew Pearson: An Unauthorized Biography* (1973) by Oliver Pilat; and *Drew Pearson Diaries 1949–1959* (1974), edited by Tyler Abell. Also consulted were *Frank Costello: Prime Minister of the Underworld* (1974) by George Wolf with Joseph DiMona, and *Kefauver: A Political Biography* (1971) by Joseph Bruce Gorman.

Research on a certain iconic beauty of the fifties included *Bettie Page: The Life of a Pin-Up Legend* (1996, 1998), Karen Essex and James L. Swanson; *Bettie Page: Queen of Curves* (2014), Petra Mason and Bunny Yeager; *The Real Bettie Page* (1997), Richard Foster; and the documentary *Bettie Page Reveals All* (2012), written by Doug Miller and directed by Mark Mori. No disrespect to Miss Page's memory is meant by the fantasy of her sexual relationship with Nathan Heller—my enthusiasm for Bettie predates by decades her latter-day discovery.

Bobby Kennedy research included *American Journey: The Times of Robert Kennedy* (1970), Jean Stein and George Plimpton; *The Enemy Within* (1960), Robert F. Kennedy; *Robert Kennedy: His Life* (2000), Evan Thomas; *RFK: A Candid Biography of Robert Kennedy* (1998), C. David Heymann; and *RFK: The Man Who Would Be President* (1967), Ralph De Toledano.

Location reference came from *New York Confidential* (1953), Jack Lait & Lee Mortimer; *New York in the '50s* (1992), Dan Wakefield; *No Cover Charge* (1956), Robert Sylvester; *The Village* (2013), John Strausbaugh; *Stork Club* (2000), Ralph Blumenthal; *The Waldorf-Astoria* (1991), Ward Morehouse III; and *Washington Confidential* (1951), Jack Lait & Lee Mortimer. In addition, WPA guides to New York City, New York State, Pennsylvania, and Washington, D.C., were consulted, including *New York Panorama* (1938). Prison reference included *Sing Sing* (2005), Denis Brian; and *Sing Sing (Images of America)*, (2003), Guy Cheli. Also helpful was a Sing Sing Internet photo gallery by Karl R. Josker.

The Internet has become an indispensable research tool for the Heller memoirs, and that I once wrote these books without it now seems unimaginable. Small facts were checked dozens of times during a writing session—for example, the spelling of once common and now obscure products, the names of radio/TV shows and popular music of the era, and the point at which slang terms and phrases entered general usage. Information on everything from the Waldorf Cafeteria to the Senate Caucus Room came from searching the Net. Acknowledging each Web site that provided a scrap of two of research would expand this bibliographical essay to an unwieldy length; my thanks to all of them.

My friend and longtime research associate George Hagenauer made a trip to Iowa for a key brainstorming session, and did much reading and digging on McCarthy, Cohn, and the Rosenbergs. A Wisconsin resident himself, George was an enthusiastic advocate for the inclusion in this novel of the day Communists "took over" Mosinee in Senator McCarthy's home state.

I had intended to open the novel with Hammett testifying to McCarthy's committee, but looking at various newspaper articles on, and magazine accounts of, this bizarre event (Racine *Journal Times*, *Wausau Daily Herald*, *American Legion Magazine*, *OAH Magazine of History*) swung me to George's thinking—specifically, that this was a perfect nutshell view of the nuttiness of Red Scare America in the fifties. There's no record of McCarthy having been present, but he should have been, so I put him there; he was certainly a key supporter and possibly an architect of the stunt. Footage of the mock takeover can be seen in the documentary *Atomic Cafe*, mentioned below.

George and I at times divided up research reading. He read the massive and essential *The Life and Times of Joe McCarthy* (1982) by Thomas C. Reeves and guided me to key pages, while I concentrated on *Shooting Star: The Brief Arc of Joe McCarthy* (2006) by Tom Wicker and *Joseph McCarthy* (2000) by Arthur Herman, looks at the man and his era from the left and right, respectively.

Other McCarthy books consulted included *McCarthy: The Man, The Senator, The "Ism"* (1952), Jack Anderson and Ronald W. May; *McCarthy* (1968), Roy Cohn; *Senator Joe McCarthy* (1959), Richard H. Rovere; and *The Rise and Fall of Senator Joe McCarthy* (2009), James Cross Giblin. *Encyclopedia of the McCarthy Era* (1996) by William K. Klingaman proved helpful as a general reference.

Any book looking at McCarthy and his era must take into account the classic documentary *Point of Order!* (1963), directed and produced by Emile de Antonio and Daniel Talbot, which skillfully (if not always fairly) edits the many kinescope hours of the Army-McCarthy hearings of 1954 into an entertaining, sometimes thrilling film. I made use of both a DVD and the published transcript. Other films viewed include *The Atomic Cafe* (1982), produced and directed by Kevin Rafferty, Jayne Loader, and Pierce Rafferty ("Duck and cover!"); *Citizen Cohn* (2001), written by David Franzoni and directed by Frank Pierson; *The Edward R. Murrow Collection: The McCarthy Years* (1991), produced by Bernard Birnbaum and written by Russ Bensley and Sam Roberts; *The Real American: Joe McCarthy* (2011), written by Lutz Hachmeister and Simone Holler and directed by Hachmeister; and *The Unquiet Death of Julius and Ethel Rosenberg* (1974) written by Alvin Goldstein and directed by Alan Moorman.

Unusual things that turn up in research often don't make it into the Heller novels. For readers who share my affinity for Mickey Spillane's Mike Hammer and the film *Kiss Me Deadly* (1955), the following historical tidbit may mind-boggle: in 1950, before any arrests in the Rosenberg case were made, an FBI agent named Spillane was searching for an iron box containing a piece of plutonium (pilfered by David Greenglass).

Thanks to my friend and agent, Dominick Abel, who has worked mightily to keep the Heller memoirs alive; and my editor, Claire Eddy, whose enthusiasm for Nate Heller and his creator is much appreciated and reciprocated.

As usual, love and thanks go to Barbara Collins—my wife, best friend, and valued collaborator—who was working on her draft of our next "Barbara Allan"–bylined novel while I was writing this one. Despite the demands of her writing, she endured my constant need for a sounding board, providing tough-minded suggestions and patient support.

## ABOUT THE AUTHOR

MAX ALLAN COLLINS has earned an unprecedented twenty-two Private Eye Writers of America Shamus Award nominations, winning for his Nathan Heller novels *True Detective* (1983) and *Stolen Away* (1991) and the Mike Hammer short story "So Long, Chief" (2013). In 2007 he received the PWA lifetime achievement award, the Eye, and in 2012 his Nathan Heller saga was honored with the PWA Hammer Award for its major contribution to the private eye genre.

His graphic novel *Road to Perdition* (1998) is the basis of the Academy Award–winning Tom Hanks film and was followed by two acclaimed prose sequels and several graphic novels. He has created a number of innovative suspense series, including Mallory, Quarry, Eliot Ness, Jack and Maggie Starr, Reeder and Rogers, and the Disaster novels. He is completing a number of Mike Hammer novels begun by the late Mickey Spillane; his full-cast Hammer audio novel, *The Little Death* with Stacy Keach, won a 2011 Audie.

His many comics credits include the syndicated strip *Dick Tracy*, his own *Ms. Tree*, *Batman*, and *CSI: Crime Scene Investigation*, for which he wrote ten bestselling novels and several award-winning video games. His tie-in books have appeared on the *USA Today* bestseller list nine times and the *New York Times* list three. His movie novels include *Saving Private Ryan*, *Air Force One*, and *American Gangster* (IAMTW Best Novel Scribe Award, 2008).

An independent filmmaker in the Midwest, Collins has written and directed four features, including the Lifetime movie *Mommy* (1996); he scripted *The Expert,* a 1995 HBO World Premiere, and the film-festival favorite *The Last Lullaby* (2008), based on his novel *The Last Quarry.* A *Quarry* television series began airing on Cinemax in 2016. His documentary *Caveman: V. T. Hamlin & Alley Oop* (2008) has appeared on PBS and on DVD, and his documentary *Mike Hammer's Mickey Spillane* (1998, 2011) appears on the Criterion Collection DVD and Blu-ray of *Kiss Me Deadly.*

His play *Eliot Ness: An Untouchable Life* was nominated for an Edgar Award in 2004 by the Mystery Writers of America; a film version, written and directed by Collins, was released on DVD and appeared on PBS stations in 2009.

His other credits include film criticism, short fiction, songwriting, trading-card sets, and video games. His coffee-table book, *The History of Mystery,* was nominated for every major mystery award, and his *Men's Adventure Magazines* won the Anthony Award.

Collins lives in Muscatine, Iowa, with his wife, writer Barbara Collins; as Barbara Allan, they have collaborated on eleven novels, including the successful Trash 'n' Treasures mysteries, with *Antiques Flee Market* (2008) winning the *Romantic Times* Best Humorous Mystery Novel award in 2009. Their son, Nathan, is a Japanese-to-English translator, working on video games, manga, and novels.